Our Lady
of the
Forest

DAVID GUTERSON

Our Lady
of the
Forest

RANDOM HOUSE
LARGE PRINT

*The Library of Congress has established a
Cataloging-in-Publication record for this title*

0–375–43293–0

www.randomlargeprint.com

FIRST LARGE PRINT EDITION

10   9   8   7   6   5   4   3   2   1

This Large Print edition published in accord
with the standards of the N.A.V.H.

To Chana, John, Mary, and Ben

Our Lady
of the
Forest

I

Annunciation

NOVEMBER 10-NOVEMBER 13, 1999

The girl's errand in the forest that day was to gather chanterelle mushrooms in a bucket to sell in town at dusk. According to her own account and the accounts of others in the North Fork Campground who would later be questioned by the diocesan committee, by Father Collins of Saint Joseph's of North Fork, by the bishop's representative, and by reporters covering the purported apparitions—including tabloid journalists who treated the story like a visitation by Martians or the birth of a two-headed infant—the girl left her camp before eight o'clock and walked alone into the woods. She wore a sweatshirt with its hood drawn tight. She didn't speak to others of her intentions. Setting out with no direction in mind, she crossed a maple bottom and a copse of alders, traversed a creek on a rotten log, then climbed a ridge into deep rain forest and began searching for mushrooms in earnest.

As she went the girl ate potato chips and knelt beside rivulets to drink. She swallowed the antihistamine that kept her allergies at bay. Other than looking for mushrooms, she listened for the lonely music of birds and—she confessed this later to Father Collins—stopped twice to masturbate. It was a still day with no rain or fog and no wind stirring branches in the trees, the kind of stillness that stops time, or seems to, for a hiker. The girl paused often to consider it and to acknowledge her aloneness. She prayed the rosary on her knees—it was Wednesday, November tenth, so she said the Glorious Mysteries—before following an elk trail into country she hadn't visited or perhaps didn't recall, a flat grown up with Douglas firs, choked by blowdowns and vine maple draped with witches'-hair. Here she lay in a bed of moss and was seized by a dream that she lay in moss while a shape, a form—a bird of prey, a luminous man—bore down on her from above.

Rising, she found chanterelles buried in the interstices of liverworts and in the shadows of windfalls. She cut them low, brushed them clean and set them carefully in her bucket. For a long time she picked steadily, moving farther into the woods, pleased because it was a rainless day on which she was finding enough mushrooms to justify being there. They drew her on like a spell.

At noon she read from her pocket catechism, then prayed—Give us this day our daily bread—before crossing herself and eating more potato chips and a package of two chocolate donuts. Resting, she heard the note of a thrush, but muted, faint, and distant. Sunlight now filtered through the trees on an angle through the highest branches and she sought out a broad, strong shaft of it, stippled with boiling dust and litterfall, and lay on her back in its luminous warmth, her face turned toward heaven. Again she slept and again she dreamed, this time of a furtive woman in the trees, lit in darkness as though by a spotlight, who exhorted her to rise from the ground and continue her search for chanterelles.

The girl got up and traveled on. She was lost now in an incidental way and the two strange dreams disturbed her. Feeling a vague desire again, she put her hand between her legs, aimlessly, still walking. A cold or flu had hold of her, she thought. Her allergies and asthma seemed heightened too. Her period had started.

The newspapers reported that her name was Ann Holmes, after her maternal grandmother, who died from sepsis and pneumonia a week before

Ann was born. Ann and her mother, fifteen at Ann's birth, had lived with Ann's grandfather, a long-haul trucker, a man with complicated gambling debts, in a series of rental homes. The newspapers, though, did not uncover that her mother's boyfriend, a methamphetamine addict, had raped Ann opportunistically beginning when she was fourteen. Afterward he would lie beside her with an expression of antic, contorted suffering etching his hairless long face. Sometimes he cried or apologized, but more often he threatened to kill her.

When Ann was fifteen she took a driver's education class, which she missed only once, on a Friday afternoon, in order to have an abortion. Eight months later she expelled her second fetus into the toilet at a minimart on the heels of a bout with nausea. On her sixteenth birthday she bought a two-door car, dented or crumpled in more than one panel, for three hundred and fifty dollars earned foraging for truffles and chanterelles. The next morning, she drove away.

Ann was diminutive, sparrow-boned, and when she covered her head with her sweatshirt hood it was easy to mistake her for a boy of twelve, fair-skinned and dreamy. She often wheezed asthmatically, sneezed feebly, blew her nose, and coughed against her fist or palm. On most mornings her jeans were wet with the rain or dew transferred from the fronds of ferns and her hands looked pink and raw. She smelled of wood smoke, leaves, and rank clothes and had lived for a month in the North Fork Campground in a canvas tent by the river. Others living there told reporters that she'd rigged up a plastic tarp with twine and often sat under it against a log, reading by firelight. Most described her as silent and subdued, though not unpleasant or inspiring unease, not threatening in her estrangement. Those who saw her in the woods that fall—other mushroom gatherers, mostly, but also several elk and deer hunters and once a Stinson Company timber cruiser—were struck by her inconsequence and by the wariness of her eyes in shadow underneath the drawn hood.

A mushroom picker named Carolyn Greer who lived in a van in the North Fork Campground claimed that on an evening in mid-October she had eaten dinner with Ann Holmes, sharing soup, bread and canned peaches and speaking with her of present matters but never of themselves, their histories. Ann had not had much to say. Mostly she stirred her soup pot, listened, and stared at the flames of the fire. She did indicate a concern for her car, whose transmission no longer allowed her to shift gears or to travel anywhere. The car's battery had petered out, and its windshield and windows appeared permanently clouded with an opaque, viscous vapor. It sat beside her canvas tent, gathering fallen cedar needles, both seats loaded with plastic bags, paper sacks, and cardboard boxes stuffed with her belongings.

Carolyn didn't tell the bishop's representative that while the soup was simmering they got high together. Primarily, it was nobody's business. Furthermore, it implicated her too. Carolyn indulged in pot regularly. It surprised her that Ann, after a few tokes, did not become effusive and talkative, like most stoned people around a campfire. Instead she became even more reserved, more hermetic and taciturn. Her face disappeared inside the hood of her sweatshirt. She spoke when spoken to, terse but polite, and poked incessantly at the wood coals. Her only subject was her dead car.

Stranded, Ann had resorted to the county bus, which stopped at a convenience store a half mile from the campground and dropped her in front of the MarketTime in North Fork for eighty-five cents, one way. She paid, the county driver reported, with exact change, sometimes using pennies, and replied in kind when he greeted her. Once he commented on the mushrooms in her bucket, on their number, size, and golden hue, and she gave him some loosely wrapped in newspaper she found at the back of the bus. On the highway, she slept with her head against the window. Frequently she read from a paperback book he eventually discerned was a catechism. When she got off in town she said thank you or good-bye, her hood still drawn around her face.

A half dozen times she accepted a ride from a mushroom and brush picker named Steven Mossberger, who wore a dense beard, Coke-bottle glasses, and a wool cap pulled low on his temples. Seeing her carrying her bucket of chanterelles and walking the road one afternoon, Mossberger rolled down the window of his pickup, explained that he lived in the campground as she did, that he picked mushrooms just like her, then asked if she wanted a lift. Ann refused him without affront. No, thanks, she said. I'm okay.

The next time he saw her, in late October, he pulled over at dusk in a modest rain and she accepted without hesitating. When he leaned across to push ajar the door, she got in smelling of wet clothes and mushrooms, set the bucket of chanterelles on her lap, and said, It's a little wet out.

Where are you from? Mossberger asked.

Down in Oregon. Not far from the coast.

What's your name?

She gave him her first. He told her his full name. He put his hand out to shake hers and she slipped her hand into his.

He wanted to believe, afterward, that this moment was freighted with spiritual meaning, that in taking her hand he felt the hand of God, and he described it that way to the diocesan committee and to the bishop's representative—a hand that was more than other hands, he said, connecting him with something deeper than his own life—but in fact, he understood privately, what he felt was probably little more than the small thrill a man gets from shaking hands with a woman.

In North Fork, Ann sold her mushrooms to Bob Frame, a mechanic who worked on logging equipment and ran his mushroom business on the side. Garrulous and jocular most of the time, he spoke with an instinctive brevity and disdain to the first journalist who entreated him. The girl's mushrooms, Frame said, were always meticulously field cleaned, and her bucket contained few culls. Only once, on an evening of bitter rain, did she drink the coffee he kept about as a gratuity for his pickers. For a few minutes she sat by the electric heater, sipping from a Styrofoam cup, watching as he layered mushrooms in newspaper and weighed the day's take on a scale. It seemed to him, working close to her, that she hadn't bathed or laundered her clothing in a long time, maybe weeks. He did recall that she kept her pay in a leather pouch worn around her neck, not in the pocket of her jeans. Her shoes, he noted, were well-worn, the sole of one of them separating from the upper so that her damp wool sock showed through. Even in his shed she wore her sweatshirt hood and kept her hands in her sweatshirt pockets.

Frame didn't tell the journalist that she could give no social security number when he requested one for his records. He'd paid her cash and noted nothing in his books of recompense made to an Ann Holmes, and because of that small worrisome omission he was angry with himself for having said anything about Ann Holmes at all. He spoke to no more journalists afterward and proclaimed in town that the media circus perpetually surrounding the visionary was a spectacle he couldn't participate in and still live with himself. In truth it was the specter of an IRS audit that made him afraid to speak of her, though he did tell his wife, swearing her to secrecy, that once when the girl freed her pouch from her sweatshirt she also inadvertently brought forth a necklace bearing a crucifix, which Bob said glowed a brilliant gold.

From Frame's shed Ann carried her bucket to MarketTime and bought a few things each evening. One checker recalled her proclivity for sugar wafers, small cartons of chocolate milk, deli burritos, and Starbursts. No one else remembered very much, except that she always wore her hood and counted her returned change. She asked for the key to the storeroom toilet more often than other customers and used the dish soap in the utility sink to wash her hands afterward. Occasionally she stuffed pennies in the cans for the Injured Loggers' Fund.

In early November, while foraging for chanterelles, two girls from North Fork came across Ann Holmes in the woods east of town. They were middle-school girls, seventh graders, who had employed the ruse of mushrooming all fall to smoke pot in the woods after school. Besides their mushroom buckets and pocketknives, they brought along a bag of marijuana, a small pipe, and matches. Deeply concerned about getting caught, careful girls who giggled for long stretches after smoking even a little pot, they were mindful of the need for chewing gum, eyedrops, and doses of cheap perfume. They were also ravenous, paranoid, and startled by noises in the forest. The singing of a bird could worry them. A plane overhead, a truck on a distant road, froze them in their tracks, wide-eyed.

They'd been stoned that afternoon for a half hour and were finding mushrooms here and there, giggling together in their usual manner, when they saw Ann Holmes perched on a log, watching them with her hands in her pockets and her sweatshirt hood drawn around her cheeks so that her face lay in shadow. At first they thought she was a boy of their own age, an unfamiliar boy not from their town, and even when they came close enough to see that her bucket was brimming with chanterelles, neither was certain that she wasn't a boy, though they inspected her face closely. Both were conscious of being stoned and wondered if it was observable somehow, if their behavior gave them away. They exerted themselves to act normal. Whoa, said one. You scored.

I should have brought along another bucket.

Amazing.

Ass kicking.

Have you ever noticed that bucket rhymes with fuck it?

Crystal.

Excuse me.

God, Crystal.

I'm sure. It rhymes.

God, Crystal. I'm sure.

They giggled now in a truncated manner, trying to stop themselves. They both put hands over their mouths in an effort to hold in laughter. Ann loosened her sweatshirt drawstring, pushed the hood away from her face, and ran her fingers through her hair. Her hair was short, the color of old straw, matted to her head, unkempt. The others could see now that Ann was a girl, which was not as good as a strange boy in the woods to talk about at school. Are you like from where? one asked.

I'm from the campground.

You were like born there?

They laughed again, covering their mouths. One of them nearly fell over.

You guys are baked, Ann said.

We're not baked we're totally hammered.

I'm like fried. Totally.

I'm like ripped.

Me, too.

They sat cross-legged on the forest floor. The one named Crystal pulled out a deck of cards. The other produced the bag of marijuana. Let's get baked, she suggested. Maybe a little, Ann replied.

They smoked dope, played Crazy Eights, ate a rope of red licorice, some Dots, and a box of Red Hots. Ann asked if they believed in Jesus. Uh oh, said one. Are you a Jesus freak?

I just wonder if you believe in Jesus.

I believe Jesus eats Reese's Pieces.

Jesus is the reason for the season.

They covered their mouths another time. Jesus saves but Moses invests, that's why the Jews are all rolling in money.

They own Hollywood.

Totally.

I have to go home.

What time is it?

It's time to go.

We need some more 'shrooms.

We need magic 'shrooms.

I'd rather do 'shrooms than get baked, wouldn't you?

I quit doing 'shrooms, said Ann.

She gave them each enough chanterelles to help them dupe their parents. God bless, she said. God loves you.

Okay. Whatever.

He does.

At school the next day they told certain people about the Jesus freak in the forest. They said she was probably a lesbian. God, what a weirdo, totally. Dikes for Jesus or something.

God bless. Jesus saves. Freak out.

Three weeks later they saw her picture in the paper, on the front page beside a long article. It's that freak from the woods, said Crystal.

It's totally her.

I can't believe it.

She got too stoned and hallucinated or something.

That little pothead lesbian bitch. I bet she makes money on this.

They told people not to believe in her. That bitch didn't see the Virgin Mary. She was on an acid trip.

Maybe she hallucinated a Madonna video.

Yeah, Like a Virgin.

No, Like a Sturgeon.

Weird Al Yankovic I think sucks.

So what are you doing after school today?

I'm totally, completely tired for some reason.

This freaks me out.

Me, too.
I'm totally freaked.
That bitch. What a lez.
She didn't see anything.

The first apparition—on November tenth at three in the afternoon, in the wake of Ann's two disturbing dreams, which she characterized afterward not as dreams but as pregnant celestial visitations—occurred while Ann cleaned a mushroom. She had taken a bandanna from her jeans pocket, folded it into a sanitary pad, and nestled it into her panties. Then, climbing over a steep hill, she'd entered a thicket of salal and Oregon grape not conducive to mushroom picking. This she passed through in fifteen minutes before coming to a sea of moss. The forest here had a dank smell. There were chanterelles, but few in number. She picked them with no particular urgency; the cold she felt coming made her feel listless, and her bucket was nearly full.

She was brushing dirt from the gills of a mushroom when she noticed a strange light in the forest. Later she described it as a ball of light hovering silently between two trees, also as a bright floating orb about the size of a basketball. It was lit from inside, not from without, not like a mirror, jewel, or prism but more like a halogen lightbulb. It didn't waver or wax and wane like a candle and appeared, like a helium balloon, free of gravity, aloft and attached to nothing. A nimbus surrounded it like fog or gauze. She thought that perhaps it revolved in place like a small planet or a moon.

When Ann felt confident it was not a mirage, a trick of the forest, or a problem with her vision, she picked up her bucket and ran. A number of mushrooms hopped out and spilled, and she lost a few dozen when she tripped on a nurse log, but she didn't stop until her lungs forced her to; then she sprawled behind a tree, pulled free her rosary, made the sign of the cross, and recited, silently, the Apostles' Creed. The light, she thought, hadn't followed her, thankfully, so she said an Our Father and three Hail Marys, and when it appeared that she was safe where she lay, hidden between two clefting roots, she went on through the remainder of the rosary, whispering all of it at high speed.

It was, she felt certain, not a fantasy or dream but more like something from a science-fiction movie, a UFO or a government experiment she wasn't supposed to know about. She didn't want to present herself out in the open and stayed behind the concealment of ferns where she could watch for it in pursuit of her and, if need be, flee again. But the woods, as always, were indifferently still; there was no sign of a traveling light. Ann clutched her rosary between her cold fingers. Perhaps, it occurred to her, troublingly, the light had something to do with Satan.

When she saw it again, off to her left, it seemed to her that it was spinning violently, or vibrating and shimmering. It was closer this time, and lower too, and feeling now that she couldn't outrun it she held up her rosary like a shield. Leave me alone, get out of here! she said. Just get out of here!

Instead, as she told her inquisitors later, it glided toward her in a frightening arc, dropping first and then advancing. It loomed larger and more distinct until it was clearly a human figure—she could make out a spectral, wavering face and a pair of incandescent hands—levitating just off the forest floor thirty yards away. It was now too brilliant, too luminous, to behold, so still staving it off with the rosary, she used her free hand to cover her eyes and peeked, squinting, between her fingers. Don't hurt me! she said, feeling at its mercy. Please, please, go away!

She dropped to her knees, squeezed shut her eyes, and told God she would never sin again in return for divine intervention. She told herself, too, that she meant it. She meant to keep this bargain. When she looked once more, a few seconds later, the light was already retreating through the trees, borne away like a soap bubble, silent, swift, and ascending through branches but touching none, no needles or leaves, avoiding obstacles as if it could see them, guiding itself in departure.

Ann, relieved, found her way out of the woods in slightly more than an hour. At her campsite she sat in her car for a long time, blowing her nose and shivering. That evening she couldn't eat anything or concentrate on reading her Bible and feeling uneasy about the coming night, went with a flashlight to Carolyn Greer, who lay in her sleeping bag inside her van, reading by the glow from a candle lantern and eating baby carrots. It's raining, said Carolyn. Come on in. You don't really look too . . . healthy.

I think I have a cold, answered Ann.

The shades were drawn and a small cone of incense burned in a cast-iron pan. Rain battered the van's roof like gravel falling from the sky. Ann's face, in the candle's glow, was grave and animated. Carolyn lay and listened to Ann's story. When it was finished she sighed, sat up, stretched, slipped a marker into her book, and pulled a rubber band around the bag of carrots. It sounds like the sun, said Carolyn.

I was in the woods. There wasn't any sun.

You must have been dreaming.

I wasn't asleep.

You don't think you were.

Well take right now. It was like right now.

Right now I know I'm completely awake. I don't have to pinch myself or anything like that. No way I'm really sleeping.

How do you know?

I'm completely awake.

Were you high, Ann?

That isn't it.

A ball of light. Floating around.

With a person in it, like I said. A ball of light. Exactly.

It sounds to me like it has to be the sun. Didn't you ever look at the sun too long? Today—today it was sunny.

But I was in the woods. In shade.

That or else you were having a dream. I've had dreams I thought were real. What else could it be?

It could be something like a UFO.

I don't think so. UFOs? That just doesn't work for me. I'm totally rational about things.

Well it wasn't normal.

A UFO?

It's crazy, I agree with you.

How can a little ball of light floating around out in the woods with a person's face inside of it be an unidentified flying object?

I don't know. It's crazy.

A UFO is a spaceship. If you believe in UFOs, they're spaceships.

I don't believe in them.

So it wasn't one.

It was something though.

It was just the sun.

You keep coming back to that.

What else is there?

I don't know. An experiment? The government doing something?

Do you mean like maybe the CIA? Is that what you think is going on here?

I don't know. The military?

The military doing something with a little ball of light that has a person stuck inside it.

Ann gave no answer to this. Carolyn tossed her the bag of carrots. Have some, she said. Go ahead.

Ann sat with the carrots in her lap. I'm a Christian, she said. Sort of. I guess. And the devil hates all Christians.

So now you're saying what you saw was the devil?

Satan hates religious people.

Then it's good that I'm not religious, isn't it.

No it's not. You should be something.

But science explains things so much better. The earth getting made in six days? Women coming from the ribs of men? Who can believe that nonsense?

That's not the right way to read the Bible. You have to interpret it.

Well what are you saying? Are you saying you were out in the woods picking mushrooms today when Satan attacked you in the form of a ball of light with a person stuck inside it?

No, but—

It sounds more like a visit from God. The bright light—it's a dead giveaway. Bright light, visit from God. Guy with horns, Satan.

They say that Satan wears disguises, though.

A ball of light with a person inside it. Satan gets creative.

Ann laughed. So I'm seeing things, she said. Maybe I'm mental or something.

Okay. I'll be candid with you. There's people around who think that's true. Because one you're kind of a loner and two you keep that hood down all the time. You do act a little bizarre.

It keeps my head warm.

It's not me who thinks you're mental.

Who is it then?

Other people in the campground.

I'm not very good at being social.

There's more to it than that I'll bet you.

Anyway, said Ann, it wasn't the sun. And I'm not going out in the woods tomorrow.

I'll go along, answered Carolyn. I want to rip off your mushroom spots anyway.

When Ann insisted she wouldn't go, Carolyn pulled from around her neck a small canister of pepper spray she wore on a loop of braided leather. No worries, she said. Because this stuff here is totally killer. We see the devil I'll spray him with this. It'll give him cardiac arrest.

In the morning they set out in a mist that blurred the treetops, the woods wet from the night's hard rain, the light gray and the branches dripping, the maple bottom and the copse of alders sodden with new lost leaves. Carolyn had a quadrangle map and she watched it as much as she watched the world, following the contours with her fingertips and taking readings from the altimeter and compass she had strung around her neck. She wrote notes in a timber cruiser's field book made of small waxed pages. When they traversed the rotten log straddling the creek she stopped halfway, above its wet boulders, and looked upstream, then at the map, then upstream again. UFO Creek this is called.

What?

Fryingpan Creek I mean a tributary of it, depending on how you read this. We're crossing it here I'm going to guess. At this little V in the contours.

Don't fall in.

Okay. I'll try.

That log is slick.

Okay already.

They found the elk trail Ann had taken and wound through the labyrinth of blowdowns. Carolyn, two steps behind, meditated on an enduring theme: that her legs were too fat and that no matter what she did, diet, exercise, both together, they would always be bloated and disgusting. Her parents' genes, she felt, were a curse. It was her fate to grow fatter despite every effort. On the other hand Ann was *too* much of a waif. Flat-chested, mousy, no hips, a boy's gait. A sickly, child-size runway model. We're headed east, Carolyn said. Isn't that like the Muslims? Don't the Muslims always face east?

They face . . . Mecca.

I've heard that too.

Christians don't do any of that.

That's because they own the whole world. They face anywhere, it's theirs already. They don't have to choose a direction.

You're not explaining it the right way you know.

This is more like south-southeast. Stop. Let me look at the compass.

There were mushrooms Ann had missed the day before and they picked them for half an hour. Carolyn pondered a plan for the evening. It didn't matter to her that Ann was slightly off, obsessive, eccentric, cryptic, a loner. Ann was inoffensive in

most regards, and her religious fervor was interesting. Carolyn decided to offer to drive her to the
laundromat in North Fork. They could eat next
door at the Chinese restaurant while their clothes
were in the dryers. Then they could split a cheap
motel room, take showers, watch television, sleep
between sheets. It would be good for Ann's cold
anyway, her incessant hacking and wheezing. It
was time, felt Carolyn, for some creature comforts, ones that didn't cost very much.

They ate a breakfast of dried apricots Carolyn
had brought folded up in a scarf and some toffee-
covered peanuts and potato chips. Ann took her
antihistamine, blew her nose, and coughed. This
seems right, she insisted. This is where I was yesterday. The hill I climbed is that way.

It's going to rain.

How do you know?

I feel it in my bones, said Carolyn.

That's not very scientific.

It doesn't prove Jesus is God's son, either.

That's not a matter of proof.

Carolyn spread her map on the ground and set
the compass on its corner. Then she rotated the
map a little until it lay aligned with the land. That
hill, she said. Here's the contours of it. It's a little
north of where you say it is if I'm reading the
contours right.

I'm sure you are.

You're more sarcastic than previously noted.

I wasn't trying to be sarcastic.

Uh-huh, said Carolyn. Okay. Sure. What's up with your car, by the way?

My car seems like it's permanently dead.

Maybe Jesus can start it for you.

I don't really know what I'm going to do.

Why don't you get it fixed or something?

Money, basically. I'm broke.

They climbed the hill and thrashed through the thicket of Oregon grape and salal. Beyond it was the dank-smelling forest in which Ann had seen the ball of light. They went in and began to pick mushrooms embedded in coverts of feather moss. Silence overtook them now. Neither spoke and while they searched for chanterelles they listened to the rain dripping out of the branches. The ground here is spongy, said Carolyn finally. I'm glad I wore my rubber boots.

This is the beginning of something new for me. I told God yesterday I wouldn't sin anymore.

You're not a sinner.

Everyone is.

Then we're all in the same boat.

It's the boat to hell.

I'm changing the subject, said Carolyn. Get yourself some better shoes so your feet aren't soaked all the time.

I'd do that if I had the money for shoes.

In the meantime let's smoke dope, okay?

I told you I can't sin anymore.

Dope isn't sin.

I don't want any. Ann stopped and pulled out her crucifix. I'm going to say the rosary, she said. It'll take me a little while.

Pray for shoes and an end to your cold.

I'm just going to say the rosary.

Pray for money.

You can't do that.

I'll wait for you. I've got a book to read.

What is it?

A travel book. I read them all the time. It's the only way I get any sun.

Carolyn found refuge under a tree and ate more apricots. What am I doing here? she asked herself. How did I end up in this spot? For seven years she'd taken classes at The Evergreen State College in Olympia, eventually declaring in General Studies and writing papers on Lewis Mumford, *Gravity's Rainbow,* Late Pleistocene burials, urban horticulture as a radical practice, and the regulation of organic farming. She'd also participated in a mushroom study in the Olympic Biosphere Reserve. It involved much camping and record keeping and a considerable amount of hash. For two summers she'd worked on a Forest Service crew, burning the slash in clear-cuts. She'd pondered a career in urban planning, also going to graduate school to become a mycologist. But both options seemed compromising. It was better to be a vagabond. Carolyn had liberated herself from the work ethic years before, shedding it like a chrysalis. She was not romantic about unemployment, but her parents felt she was. They lived not far from Terre Haute, Indiana. Her father sold life and car insurance; her mother owned a laundromat. They were banal and overweight Midwest people who incited in Carolyn a deep rage. She rarely visited them and when she did, she sat in terrible judgment. Her father wore wing tips and ate fried chicken gizzards. Her mother smelled like sweat and bleach. Carolyn didn't admit to them, in private or in public. Together with her sisters she laughed at them both and engaged in parody and ridicule. Carolyn was the youngest of three big-boned girls and knew this truth about herself: that she was indolent, self-serving, and unsavory, like the Beatniks of the 1950s. Sometimes she wished she could have been a Beatnik, but it wasn't a philosophical proposition. Her ideology about work and freedom was utilitarian, little more. She could present it to her parents as an intellectual construct or eclectic moral regimen beyond their midwestern ken. It made a comfortable argument, an easy false bastion that kept her disengaged from them, freed from obligations.

Though it felt like voyeurism, Carolyn peered

over the top of her book to watch Ann's devotions. She herself, who didn't pray, who didn't believe in any faith, felt pierced by loneliness. She indulged a sadness about the tone of her life, then focused again on travel. *Down by the water a large herd of black and white cattle, smallish beasts with humps, were feeding on the grass that grew in round pin-cushions among the stones.* Carolyn mentally tallied the sums in her checking and savings accounts. To this she added two more weeks of mushrooms. Her hope was to pass the winter in Mexico, though she was overweight, right now, by ten pounds at least. Definitely, she told herself, she would have to drop at least five of them before she could even cross the border, she couldn't be seen on a beach like this, a veritable butterball, a walking advertisement for Weight Watchers but only the BEFORE part. *There were also flocks of fat-tailed sheep high up on the hillsides and some angry-looking goats.*

There it is, she heard Ann say. There it is again.

I don't see it.

Right over there.

You're seeing things.

No I'm not.

Carolyn stood. It's what I thought, she said. You're seeing things. You're psycho.

Ann stood, walked twenty yards, dropped to her knees on a bed of moss, and clasping her hands in front of her, gazing up between two trees, said Yes, yes, I will.

Carolyn reported later to the bishop's representative that Ann's gaze remained fixed, that three times she tilted forward, that once she smiled and gasped softly, and that her eyes welled up and overflowed. At the end of her ecstasies she collapsed as if the breath had ruptured out of her and finally she deflated—that was Carolyn's word—with her face settled in the moss.

Are you all right?

I'm called. I'm called!

Take it easy.

Give me a second.

What happened?

Just give me a sec. Let me catch my breath for a sec. It's like . . . I can't even breathe.

When Ann rose to her knees again, her face was so thoroughly stained by tears she looked as if caught in a rainstorm. Carolyn noted the convulsive trembling seizing Ann's chin and shoulders. The girl pulled back the shroud of her hood and dried her cheeks with her forearm. She blew her nose on the sleeve of her sweatshirt. Why me? she asked. Who am I?

You're somebody who's seeing things out in the woods. Do you grasp what I'm trying to say to you? You're having delusions, hallucinations. You need professional help.

Ann held her face in her hands and rubbed her eye sockets with her palms. What? she said. You didn't see her?

I didn't see who?

The Blessed Virgin.

Jesus Christ.

She spoke to me.

Oh Jesus Christ. You're certified.

She called me to her ministry. I have to come back at this time tomorrow. Right here. I promised her.

They're going to have you in a straitjacket by then.

I'm not insane. I saw Our Lady.

You are insane. You just can't see it.

It's you who can't see, answered Ann.

By late evening there were two other women who wanted to witness with their own eyes the ecstasies of Ann Holmes. Carolyn had mentioned to another picker that the strange girl who wore the sweatshirt hood had claimed to see the Virgin Mary while picking east of Fryingpan Creek, and by 10 p.m. a number of people living in the North Fork Campground had heard it mentioned, questioned, or scoffed at, or had scoffed at it themselves. The idea of an apparition was mostly disparaged but in the case of the two women there was zeal for it, enough that they came forward the next morning hoping Ann would permit them to go along, the first out of a fervent Catholicism, the second because it occurred to her that what Ann had seen was not the Virgin Mary but the ghost of a girl who'd been lost near the campground eleven years before.

The mystery of this lost girl no longer disturbed North Fork, a town beleaguered by newer discontents and by a sense of deep injustice. It had thought of itself until recently as a prosperous timber community, had sawn down its adjoining forests with purposeful enthusiasm, but was at the time of the purported apparitions a place impoverished and psychologically defeated, a casualty, in its view of things, of urban liberals and their representatives in government, who wanted all the trees left standing. As a result, stores were closed on Main Street. The Chamber of Commerce encouraged tourism by opening a History of Logging Museum, but few travelers visited. A prison was built in the vicinity, a baleful presence south of town that hired ex-loggers as guards and clerks, but many in North Fork stayed unemployed.

There were clear-cuts on the edges of town in the sullen, mangled state of disrepair common to war-torn landscapes. In side lots the tackle of logging operations was already seized by blackberry creepers and rusted in silent heaps. The sawdust and sluff at mills rotted. Mildew stained certain trailer homes. Sheds and buildings sat boarded up, and the mud puddles in the side streets, iridescent with motor oil, were as long as logging trucks. Rain fell from a leaden sky, which cast a permanent pall over North Fork even in the best of times, and these were far from the best of times, these were closer to the worst. No one quite knew what to do now that the era of logging was past, a chapter in history with a museum to commemorate it. A number of families moved away to wherever the hope of employment took them, selling their homes at a loss without exception or turning them over to the banks. A few ex-loggers became fishing guides, working the rivers in drift boats, making sack lunches at 4 a.m. Others living up in the hills or along spur roads in old clear-cuts took to growing marijuana in pits dug under their trailer houses. As a result it was not considered safe anymore to drive back roads inquisitively or to poke around very much. Mushrooming for cash was popular, as was brush foraging, seed-cone gathering, and scavenging the last of the cedar stumps. The taverns still did a viable trade: the woman who thought of the lost girl's ghost had worked in one until recently, drawing beers, mopping the bar, leaning against the cash register, chain-smoking, and watching football. She was let go because, after separating from her husband, she began to drink unreasonably, and then she lost what was left to her and ended up in the campground.

On the evening she heard of Ann Holmes' apparition, she went to the phone booth outside the convenience store and called the lost girl's mother in North Fork, a woman whose husband still had a job as a custodian at the high school. There's somebody picking mushrooms out here who saw a ghost in the woods, she said. Maybe it was Lee Ann.

I don't think I believe in ghosts. But sometimes, you know what? I feel her nearby. Lately I feel her. Her presence.

There's more to the world than what we see.

I guess so, said the lost girl's mother. Anyway, it can't hurt anything if I come out there around ten o'clock, which is the earliest I can come tomorrow. And hey—something else. One more thing. Please don't tell my husband.

And so by midmorning they were a party of five: the fervent Catholic, the mother of the lost girl, the onetime bartender with the drinking problem, Carolyn Greer—appalled by her own interest—and finally the visionary, carrying her catechism, her hood drawn tightly around her face.

They set out in a file through the woods, underneath a light rain. Carolyn and the ex-bartender had brought along their picking buckets but for the others this was an expedition whose purpose was a scrutiny of Ann and not the gathering of mushrooms. In fact as they were crossing Fryingpan Creek the Catholic woman ventured the opinion that gathering mushrooms, for her at least, might indicate a kind of irreverence. If in truth Our Lady was present, who would want to stand in Her light with a bucket of mushrooms at hand? The Catholic woman felt that the loss of income accruing from a missed day of picking was a small sacrifice. But it's up to the individual, she said. I'm not going to judge you for picking today. Go ahead and pick away. But to me, it just doesn't feel right.

I feel judged whatever you say.

I'm sorry. What's your name?

Carolyn.

I'm sorry, Carolyn.

I see you don't mind bringing your camera.

I always carry it. I take photos as a hobby.

Well maybe you can sell your Virgin Mary pictures to a tabloid magazine.

They stopped to rest alongside the elk trail, under the shelter of a blowdown fallen across another blowdown. Ann swallowed her antihistamine with a draft from a water bottle. They sat on the moss in a semicircle and the Catholic woman, apologizing first, asked about the lost girl. She was seven, said her mother, so if she was here she'd be graduating from high school this year.

Going to the prom.

All those things.

How did it happen?

She was fishing with my husband.

You weren't there?

I was home that afternoon.

She just walked off?

No one knows exactly what happened. There wasn't a trace of her—okay, I apologize. I can't really talk about it.

The mother of the lost girl hung her head. The Catholic woman plucked at something that looked like clover festooning the bed of moss. What is this stuff? she asked. I'm sorry.

It's oxalis, said the mother of the lost girl. Some people actually plant it.

They traveled on through the labyrinth of blow-downs and climbed the steep hill northward. Ann seemed to the others aloof, traveling at a slight re-move. The rain had penetrated through the trees now, and passing through the Oregon grape and salal they were all soaked to the knees. The ex-bar-tender pulled a scarf over her head and snugly knot-ted it under her chin until it made a dimple in the fat there. I look like my grandmother this way, she said. But at least my hair won't be wet.

We all look like our grandmothers these days, the mother of the lost girl answered.

It's disconcerting.

I'll say it is.

What's to be done?

Nothing I don't think short of botox.

Well I can't afford a new face.

They came into the deeper forest, home to the purported apparitions, before twelve o'clock. I'm going to say the rosary, announced Ann, when they reached the spot she had led them to, a bed of moss beneath fir trees whose tops they couldn't see. Also a prayer for your missing daughter, if that's all right with you.

Yes, of course. I want you to. I've said plenty of prayers myself over the years and I'm not even religious isn't that strange?

Inside, said the Catholic woman, your heart wants to be.

She turned to Ann, put a hand on her shoulder. If it's okay I'll join you because I brought along my rosary. I checked my calendar last night, too. It's the feast of Martin of Tours.

Who's that? Ann asked.

The patron saint of horsemen and tailors. He joined the see in animal skins and was a conscientous objector.

Horsemen and tailors, said Carolyn. What a great combination.

Ann and the Catholic woman began their devotions. The others sat on a log nearby. The ex-bartender lit a cigarette. The mother of the lost girl produced from her backpack a Tupperware container of oatmeal cookies and a jug of lemonade. All right, she said. Help me, please. You two eat up.

They look great, said Carolyn. But I'm supposed to be watching my waistline.

I cut the butter back by half so you can probably get away with these.

It's the sugar that gets made into fat. I'm going to pass, thank you. Discipline. Control.

That only works for so long you know.

I know it better than anybody.

I've been reading about this thing called the Zone Diet. Thinking I'd better get myself on it before I turn into a cheese blimp.

Cheese blintz, said Carolyn. But I like cheese blimp better.

So, said the ex-bartender, taking a cookie. Where are we anyway?

This is Stinson Timber land. The mother of the lost girl took a cookie too. We went all through this years ago. When my daughter was lost. Stinson Timber. They own every stick of timber here. From here and down to the highway.

Stinson owns everything.

Just about.

It's hard to believe how much they own.

They're ruthless about it. That's how they do it. Or that's what my husband says.

I've been meaning to ask, said the ex-bartender. I won't say a word so you don't have to worry. But how come you're keeping this a secret from Jim? Why don't you want him to know?

Jim is Jim, he always has been, but somehow our marriage is stable right now. Right now things are on the upswing.

And? said Carolyn.

This is supposed to be behind me.

How can that ever be the case?

You have to go on, is what he says. And the marriage counselor is on his side. So I'm the bad guy, I guess.

Quiet, said the ex-bartender, snuffing out her cigarette against the toe of her boot. She's doing her thing over there.

My God, said the mother. She is.

None of them would say later that they saw the illuminated figure of a woman, smiling beatifically and clothed in shimmering vestments, that the visionary claimed was the Virgin Mary come to speak with her again. They heard nothing either, except for an occasional gasp from Ann, who seemed otherwise in the grip of catalepsy and was tilted forward in a kind of arrest that defied gravity. A girl in rapture turned to stone, except that now and then she trembled. The others present could not report that they too beheld a vision or received a Marian communiqué or saw the traveling light in the forest that Ann was adamant about. Yet for the mother of the lost girl and the Catholic woman kneeling at prayer there was a charged and numinous atmosphere and the aura of an otherworldly presence inhering in Ann's rapt attention. The Tupperware container fell from her lap, the oatmeal cookies spilled into the moss, and the mother of the lost girl took three steps in the direction of the visionary. Is it her? she asked. Lee Ann?

The ex-bartender held the snuffed-out cigarette as if it was evidence of her culpability in the crime of leading an abject life and considered only her next small move, whether she ought to tuck it in her pocket—and signal further her indigence—or drop it furtively into the moss and hope that this defilement of nature would not be noticed by anyone. Meanwhile the Catholic woman, still kneeling with her rosary, watched Ann with an expression of dazzled pleasure and said Bless and Hail Our Lord, Bless Jesus, Bless Our Lady. Carolyn picked up the oatmeal cookies. She's maybe on uppers or an epileptic, she said. Or I don't know. She's crazy.

Quiet, said the ex-bartender. Let's just watch for a while.

She hadn't seen anything like this before. The

girl was in the fixity of seizure and her face was awash, a-shine. The girl kept her gaze fixed steadily, she didn't blink or waver. Clearly this Ann was seeing something no one else could see right now, clearly she saw the invisible. And no one could keep from blinking that long or kneel so tilted without falling over unless there was supernatural assistance or something weird going on. The ex-bartender pondered the chances that perhaps, indeed, the Virgin Mary was present. It wasn't an impossibility, and thinking this, and feeling afraid, she knelt on the forest floor. It's the safe thing, she told herself.

The mother of the lost girl knelt as well. Is it Lee Ann? she pleaded. Lee Ann?

Now all had knelt except Carolyn, who saw the others in a kind of tableau, four women kneeling in forest rain like one of those tacky Christmas crèches, bewitched, felt Carolyn, by a shared fantasy that a ghost or something stood before them, ensorcelled by their own hopes. And she felt more powerfully alienated from people susceptible to these things. She fingered the cord from which her compass hung and clutched absentmindedly at her pepper-spray necklace. She felt alone, and feeling this, she took a large bite from a cookie. What the hell, she told herself. I haven't eaten today.

Ann in ecstasy, Carolyn thought, was something

like a theatrical performance that even Ann believed in. It was something like playing with a Ouija board. It was like the eyeballs that were really peeled grapes or the intestines that were only noodles in a Halloween haunted house. If you believed then what you believed was real and if you didn't believe there was pasta. It wasn't deceit or sham or swindle. The more accurate word was probably delusion, encompassing the appropriate psychological origins and including the notion of collective delusion, which embraced all four of these forest-kneelers clearly prone to believing something otherworldly was present. When in fact whatever was there was only there in the girl's addled mind, a desperate projection of her inner life with all of its high-pressure turmoil. Ann's self-arrest was self-imposed, her dialogue with herself. Like the jet of steam from a boiling pot a shade comes into this world. Like the sleepwalker engaged in a conversation with nobody in the room. Like the dreamer who falls from bed at night in lieu of a dream-world death. Carolyn chewed her cookie and watched while Ann's tortured face constricted and contorted through the myriad expressions of the listener, the histrionic listening face that shows everything, like a mime's. Mime was not a bad comparison, if the mime could be construed as having studied with Lee Strasberg. A mime hallucinating.

When Ann was done she collapsed on the moss

in the same manner as the day before, then sat up and swabbed her eyes. The mother of the lost girl wept, gasping: grief collected over many years. Our Lady knew you were here, Ann told her. And she says Lee Ann is in heaven.

What happened to my baby?

I don't know what happened.

Can't you ask?

I don't know if I can. The Blessed Mother came to speak to me, not for me to speak to her.

The mother of the lost girl clasped her hands. Couldn't you try, though? Please?

I guess I could try.

God bless you.

She wept more, and the visionary held her lightly in her arms and stroked her wet gray hair. It's all right. Your daughter is with Jesus. Stop crying. Everything is all right.

I'm sorry about your daughter, I truly am, cut in Carolyn, and I imagine that your life has been ruined by losing her, that it's been easily the most difficult thing ever and that the rest of us don't know a thing about it, can't relate, don't understand, have no idea how it affects you really, how it colors everything every day and is absolutely the worst thing that could happen to a person, but anyway I have to say, Ann you sound like a radio talk-show host, a Bible station call-in show to Dr. God or something. I—

She's helping me, said the mother of the lost girl. Don't be critical. Please.

When she was calmer and had stopped sobbing they all sat under the cover of trees and tried to collect themselves. The ex-bartender, apologizing, lit her cigarette again. A cigarette helps me relax, she said, so don't lecture me about lung cancer please. But getting to the point here: What did she say? The Virgin Mary? What did she tell you? Aren't we all interested in that?

I won't lecture, Ann said, and took the ex-bartender's hand. But God wants you to quit smoking. I'm going to pray for you to stop this habit of needing nicotine.

Whoa, said Carolyn. Come on now.

And these warts on your fingers, Ann added. God can make them go away. I'll pray for that at the same time. All of us should include her in our prayers. Prayers of healing and redemption.

No cigarettes or warts, said Carolyn. Are you David Copperfield?

But the ex-bartender could not easily shrug off the heightened feelings of the moment. What she felt was a jolt of assurance passing from Ann's hand to hers. I hope it works, she said earnestly. I'm not against anything successful.

A pragmatist, said Carolyn. You remind me of Blaise Pascal's wager, which holds that the skeptic should believe in God, since if there is a God belief's the right call, and if there isn't, no harm, excellent. Whereas the nonbeliever might burn in hell. So now that I think about it, count me in! Count me a believer!

Hold up, the ex-bartender said. Let's get back to the subject here. What did the Virgin say, please? Aren't we all dying to know?

Besides Lee Ann, the mother said. Yes. There must have been more . . . revelation. Isn't that the word?

In God's glory, said the Catholic woman.

The message was this, Ann told them. One: All good followers of Christ were called immediately to renewed service in the name of the Mother of God. Two: Our Lady had come to warn the world and to implore in particular the selfish and greedy to change their ways immediately, lest it be the case soon that she could no longer restrain her Son from wreaking a general destruction. Three: True believers were called upon to spread Mary's message of dire consequence if sin were not energetically thwarted and also of hope for a better future in which few, if any, were still impoverished. Four: Our Lady would return on four successive days to deliver further messages and to elaborate her themes. Five: A beautiful new church and shrine to Mother Mary should be built at this very place in the forest where they now stood together. Six: Ann was to go to the local priest and tell him everything.

They ate the cookies, drank the lemonade. They had all gotten wet in the soft, steady rain and had the bedraggled look of lost travelers, except for Ann, who still wore her hood, and the ex-bartender, who wore her scarf. Well, said Carolyn, standing up. I guess this is farewell for me. She tied a bootlace and picked up her mushroom bucket. I have to try to make a living.

Go in peace, Ann said. But when are you going to admit to yourself that you didn't come out here to pick today? That you came here looking for the Lord?

Go in peace? Are you serious? Are you starting to believe in yourself?

I believe in the Father and the Son.

And what about the quote Holy Ghost?

Answer me and I'll answer you.

Okay, said Carolyn. Once and for all. It's a big gamble but here I go: If there's a God may he strike me dead right now, in front of you all, as evidence and proof! Hello? God? I'm waiting.

She stood there. Ring him up, she said. Or talk to his wife—get her on board to talk to him about penciling in my death. Come on, Ann. Dial up. Order a bolt of lightning.

She isn't his wife.

That's not the point.

And the Lord doesn't have to prove anything.

Anyway, said Carolyn. I have to get busy.

You didn't come for mushrooms, insisted Ann.

Carolyn swung her mushroom bucket. Get help, okay Ann? I think you need professional help. You're seeing things, okay?

She turned her attention to the Catholic woman. What was that? Horsemen and tailors? Well who's the patron saint of lunatics?

Strange you should ask because I happen to know. Christina the Astonishing, she was called. Her feast day is my birthday, July twenty-fourth. She's also the patron of therapists.

Doctor and patient. How convenient.

The Catholic woman lifted her camera. No one helps himself by hurting another. Those words are ascribed to Saint Ambrose. Now do you think it would be okay, would everyone agree to a group portrait?

And so they arrayed themselves, if sluggishly. The Catholic woman set her camera on a log and peered for a long time through the viewfinder, making minor adjustments. There, she said finally, pushed the timer button, and hurried into the photograph. They sat there waiting for the click that meant the camera's shutter had opened and

closed and in that interim the Catholic woman
said: Thank you all for doing this. Because I like
to remember things.

You know the Simon and Garfunkel song? said
the ex-bartender, and the timer clicked. This reminds me of that.

Which one? asked the Catholic woman.

Kodachrome. What else would it be?

I know it well, it's a song I like. I think Paul
Simon is kind of a genius. Anyway, we've commemorated this day. We've hallowed it with a
photograph.

The song's sarcastic, Carolyn pointed out.
They're anti-photo, not pro.

Going back toward the campground, the
Catholic woman turned her camera on the rain
forest and snapped four photos for her memory
book—a bed of rotting vine-maple leaves, a boul-
der encrusted in hoary lichens, the monstrous fo-
liage of a skunk cabbage, raindrops on a frond of
fern. She did not believe in the literal sense that
the Virgin Mary had made an appearance, since
hers was not that kind of Catholicism; she had
gone to church consistently except for a period in
her early twenties when, briefly, she'd been attracted to Buddhism, then she came back, immersed herself, had flirted with the thought of
becoming a nun—but even in her piety she was
cognizant of her skepticism, a deep and quiet cur-

rent. She did not believe in apparitions and could not believe in apparitions and even to believe in God was an effort for an honest person, just read Saint Augustine. On the other hand, who could be certain? In the girl's rapture there was possibly some spark of another, larger truth. The point, for the Catholic woman, was that she wanted to believe, which she didn't tell the diocesan committee or the bishop's representative when asked sometime later. Instead she described the consecrated atmosphere, the feel of something hallowed in the forest while the visionary knelt in ecstasy. She made no reference to doubt.

The ex-bartender told herself that the day had already culminated. The expedition with the visionary meant that now it was too late to forage for mushrooms and besides she was wet, she didn't feel like working, and she felt an obligation to the mother of the lost girl to hike back with her. Also in her car at the campground was approximately one sixth of a bottle of gin and with the engine idling she could run the heater and drink and listen to the radio and clip her fingernails. A little drive first would warm up the car, it was seven miles into North Fork, besides she needed a quart of motor oil, the pistons were worn, which worried her, the car drank a quart every five hundred miles, and she wanted a *People* magazine and a package of low-tar cigarettes.

Now she remembered that on Friday afternoon during happy hour at HK's Tavern a tap beer was only seventy-nine cents, meaning that for a price almost in her budget she could sit inside and watch television, smoke in peace and ponder what she'd seen—this ragtag girl with the sweatshirt hood who claimed to commune with the Virgin Mary, who claimed she could heal warts with prayer and thwart the power of nicotine. The ex-bartender could already predict what kinds of things she was going to hear, the kind of resistance she was going to meet by talking about the girl at HK's—Those doper mushroom people in the campground, they're all on acid anyway, they probably all see things in the woods, Snow White and the Seven Dwarfs, Little Red Riding Hood, Jimi Hendrix, the naked Indian from that movie The Doors. Heh-heh-heh. Haw-haw. They don't call them mushroomers for nothing.

The mother of the lost girl walked behind Ann and asked herself repeatedly what to tell her husband. That she'd followed this penniless waif into the woods while he was at work, earning their keep, and searched for Lee Ann's ghost? That this waif had seen the Virgin Mary and been assured that Lee Ann was in heaven and had promised to make further inquiries into the mystery of Lee Ann's disappearance? Jim would sit with his head between his knees, fingering the bristles on the

nape of his neck, gray now but not unattractive in
the way they contrasted with the deep red crevices
in a patchwork below his hairline. His neck had
the raw painful look of sunburn even in the middle of winter and he wore white t-shirts and black
plastic glasses without realizing they were sort of
hip. If he'd known he would have done something
about it. That was one of the differences between
them. It was all convoluted over many years but
even the marriage counselor agreed that part of
the problem was selfishness, that Jim cared moderately about how she felt but more about pre-
serving a status quo in which there was sufficient
equilibrium to ensure fairly regular sexual en-
counters—at this point twice a week was adequate
to keep him satisfied. It would have been nice if
somehow the result had been another child to raise
but after Lee Ann she was utterly barren; they'd
been lucky, in fact, to have Lee Ann. An upright
tree in winter with no leaves, was how she thought
of herself. Or as old and weathered like a shed or
barn, or like a starving sow with empty teats.
Anyway, their marriage had improved. It was all
calmed down like torpid water. Stirring it would
only corroborate Jim's unarticulated but obvious
suspicion that she harbored permanent hope. She
did like to think that it had happened before—
strange teenager knocks on the door, says I'm the
child you lost years ago—every time she heard a

knock, which almost never happened in North Fork, that was the thought that rose in her, a flighty little leap of hope. No, she just couldn't tell Jim anything, divulge to him her enthusiasm for what had unfolded this day. Jim would sit there shaking his head and maybe turn on the television, telling himself he didn't need to shave, didn't even need to jump in the shower, they were back in sullen contentiousness, there wouldn't be sex tonight. Of course, that was just one big question. The other—less personal but more spiritual, or maybe more personal because it was spiritual— was what she was going to do about it if the Virgin Mary was real.

They walked together but separately, a small group weaving through monumental trees, insects threading through blades of grass, Ann silently in the lead. Even Carolyn had not branched off. I want to pick somewhere new, she told Ann, catching up to her. What I want to find is the mother lode, not the Mother Mary.

I have to go see the priest in town.

See a shrink.

Come on, Carolyn.

Get a ride with what's-her-name. The woman who lost her daughter over there. And have her stop at the drugstore for you so you can get some cold medicine.

Ann stopped and pulled off her hood. Now she

appeared to be twelve years old, somebody's little sister. What if I asked you to take me? she said. I can give you gas money for it.

If you asked me I guess I'd have to say yes, but that doesn't mean I'm helping you because I still think this is psychotic behavior. And what's-her-name would do it right now because she has to get home anyway so why not just go with her?

I don't have a reason.

That isn't an answer.

If you're going to pick I'll wait for you.

Well I don't want you giving me gas money. And after the priest, listen to me, we hit the psycho ward.

I'm not psycho, said Ann.

At six-fifteen they knocked on the door of Father Collins' trailer home in the North Fork Mobile Home Court. There was something unseemly about the notion of a priest who lived in a mildewed trailer court, in part because it seemed to them that the church must provide for its clergymen a rectory or permanent lodgings, in part because the trailer court was known to be a place of discords. Drunks and criminals lived there. It was regularly visited by the sheriff. Vast puddles stood in lieu of landscaping outside Father Collins' door, and his car, a worn station wagon made in Japan, had a bent coat-hanger antenna. His trailer sat at the end of a row of trailers closely resembling it and was difficult for Ann and Carolyn to find, their journey starting at Saint Joseph's of North Fork, where they'd rattled the doorknob, peered through the windows, and noted his name on a placard. At MarketTime they'd found no information in the white pages cabled to the telephone booth but asked around until a boy stocking shelves said he thought Father Collins lived in the trailer court. Carolyn bought Ann a package of Sudafed to go with her antihistamine; then in the rain they knocked on trailer doors, more than one person noting, concurring, that it was odd for a priest to be living there, something you wouldn't assume or expect; nevertheless, he did. Doesn't even look like a priest, one man had added suspiciously. I've never seen him in that collar getup priests are supposed to wear.

With time they'd been led to the proper dwelling, but only after a series of mistakes—knocking on the wrong doors, misunderstanding what they were told, once even leaving the trailer court for another three miles up the highway. We're looking for a Father Collins, Carolyn said to everyone, until finally someone answered, I'm him.

You really are?

I'm the guy.

Where's your collar?

I don't wear it all the time.

You're really the priest from the Catholic church?

I pinch myself sometimes. But yes.

He was slight of build, maybe thirty years old, with thin hair like cornsilk. With his index finger tucked into a book he looked more like a graduate student studying for final examinations than a priest at home for the evening. He wore sweatpants, a t-shirt, a button-up sweater, wire-rimmed glasses, and slippers. While he spoke he looked with curiosity at Ann, whose face was concealed under her hood—he even bent at the knees a little, to peer more closely at her features. A little lost soul with a cold, he thought. And a rather stunning immaculate complexion. Hello, he said. Obviously it's raining. I'm losing my heat with the door open like this. So if this isn't a quick question, something quick I can do for you, it's probably better if you come in for a bit, except that the place is a mess.

This isn't quick, warned Carolyn.

Then, okay, come in.

The heat was on very high in his trailer, which smelled of mold and fried onions. They sat on his sofa. He turned off a lamp. I was reading but I'm not right now and I think that lamp is just too bright. It blinds my many visitors, the endless parade of guests.

We got your name off the church door. Father Donald Collins.

I could show you my ID if you want.

You just don't look like a priest is my point.

Well what's a priest supposed to look like?

Like Karl Malden, said Carolyn.

Father Collins smiled broadly, revealing that his teeth weren't straight. I think of him, he said, from The Streets of San Francisco. His partner was Michael Douglas, right? Back when Michael Douglas was young. Michael Douglas was the young tough guy. Karl Malden slowed him down. But a priest? Was he ever a priest?

He played a priest in On the Waterfront. Also—kind of—in Pollyanna. That was Karl Malden. The Reverend Paul Ford.

I don't remember seeing Pollyanna. But you're right about On the Waterfront. He was superb in that.

I coulda been somebody too, said Carolyn, and her Brando was not that bad.

Father Collins sat in a ratty reading chair with one leg hooked at a feminine angle across the knee of the other. With his plate of orange slices on the table beside him, their membranes dry and hard in the swelter, he seemed to be a homebody. His hands were small and looked fragile and pale. He had bitten a few nails to the quick. So what's this about? he asked now. Are you with the Karl Malden Fan Club?

Not quite, answered Carolyn. She turned to Ann and touched her knee. My friend here wants to tell you something.

I'm happy to help if I can, said Father Collins. But is this an emergency?

Not like a nine-one-one emergency, if that's what you mean, not like that, but as far as my friend here is concerned, this couldn't wait for your church to open.

The priest took in the girl again; she hadn't yet removed her hood. Please, he said to her. Speak.

This is hard, Father, said Ann.

The priest didn't think of himself as "Father," and the word persistently surprised him. He thought of himself as Donny Collins, a boy grow- ing up near Everett, Washington, the name he'd been given to distinguish him from Don Collins, his father the machinist and Cub Scout leader, Jack Russell terrier enthusiast, remote control glider airplane hobbyist, church treasurer and Rotarian. Much has been made in psychoanalysis of the son burdened with his father's name, of the name that is like a noose or straitjacket or the ut- terance of a willed fate, for to be named for one's father makes more desperate the struggle to sub- due and kill him. As a result, the priest had not been among those boys who rolled their eyes at their tenth-grade English teacher as she explicated Freud's embarrassing theory in accompaniment to *Oedipus the King*. Don Junior didn't desire his mother, or didn't believe he desired her, his denial consistent with the theory of the unconscious—with the father of psychoanalysis you couldn't win either way—but he knew he wanted to kill Don Senior: for him, Freud was half right.

Go right ahead, he told the girl. But maybe—first—you should take off that hood. Because I'd like to see your face while you're speaking. It makes it easier for me.

He didn't want to be overbearing. He knew that overbearing didn't work and was of the opposite school. Father Collins' father had been overbearing, which in combination with his doting mother was supposed to produce a Stalin or Hitler but in his case produced a priest. In college Father Collins had mulled that irony, read *Mein Kampf* and the accounts of Hitler's life, the library of psychological theory, read about Stalin, then about Mao, who suffered a similar family dynamic, a fact little known in the West. Father Collins was dismayed to find that like all three members of this mad triumvirate he'd grown up ashamed of his provincialism—in his case a lower-class, suburban, American, West Coast, blue-collar provincialism—but relieved to note that unlike them he hadn't suffered in the crucible of a terrifying war. Perhaps, he'd speculated, but for that element he might have annihilated his own millions, though at the same time he understood that nothing really worked that way and that causal theories about the deeds of men were often completely facile. He was a total physical coward, for one. He could not have taken the life of another, even by an abstract command. *Look, with a spot I damn him* was, to his way of seeing things, the most chilling line in his eleventh-grade reading of *The Tragedy of Julius Caesar.* With Hamlet in the twelfth grade, Donny identified utterly.

The girl before him slid back her hood and her pale young face emerged from it, a white chrysanthemum. It seemed she had barbered her own hair without the fundamental assistance of a mirror, scissoring it off in hanks. She was slim, wet, and plainly ill, and she evoked in him both professional pity and a burst of sexual desire. The latter was more than incidental, as it always was for Father Collins, whose vow of celibacy was in part a life sentence to struggle with carnal yearnings. The girl's youth was highly disturbing, a girl of her age was clearly off limits, the ineluctable craving he felt for a girl just recently of childbearing age must not be consummated. The irony being that for a priest like him, all people of all ages were off limits.

Father Collins didn't desire Ann Holmes any more than he desired most other women, which is to say that as best he could he put his corporeal desire aside from the moment she pulled back her sweatshirt hood with her cold, pink, small fingers. Thank you, he said. I can see you now. Why don't you tell me what your name is?

I don't know if I should give it or not.

This sounds like it might be complicated.

It's the most complicated thing that's ever happened to either one of us.

Except that it hasn't happened to me yet.

In a way it has. I guess you could say that.

Okay, said Father Collins. Whatever it is. Have you committed some kind of crime?

No.

Is there something you feel you have to confess?

I've been sent to you, said Ann.

The priest had to ask a great variety of questions, so they were there for a long time. At first he sat with an elbow on his knee and a hand clamped over the lower half of his face, as though afraid that but for his hand he might be compelled to interrupt. He was a good listener, his posture intimated, though at the same time he appeared eager to retort at any point. At moments in the narrative most outlandish—the attack of the ball of light, the advent of the Virgin, Our Lady's six-point bulletin—he pressed his hand even harder to his mouth in order not only to maintain his composure but to keep himself from responding in a fashion derisive or prosecutorial. Father Collins had a modest familiarity with prominent apparition narratives like those that unfolded at Lourdes and Fátima and was aware that in their standard tellings the local priest was an insular bureaucrat, at odds with the inexorable groundswell of sentiment in support of the peasant visionary. Given this, he did not interrupt. He would not play the role of ecclesiastical authority. His view of himself was adversarial. He wanted to reform the church.

He had wanted to reform the church, in fact, ever since middle school. He'd incited concurrently running arguments with the instructor of his confirmation class about the pope's positions on abortion and birth control, the existence of the devil and hell, and the nature of the Holy Trinity. He was one of those pent-up sensitive boys whom classmates mistake for a homosexual because he did not express himself crudely, was open about his intelligence, wore saddle shoes and corduroy slacks, and was passive during gym class. Faggot, other boys said to him. I'm not a faggot, he answered. But why would you care if I was anyway? How come you're thinking about faggots constantly? Why is it such a big deal to you? What is this weird obsession you have with faggots all the time?

He'd been shoved against a locker once for saying just this sort of thing, the other boy closely breathing on his face, fist poised, waiting. I have an idea, said Donny. If we're going to get in a fight over this, why don't we do it where we can impress some girls? Or maybe you don't care about girls. Anyway, there's guys around, and maybe you're okay with that. So go ahead, hit me!

Donny had smoked a lot of marijuana as a preventative against school boredom and because it made large questions palpable, allowing for their contemplation. As a teenager he'd formulated a metaphysics that was sequenced like a geometrical theorem or a formal causal argument and had presented it, stoned, to a friend named Jerry: that human behavior acts like a wave, a wave has mass as in particles of light, mass has gravity and as cosmologists know, gravity determines the fate of the universe, therefore the behavior of individual human beings, good or bad, right or wrong, contributes either to eternal oscillation or to a cold and lifeless steady-state entropy, to fire or ice, darkness or light, we each make our personal contribution, that was the critical thing about free will, the fate of the universe was literally at stake, the word *gravity* had two meanings, now do you think maybe you could be less selfish and stop bogarting that bong, Jerry? Wait, answered Jerry. There's a major flaw. You presuppose action is like a wave. It's all contingent on that being so. Karma, said Donny. Cause and effect. Now quit stalling and pass me the bong. Effects aren't waves, Jerry said.

Donny's parents, eventually, had become unin-flected background noise, Muzak played in an elevator. Their moral impact dwindled steadily until he was able to lie to them with pleasure and aplomb. Chess Club meeting at Jerry's house. We're going to watch hockey. The International Brotherhood of Left-Handed Basket Weavers' Fifteenth Annual Rendezvous. It hadn't always been that way. The prepubescent Donny and his sisters were sometimes arrayed as though for a firing squad, his father pacing, his mother at hand, his father fulminating and venomous to a degree incommensurate with circumstances, his mother obviously rent by crisis, yearning to support her spouse and also yearning to protect her children, by these opposing intentions paralyzed, and his father might say—his father had once said—I'm asking only one more time, and this time I want an honest answer: Which one of you got into the hi-fi this morning and scratched my Sinatra record?

They would have been sequestered in their sev-

eral bedrooms for two hours and forty-five minutes with a decree to give this question thought
since none of them would admit their guilt, all
three deflecting blame when asked, and so, it was
certain, one of them was lying, a crime far worse
than touching the hi-fi, which heightened the
stakes, compounded the mystery, and left Donny
feeling deeply troubled about the looming culmi-
nation of events. The innocent had already suffered because of the persistent cowardice of the
guilty, a cowardice charting a line parallel to the
line of the father's wrath. The culpable party was
keenly aware of the moral complexity of the situation and of what that meant for sibling relations
but also admired the father's strategy, so Machia-
vellian and fantastically medieval, to divide and
conquer was an art. Which one of you? his father
said. Which one did it? Or do you all want to
spend the whole day doing nothing in your
rooms? Or the whole weekend as far as I'm concerned. And you can miss school on Monday too
because we're going to get to the bottom of this. I
want to know who scratched my record and who
answered no when the truth was yes, that's the
thing that's got me. If it was just the record that
would be one thing, that was something I could
have addressed, but the lying, the lying, that I can't
accept, I can never trust you again if you lie, and

in a family you have to have absolute trust, now which one of you scratched my record?

Donny's endurance wilted. He was whipped ten times on his bare backside, the number ten emblematic of order—his father was a proponent of the metric system—not too many but not too few, an amount that would have to be endured and was not mere symbolic punishment but the real thing, authentic pain. His father, it was obvious, held something back but nonetheless delivered pain in a measure intended to be permanently memorable and forever associated with the notion of lying, using the belt holding up his pants, then threading it back, retucking his shirt, yelling hysterically all the while in a reedy shrill voice they all recognized, Don't you lie, don't ever lie again, don't you *ever* lie to me!

His father became inarticulate. He sat down on a chair and checked his belt. Look, he said finally, I don't want to be mean. Now wait a minute I take that back. Yes I do really want to be mean because I want you to learn a valuable lesson and there just isn't any other way besides a real punishment that will make an impression. Right and wrong, Donny, right and wrong, it's not about the Sinatra record. I can always buy a new one of those. Now pull your pants up and buckle them. And stop whimpering like a little girl.

OUR LADY OF THE FOREST

Don't call him that, Donny's mother said. I
don't approve of this.

You be quiet, said his father.

They went to Alaska one summer on the ferry
and there was a girl with red hair and a backpack
on the top deck who had staked out a chaise
longue, laid her sleeping bag on it, and passed the
miles reading John Muir and eating soy nuts from
a bag. She and Donny smoked pot together and
rummaged inside each other's clothing until the
ship was halfway to Sitka. The logistics of their li-
aisons were particularly challenging because pas-
sengers tended to linger at night to gaze in search
of the northern lights and generally to partake of
the solstice dusk, so there was little in the way of
darkness or privacy; nevertheless they found
furtive corners, places where she pushed against
him, reached inside his pants with a cool hand,
and whispered encouragements in his ear like
Love the one you're with.

He was sixteen. He became ill while they were
under way and could not continue with these
assignations, but in Sitka he saw her at the Raptor
Rehabilitation Center—a ceremony for setting
free an eagle that had successfully convalesced.
How are you? she said. Better, he answered. I
think I'm in love with you.

I'm not with you. What is love? I think you
mean lust, not love.

The liberated eagle flew two hundred yards, settled on a limb, and looked back. Some of the tourists clapped and cheered but something about this conventional response, as if they were spectators at a football game, seemed inappropriate from the moment it started, and a hush soon descended. They stood waiting for the eagle's next move.

I mean love, insisted Donny. I think I know the difference.

No guy knows, said the red-haired girl. Don't be completely ridiculous.

Jilted, he mooned through the chamber musical festival. She was there, too, and afterward he approached her. You're not for me, she said.

Why not?

You're too intense.

What do you mean?

You're just too wired. You think too much. It's not something I want to deal with. I didn't come up here for spiritual angst. Is there a God, isn't there a God—I don't want to approach it with words.

Sorry for ruining your vacation, said Donny.

Fuck you, too, she answered.

Ann told her story with chronological precision, as if the order of things was the point. Finally she pulled out her rosary. Everything is totally true, she said. In Jesus' name, Father. I swear.

Father Collins scratched his brow, shook his head, and sighed. This is—how to put it—I don't know. This is just really . . . mind-boggling.

Nice description, said Carolyn.

This is a serious claim you're making.

All I know is what I see. And hear, too. What I hear.

You see and hear her.

Ann nodded.

But no one else does. Not these others. Not your friend here or any of these other people who went into the woods with you.

I didn't see a thing, said Carolyn. And didn't hear anything, either.

I did, said Ann.

But, said the priest, like you see and hear me?

No. Not the same.

Well how does it differ?

I can see through her. Like she's made of light. I can't see through you. You're solid.

Like looking through a window?

No. Not really.

Like what then?

I can't put it into words.

Well what about her voice. Is it just like mine?

It's a woman's voice.

But is it like a person speaking?

It's far away. Like under water. That's the best I can describe it.

People can't speak under water, said Carolyn.

I think I can see what she means, though, said the priest. It's a figurative description. Not literal.

I mean *if* you could speak under water, said Ann. If you could, that's what you'd sound like.

Right, said the priest. But does it seem to you that the words you hear from her travel to you directly through the air—like ordinary words, like my words, sound waves—or is it that you hear them in your head as if they arrived there by telepathy? Instead of hearing them through your ears?

Telepathy. In my head.

A telepathic voice then? Not like thoughts? Not the sound of your own internal voice? Not the sound of your own thinking but somebody else's voice?

It's the sound of her voice in my head—her voice. That's how she speaks to me.

But do you see her lips move? Is it something like lip-syncing? Her lips move, and telepathically, you hear her words in private?

Her lips aren't moving, no.

You can see that clearly? She's close enough?

Her lips aren't moving. Definitely.

And how close is she?

Like twenty yards.

Does it seem to you that you could touch her, though? If you reached out, could you take hold of something? Or would your fingers—I don't know—maybe go right through her? Like a ghost or like us, three dimensions?

You'd go right through her. I guess. Sort of. I can't explain it very well.

Would there be, say, a ripple, do you think? Like parting water with your hand? Or nothing—like parting air?

I think it would be more like parting mist. Like putting your hand through a cloud.

What makes you say that?

It's just an impression.

An observation?

Yes. Observation.

So her texture is like the texture of a cloud?

I guess so. I don't really know.

Well how does seeing her compare to a dream? Is it the same sort of thing? Like dreaming?

No. I don't think so. I know it isn't. It's not like dreaming, no.

How is it different?

What do you mean?

What are the differences between this experience and the experience of having a dream?

The difference is, it's not dreaming. I'm awake when this is happening. It's more like now—like right now. Don't you know for sure right now that you're awake and not asleep?

Yes.

Well that's what it's like when I see her.

I didn't mean to imply otherwise at all. I'm sorry if it seemed that way.

It didn't.

I apologize.

It's okay, Father.

I'm pressing you, forgive me for that. He lifted his crossed leg, set it on the floor, and brought the other up. I'm acting like a lawyer, he said.

Not really, answered Carolyn. You haven't billed us yet.

Do you think, said the priest, that you could tell me the whole thing again, just repeat everything that happened? And would you mind if I stop you along the way and ask a few more questions?

It's after seven, said Carolyn. Maybe we'll go eat and come back.

Please, said the priest. Eat with me. Stay. I was just about to throw something together when you two knocked on the door.

He noted the disdain of the visionary regarding the subject of dinner. It was clear to him from the tension in her posture that she had no inclination to eat. He thought it was in part the malaise of illness, in part her Marian obsession. Let's just take a time-out, he said. I'm going to cook—linguini marinara. I'll be in the kitchen. Read something, or take a nap. Nurse your cold, turn on the television. Relax for a little while.

I'll help, said Carolyn.

No you won't. The kitchen's too small. Let me handle it. My blessing.

What a priest, Carolyn said. Equally adept on the pulpit and in the kitchen. Most priests I'm guessing do frozen pizza or microwaved Mexican food.

I do those too, the priest answered.

He served pasta with basil tomato sauce from a jar, warm bread with butter and garlic salt, steamed string beans and a salad of iceberg lettuce dressed with ketchup and mayonnaise mixed to approximate Thousand Island dressing. While they ate on the sofa, holding their plates, he played a tape called *Beethoven Breaks Out:* the second movement of the Ninth Symphony, the Apassionata, the Kreutzer sonatas, the Egmont overture. Lively inoffensive music. Carolyn ate with gusto, Ann with a perfunctory charm. Afterward the priest did the dishes rapidly, then gave them bowls of Neapolitan ice cream, set out a plate of sugar wafers, and made them Darjeeling tea. Finally he told them that if they used the bathroom it was necessary to keep the toilet handle lifted in order to achieve a decent flush and apologized for not having cleaned the sink—I'm not very neat and clean, he confessed. I don't stay on top of the housekeeping.

It was true, Ann found, that the bathroom sink was flecked with shaven facial hair and stained with nasal mucus. On an open shelf stood a package of disposable razors of the sort purchased in preposterous volume at warehouse discount stores. There was a twelve-pack of toilet paper, ten bars of soap, a large bottle of Tylenol, and a half dozen large toothpaste tubes—it was as though Father Collins expected a siege or sudden economic turmoil to disrupt the flow of goods. Two magazines and two books lay on the floor beside his toilet—*Travel and Leisure, Vanity Fair,* J. P. Donleavy's *The Ginger Man,* and Norman O. Brown's *Love's Body.* The visionary, seated on the toilet, pigeon-toed and cramping now, the flow of her period at its heaviest pitch, blew her nose into a wad of toilet paper, opened the Donleavy to its inside cover, and read: A PICARESQUE NOVEL TO STOP THEM ALL. LUSTY, VIOLENT, WILDLY FUNNY, IT IS A RIGADOON OF RASCALITY, A BAWLED-OUT COMIC SONG OF SEX. What was the priest doing with a book like this? Curious, she opened *Love's Body* randomly, to page 63, noting on her way how the text was permeated by incessant line breaks, diced into endless cryptic snippets: *The vagina as a devouring mouth, or* vagina dentata; *the jaws of the giant cannibalistic mother, a menstruating woman with the penis bitten off, a bleeding trophy—Cf. Roheim,* Riddle of the Sphinx. She combed through the rest and found that much was much like this, passages about sex and other matters lifted from writers she'd never heard of and placed back-to-back and side by side, as if they added up to something by virtue of juxtaposition. And maybe they did. She didn't know. But why was a priest reading this sort of thing? While sitting on his toilet or anywhere else? She'd assumed when she came in that the magazines would have titles like *Priest Quarterly* or *Catholic Review* and the books would be Saint Augustine's *Confessions* or a Mother Teresa biography—not *Travel and Leisure* or *Vanity Fair,* not a woman with her penis bitten off or a bawled-out comic song of sex.

She couldn't help herself. She peeked into his bedroom. She saw where he slept under an unzipped sleeping bag with two empty pop cans crumpled on the nightstand, more magazines and books on the floor, a digital display alarm clock flashing all red zeroes in the dark. A towel had been thumbtacked over the window, and a pair of dumbbells languished in the corner. What would a priest do with dumbbells? she asked herself. Why would a priest want muscles? He had nailed a crucifix over his bed, a two-foot Jesus long and black, sternum high and exaggerated, chest pronounced like the chest of a great bird, the gut shrunken and shriveled tight beneath the stripes of the rib cage. Ann took three steps into the room where she smelled the sheets on the priest's rumpled bed, nervously touched Christ's thigh with an index finger, crossed herself, and kissed her rosary. Hail Mary, full of grace, she whispered. Then she hurried back into the living room.

The rain sounded like shotgun pellets against the priest's trailer-house window. He had turned off a second lamp, and they spoke now in the glow from the kitchen spilling across the sofa, concerto music turned so low it was only audible during the brief silences between their uttered thoughts.

So there were six points, the priest was saying. And she mentioned, specifically, selfishness.

Greed too, Father.

But there are so many other forms of sin.

Those were the ones the Blessed Mother mentioned.

Why those?

I don't know.

She didn't say?

No, she didn't.

But the fourth point was her promise to return. For four days in a row, you say. So perhaps we'll find out more.

I can't say, said the visionary.

The priest nodded soberly. Did you ask or did she volunteer her revelation regarding the missing girl?

I didn't ask anything. I listened, Father.

I ask because it differs in substance from the rest of the message you received. It's specific while the rest is general. That's why I ask. It's different.

It's her fifth point that's . . . different, Ann said. That we have to build a church up there. A church and a shrine to Our Lady the Blessed Virgin. She gave us something we have to do. So on that—we have to get started.

Well, said the priest, sitting back. Big challenge. Big task. I've been trying myself ever since I got here to get a new church built in town because the current version is falling apart, a drafty barn, it smells like mildew, but if you don't mind, let's concentrate on your vision. I, for one, am prompted by your vision to meditate on the nature of illusion. On the seeing of extraordinary things.

Me too, said Carolyn.

I'm interested, said the priest, in the forms of illusion. The various forms of mirage and apparition. Take, for example, crossing your eyes. I can hold my fingers in front of my face and by merely allowing my focus to soften produce the illusion of two index fingers, one immediately beside the other, and that's one form of illusion. Different from a magician's illusion that he has pulled a rabbit out of a hat or cut his assistant in half at the waist—that's just sleight-of-hand and mirrors, I'm not raising the specter of that. If you're camped beside a river at night and sitting dreamily by your fire you can begin to imagine that the sound of the river is really the sound of voices in the woods or when you're falling asleep or in reverie you can feel that somewhere in the drift of your thoughts is something vaguely repetitive of the past, as if you've been in this moment before, but—

Déjà vu, said Carolyn. I'm having one right now.

That's an illusion, said the priest. Though it's entirely possible that in point of fact you might have been here before.

You said that last time, exactly.

The priest smiled. Did I smile? he asked. Did I ask you if I smiled?

I'm completely not religious, said Carolyn, so I don't care if you know this or not you can take it or leave it for whatever it's worth since it's probably some kind of sin or something but I've been on probably two dozen acid trips and seen things like seagulls flying in slow motion and a cat multiplying into twenty cats sort of like in a hall of mirrors and also a tree squeezed so tightly by a cable that I could literally hear it . . . weeping. And it all seemed more real than real, more real than normal does, but it was just inside my head in the end. It was just something my head made up. It was just a trip I was on.

I know what you're saying, Ann said. But this isn't like that. It's different.

Different how? said Carolyn.

I remember, said Ann, my science teacher in the ninth grade saying that if you were a dog or a bee, everything would be different. You wouldn't see what we see. If you were a fly this teacup wouldn't be here. If none of us were in this room and just a fly was buzzing around there wouldn't be this cup.

What is this, Ann, Philosophy One-oh-one? I thought you believed in God and Creation. What are all these deep thoughts?

I'm just saying—I saw the Blessed Mother.

Look, I have to pee, said Carolyn. So hold the phenomenology, please, until I empty my bladder.

I saw Mother Mary, repeated Ann.

Carolyn got up and went toward the bathroom. Remember to lift the handle, called the priest. You have to hold it for about three seconds if you want the thing to flush right.

Then they were alone together, the visionary and the priest. He could hear her rough, asthmatic breathing. He became self-conscious and began to worry that the fine hairs shooting from his ears now that he was close to thirty were highly objectionable. Ann, he said. That's your name, I guess. The epistemological argument can be a compelling one.

Sorry but I don't follow you.

It doesn't matter when I think about it because your argument isn't really epistemological, it's empirical to its core. It's based on data, raw evidence. It's based on knowing something definitively because you've experienced it directly and explicitly and without questioning the validity of your senses. There's no deduction or induction. Just your sensory impression.

Anyway you don't believe me, Ann said.

I do believe you. I didn't say that. I believe you saw Our Lady.

But you don't believe she was actually there.

That's what I've been talking about. That's exactly the question at hand. What do you mean by actually?

Really there. You know. Not just something that came from me. Something that came from outside of me. That's what I mean by actually there. Really there, Father.

Really there is the central question.

And I can tell you don't think she really was.

I'm just saying honestly that I don't know. I'm just saying it didn't happen to me. I have no direct experience of Mary, unlike you, can you see that? For you, it's one thing, for me it's another. What I have is your report about it which I am not criticizing in any way, but still it's important for me to be certain before I decide that the Mother of God is really, actually present. It's just too important to accept on its face without asking fundamental questions.

She told me I should come and tell you everything.

And in what way would you describe her tone?

I don't know. What do you mean?

I mean is she giving you a firm command when she instructs you to come and talk to me? Is it an order, a request, a suggestion maybe? How would you describe her tone?

It's a command, Father. She commands me.

A command sounds . . . scary. Is it scary a little? Is all of it kind of frightening?

I'm scared about one thing.

What is that?

I'm scared about the devil, Father.

There isn't any devil, Ann.

Yes there is. I feel his presence.

The priest appraised her disconsolately. It's normal to feel unsettled, he said, in a situation like this.

Ann leaned toward him desperately. Suddenly my whole life is different, she said. I didn't ask for this to happen. But it did happen, and I'm here because of it. Because she told me to come to you.

I'm trying to understand this, said the priest. I think I can guess how it might feel to be seeing the Mother of God, yes.

You think I'm crazy. That I'm seeing things.

I'm a cautious believer. Inherently.

And I've been chosen. I don't know why. Just chosen by the Blessed Mother.

That puts us clearly on two different levels.

Well I saw Our Lady out in the woods.

I don't deny that. I don't deny or affirm. I only ask questions, Ann.

The girl shook her head. Why me? she asked. Why me of all people? I never went through confirmation and I wasn't ever baptized.

Father Collins considered this. You're obviously devout though, he answered.

I've never even been to confession, I've never taken the sacrament, I'm not even officially Catholic, I only got started being religious the last year or so. So why? Why did she choose me?

Because you're pure and innocent, I'm guessing.

I'm so not pure it isn't even funny.

What do you mean?

I'm just not pure.

How exactly?

Everything.

Carolyn tiptoed into the room. You two are whispering, she told them.

He agreed to accompany them the following morning on an expedition to the woods in question, though not without making it explicitly clear that by so doing he offered no sanction or any imprimatur of the church, the trip was merely exploratory, he undertook it speculatively, he would meet them at approximately ten-thirty with his raincoat and his boots. He was casual in manner throughout his farewell, but when they were gone he couldn't concentrate on his reading—*Fear and Trembling*, by the angst-ridden Kierkegaard; the priest always read five things at once—and browsed through the *National Catholic Reporter* with its ads for spiritual retreats and sabbaticals, for hermitages and conferences offering massage or tai chi, one quoting the mystic Rumi in a banal and embarrassing marketing ploy: *Out beyond ideas of wrongdoing and rightdoing there's a field. I'll meet you there.* Father Collins combed the classifieds and considered the parish position in Ecuador, *Fishing villages on the sea,* and the pilgrimage to Spain and the Celtic pilgrimage and the possibility of Florida Priest Week, to be held at Boynton Beach. Was there really something called Florida Priest Week? A coterie of priests in bathing suits and zoris, discussing, say, the communion of saints or the origins of the church's sacraments? God be with you, Brother William— and now could you please pass the cocoa butter? Father Collins laughed out loud. He was laughing out loud when the phone rang.

It was Larry Garber from his congregation, who out of both religious zeal and a yearning for perpetual self-flagellation was developing in his evening hours a pro bono set of architect's plans for the proposed new Saint Joseph's Church of North Fork. Father, he said. I'm calling late. I don't like to call anybody this late at night—especially you, a clergyman—but I have a few small questions I need to ask if you don't mind for a moment.

I'm always here if you need me, said Father Collins. Besides, it's only nine-thirty.

Well, regarding, again, the elevation of the altar. Have you given any more thought to that? And the three options I presented you with last week for the dimensions of the sacristy? Can we spend a few minutes on those two things? And briefly—again—about the soffits?

I'm glad you called, said Father Collins. I'd love to discuss the sacristy in particular. I've been giving it substantial thought.

White lies are loved by God, he told himself. Because the last thing he wanted to do right now was discuss a hypothetical sacristy. Hypothetical because the new church was hypothetical: there were no funds for it. The town's economic demise and the general indifference of the larger diocese toward its much-beleaguered North Fork parish made certain of that. The new-church notion had been conjured up almost two years before Father Collins' tenure and the account that had been established for it was now at seventeen thousand dollars and earning three and a half percent. The whole thing seemed, to Father Collins, like an empty and ultimately fruitless hobby, this endless tinkering with lines on a blueprint, worrying which way the doors would swing, what sort of finish to put on the hinges, it seemed to him like a child's project, like Tinkertoys or Lincoln Logs, he could no more imagine being an architect and spending his working life on these things than he could imagine worshiping Satan. His "work" on the new church was theater, a performance. It was also unexpectedly therapeutic, like woodworking or building model boats. A pastime that felt to him ominous and boring, a staying action, a siege. He wasn't doing anything important and that fact elicited a fundamental angst not even Kierkegaard could vanquish.

I prefer, he said to Larry Garber, option two for the sacristy. I think it gives us more room to work with. And I'm willing to give up the office space. The third option—that's too much. I lose the entire nook for my files. I don't think we want to lose that flush face, the files pushed back, like we talked about.

There was at least ten minutes of this sort of blather, and then Larry Garber asked, tentatively, if Father Collins had heard the rumor about a girl who claimed to see the Virgin Mary.

Yes, said the priest. I've heard of that.

What do you think?

As you say—it's a rumor.

What have you heard?

Various things.

I understand she's a mushroomer-type person.

Yes, well. We'll wait and see.

I understand she's a runaway or something. And maybe—mentally unstable.

Mentally unstable, said Father Collins. All the saints were mentally unstable. Saint Teresa of Ávila was mentally unstable, as was her friend Saint John of the Cross. As was Saint Francis of Assisi.

Yes.

So look, we'll talk about the footing drains soon.

After I hear from the engineer. I'll give him a push. Tomorrow morning.

There's no hurry, said Father Collins. And God bless you, Larry, in your work. God be with you in it.

After he hung up he dropped the newspaper on the floor and examined his bookcase for anything pertinent to Marian apparitions. There was nothing so he did the remaining dishes before falling onto his bed still clothed where idly he remembered with disturbing clarity the sallow beauty of the girl's complexion and thought of her saying *I'm so not pure,* and then he recalled the redhead on the Alaska boat exhorting him to greater heights. These images waned, his fantasies dwindled, and he recollected that his mother had been a dues-paying member of the Marian Helpers and a supporter of the Legion of Mary, had sometimes practiced the First Saturday devotions, had kept Lourdes photos in a keepsake book, had made a trip to Our Lady of Scottsdale in conjunction with a convention of remote-control glider enthusiasts held near the Grand Canyon. He was in seminary and she sent him a postcard depicting the Arizona apparition with a countenance resembling a Barbie doll's. *One hun-*

*dred and two degrees but very dry, with redrock moun-
tains. Your father's stomach has been a tad upset but he
is finally taking something for it after a little bit of con-
vincing. The convention was a big success and the
Grand Canyon had a spectacular sunset and then we
drove here to Our Lady of Scottsdale which frankly is
disappointing. Looking forward to seeing you Labor
Day. Proud of you—Dad too. XXX Mom*

She no longer sent postcards. Recently his
mother had discovered e-mail, ensnaring him in
an instant messaging relationship that made him
loath to go on-line. Just checking in, she would
write invasively. I'm still here, he'd reply in surrender. When do you think you might come
home? I am home, so to speak, I guess. You know
what I mean. I have some free time in 2013. Your
father's birthday is coming up. Dad's getting old—
is he depressed about it? Your father doesn't get
depressed. Maybe he should, wrote Donny.

He put his sisters on his buddy list. Forgive me
Father for I have sinned—something of that ilk
would pop onto his screen. So what else is new?
I'm sleeping with my lover's lover—do you think
that's okay with God? I'd ask for you, you know
I would, but I don't want to bore Him with the
details of your sex life. I'm also sleeping with my
neighbor's black Lab. Cruelty to animals. Better
than nothing. Two-word limit. You lose. No
way. Make it one. Okay.

Or: How many loggers have you converted this week? I stopped counting when it got to be a problem. I want to visit. Well don't wear Gore-Tex. What's acceptable? Nothing, really. It's a town with NAKED ONLY signs? It's a town with YOU'RE NOT WELCOME signs. I feel so welcomed in places like that. EARTH FIRST: WE'LL LOG THE OTHER PLANETS LATER. So—ahem—you're doing okay? HUG A LOGGER: YOU'LL NEVER GO BACK TO TREES. Gee I guess you're doing great. I LOVE SPOTTED OWLS—FRIED.

Or: You've been a priest for almost a year. You're excellent with a calendar. No regrets you ex-pothead? It isn't possible to have no regrets. Mother Teresa wouldn't say that. Mother Teresa's not an ex-pothead. You have to miss the act of fornication. Fornication remains inviting. Satan is powerful, Father Collins. But I don't want fornication, really, what I want is meaning. Fornication's meaningful. For however long it takes, agreed; then postcoital depression, in my case. You're a very heavy dude, Father. It's a heavy job, sister—very weighty. Couldn't it be like one-year probation? I wouldn't have to wait a whole year. Well Jesus Christ. Quit.

Quit? He'd arrived in North Fork the previous November and found that his congregation was twenty-seven families, half of them out of work.

There was a core of twelve families regularly at mass, a gathering of forty to fifty people, the majority with Teutonic or Anglo-Saxon names like Goble and Pendergast. Half of these were staples at confession, which he sat for fascinated three times a week: I got drunk and shoved my daughter against a wall when I caught her with a six-pack. I ripped off the clinic for these pills I like. I stole a T-bone at MarketTime by shoving it down the front of my pants. I cheated on my Food Handling test. I hung around till they were just bout closed and when she went into the back to get something I took a bottle from behind the bar and stuck it in my coat. Or: I siphoned gas because I didn't have none and didn't leave a note or nothing. I didn't go all the way but I sure came close and I didn't tell my husband about it. I took some paper clips at work and after that it was like a flood and I just filled my house with office supplies and with cleaning stuff from the closet. Or: I rammed a Forest Service gate last night. I borrowed a chain saw from behind Pete's shop and just didn't never return it. I was out elk hunting with no success and out of sheer frustration I guess it was I shot somebody's cat.

There was the woman with persisting sexual thoughts about her teenage son's best friend. There was the girl considering birth control measures whose virginity was under siege. There was the man who was only recently remarried but sleeping with his ex-wife again, to his endless astonishment. There was the grocery store checker upbraiding herself for ignoring her mother in Alabama, where she was dying of kidney failure. There was the divorced man whose daughter hated him, the divorced woman whose son hated her, the former car-parts sales clerk who hated everybody. There was the woman who felt she was uncharitable because she hadn't made enough hospital visits since her confession the week before. Then there were the members of the Tom Cross family with their highly appropriate surname. The girl of fourteen sat with her mother near the middle front every week but Tom Cross always sat by himself farther toward the rear. No matter that they were separated, as a whole they were a disturbing reminder of God's capricious mystery. They'd been visited by the worst sort of accident. The Cross boy, nineteen, was paralyzed. A committee had formed to attend this tragedy, and like the chorus in a Greek play its members felt called upon to comment. Be prepared, its chairwoman had written Father Collins, a week before he came to North Fork, for a family in a state of disarray, a family much in need of your ministry. Perhaps it is for them as much as for anything that you've been summoned to us.

But did Father Collins feel summoned? Not in

that way, not called. He had simply replied when asked by the bishop that he was willing to go where he was needed. And he had only said this because to his ear it sounded like what a new priest should say, a properly pious and humble new priest who understood his vocation. So in truth it was via this momentary playacting that Father Collins was summoned. He had practiced a small heroic deception. By the route of his own deceit he had landed in a dying timber town. Now and again he tried to convince himself that in fact he had not engaged in a falsehood but had declaimed before the bishop instead his truer and more noble self, discovering it in that moment. As if the words had surprised even him—*wherever I am needed.* As if inspired by all his training to rise to this occasion. But most of the time, alone in his trailer, his self-effacing pronouncement to the bishop felt like circumstantial theater for which he now paid dearly. At the moment of truth he had not been true and North Fork was his daily penance for the sin of obfuscating.

However dull and rain-stricken his gulag, however sluggish and leaden his soul, Father Collins did indeed find the Cross family a challenge to his heart and mind. Forgive me Father for being a sinner, Tom Cross had said, very softly, when the priest first met him at confession. Father Collins couldn't help but observe that the ex-logger who'd come to expiate his sins looked very much like the Marlboro Man at a juncture in his life a bit down the road from the era in the sun-swathed advertisements. After all the dusty rides, the campfire brooding and sunset gazing, he'd arrived at a place where his pain went beyond the romantic loneliness of the plains. The windy cracks in his face had blown open to reveal more than the existential suffering the cowboy feels by his coffeepot, and the points of his sideburns terminated steeply in the too-dark abysses of his cheek pits. You're new here, Tom Cross whispered hoarsely, so you're probably the only person in town who doesn't know about my boy.

And what about your boy?

He's quadriplegic. He's nineteen and paralyzed, for the rest of his life he'll never move anymore. And it's because of me. It's my fault.

But I heard it was an accident, what happened to your son.

Accidents aren't always accidental, if you catch my drift, Father.

I'm not sure I do.

Well the drift is, I caused it.

But why would you do that?

Cuz I hated his guts.

You hated your son.

I have a lot of hate, said Tom Cross.

The Lord has a reason for everything, but this, a father's hate—who can say?

I'm here for answers.

As am I.

I want to confess.

Go ahead.

I'm evil, said Tom Cross. There's a hole in me. I just go dark a lot of the time. I lock down and then, look out. I'll roll right through you and don't give a damn. Forgive my language, Father.

The man had the eyes of a bird-hunting dog—specifically Don Collins' beloved Prince, the rangy English pointer of Donny's youth—who has been aprowl in heavy grasslands. In all that strung-out, high-wire bird searching, grass seeds lodge beneath the dog's eyelids, where unhappily they try to grow in the medium of his tears.

Mostly you don't want to know me, priest. Because I'd just as soon kill you as look at you. That's how I feel: cold.

You'd want to kill *me*?

Not you in particular.

You sound to me like a war veteran.

I never went. I didn't need a war. If there'd been one for me I'd been king of it, though. I probably would have been just what they needed. The guy they were looking for.

I can see that, answered Father Collins.

Before Donny went to seminary, his father gave him a copy of Kipling's "If" and professed that he was loath to give advice but since the moment seemed to call for it he would only say one that there was nothing wrong with being a priest so long as he made himself the kind of priest who served the Church to the best of his abilities and two if he was going to stick it out and actually become a priest he should accept the seriousness of his profession's vows and never abridge or demean them. The Kipling poem made Donny fume at its ponderous and repetitive proposition that British conduct made you squire of the world, supplied you with everything in it too, and what could that possibly have to do with the decision to become a priest? *Yours is the Earth and everything that's in it/And—which is more—you'll be a Man, my son!* with the exclamation point heralding a shallow victory and the meaning of manhood remaining indefinite, unless you were willing to take it to mean reserve, mad dogs, and tea.

None of it—his father's advice, the Kipling poem—was doing him any good now.

Well maybe, he said to Tom Cross, you're here because you want to change.

Do people change?

They do in stories.

Too bad this isn't a story then.

How do you know this isn't a story? Maybe

your whole life is just a story—one that God has written for you but within which you must act with volition.

Assign me an act of contrition, Father. Assign me my penance. Please.

Pray as much as you can, I assign. I know that sounds vague and ridiculous to you. But in the sheer beauty of holy words lies succor and salvation. Like carrying water and hewing wood. Aren't you a hewer of wood, Tom? Strike upon strike of the splitting maul, according to the will of God, until your penance has been realized, achieved, that's what I ask of you. The words themselves, their utterance bringing His light to the world, their utterance lighting your path through a dark wood. So for the rest of your life say as many as you can. A million Hail Marys and a million Our Fathers. That's what I ask from you.

Words?

Yes.

Okay, said Tom. But they won't help.

And why is that?

They're only words.

It had later been Father Collins' duty to call on Thomas Cross the younger—Junior as he was widely known, or Tommy as his mother called him—to take confession from this paralyzed boy who breathed with the help of a ventilator. On his first visit the priest had been apprehensive and felt a stirring of tension and dread: I'm the new priest, he'd said with false cheer, his voice echoing in the Cross family kitchen where the boy sat lashed to his wheelchair, looking out the window into the backyard at nothing of genuine interest. Nothing, really, to look at for very long, a ragged square of mossy lawn, fallen cedar needles, copious blackberry, rotting firewood, a mildewed truck canopy, moss-covered roofing shakes. The kitchen itself was clean but depressing, the pattern in the linoleum worn to a yellow sheen from years of work-boot traffic. Tom Junior had been dressed and groomed for this audience—a turtleneck shirt to conceal from view the tracheostomy hole in his throat, his hair wetted and parted. I have to confess, said Father Collins, that I don't know what to say in your presence. Forgive me for that. This is new to me. I feel more than a little awkward.

The boy looked a little like Stephen Hawking, Hawking if younger and not quite so curled, his left shoulder twitched every now and then and he smelled faintly of urine. He was thin with a high Shakespearean forehead, his ears were large and canted out, and his head appeared to be perched precariously on top of his frail neck. His mechanical breathing was so disconcerting that the priest felt panicked and metaphysically distressed. Steady, he told himself. Try to feign calm. Hi, said

Tom Junior robotically, on the exhale. There was a pause while the pump inflated his lungs. My name is. Tommy Cross.

Father Collins remembered that Tibetan monks were made to sit in graveyards at night to thwart their fear of the supernatural and he wished he'd had that sort of training. How could you be human but unable to breathe? The breath of life was infused at birth and left again at the moment of death, which meant that somebody like Tom Cross Junior was in no-man's-land or purgatory. An interesting locus for spiritual questions of the sort priests asked at seminars. I'm very pleased to meet you, Father Collins said. After hearing so much from other people it's good to finally meet you.

Tom Junior's eyes swiveled to take him in and Father Collins, aware of his thoughtlessness, moved immediately in front of the boy—wishing in his rapidity to signal apology—and perched on the edge of a chair. The chair, he saw now, had been placed for him, the boy's mother thinking of this, leaving the chair where it needed to be, the priest felt compelled toward a formal posture and sat with his hands clasped humbly in his lap. Here I am, he said.

The boy packed as much as he could into an exhale. It's really hard to talk. A big effort. An effort for me. I'm sorry.

Don't apologize. Please—don't apologize. But if you need to, whenever you're ready, go ahead and confess.

It's hard to sin. Sin from a wheelchair.

One of the benefits, maybe. I suppose. Although it's possible there aren't any benefits.

No, said Tom Junior. None.

The priest felt certain that a statement such as this was harder to hear than to utter. The rest of us don't want truth, he thought. We only want to hear success stories. Cup-half-full stories. Tales of triumph. I appreciate your honesty, he said.

Being a quad. Quadriplegic. Sucks.

I'm not going to doubt you on that for a moment.

In a movie. About gimps. It's over. In two hours.

Do they make any movies about gimps do you think?

No. Too boring. Nothing happens.

Father Collins nodded grimly. Not entirely true, he thought. Daniel Day-Lewis in *My Left Foot*, Tom Cruise in *Born on the Fourth of July*, Peter Sellers in *Dr. Strangelove*. Gimps could be interesting for maybe two hours but after that, thank God, no more, let's gratefully walk out of the theater.

Since I last. Confessed. I told God. To go to hell. A thousand times. At least.

I have a feeling God'll give you a pass. As your priest I'm giving you a pass for that. A free pass. A get-out-of-jail-free card. You can say that to God a thousand times and God will not drop a thunderbolt on you. But I'm sure He's glad you've confessed to it. And more—do you still feel like cursing him? That's the important question.

Yes. Not as often. Sometimes.

Good. That's progress. And for your penance I assign you to seated meditation on the first of the Ten Commandments.

Okay.

So what were you looking at when I came in here? Out the window there?

I was thinking about. Thinking about stuff.

What kind of stuff?

That my lungs. Feel dry.

Anything else?

Zanaflex.

Zanaflex?

To keep me from. From twitching.

What else?

My leg bag. Stinks.

No it doesn't.

The truck canopy.

What about it?

We camped. With it. In Montana. I was eleven. We went. To a rodeo.

Who went?

My father. And me.

How was that?

Good. Good time.

So you have good memories?

No. A few.

Most aren't good?

Most. Are bad.

How so?

My father. Was mean. Was mean to me.

I'm sorry to hear that, said Father Collins.

The boy made no answer to this. They sat there together listening to the ventilator which was a little like Chinese water torture. Father Collins felt a frustrated pity and profound helplessness. A priest was only a man, after all, and not a magician, wizard, saint, miracle worker, or angel. I don't want to make you talk, he said. I don't want to wear you out.

Sorry. Already. I'm sorry. Talking is hard.

Then, all right, let me do this now—and the priest muttered rapidly the formula of absolution and reached into his pocket for the small silver box in which he carried Tom Junior's communion wafer and his vial of eucharistic wine. Don't, said the boy. Don't touch it. Please. I get. Infections. From people.

So what should I do?

Over there. Are gloves.

Father Collins washed his hands at the sink. There was a box of surgeon's gloves on the counter and he pulled on a pair. The ventilator reminded him of the devil's breathing and made him think of *The Exorcist*. He composed himself. He sat down again. He took Tom Junior's hand in his and said Are you comfortable with me doing this?

I don't. Believe in God, said the boy. But go ahead. If you want.

Father Collins performed the Eucharist with an empty heart. The boy's tongue looked dry and pale. His exhaled breath was sour and sweet. The wafer disappeared down his raw red gullet and his eyes bulged with pain. Father Collins avoided looking at the place where the vent tube penetrated Tom Junior's throat, visible at the sagging lip of his turtleneck. He felt wholly ineffectual. The smell of urine nauseated him. He was frightened and wanted to leave right away. He despised himself and nearly said so. Weren't there priests who worked among lepers, wasn't Christ himself a physician, wasn't he called upon by his very office to salve wounds, anoint the sick, heal, bless, and make hospital visits? Wasn't he called on to look at death, as Mary had looked at her Son's crucifixion? I'm weak, he thought. My soul is weak. You're tired, he said to the paralyzed boy.

So I'll leave you now. I'll leave you to rest. And he left with that paltry excuse.

On the morning after meeting the visionary, the priest packed a lunch of a cheese sandwich, an orange, and raw almonds mixed with raisins. There was no rain, which cheered him a little, and as he drove out of the trailer court with the defroster fan screeching and scraping against its housing he played his *Miracles of Sant'iago* cassette and plowed directly through the puddles. He was aware that his infatuation with the visionary had expanded slightly overnight, surprising because he had come to expect that his crushes would constrict immediately. In the case of the visionary, Father Collins decided, his attraction was held aloft this morning by the prospect of their campground rendezvous—toward which he sped beneath drab skies—which felt to him like a tryst.

He was surprised to find, though, on arriving there, that a party of more than a dozen pilgrims had gathered around the girl's morning fire, where they drank from thermoses, poked at the flames, and milled with their hands in their pockets. A blanket of heavy, smothering mist pressed against the treetops. Sparks spiraled through moss-hung maples and the river just beyond her camp ran the hue of dulled gunmetal. The girl's car

looked derelict, her canvas tent improbably an-
tique, like something from World War II. The
morning air felt rheumatically damp and the
ground seemed permanently sodden. The priest
thought it an ill stroke of history that the Romantic poets had not come here, since these
woods might have fully drawn out their lyric
melancholy. He imagined the sickly Keats,
coughing, seated under a hoary spruce and pondering the tubercular chill in the air; Byron about
with his walking stick, brooding and poking
dashingly at the moss; Shelley the atheist; the restless Wordsworth; all grappling with odes to
gloom. The mossy coverts and vales of the rain
forest would have spoken to their forlorn souls,
and the clean and desperate beauty of the trees
would have spurred them to new flights of fancy.
What a marvelous place to be depressed about the
very conditions of being, thought the priest. The
constitutionally philosophical, those with a tender
awareness of mortality, had simultaneously no
business here and no better place to go.

Feigning calm, he approached the fire and held
out his hands to warm them. There were seven
members of his congregation, a trio of dogs, five
utter strangers, and the two who had come to
him the night before with news of the apparition.
The girl's cold, he thought, had worsened; she
appeared more spent and pale. Why are you here,

Father? a bearded man asked. What's your purpose here?

Those are the fundamental questions of my life. I wish I could answer them.

What have you heard? What do you know?

I've heard no more than what you've heard. So I've come to see for myself.

Praise the Lord, a woman said—a stoop-shouldered widow from his congregation whom he knew to be half blind. She was overly fervent at prayer, he thought, and trembled when she sang, a charismatic Catholic. Behold, our priest is among us, she croaked. We can count our priest among our numbers. As it is written in Revelation: There appeared a great wonder in heaven: a woman clothed with the sun, and the moon under her feet, and upon her head a crown of twelve stars!

Yes, said the priest. I'm here, as you say. Good morning, Ann, he added. I hope you're taking care of that cold.

I'm trying, Father, said Ann.

I didn't sleep.

Neither did I.

I stayed awake in anticipation.

The same with me. All night.

Not with me, said Carolyn. I crashed hard. Completely tired. I slept the sleep of the dead.

They set out in the manner of an expeditionary force—after the priest, ten others showed up—their trampling pace and enthusiasm for travel at odds with the muted woods. They were like a race of warlike ants advancing fanatically through the forest, some of them vaulting over logs and deadfalls and getting ahead of the visionary before slowing against their will. The dogs, like most dogs, were impressionable and, feeling the fervor of the situation, became manic and feverish and could not be checked from dashing forward far into the distance. One took up the trail of a deer and could be heard barking at a considerable remove until its owner began blowing on a pocket whistle in such shrill, piercing and strident blasts that nothing else could be discerned. I'll tell you what, said Carolyn to the priest. This is probably what the Crusades felt like. An invading force. With zeal.

Except that there aren't any Turks with scimitars.

We've got loggers.

Are they out here you think?

Like Saladin. But with chain saws.

The priest assisted the stoop-shouldered widow through the log crossing at Fryingpan Creek and afterward took her arm at the elbow as they wound through the forest of blowdowns. The flaccidity of her triceps muscle was so complete as to disturb Father Collins with its intimations of mortality and her odor was of ill digestion. I have a son in Toledo, she told him. So I've been to Our Lady of America.

Our Lady of America?

The Blessed Virgin appeared there too. To a Sister Mildred. In 1956. In a hallway—isn't that interesting? The Virgin appearing in a hallway.

The priest didn't answer. He steered her through the woods. Sister Mildred of the Sisters of the Precious Blood in Fostoria, Ohio, said the widow. You ought to visit sometime.

Another woman, who walked just behind them, exclaimed that she'd been to Knock on Feast Day in 1987 and to Moneyglass in County Antrim. There's a folk museum in Knock, she said, that is well worth visiting.

I'm aware of Moneyglass, said the widow.

There's a carved cross at Moneyglass and at the bottom of it is carved a pot and what I guess is a chicken but what they called in old Ireland a cockodel. I think.

It's a cockerel, a young rooster, said the priest. Why a cockerel?

Because Judas' wife told him not to worry, Jesus couldn't anymore rise from his grave than the cockodel she'd boiled could fly from his soup pot—at which point the cockodel did fly from the soup and said something I don't exactly remember like, The Son of the Virgin is safe in heaven! Or something to that effect.

There's a fascinating place in California, said the widow. Out in the Mojave Desert.

I've been there, the other woman said. California City, it's called. It's not as good as Our Lady of Snows. I used to live near Our Lady of Snows. But what I really want to visit is Medjugorje.

My daughter-in-law went. But it scares me too much. I wouldn't go anywhere near that place until these Slavs get things worked out.

That means you just won't ever go then.

Probably. But that's fine with me. I'd rather go to Lourdes.

The visionary stopped to sit on a log and they all took her signal and stopped too, like an infantry at rest on the order of its general, and the priest shared his orange with the widow. He pried the segments apart gently and deliberately and tried to remain inconspicuous, looking down, but the business of the orange attracted a dog who clearly wanted something to eat and the bearded man who'd spoken at the campfire said The poor soul. He's hungry.

Does a dog have a soul do you think? someone asked.

Is the pope Catholic? someone else answered.

I don't know if it's that simple, said the priest. The question of the souls of animals is much debated. Rightly so, I feel.

My dog has a soul, the bearded man said. More

than some people, I have to say. Some people seem to lack souls.

Then there's the people who care more about animals than they do about people, someone put in. Those types are all for capital punishment but against cruelty to animals.

And you're for cruelty to animals?

That's not the point.

Look into the eyes of a dog sometime.

You're missing the point. Intentionally.

The priest, picking out the raisins first, gave a handful of almonds to the dog. That food is blessed, pronounced the widow. Fed from the hand of a priest, you are. Fed from the hand of Saint Francis.

They climbed the hill and three times the widow stopped because she was short of breath. She hung her head and leaned on her knees, waiting for her trembling to subside, and the priest impatiently waited with her. Do the right thing, he told himself. She's an old woman and she needs you. The others went ahead, abandoning them, except for a dog of indeterminate breed, a tired black dog with clouded eyes, who took up their cause instinctively. The infirmity of the aged is a curse, said the widow. I grow old, I grow old, I shall wear my trousers, et cetera. In the room the women come and go . . . I do not think they will sing to me.

I do not think *that* they will sing to me, the priest corrected her dryly. It distinctly changes the rhythm.

Here I am, an old man in a dry month, being read to by a boy, waiting for rain.

A boy, yes—appropriate. Forgive me I apologize. But how does someone in a logging town get so impressively intimate with T.S.?

I'm a UW graduate, I'll have you know. I studied with Ted Roethke ages ago. Would you believe I was once a girl beat poet hanging around the Blue Moon Tavern and skinny-dipping in Portage Bay? Of course you wouldn't. Who could believe that? But I've published my poetry here and there in small journals and periodicals over the course of eons. Never a published collection, though—I'm a firefly, so to speak. But you're our brand new lovely young priest so I must tell you that it was Kierkegaard who caught my interest centuries ago and turned me toward the Lord. My master's thesis was a perambulation on his *Concluding Unscientific Postscript*. I was thirty-seven years old then. My husband was a struggling, tender playwright who taught theater at Lincoln High School. Now I'm an old widow in a logging town, that's the way life goes. I do not genuflect to time or circumstance but move forward in the name of Jesus and have at times been enamored of the Quietism with which you are familiar from seminary, particularly the Quietism of François de Fénelon which you touched on so briefly in your sermon three Sundays ago. On another topic, I reread my V. L. Parrington last summer. And three volumes of the Great Books series. Lately I've been making a little study of Aquinas and Bishop Berkeley.

In large print?

With a magnifying glass. Built into a kind of helmet. I found it on-line two years ago. It's something like a watchmaker's visor.

I've never seen that, said the priest. So Aquinas and Berkeley lately, you say. Then you must know the answer to the age-old question: How many angels is it, approximately, that can dance on the head of a pin?

Twelve, I suppose. I don't know for certain. If only Saint Thomas had thought of us here, out in these woods asking humorous deep questions, he might have finished his *Summa Theologica* and we would have that information.

Are we ready to catch up to the others, my dear?

A cold coming we had of it, just the worst time of the year for a journey, and such a long journey—let's go.

They made the crest arm in arm, waded through the Oregon grape and salal—following the lead of the old black dog, who seemed to have fixed on the scent of the others—and entered the dank-smelling forest. The priest felt happy to have found somebody who was reading Aquinas and Bishop Berkeley as opposed to *Fishing and Hunting News* or *Cosmopolitan* magazine. In ten minutes they found their fellow pilgrims, now milling like a restive theater audience, and the widow whispered, Set me down now, it's dry right here, and you go among the others.

All right, said the priest. Bless you.

They were in a forest mostly of firs, most of which wore moss on their branches—moss draping the vine maples and deadfalls and hanging over everything smotheringly like a botanical parasite. The priest recognized feather moss because he had taken a handbook to the forest on two successive gray afternoons and thought he recognized nearby as well something called old-man's beard. It confounded him that his memory for flora was so poor, an insufficient and paltry instrument; he would learn a plant's name and then, within days, it was as though he hadn't learned it. He did recall reading or hearing somewhere that moss grew only on the north sides of trees, a theory of nature flagrantly at odds with the reality of these throttled firs which were slightly sinister, slightly macabre, as though dipped in some green virus.

The visionary knelt in a bed of moss with her hood pulled tightly around her face and her rosary clutched in her hands. Most of the pilgrims knelt now too, and one in an elegantly wavering voice read solemnly from the book of Acts And it shall come to pass in the last days, saith God, I will pour out of my Spirit upon all flesh: and your sons and daughters shall prophesy and your young men shall see visions, and your old men shall dream dreams. Someone else shouted Behold the handmaiden of the Lord be it done unto me according to Thy word! and a shrill, addled voice cried Hail Holy Queen Mother of Mercy our life our sweetness and our hope to you do we cry poor banished children of Eve! Another pilgrim lit a candle and pleaded Mirror of justice, vessel of honor, virgin most venerable, virgin most renowned, eliminate all sin. The priest heard the half-blind widow, too, Were we led all that way for Birth or Death? and saw that her hands were clasped in prayer while she recited T. S. Eliot.

The visionary's ecstasies began in earnest in the midst of these exhortations. The gathered host fell gradually silent and the priest, too, dropped to his knees because he felt loomingly conspicuous. He observed that in the throes of rapture, Ann appeared more diminutive than ever, her hood close like a monk's cowl, her angle of carriage preternaturally forward, her gaze directed toward the tops of the trees, her hands clasped in desperate supplication, and he tried to commit her image to memory since he was convinced now by the scene at hand that inevitably he would be required to participate in the unfolding of this spectacle, that this was to be an apparition, with its accompanying inquest and hysteria, he could neither avoid nor escape. It was going to have an effect on him, an impact on his ministry. When she fell forward someone cried Lady of the Holy Rosary, consecrate our hearts this day! but no one else took up this call or felt it proper to renew their prior clamor and there was again silence while the visionary lay like a small heap of lost children's clothing on the wet forest floor. It was like that moment at the end of a symphony when no one is certain that indeed it is ended and for a brief hiatus there is no applause because each member of the audience fears leading the rest toward embarrassment. No one did a thing, not even the priest, who had to admit that he too felt spellbound and in the presence of something holy.

The moment passed. His wavering skepticism righted itself. The priest felt certain that a literal interpretation—the actual presence of a Madonna from heaven—was absurd and erroneous. He did not believe that Mary had descended from her blissful place at the right hand of God to speak to a mushroom picker. He did not give credence to apparitions, not even to the seven the Vatican had legitimized, believing instead that the deposit of revelation ended with Jesus Christ. The priest understood his spiritual frisson, his moment of yearning toward a facile acceptance, as a small leap of natural desire, undoubtedly archaic at source— autonomic fear of stars, of thunder, lightning, the shaking earth, of large waves, darkness at noon, a shadow across the sun. A polytheistic urge or impulse to meet a forest wraith. In his role as self-reflective anthropologist, the priest thought of pagan seekers who starved themselves intentionally in the hope of passionate revelation, in the belief that the hallucinations of hunger would grant them dreams and names. Pain, sex, crack cocaine, copious sweat, a near miss with the reaper—by these means are spirits induced when otherwise spirits are most reluctant to show their hideous faces. By these means, the dying beast seeks life. By contrast the priest's elected route was a stark one of scholastic contemplation. There was no drama in that, of course, which was precisely what made it difficult. Blundering on like the magi in the widow's poem could not hold a candle to the advent of a ghost who speaks to a pauper in the forest. *There were times we regretted / The summer palaces on slopes, the terraces, / And the silken girls bringing sherbet*—the widow's recitation still echoed in his ears and he regretted it all, a familiar regret. He didn't know why he was a priest.

When the visionary stood and faced the crowd

he noted again how small she was—*And a little child shall lead them,* he thought. She now looked clearly feverish, ill, someone who should be in bed. She clasped her hands in an attitude of prayer and said in a thin plain-speaking voice, Our Lady asks me to share Her message, and still she hadn't removed her hood, her face lay hidden in its shadow. Dear children, she said, put your faith in Mother Mary and answer her call to Christian service which means to serve Our Lord Our Jesus through acts of loving-kindness. Pray for the sinners that they might be made whole again and freed from their selfishness and greed before Jesus in anger visits destruction on us. Carry Our Lady's message of hope to the ends of the earth with your whole soul and for sure you will bring an end to poverty. Build a church at this very place which will be like a beacon to unbelievers and bring them into the presence of God your Father your Protector. Give your hearts to the Precious Son and take refuge within His wounds and He shall protect you always. I am as your own Mother and gather you here as a Mother might to keep you safe from the hand of evil and to deliver your petitions to the Lord Himself, in Jesus' name, amen.

As for the grieving mother who has petitioned Me on this day, Lee Ann went peacefully to the embrace of Our Lord after wandering alone in this very forest and didn't suffer but was cold toward the end, was hungry and finally reached exhaustion, at dusk she curled beneath a tree where she slept deeply to fend off the cold and in sleep rose to the kingdom of heaven on the wings of loving angels.

My children, said Ann. Jesus is merciful and will keep all believers safe from the Evil One. Rest assured your petitions shall be heard in the name of Jesus and of Our Lord God I take leave of you now, amen.

To me it's like she freaks out and everyone goes for it, said Carolyn to the priest when they were walking back toward the campground afterward, the crowd dispersed in the gloom of the woods, reduced to small excited groups speaking rabidly of what they'd seen and to lone spellbound sojourners silenced by the spectacle they'd witnessed. Perhaps, said the priest, that's the nature of revelation. How could it happen otherwise? How else to define belief?

I don't think so, said Carolyn. That kind of thing is circular. The Virgin Mary is either there or not there. It doesn't work some other way.

And in your opinion?

Two thumbs down.

You doubt with enormous certainty.

No I'm certain without any doubt.

I wish I could do that, said the priest.

For a while he gravely accompanied the widow, arm in arm, guiding her, taking comfort from her scent of decay, of garlic, dried flowers and old Mason jars, from the way it shrunk his earthly needs and humbled the demon in his groin, until the visionary appeared out of no-where at his shoulder and walked beside him in unnerving silence.

Excuse me, the priest implored the widow. A moment privately if you don't mind.

I'm perfectly fine on my own, you know. I merely go a bit slower.

You'll need help at the creek crossing, though.

I suppose so. It's very sad.

Then the priest walked alone with the vision-ary, whose face was still luminous with tears. He could not stand the loveliness of that and bit his lip about it. He sauntered along with his hands behind his back like a monsignor in the movies, like a cleric in a multibuttoned frock. He felt he needed a magenta-hued sunset and more somber, oval glasses. The visionary smelled of mossy humus and had pulled back her sweatshirt hood so that he caught a hint of wood smoke mingling with the rankness of her clothes. She was more enticing than before. She had not lost any of her luster to excess, as can sometimes be the case. It was her purity that moved him, he thought. Her essential, if sickly, purity. The church, she said, pausing among ferns. When do you think we can start?

I'm going to contact the bishop, said the priest.

Why him?

He'll know what to do.

The visionary put a hand on his heart. In the forest's deep shade he felt its warmth. You know what to do, she told him.

II

The Adornment of Worship

NOVEMBER 13–NOVEMBER 14, 1999

Tom Cross was one year separated from his wife and had lost his logging company, so he was now a guard at the North Fork Correction Center and encamped at a motel on the south edge of town for forty dollars' rent a week and on-call maintenance work. The motel, once called the R&M but now called the Tired Traveler's Guesthouse, was a row of cabins beside the highway owned by a Punjabi couple. The Punjabis sent Tom from cabin to cabin with a list of menial tasks. He cleaned pea traps and pinched between his fingers the hair and scum clogging the drains. On a Saturday afternoon he was out in the rain taking the motel's icemaker apart when a car pulled up and a man handed him a laminated road map and asked directions to the North Fork

Campground. What have you heard? the man asked.

Haven't heard anything, Tom answered.

I heard there was a Virgin sighting.

There's no virgins left up here, said Tom.

That's a good one, answered the man. But's it's the Virgin Mary I mean, Mother Mary, not a sexual virgin.

This is the first I've heard of it, Tom said. What's that about? A Virgin sighting?

Have you heard of Lourdes? Lourdes in France? A place where Our Mother came to earth and made herself known to human beings? Is that what's happening out here?

The icemaker needed a new compressor. Tom went inside to discuss that with the Punjabis. The motel office smelled of curry and pomade, and the Punjabi children, a boy and a girl, watched him with cavernous, doleful gazes. The Punjabi man was emaciated and wore thin cotton shirts and sandals that made him look like an extra from *Gandhi*. In the flaccid, fluorescent light of the office, his carefully combed hair shone with motes of dandruff. His wife was silent and homely despite her beautiful skin and hair and despite her beautiful teeth. The Punjabi's name, Tom thought, was Pin, though probably that wasn't the proper spelling. Pinh? Pen? Pem maybe? The wife was Jabari, Tom guessed; that was what he thought he overheard when the Punjabi husband addressed her.

Bagged party ice, Tom told them now, was available at the convenience store down the road. No, it was not necessarily the custom in America to offer complimentary ice to motel guests. Some motels had it, some didn't. It wasn't a crucial amenity on a par with towels or soap. No one made their choice of lodgings based on the availability of ice. While he was explaining these deep American things a pair of travelers came through the door, a man and a woman leaving behind a white Lincoln Continental idling in the rain. It's pouring, the man observed. They already know that, the woman answered. They're capable of looking out the window.

Excuse me, said the man, for stating the obvious.

Okay, you're excused, said the woman.

Pin performed a fastidious check-in. His little fingers with their long nails picked up the credit card. Dogs were allowed, he made it clear, but please that is ten-dollar surcharge. He was formal and polite about it, softly belaboring his explanation—The bedspreads must need get little hairs in them that are very difficult for me to remove so you must please be so careful that the dog is comfortable to be sitting on the floor rug and no pet is sitting on the bed. We don't have a dog, the man said. Or we do but we didn't bring him with us.

What have you heard about the apparition? asked the woman. Have you heard anything up here?

I don't know what you are talking, Pin answered.

A girl up here saw the Virgin in the woods.

It's a sighting of the Virgin Mary.

They're Hindus, the man said. Are you Hindus?

All that evening, more travelers checked in. For the first time in Tom's brief tenure, the Punjabis turned on the NO VACANCY sign, which cast a bleak red glare. Tom stood smoking beneath the eaves and watched people unload their cars. The couple with the Lincoln did in fact have a dog with them. Pulled up to the cabin beside theirs was a car with two bumper stickers: A JEWISH CARPENTER IS MY BOSS and DON'T TAILGATE—GOD IS WATCHING. On a truck was one Tom hadn't seen before: JESUS DOES IT BETTER. A trailer across the parking lot was emblazoned with a cross and inscribed with a name—Greater Catholic Merchandise Outlet.

A man came under an umbrella to the office and in a stringent voice, complained. So Tom had to fix a leaky toilet while Pin and Jabari shampooed the carpet in a cabin that smelled of cat urine. Jabari's hair, Tom couldn't help noticing, was bound in a thick glossy braid. Surreptitiously, he watched her at her work; how poignant were her flat thin forearms. Immigration, he supposed, had etched her face with tiny fissures. She and her husband both were soft and measly little people. It seemed to Tom that all through the day the two of them were dressed for sleeping. They both wore extra-large sweatpants. While they worked they ignored him and spoke their own language, mellifluous and exotic. Tom liked to hear it and kept his head down, pretending not to hear in order to listen. He examined the toilet ball valve, a ploy, and let their subdued married chatter move him. He liked the way it left him out. Here were two people, their own constellation, alone in a strange place on the far side of the planet. Their curry-scented, dark-brown presence reminded Tom of the fullness of the world. The planet was larger than North Fork—this thought soothed him a little. His own problems, however deep, were nonexistent in India.

When Tom finished adjusting the toilet's lift rod, Jabari put on rubber gloves and a surgical mask to clean the bowl. It was the beef-eating sickness of American excrement she took such pains to avoid, thought Tom—in her mind, we're the unclean ones, though she would never admit as much. She had things to be afraid of. White supremacists in particular, but she and Pin did an excellent job of appearing not to notice. Did they know how much everyone hated them? He felt they had intimations of it but found strength in denial, like the Jews before Hitler got serious, like ostriches in children's books or stockbrokers.

Please what is a sighting of Virgin Mary? Pin asked in his syncopated diction. It is bringing so many customers.

It's hard to explain. I don't get it myself. A religious gathering, I guess you could say. Like a pilgrimage in India. Like people going to the Ganges, maybe. Don't you go to the Ganges?

In India we go to the River Ganges every year to make us clean. The toilet is so much quiet.

That guy was just a royal complainer.

So now the toilet is very quiet and you are all done fixing.

Tom repaired to his cabin. He pulled off his boots and locked the door. With permission from the Punjabis he'd installed a deadbolt; he didn't want to lose his fishing rods, his waders, his binoculars, his knives, his .44, his shotgun, his rifles, or his tackle boxes. Tom lay surrounded by his outdoor gear and watched a football game. The place smelled of mildew, but he only noticed it when he first came in, turned up the heat or raised a window. There was no phone in his room. His shift at the prison ran from midnight to eight, which meant that on off nights at 3 a.m. he was wide awake in his cabin. Bored, he'd appointed himself security officer and made up noise complaints. There would be a room full of young guys, contractor crews, but they wouldn't like the way Tom looked in the doorway with his long-distance, hazy, out-for-blood pupils and his broad-shouldered posture of logger's aggression and most were poor at feigning disdain for what he said to them. Tom made it up as he went along. It's late and we got fishermen with early starts complaining about your little party. So no bullshit, tone it down, and don't fuck with me. A brief interlude of nervous machismo. Someone would look ready to call his bluff but that was as far as it went. Come on in—he could predict hearing that. Someone would turn the music way down. Do you want a beer, guy? Sure, he'd say, take one, pop the top and walk away.

And why not? A free beer was not to be scoffed at since Tom Cross Logging went defunct. Tom's two log loaders and his D-7 Cat had gone for ten percent of what he'd paid, so the bank was taking his house. Eleanor and the kids were there for now—Junior in the living room with the television in front of him—until Tom figured something else out. Another logger without Tom's payments was making a go of it with Tom's machines, bidding lower than Tom ever did because his books looked better. It irked Tom that it worked this way, that vultures were in ascendance. What he had left was a contract from Stinson set to expire in about four months—which maybe he could pass along at a loss—and his saws and hydraulic jacks, worth nothing. And his pick-up: five grand at best.

More, there was his looming divorce, which he didn't care to think about. Putting a number on it at this point anyway was only self-flagellation. Tom rearranged his limbs on the bed and thought, morosely, of Junior's medical bills, numbers so difficult to comprehend the insurance company might as well present them in cuneiform or hieroglyphs. Tom's books were a morass, like jack-strawed blowdowns: where should he start untangling? In the past he'd worked his way out of problems; a 4 a.m. start had been the answer. This was during his high-lead days, when he smelled perpetually like diesel and wood shavings and his cuticles were rimmed with grease. He'd run the loader, done the sorting himself, and contracted out the falling. At high pitch twelve people worked for Cross Logging; later Tom streamlined and went into shovel logging. It began to slip with the spotted owl, so he'd auctioned off his machinery. He tried contracting out of his pick-up, his cab a kind of office, a desk job on wheels. But there were fewer contracts, more bidders.

Somebody had to go under. Tom went—he and about half the town. They blamed the spotted owl, the Wild Rivers Act, the Sierra Club, and EarthFirst!, not to mention the marbled murrelet and anybody from Seattle. Tom seethed. He increased his communal drinking. Then he took work felling trees for hire. That meant free time in which to grouse and attend seditious meetings. People pushed him to the forefront of the movement because they thought he was less stupid than they were and he ended up in DC finally with five other timber-politics honchos on behalf of the Forest Action Committee. But they were Indians visiting the Great White Chief. The reservation was going to get smaller. Tom went home a treaty Indian. It was in this period of helplessness that he and his son dropped trees together and Tom Junior's neck got broken.

Tom slept and when he woke it was ten and he felt afflicted by his detachment from life, by a headache and aching hip joints. His years in the woods had turned him to wire, his tendons and ligaments weren't spruce anymore, and the truth was he felt ginger a lot, like somebody about to fracture. Was that aging or overwork? A theory he had was that less was better, you could wear yourself out with exercise or labor, each heart having only so many beats, each joint only so many articulations, use it or lose it, maybe that was wrong, maybe if you used it you just used it up, that made more sense—decay. A lot of these lame weary gimps around town were wounded veterans of the timber wars, guys with tight shoulders, lumbar complaints, calcified knees, dead toes. Guys at MarketTime with a six-pack of Bud, a loaf of bread, a tall can of chili, a bag of M&Ms and the newspaper. Tom watched them with morbid reluctance, recalling how it had been for his father, who toward the end couldn't turn in bed or find a posture to sleep in. He'd sat on the toilet to piss in the wee hours and had begged for cortisone. Tom remembered him bitching and moaning with glum humor and sour resignation: Nothing works, not even my pecker, I can't even bend down to touch my toes, the only thing left's a good shit now and then, I ought to be put out to pasture I guess, I'm used up, leftover kibble. I'll tell you, Tom, whatever I eat, it gives me gas like no tomorrow, I'm a god damn wind machine these days, your mom's got me taking something called Beano but you know what? It just makes things worse. You wouldn't want to ride with me no more without the windows open.

Now Tom wished he'd encamped with a dictionary. He needed one for his paralysis research, which he did with the nine-dollar reading glasses he'd bought off a revolving display rack. Impenetrably distant science writing, but the point was that when the spinal cord went it couldn't be healed, you didn't need a dictionary to get that right, for nine dollars Tom had that sussed. He knew the question, but not the answer. Was there a greater helplessness anywhere in the world? Like watching your child stabbed to death while you're bound to a post and gagged. Like watching your child flail in a lake through a telescope on a mountaintop. Except that in a stabbing or drowning a finite if horrible end is achieved. To get Tom Junior into his underpants you had to roll him around on the bed, treat him like the fetus of a whale or a blob of protoplasm. You had to splint him every night, arms and legs, a trussed human pig, or he'd permanently curl like a slug. You had to floss his teeth and shave him. You had to clean his ass with a rag, swab his ears, sponge his testicles. You had to listen to his mechanical breathing—the ventilator's endless hiss and squeak—and empty his stinking piss bag. In short, you had to devote your life to his until your own was obliterated, until it vanished.

But Tom's had already vanished. Tom was already dead. That was why he went to mass each Sunday, watching the back of his wife's head and hoping his daughter would turn around, catch his eye, acknowledge him, maybe smile. But what did she have to smile over? Those days were behind her now. Since Junior's accident she'd become a teenager; she'd been suspended from school that fall for smoking dope with an older girl, driving aimlessly, listening to music, then pulling into the parking lot where the teacher on lunch duty smelled dope on her breath as soon as she stepped from the car. Colleen was apathetic about this trouble and passed her suspension in front of the computer with headphones on, snapping gum. Her face wasn't the same as before, was full of truths life ought to reserve for older people closer to death—there was no God or, if there was, He didn't feel love or pity. He didn't feel human pain. He was too far beyond interpreting—so far beyond He didn't exist or had no shape, like water. Tom half concurred with his daughter on these things but tried not to think about them. Lolling aimlessly in his motel cabin, he tried to turn off his brain. The thing of it was, not thinking was as hard as thinking, maybe even harder. After a while, thoughts crept in. The brain did not much care for lulls. Once it had slept it was ready with a vengeance for constant cogitation. Tom washed his face, laced up his boots, went out and lit a cigarette. He had fought with going to the Big Bottom long enough and now it was time to go.

Every cabin was taken tonight. The lights were on in most of them. It was raining with a genuine fury, as though the sky had been torn open by a God bent on angry floods. It was raining as if to beat the earth into a wet submission. You couldn't hear a truck on the highway.

When Tom drove past the motel office he peered beyond the sweep of his wipers and through the picture window there, hoping to glimpse Jabari. He wanted merely to see a female, for whatever that might be worth. But behind the desk, the television was on and Pin was watching with his head on the counter, his fingers limp above his greasy head—small, caramel-colored fingers. It was the fingers that bothered Tom the most—something like that could get to him. He was weak and tender underneath. It's all too sad, he thought, and drove off. Even just ordinary sadness.

The Big Bottom was crowded but not lively. Despite the impoverished tenor of the times, drinking establishments still flourished in North Fork as though it were a frontier boom town. The Vagabond, the Big Bottom, HK's, and TJ's were filled with dipsomaniacs. Almost every patron's life was complicated by debt, by decisions devoid of the most basic logic, and by a generalized confusion. Somebody would lose half their teeth, a couple of fingers, a spouse and a truck in seven days' time. Somebody else would shoot a horse in a field, drive a borrowed car into a ditch, stumble drunkenly into ferns and sleep, bleeding, until 2 p.m. It was inexplicable by the more reasonable standards of the American upper middle class—people who folded their underwear at night and watched their mutual funds in on-line portfolios—but there it was, another slant on things without roots in better judgment. How to explain two unemployed loggers who smashed in the door of HK's one dawn, then sat at the bar drinking shot glasses of Jack Daniel's until the sheriff finally loomed over them? We needed a place to sleep was not a viable explanation. Or the logger who heard at the Vagabond one night that laughing gas was an aphrodisiac and so broke into North Fork Dental, sprawled in the chair with his pants at his ankles, twisted a valve, pulled on a mask, groped himself, and died? Or that already on probation and in disobedience of a restraining order by virtue of being in the tavern at all, an ex-con left TJ's at 2 a.m., crept into a van, hot-wired it—melting a nest of wires beneath the dash—then put the van in first gear, not reverse, and drove through TJ's rear wall? There was no explaining these things. It was all one tale, like low-rent soap opera. The town was an extended family teeming with dark associations. Stories of loss were loved in North Fork: episodes of inexplicable behavior exhibiting a feckless and reckless bravado; head-shaking morality tales from a twisted universe. They mostly corroborated what North Fork knew: that an orderly life was unnatural, lived against the odds. Things happened because of the Sierra Club, the ACLU, and Jane Fonda. CHARLTON HESTON IS MY PRESIDENT a ubiquitous bumper sticker read. There was another that said KILL DOLPHINS. No one knew why all this was so and you couldn't really blame the rain for it because rain is as much a cathartic precipitation as a purveyor of ridiculous sorrows. Monstrous, dark and claustrophobic woods could not be imputed either. A dark rathole, wrote one explorer. A weight upon my sensibilities, added a nineteenth-century reporter. They brought their unhappiness with them to the woods. A billion places are ripe for discontent. You can't blame trees for your soul's condition. Was it perhaps the absence of light, then, a condition medically named?

At the Big Bottom Tom Cross sat by himself and stared at a football game. It was Saturday night and raining so hard that the Big Bottom's windows were translucently smeared and beyond them in the parking lot the rain was like an electric field illuminating the windshields of trucks and sparking off the ground. Rain rumbled outside, a dissonant, percussive chant. The out-of-work loggers sat at lone tables or in small clutches with pitchers in front of them, blandly cursing at the television. There was little enthusiasm or animation. No music played. Serious drunks in this atmosphere simply became more sullen. Someone shouted a football comment—These guys better get a nigger running back like all the good teams got these days—and this initiated a sporadic dialogue, more random gridiron commentary. Third and long's starting to make me sick. Whatever happened to the forward pass? That guy's worse than the Boz ever was. Maybe the Seahawks should bring back the Boz. Where's the Boz when you need him anyway? He's smeared to the bottom of Bo Jackson's shoe. He's Hollywood. He tried to be Arnold. If the Boz had been a big fast nigger maybe the Hawks coulda been in the Super Bowl. Niggers can't throw, someone said.

A row of women hunched over the bar, talking in furtive undertones. They'd arranged themselves in an elaborate betting pool that involved guessing the score of the game not only at the end of each quarter but also at the two-minute warnings. The bartender had strictly attached herself to them—a comforting klatch of old crones, she thought—and made only obligatory forays to serve the men at their tables. She stood posted by the cash register, smoking with obvious craving. What about this girl seen the Virgin Mary? one of the crones ventured. Or suppose to seen the Virgin Mary I don't know which it is.

I heard she seen that little girl's ghost. That one was lost—you know.

That one who works at the school cleaning up.

Jim Briggs. His daughter.

I heard she seen the Virgin too. It's Jim *Bridges.* Bridges.

I heard she seen them both is what I heard. From somebody who went up there, went with her up into the woods.

Who went?

Pat Mendencamp.

Going into the woods like that? No thanks they can have it.

A group of people went up there.

Well they can all have it, far as I'm concerned. I'm not going out into the woods like that to be abducted by a UFO.

Is that what you think?

Who knows? It maybe could be. That's how these things get started, don't they? Someone thinks it's one thing or another and it turns out to be something else. There's a lot of stupid people'll fall into anything and they're the ones end up in spaceships.

Maybe it's the devil, the bartender said. Doing his dirty work.

For the ten millionth time in her professional life, she scanned the tables of men. What did they want? What did they need? Where were they in their drinking? She went to pick up their empty glasses and to find out what came next. The devil she meant was just a notion—still there was clearly bad shit in the world, and it had to come from somewhere. Hey, she said to two pool players. You heard about this girl at the campground seen the Virgin Mary?

Bloody Mary, one of them said. She seen the Bloody Mary.

She didn't see jack.

Maybe they should make her coach of the Hawks.

You guys need another pitcher?

What I need is a Bloody Mary.

We don't have those. Who else needs what?

Bring another pitcher, Tammy.

What about you guys over here?

Two more pitchers. And watch the foam.

Make her coach of the Hawks, I say. Or give her some more magic mushrooms, maybe. Or hey—burn her at the stake.

Tammy went back to the sanctuary of the crones and began to fill orders at the tap. She was halfway to being a crone herself but nevertheless stuffed her thighs every evening into a pair of wide jeans. There were two guys in the place tonight she'd slept with out of drunken stupidity, but neither had been good to know, fun or interesting. One of them was Vaughn Maynard, who since then had lost an eyeball to a two-by-four launched out of a table saw, and the other was

Tom Cross. As long as they don't get violent, she said, to nobody in particular. Just keep them in suds and they're all right.

What did you mean by saying it's the devil?

I mean people seeing things in the woods it could maybe be Satan just as easy as anything. I mean it could be a bad thing.

Tammy carried three pitchers in one hand, a full glass in the other. The satellite dish on the roof was acting up. Sometimes in the rain the signal broke apart, something the satellite company called rain shadow. The whole idea of a TV signal was mind-boggling in the first place. How did it happen? Did anyone know? If the image of a football game could travel through the air from Texas, couldn't there be a Satan? Anyway, the game looked odd. She hoped the picture would improve.

Tom Cross was drinking in a self-possessed way, but finally his glass was empty. You doing all right here? Tammy asked.

Another.

Why is it you always give me just a little old one-word answer?

Could you please bring me another beer, Tammy?

A whole sentence.

Yes.

She moved out of his range. Tom gave her a case of ill nerves. Partly she wanted to sleep with him again, now that he was beaten by tragedy. Maybe he would be more tender from it. Not so aloof and cold, not so terse and uncaring. After they did it, when that part was done, maybe they could talk about things that mattered, something she felt she needed to do, talk to a man about her life. She imagined them in bed with cigarettes, speaking of what was inside them both, his private world and hers as well—she had her own sore subjects, after all, though nothing close to Tom's. His were enough to ruin somebody and that made her want to pursue him again, to find out if Tom was someone she could talk to, a person she could peel open, reveal, because of all his wounds.

But more likely, she guessed, he was worse now. It seemed that way to her, watching. Getting tangled up with Tom in the hope of finding a moment's tenderness was plainly asking for trouble. That was one thing Tammy knew about—thinking that sleeping with a man was one thing, finding out it was another. No, she told herself, I don't need Tom. Curiosity killed the cat and I've already used nine lives.

When she brought him his fresh beer and took away the old one she said, That ought to hold you for a while and Tom answered, Maybe. Then she lost her will about him and put her hand on his table. Your son, she said. How is he?

Paralyzed.

I know that. But how is he?

How would you be if you were paralyzed?

Not too good. Terrible. But maybe he'll get back on his feet.

Tom drank, wiped his lips on his coat sleeve, and looked at the football game. Okay, said Tammy, fair enough. I can see you don't want to talk about it.

Tammy?

What is it?

That guy over there is calling for a beer.

Tell him he can get it himself.

It doesn't do me any good to jabber. I'm not game for beating it to death, talking it over all the time.

If you say so, Tom.

This girl that's seen the Virgin Mary. What's that about?

She's a mushroomer. That's all I know.

He's pissed because you won't look at him.

Tell him I'm busy looking at you.

Go on, Tammy. See to business.

I'm not going to speak for you, but me, I had a lot of fun. That's all, Tom. Otherwise, it's raining. Just a little fun.

It never works that way. You know that. There's no such thing as a roll in the hay and everyone goes away fine.

You turning me down?

Probably. I guess.

That's a mistake, said Tammy.

By closing time, she'd gotten to him; he'd also been drinking a little. But as it turned out Tom was still bad to sleep with. He did it quickly with his pants at his ankles, his boots still laced, his shirt still buttoned, and his big moment arrived without fanfare. Oh God, she heard him say, and when he opened his eyes, they were misty. He pulled out with no inkling of affection and zipped himself up right away. Then he sat in a chair and smoked, looking out the window. Immediately it was as if the sex hadn't happened; it barely had, in her case. Yet she held out hope for an emotional exchange, some kind of intimate dialogue. Tammy remembered her disappointment from the last time, how Tom had been so quick about it then; now he was even more of a mistake, didn't kiss her, didn't look, just did what he had to, took care of his business in the perfunctory manner somebody might piss in the woods. But where before he'd mainly been cold and impersonal, now there was mostly this layer of sadness slowing his every move. Now he was empty and a cause for distress, his unhappiness a transferable stain, so that as much as she'd wanted to probe into him she found herself wanting a quick exit.

At least there hadn't been any trouble; he'd been in and out in no time. There hadn't been logistical fumbling or the awkwardness of coaxing an erection. What had possessed her to give Tom a whirl? What new low had she sunk to? Tammy sat up and started gathering her clothes. How'd you get here? she asked.

I'm motel maintenance. Plus cash every week. It's what I'm able to afford.

You get kicked out?

I walked out, Tammy.

Over what exactly?

Over everything.

She knew the story. Everyone did. The Cross family tragedy was a public meal, all-you-can-eat night at the Elks Club. Still, there were multiple versions of it—a kind of smorgasbord. Some said Eleanor gave him the boot, some said Tom left breaking things, some said they parted amicably, some said the two of them still slept together but were nevertheless full of hatred. Everyone knew, obviously, that their differences were over the boy and his troubles, but what sort of differences were they? Everything, said Tammy. That's a lot.

Tom got up and tossed her jeans on the bed. A car went by on the highway, wet tires, and she watched while its headlights swept through the curtains and swam across his face. A fleeting underwater glow, like glimpsing Tom's face through a porthole. His lone rider's profile pockmarked by shadows. A momentary illumination; from one shade to another. Let's not go there, Tom said. I just couldn't take it, that's all.

Take what?

Get dressed.

If you had any tenderness in you at all you'd snap this bra for me.

Snap it in front and work it around.

That's not my point.

I know it isn't.

Don't you talk to anybody?

I go to confession once a week.

You tell your priest about nights like this?

If I don't I can't take Communion, so yes.

What's he say about the mushroom girl?

I haven't heard him say anything.

Seeing the Virgin Mary, Jesus. How can something like that be true? Tammy wrestled into her shirt. Toss me a cig, she said.

She got into her jeans, lit up, and smoked, pulling even harder than he did. For a long time she'd accepted the risk that she could die from lung cancer or emphysema; in the meantime there were cigarettes. She'd also promised herself that one day, when she ended up breathing through a hole in her throat, she wasn't going to whine about it but instead quell the urge to whine by remembering the joy of smoking. You know what it is about you? said Tom. It's the way you smoke a cigarette.

I smoke with a death wish.

Yeah. That's it. And your cheeks get kind of hollow.

Like a blow-job queen.

I didn't say it.

Well what if you did?

I didn't, said Tom.

Why are you such an uptight Catholic?

I'm not uptight. But I believe in Jesus.

What if that's just a life preserver? Here you are thinking it makes things all right but you know what about a life preserver? You fall in the sea with one of them on you're still dead in an hour, Tom. From cold water or sharks.

No you're not. You're saved.

Saved. I've never understood that. Saved from what exactly? I don't see how you yourself are saved. And you're a church-going guy.

This is the problem with balling somebody. You feel obligated to talk.

Balling somebody, Tammy said. Your kind of balling, you owe half a sentence. Half a sentence or a word. A cough.

I never promised anything, Tammy.

The promise is—what do you call it? Implied, Tom. It's implied.

She tied her shoes and got her jacket on. This

place is depressing, she said. It smells like mold in here.

I didn't make any promises.

Okay, you didn't make promises.

He was sitting by the window, low, with the cigarette hand against his forehead, and with the light from the bathroom across his face she could see his chin stubble flecked with gray; the light was at just the right angle. Tammy, he said.

I have to go. I'm out of here.

I can guess what people say about me.

That doesn't do you a lot of good, Tom.

You believe what you want to believe.

To tell you the truth I don't think about it. Except to feel sorry for your son.

Tom got up and threw his butt in the toilet. You offered, he said. I didn't lead you on. I even tried to talk you out of it.

Right, said Tammy. My mistake.

She stood in the doorway and tossed her cigarette at the rain. You're pathetic, she said. Go to hell.

Tammy left and he lay on the bed, waiting for her residue to dissipate enough for him to consider other matters. It took a while and some effort. The room smelled of their encounter. He imagined telling the priest about it: I slept with the bartender, Tammy, from the Big Bottom. Those nouns in combination sounded so sordid. Was there an act of contrition that would make it less so? He was married only in the technical sense, so the sin in it really was somewhere else, he didn't know how to name it. He'd been impersonal, he knew that. He hadn't reckoned with Tammy's soul. That was one of the problems with problems: they didn't leave room for other people. Reserves of understanding dwindled under duress, were pared down by despondency or depression. Whichever you called it, Tom woke with his and it inhabited even his snatches of sleep, his dreams and drunken interludes. He was trimmed for descent even while he fornicated and he thought he knew how craziness felt—it was just growing tired of being unhappy, it was what came after unhappy. Then you either had a heart attack or a switch flipped in your head. Things went dark and you weren't there. What held him back was the prospect of embarrassment; it kept him in the realm of the unadmitted, except that who would blame him if he lost it? Didn't he have the perfect excuse for checking out of this world?

In the morning Tom raked fallen cedar needles and cleaned them from the culverts. There were new rivulets in the parking lot: water finding its way. With a wheelbarrow of gravel he filled the potholes. He raked in grades to make the water run. The couple with the secret dog emerged. The man was pulling a suitcase on wheels, the woman had the little animal wrapped in a red checkered blanket. Good morning, said Tom. Did you sleep all right? Tom knew how to fly on automatic pilot. There was a certain degree of theater in his everyday behavior.

Fine, said the man.

The heater ticked, said the woman.

We're thinking of taking them out, said Tom. Installing fan-driven heaters.

Well you can listen to the fan, said the woman.

You can't win, said the man, and winced.

On request Tom showed them the campground on a road map. Then they spoke about the Virgin sighting. The couple had been to apparition sites in Conyers, Georgia, and Cold Spring, Kentucky, but this was the first in their own backyard. They were excited, they said, to be there at the beginning. Miracles might be accomplished, said the woman. Who knew what could happen?

A lot of people seem excited, said Tom. But how did everyone find out about it? How does everyone know so fast? That's the surprising part.

The Web, said the man. Boom.

On the way to church Tom drove by his house—it really wasn't his house anymore—a mildewed rambler with a carport, a toolshed, and a square of moss-throttled lawn. He stopped to spy on his former life from the cab of his idling pick-up. The gutters were choked with black needles, he saw, and the front gutter was no longer attached to the drainpipe, so half the roof was pouring its water right against the foundation. Probably the basement smelled like a sewer. And the toolshed door wasn't shut all the way. Then he noticed what he would have expected, that Eleanor didn't keep the firewood covered, the plastic tarp sat bunched up against it; she was no doubt spending a fortune on electricity instead of using the woodstove. She'd never had any appreciation of money and didn't have any now. What did he expect—change? She'd always bought expensive produce—kiwi fruit and avocados—and had let the kids' dentist swindle her, but did any of that matter anymore? They were both spending money they didn't have, so what difference did any of it make? He tried to let go of caring about it, her shopping out of mail-order catalogs, things going bad in the refrigerator. The bags of expensive fertilizer—shit for sale—and the rototiller she saw on television. Or that his wife was a sucker for infomercials and straight-faced sales pitches. The sort to buy the slicer-and-dicer after seeing the demo at the county fair, the electric back massager, the nonstick pans, the juicer and the set of steak knives. There was never any arguing about it: these were necessary purchases. I'm not extravagant, you know that, she'd say, so why do you accuse me of being a spendthrift? I shop the sales, I cook from scratch, I darn socks, I clip coupons, so I don't want to hear any more of this, it isn't fair to me.

I won't say anything then.

Well why do you all the time?

I'm all done now. Believe me.

But all of that was petty wrangling from a long time ago. It was just one area of picayune dissension that went with being married. He was pretty well worn out with Eleanor way before the current business, but in a minor key, like anyone else—it wasn't any big thing. He probably could have lived with it, made it to the end of his marriage when a heart attack or stroke would get him, but then along came Junior's "accident" and that was the beginning of the end of their arrangement, which until then had worked well enough: to live without any expectation that love would satisfy. In the long bitter run of bad blood that ensued he'd said more than once It's exactly what they say, something like this really tests a marriage. I'm tired of that, answered Eleanor finally. Pointing that out doesn't solve anything or take us anywhere, does it? Tom snapped then: What are we trying to solve? he asked. If you don't know that then I can't help you. I wasn't asking for help from you, though. There you go twisting things again, you asked for help ten minutes ago, you definitely asked for help, Tom, your memory is incredibly selective, I mean I remember exactly what you said but you can't even remember from yesterday when you told me this was all my fault and you didn't want to talk about it. Damn, said Tom, yesterday, here you go back to yesterday. Well this is a continuation of yesterday, I don't think we ever finished that, I know I wasn't done with it but you just swore and stomped out of the kitchen and what was I supposed to do, be nice to you and sweet? Sweet, said Tom. Don't give me that. When was the last time you were sweet to me? I know, you have a perfect memory, it was the day before yesterday or something like that, something I don't remember right because I'm a god damn idiot. Listen, said Eleanor, who has time for this? It's just endless circling, over and over. Talking to you doesn't go anywhere. I'm going in to help Tommy now. I can't waste any more time on you. That's fine, said Tom, go help Tommy. I'm sick of talking anyway. It's fine with me if we don't talk at all. Talk doesn't do me any good. See? said Eleanor. That's the problem. Your attitude is you don't want to talk so how are we going to get anywhere? You were the one done talking, said Tom. I thought you were going off to help Tommy. Why is it you don't answer me? asked Eleanor. We went all over this yesterday, answered Tom. Maybe you just don't remember.

Tom draped his arms across the steering wheel and pondered the gloomy facade of his house, its rain-beaten, slatternly profile. He knew that Eleanor had Junior in the living room where he could see outside and watch the street, so it was a bad idea to linger. Maybe the boy, with nothing better to do, was staring out the window. Tom didn't know because he couldn't go inside; there was a restraining order against him. There was a legal writ imposing exile concocted by Eleanor's attorney. After Tom's separation from his wife he'd showed up at the house persistently unannounced until, apparently, this had vexed her sufficiently that she'd retained legal counsel. So Tom had this . . . adversary. Some kind of junior partner Jew. Ostensibly because he'd made it a habit to amble into his own house and peruse the contents of his own refrigerator, select a can of pop or an apple bought with money he had earned, and sit at his own table with his feet up. After too many visits of this sort Eleanor had forced him to arrange a schedule, the attorney wrote him a letter about it, surprise visits were not acceptable, the letterhead named a firm in Tacoma, three Jews plus Garr and McMillan. They agreed on the hour before Tom went to work—this was when he was still on day shift—since that would enforce a reasonable time limit, at a certain point he would have to leave, it wouldn't be strained or ambiguous, a natural end-point was implied by this plan, if he started work at 9 a.m. he could visit from 7:30 to 8:30 a.m. and still have time to drive to the prison, either that or be late for work, the attorney considered himself a creative genius for coming up with this timetable, Solomon, his smugness about it made Tom want to break every bone in his arrogant face. Sometimes while this attorney blathered Tom focused on the space between his nose and moving mouth or on the crescent under his right or left eye, selecting a place to hit him, shut him up, cold-cock him, deck him, no warning. So extreme restraint was required. The attorney had civilization on his side. Tom regained the upper hand by switching shifts with another guard, getting himself transferred on a Sunday to swing shift, then arriving at the house at 4 p.m., waltzing into the kitchen humming, grabbing a can of pop from the refrigerator while Eleanor was chopping celery. Do I have to call my attorney? she asked. Wait, said Tom. Oh, yeah. Our agreement. Don't play games with me, answered Eleanor. Games, said Tom, and popped open the can. Word games or mind games—I'm up for either. We have, said Eleanor, a specific agreement. Read me the language carefully, said Tom. You're not supposed to be here, Tom. I am supposed to be here, darling. You know I don't have the physical strength to simply boot you out the door, said Eleanor, so why do you play these games with me, if the tide was turned you'd use your muscles to get your way you know you would, you'd just shove me out into the yard, so this is typical of your behavior, this is what makes me so sick of you. You're off the subject, Tom replied. The subject here is our agreement not your version of what I'm like which you always make up to serve your purpose. So call your attorney if you want darling let's get it on him and me.

She called the attorney. She had his home number. We're having a little problem, she said. Tom's here. And I can't make him leave. Then she handed the phone to Tom. Sorry to bother you at home, said Tom. I'm sure this isn't exactly your idea of how to spend a Sunday afternoon but Eleanor insisted we had to call you which I tried to talk her out of, sir. Anyway, please forgive her.

Your tone is supercilious, Tom. Let's not play this sort of game. Let's at least try to be serious.

I'm dead serious, Tom answered.

Then you understand there are legal implications for breaching your agreement, don't you? Don't you understand that?

I'm sorry, said Tom. Read me the language. I'll do whatever it says.

You know what it says.

I'm trying to remember.

Don't play games.

I'm not playing games.

So why are you there?

I'm following the agreement. I'm doing exactly what you told me to do. I'm doing what you commanded.

I didn't command. That's not the right word. We agreed, Tom. Mutually. You put your signature to the document. And the agreement was, one hour before work. Not on a Sunday afternoon.

Does it say not on a Sunday afternoon?

Why do I have to walk you through this? I'm sitting here with my son and daughter, we're playing a board game at the kitchen table, and here you are exasperating me for no discernible reason. I just can't fathom this.

Which board game?

Very clever.

Sorry again. Sincerely, sir. I didn't mean to ruin your family time. Cut into your quality time. But it was Eleanor who called. Not me.

If Sunday afternoon is not included in the category of One Hour Before Going To Work then no, no visiting on a Sunday afternoon. That should be patently obvious.

Please go back to your board game, okay? We're very sorry this happened, sir. I'm sure Eleanor apologizes.

Tom hung up. He shrugged at his wife. It's all clarified, he said.

What?

I get it now. One hour before work. And I've been transferred to swing shift at the prison, which starts in fifty-two minutes.

This visit is unannounced, said Eleanor. And I—I want you to leave.

Just sticking with the contract, answered Tom.

But she was unimpressed, unfazed. Very original strategy, she said. You're hugely thinking on your feet again, Tom. Using that enormous brain power to come up with something like this.

He stood and kicked his chair behind him so that it skated and toppled over. Don't start breaking furniture, said Eleanor. That'll just get you in more trouble.

It was an accident, said Tom. The chair.

No it wasn't, said Eleanor.

I came here to see the kids, not you.

The kids don't want to see you, though. And anyway, Colleen is out. And if she wasn't she'd be hiding in her bedroom.

That's what you say.

That's what *they* say. They hate you, Tom. Your own kids. They—

Tom half raised a hand to slap her, Eleanor cringed, he stopped himself, Eleanor ran to the telephone, Your lawyer's a piece of shit, said Tom, go ahead and tell him whatever, I don't give a fuck. Hello? said Eleanor. It's Eleanor Dillon.

Eleanor Cross. What? Yes. My maiden name. I'm being assaulted by my husband right now, he's breaking the terms of his visitation rights, he's slapping me and smashing the furniture, I can't seem to make him leave. Tom ripped the receiver from her hand. I didn't, he said, touch a hair on her head. And I haven't broken anything either. Give me back the phone, said Eleanor. She tried to pry it away from him and he put one hand out to stave her off, hold her at a slim remove, she feinted once and came in from the left, he caught her forearm in his logger's grip and twisted it while he spoke into the phone, No one needs to come out here, no one's hurting anybody, He's twisting my arm right now, shouted Eleanor, Well she's god damn attacking me in the middle of everything, and so a deputy was dispatched.

End result: restraining order. And Tommy had "signed" an affidavit—marks inscribed with a pencil between his teeth—citing psychological and emotional abuse, so Tommy was off limits too. Tommy, Eleanor, his own house. Fortunately there'd been no criminal charges for domestic assault or spousal abuse or obstructing a call to 911 so his job at the prison wasn't jeopardized. His daughter he could see two afternoons a week and Saturday and Sunday afternoons but they had to meet at Burger Barn or Gip's and three quarters of the time she didn't show up so he sat there drinking coffee by himself, a public spectacle, Tom Cross. He didn't blame her for jilting him; he knew he was morose, a drag. And in the months of his separation from his family Colleen had sprouted a case of acne and had also begun to wear a bra, which evoked in Tom mixed feelings. How could it not evoke mixed feelings? How could a daughter's bra be otherwise? His daughter was at a time in her life when she was temporarily unattractive, and this, he could see, bothered her, for her it was a tragedy. Lately she asked him to buy her teen magazines with articles about how to doll herself up, clothes, cosmetics, hairstyles. Having never been unappealing before, she didn't know how to handle it. Neither did Tom. The bra and the shape of her backside, like Eleanor's—athletic, winsome, beckoning—made him afraid of her. He couldn't touch her anymore without stirring up weird questions. What made it complicated was that she looked like her mother. She was a miniature version of her mother, it was frightening, proof of the tenacity of genetics. She also had her mother's demeanor, her mother's habits of being. She could be ironic in a charming fashion and she could also be imperious. She bit her lip to think about things, brooded over imagined slights, was plaintive for days inexplicably—in all these ways like her mother. A moody and sensitive presence in Tom's life, but as his deposit of feeling for

Eleanor emptied it had naturally flowed into the vessel of Colleen, who for her part had no time for him, no inclination to sit in the shadow of his sad unarticulated rage. Another loss. He wasn't prepared for it. Junior, Eleanor—that made sense. But Colleen? He hadn't reckoned with that. He still couldn't reckon with it.

So now he sat on the outside looking in, a logger with no trees left to cut. An out-of-work logger in the cab of his pick-up, a sad fool pining for his old lost life, a dog left out in the rain. He didn't want to be caught like this, spying on his past so pathetically, caught red-handed in his misery, he didn't want people looking down on him, especially Eleanor. She'd find a way to use it against him, second-guess his thoughts. She'd make up something that wasn't there and add it to her list of grievances, which by now stretched to the moon. Why give her the satisfaction? Why give her an advantage? For a year he'd alternated between sadness and anger about what had happened and not happened between them, he'd passed too much time in the silence of his cabin remembering how things used to be. Sappy, sentimental, separated. Mired in marital memories. Yes, in the beginning they'd both been insatiable in the happy, dreamy fashion of young lovers which is something he'd hoped would continue unabated and last indefinitely. They were twenty years old and Eleanor Dillon, the youngest daughter of a North Fork logging family, had high, fine, middle-sized breasts he constantly wanted to slobber on and a hard high butt he could not keep from kissing and all he'd wanted to do back then was disappear inside her forever, in the morning before he went to work, in the late afternoon when he came home again, on the weekends at noon with the television on, on the floor, in the shower, on the kitchen table, in his truck, in the woods, in an easy chair, a few times bent over his workbench in the shop but more often against the bathroom wall or on the couch in front of the woodstove. Tom walked around with a smile on his face. He carried a secret wherever he went. He was careful at work because he didn't want to die—if he died he'd miss out on more of Eleanor. He knew he was a slave to her flesh. But that was okay. He could live with that. He got inside of her whenever she'd let him. He buried his face in her wet smelly pubic hair in order that he might stop being himself, find refuge from being Tom Cross.

Lo and behold: Tom Junior. Tom didn't mind at first. He'd liked plying Eleanor from behind while she was hugely animal pregnant by him, a female mammal who'd started his seed, he'd liked her taut impregnated belly, he licked her belly button, he nibbled her ear, when the baby was born Tom drank at Ellie's breast, he made her get on top, ride him, and he squeezed mother's milk all over his face while she came with contented sighs. Moo!

Then what? He couldn't place it. Things go wrong but they go wrong slowly. The baby had colic and screamed all the time. The little son of a bitch wouldn't sleep. And people are always changing too. Maybe Eleanor was played out, exhausted. Okay: he could deal with that. He adjusted his sights like a good married man and fucked less often, satisfied. A time for everything—they'd been there, done that. Been young and humped like donkeys, monkeys. What was wrong with this languid version? Nothing, really, nothing at all. He liked the married alternative, too. Skill, consideration, delicacy. He applied himself. They still got it on. It even got wild sometimes.

Why was everything about sex anyway? That was what Eleanor wanted to know. She read him like a book. She knew his thoughts. He began to be subtle, manipulative. The day was one long careful seduction. If he was good he got some when the sun went down. If he was bad, forget it, don't try.

But he couldn't help himself. Tom Junior drove him crazy. Tom would screw up, be mean or impatient, and then he wouldn't get laid. She'd carry a grudge against him, close down, until he paid one way or the other. Sexual blackmail. She had him not by the proverbial nuts but by his literal ones. He discovered that he wanted to go to work, wanted to get out of the house, ride. What a relief to be in his truck, heading out to play in the woods with his D-7 Cat or his loader or his chain saw. Afterward a few beers in the shop while he greased his equipment or worked on his saw would set him up to come home.

You smell like beer, she'd say in the kitchen. You try working in the woods all day. You're god damn thirsty afterward. You know what? Your son hears you use that language. Do you want him growing up like that? He absorbs everything coming out of your mouth. You better watch your language, Tom. Shit—I'm sorry. It's not a joke. Okay—I'm sorry. He's watching you. You're his example. Whatever he turns out, what kind of man, it's going to be because of you, Tom. Because of what you are.

Tom took the boy in his truck to the shop and let him poke around at things, get sawdust in his hair. He bought him suspenders and a toy plastic chain saw and when he did he felt that good paternal glow but more he knew he was going to get laid, he would drive down Main Street with the boy beside him, four o'clock on a Sunday afternoon, a half gallon of chocolate fudge ice cream in a white freezer bag on the seat between them, and he'd say Okay now you little son of a bitch we're bringing the ice cream home, all right? And you can eat some after dinner tonight, get fat if you want to, smear it on your face, make a mess, I don't care, but then you have to go to bed early, otherwise—no ice cream.

He took Junior fishing but Junior, it turned out, was afraid of fish and couldn't cast. What's your problem? Tom said, livid, you're ten thousand times bigger than that little trout, just grab the god damn thing in your hand and chew its god damn head off if you have to, and then Junior started to cry. He took him grouse hunting, shot a grouse, the boy wouldn't go near the thing when it was all done fluttering on the ground, wouldn't pick it up or even touch it. Jesus, said Tom. What's your problem? He signed up the boy for Pee-Wee football but Junior quit after three practices, complaining that he didn't like to run, the practices were too taxing, too hard. Eleanor thought this was perfectly okay, the boy's choice, he hadn't wanted to play football in the first place, it was something Tom had forced him to do, and Tom didn't get laid for thirteen days straight when you combined the argument over Junior's football with the six days of her period.

Sometimes he truly loathed himself. I'm wedded to, a slave to, my appetites. They run me around, ruin me. But that thought was rare. The tenor of his life didn't call for it. He was a logger except on Sunday mornings when they went to the Catholic church together, the only interlude in his weekly existence that didn't encourage meanness. Tom went at first because Ellie was a Catholic, it was just a place to park his butt, rest, an easy way to score a few points, get laid on Sunday night. But the funny thing was, he liked what he heard. Jesus had died for his sins, et cetera. He attended the class, did the conversion, was baptized, confessed, and took the Eucharist, all of this was cleansing a little, it made him feel there was something more than this bleak rain-wracked life of his, eking out a living dropping trees, everyone around him doing it too, this blunt, mechanical resource extraction, noisy huge machines in the forest, bad beer, televised foot-ball, mud and cigarette smoke in the taverns. He surprised himself and became sort of Catholic in a mild, confused way.

But that hadn't helped with Tom Junior. It was probably ancestral, like Abel and Cain, if a brother could hate and slay a brother, why couldn't a father hate a son? Was there some sort of mythical story for that, something sternly Old Testament? Abraham arranging Isaac's head on the block in part to placate a bizarre insane God, in part because he enjoyed it? Or was it some dark animal instinct, hungry lions eating their offspring, the primal paternal predator in the night, a freighted domestic cannibalism, a perverse meat-eater's blood lust? Or to be plain and concrete about it: the boy hadn't met expectations. He could never figure things out. He was dumb as a plank about important matters. What use was he to anyone? When they worked together, Tom worked, Junior didn't. A so-called father-son falling team. Junior thought they were out there to talk. Focus, Tom told him. Stop bullshitting and work. The boy would focus for fifteen minutes or pretend to focus with his mind still dedicated to everything but what was in front of him. Fifteen minutes. Twenty at best. Then back to rock bands, television, movies, magazines, Web sites, computers. He didn't really want to exert himself or do a full day's work. Even when he was a little boy, Junior had been distracted, pitiful, timid playing around in the yard, always crying about something or other and getting his ass kicked at games. In high school he was a lump of shit, unwilling to try out for football or wrestling, for a while he ran on the cross-country team with all the other nonathletes. Then he quit because, he said, running was too much hard work. You're just lazy, Tom told him. Why don't you go out for a real sport this winter and take the pain, stick with it? Because I don't want to, I guess, Junior answered. I'm not interested in any winter sports.

Interested? Tom said. Who gives a shit? Just get out there and take some pain and stick with something you don't even like. Because that—you're going to need it.

I don't think I'm going to need it.

The hell you won't. Everyone does.

Taking pain?

You're god damn right.

I'm not really interested in sports.

What did Junior do? Nothing. Sat in front of the computer at home drinking chocolate milk and eating cookies, bullshitting with people in chat rooms, strangers, every time Tom looked over his shoulder the boy clicked the mouse, switched the screen, waited for Tom to go away. You're tying up the god damn phone. I'll be off in a couple of minutes, Dad. We can't have the phone tied up all the time. Why don't we get a second line? Go ahead if you want to pay for it—why don't you get a job or something? You don't do shit after school anyway. What is it exactly you want from me, Dad? I want you to grow up and take care of business, square your shit away, Junior, okay? I mean right this second, not my whole life—what do you want exactly? I want you to get off that god damn computer and stop tying up the telephone line. There's more important shit going on than you just bullshitting all night with strangers. All right. God. I'll be off in a minute. Don't you raise your voice at me. Jesus, Dad. Leave me alone. You get off that computer.

Tom would find him at two in the morning clicking the mouse, typing. How the hell will you get up for school? I didn't want to tie up the phone, answered Junior, and nobody needs it late like this. Go to bed. I'm almost done. What a waste. I don't think it's a waste, okay? Pushing all those little buttons. What a waste of energy.

But the worst of it was that Eleanor got involved, had to put in her two cents, coddle him, keep Junior from growing up. She had to have her say about everything, make Tom pay, wound him. You always protect him, Tom would tell her. Even when he's wrong you take his side.

No I don't.

Yes you do.

Don't tell me things about myself. I know who I am, Tom, what I think. I'm my own person, I have an opinion. A legitimate, important opinion.

You take his side no matter what. And that's something I really don't get. Because I'm only trying to help him.

Right.

Otherwise why would it be worth my time? I have better things to do than deal with him. But I do it, okay? Because I want him to grow up. I want him to turn out all right.

You do it because you're messed up, Tom.

You always let him drive a wedge between us. You let him get between us, ruin things. I—

I just can't let you abuse my son.

That's bullshit.

Good night, Tom.

That's just completely bullshit.

So see? It cut into his sex life all the time and forced him to pretend, lie, in order merely to get laid by a woman he didn't even really like. There was no way to win and it angered him. So when the boy went through puberty, got a little stronger, Tom took him out to do some falling, as always hoping a leaf would turn, that metamorphosis was imminent, that it was possible the boy would be transformed, by hormones maybe, or just by the work, suddenly the boy would become someone else, but Junior turned out to be who he was, he couldn't figure out what was going on, he was passive and didn't absorb anything, couldn't learn how to sharpen the chain saw, didn't want to focus on trade secrets, technique, on undercuts, back cuts, felling against the lean, side notching or using the dutchman. Then he was constantly ruining good timber by fucking up on the simplest bucking and getting into the same kind of top bind over and over, a hundred times, even though the physics at work had been explained to him repeatedly, the god damn weight of this whole entire log wants to ride down right against your saw blade as soon as you start releasing the tension, just take a look and think about it, try to project yourself into the future—if you make this cut what's going to happen?—and the boy made noises like he understood and proceeded to another top bind. You dumb fuck, Tom would say, and wedge or cut him out again, and the boy would stand there, watching. What he wanted to do was just stand there. Not get the job from the inside, feel it, understand what had to be done and do it without ever having to be told, he couldn't think for himself and contribute to the program, he had to wait to be shown everything and even then he fucked it up, he wasn't going to be a logger. He wasn't going to be one. All you could do was order him around, tell him to go do this or that, then listen to his whining and complaining. Go back to the rig and bring me both jacks. All the way back, do I have to? By myself? What kind of pussy shit is that? Jesus Christ you little fuck you ought to be proud to bring the jacks and not say a single word about it just get them here pronto without a word and let that action speak for itself not this whining shit you give me when I ask you to do one simple little thing you little fuck you shithole.

He always went, Junior. Tom could make him go. It reminded Tom of dog training. You beat the dog down just enough to make him heel or retrieve a stick and the dog stayed with you long enough to keep from getting more of a beating, as soon as you were out of sight he dug a hole or chewed up something unless you attached to that, too, more unhappiness.

Usually, Tom felt bad. The boy was so easily cowed. What a pathetic drip his son was, you had to feel bad for him. Thanks for bringing the jacks, Tom would say. He meant it too, sort of, maybe. So what was Junior supposed to think? That his father was one confusing bastard, a puzzling son of a bitch? Sometimes Tom just didn't make the gesture that meant he wanted to apologize, he thought it better to be consistent, even consistently an asshole. But wasn't the answer right there in the Bible? How many times did God the Father get so pissed he killed men in droves, wiped them out and then changed his mind, here, have a city or a fertile valley, sorry I murdered a bunch of you, I'm feeling a little calmer now, wrathful carnage is a great cathartic, God's ambivalence was so familiar, and wasn't man made in God's image? And when you thought about it even merciful Christianity with all of its talk of a forgiving God had this disturbing mystery at its heart: that God gave his only Son to murderers and had him crucified. Had him nailed through the hands and ankles, then stabbed in his frail gut. Where was the

Father's mercy in that, where was the Father's love? It was a boon for everyone on earth but the Son, the Son who was the ultimate victim in a history fabricated by—who else?—forefathers. Fathers of yore who understood their yearnings. Who needed that story to quell their dark thoughts. To kill one's son was unnatural, probably, but also, probably, an instinct. To blindly wipe out the competition was to blindly obliterate your own bloodline but also an immediate animal urge that didn't require thought. The ultimate taboo was the ultimate symbol in the Western World's penultimate religion as formulated by bearded patriarchs. God couldn't love until his hate was purged. A man was finally civilized by guilt, tamed by his own transgressions. And what was the worst trangression possible? Kill your own son, like God.

But in the case of Jesus there was resurrection, proof that God had grown, was merciful, whereas Junior suffered on. Junior was permanently crucified. And whose fault was that anyway? Who was responsible for it? Tom remembered his words from the time, less than a minute before Junior's "accident," they'd been logging a steep knoll for the state highway department, taking out an S curve. You god damn pussy piece of shit, I wish you were never born. You fuck, you girl, you faggot little fuck. You finish the job or go fuck yourself. You finish dropping that tree you fuck. Don't talk to me until you're finished with it. I want that tree on the ground you fuck or I'll cut your god damn dick off.

A day of hot sun, addled flies, litter fall, wood chips in Junior's hair. But there was very little else to see, most of Junior was pressed into the ground, just a part of him visible beneath the tree, his legs twitching, splayed. Tom and another man cut Junior out and with his saw Tom recognized dead wood. The nine men present on the job got together and lifted the freed piece of snag off Junior. Then they knelt or stood in vigil. Don't move him, said one man. It's liable to make things worse. They listened at his mouth and felt with their fingers. Breathing a little. Still had a pulse. But Junior was mangled. Flattened unnaturally. His tongue hung out, his face was dark. One man stood with his radio crackling and stayed in touch with the medics from town. But Junior was squashed like an ant, ruined. Jesus, Tom had said. Save Tommy. Please! He was trembling and making a fool of himself. He heard the siren far down the road. Get ahold of yourself, said another logger, who stood watching Tom and smoking a cigarette. It isn't going to help anything for you to fall apart.

Tom gave up spying on his family's house and drove down Broad Street and north over Main,

which on this Sunday morning appeared to him
sullen, leaves turned to mire in the gutters. The
surrounding hills were a patchwork of clear-cuts
that had not been burned or replanted. Like an
incidental bombing run—ravages no one cared
about. Here was all this devastation, thought
Tom, this foolish disregard for the view, and still
the town leaders spoke of tourism as if it were salvation. A proposal with serious clout behind it
called for dressing the loggers as loggers and arranging them jauntily around their trucks in red
LOGGERS WORLD suspenders. Tom, flabbergasted,
had asked the town's hired tourism consultant—a
Jew with slick hair named Appelbaum, from
Seattle—if the loggers were meant to sing in chorus once the tourists were comfortably in their
chairs or get drunk and pretend to break things.
Which was it, he wanted to know—were they
extras in a musical production or extras in a
Western bar brawl? Appelbaum had described an
hour-long program to unfold in something called
the Old Forest Fire Pit with tourists seated on
split-log benches under a cedar-shake faux-mossy
roof while Pete Schein showed them how to
sharpen a Stihl or fell a tree using the dutchman.
The tree would be held together with hinge pins,
and Stihl would be advertising. It was the Buffalo
Bill Wild West Show in Prague with the loggers
starring as Indians. Schein's staged jeans would

be stagged so high he might be wearing knickers on the Disney Channel. A props crew would invent the creases in his neck and his caulk boots would be made by an effects company specializing in distress.

Already, Tom recalled, a diorama under glass in the museum depicted a high-lead logging operation. The loggers were handmade painted lumps, about half an inch in height, resembling Lego figurines. Someone had earned a few dimes making them, along with the Popsicle-stick trees. Now there was talk of a Dead Logger Memorial, but was that too morose? A sculptor from Seattle made a presentation but the dead logger he wanted looked too much like someone from the hammer-and-sickle department, a barrel-chested guy with the jaw of Arnold Schwarzenegger, a proletariat hero. He died so tourists might have houses. He died delivering newspapers, literature, and most of human thought. Overblown and sad, some suggested, but what if it got tourists buying the myth long enough to stay around for a hamburger at Smitty's and a souvenir chain-saw key ring? That was the yes argument in a nutshell; the no argument favored the denial of death and plenty of salt-water taffy. Still there were those dreamers who declared that Tourism A and Tourism B were really neither here nor there, the only future was with high-speed cable and Internet start-up companies. Loggers with thumbs de-soiled, thought Tom, pounding away at the return and shift keys, hauling laptops around in their pick-ups—did that make any real sense? The governor thought so and had come to town to describe North Fork's e-destiny. What North Fork needed, he said with a fist raised, pounding a lectern in the high school gym, was more consultants, community college night classes in programming, and a vision that went beyond cutting timber. Then don't put a Christmas tree in the Governor's Mansion! somebody had duly shouted. There was an interim devoted to loggers at the microphone, the governor blinking and scratching his head: We don't want to be computer geeks, I'd rather be poor and look like me than have to look like Dollar Bill Gates, You ought to be serving spotted owl to those guys in the legislative cafeteria, What do you think you're doing up here, you're a god damn liberal-Democrat governor, why don't you climb into your tax-paid helicopter and get the hell out of Dodge? Oh hopeless, hapless, helpless, said the merchants. Oh dull, misinformed cretins. Naturally, North Fork had screwed up royally in its best self-destructive logger's manner—or so asserted the president of the Chamber of Commerce at an emergency City Council meeting—the loggers always wanting to break things or to toss someone through a window. It was true, thought Tom. Loggers gone wild. His cohorts were doing their ghost dance now, thinking that if they stomped around long enough, revving their chain saws and gumming their snoose, the tide of jogging-shoed, tree-hugging, latte lovers would disappear into Puget Sound, taking their cell phones with them to fifty fathoms, their stacks of Helly Hansen catalogs and their World Wraps fast-food outlets. The grandfathers of loggers would rise again to cut all the trees in the national parks and the buffalo would return. It was a future that demanded considerable drinking by those present in these bad times—but how else to get to the world of dreams, where the future was always the past?

Tom pulled up to the minimart pumps and was standing there rubbing his temples and coughing when Jim Bridges pulled into the adjoining bay and waved at him through his windshield. Tom opened his truck's hood so as to fend off requisite gas pump socializing, but Bridges, once his gas was started, called out, hoarsely, I'm basically bad hungover this morning there's no other way to describe it.

I second that, answered Tom.

I went to Tacoma yesterday: traffic. There's a girl I see every now and then. Twenty-seven. Dishwater blonde. Works out. No makeup. I found her through an escort agency. And get this—her career goal is, she wants to be a counselor to other whores.

That makes you research material, Jim.

She can use me for that it's okay with me.

You can tell her you're doing research too. Get the nonprofit discount.

Bridges laughed with silent blue mirth. That's good, he said. I'll use that on her. Professor John's nonprofit discount.

Bridges popped open his truck hood. He pressed his glasses to his nose with his middle finger and stood there examining his engine.

Get this, Bridges said. You heard about this mushroom girl? Well Bridget went up in the woods with her to look for the Virgin Mary.

Bridget went?

Day before yesterday.

Bridget's in with the mushroom girl?

Bridget's one of her followers now. She's dropped everything else.

Tom worked the pressure off his radiator cap. I wouldn't have thought it, he said.

Well Bridget loves this kind of stuff. Television psychics, hypnotists, séances, ghosts, horror movies, the works. She cried all through *The Sixth Sense*—did you see that? Bruce Willis as a dead guy? Bridges shook his head and released a sigh that was meant to suggest the idiocy of the world, then gently pressed his hood shut. The mushroom girl—get this, Tom—the mushroom girl mentioned Lee Ann.

What?

She's up there where we lost Lee Ann.

How did she know about Lee Ann?

She told Bridget the Virgin told her.

The Virgin knew about Lee Ann?

She said Lee Ann went to heaven, which is good. She said Lee Ann passed on in the woods. In her sleep. Or the Virgin said it.

Bridges walked around his truck. Tom could see how he felt about the subject. Bridges stood reading his gas pump receipt. I bet she wants money, he said.

Maybe, said Tom. But who doesn't?

I'm going to take some aspirin, said Bridges. And sit on my ass watching football.

Don't hurt yourself.

Okay, said Bridges.

You've got it pretty hard, said Tom.

He went into the minimart for breakfast. The place was busy for a Sunday morning; three of the four tables were occupied. He poured coffee into a plastic cup, bought a donut and a maple bar, and sat down with a will to eat in expeditious solitude, but boredom seized him immediately and he ended up listening to the talk at other tables for its entertainment value. Someone had rented a trailer to Indians: Their six hundred cats shit on everything so I had to pull up the rug.

You can call a guy to take carpet away.

If you can get him to show up before you die of old age. I took it all to the transfer station. Pad and everything. Gone.

Sometimes you do that but it's more expensive.

Let me give you a piece of advice. Don't ever rent to Indjins.

I don't have nothing to rent, Ken.

Leave it like that if you want to stay happy.

Why don't you give me one of those smokes? Your Indjins can get you new ones at discount. Don't they like to barter?

What are you talking about? I'm all through with them. Jim Billy, you know that guy? Indjins have those names like that. There was one I knew named Dick By The Fire. We called him Roasted Weenie.

Dick By The Fire.

That was his name.

How'd you like to be Dick By The Fire?

Jim Billy. He was the guy. The cat master. The cat chief. I had to kick him out last week. The whole bunch of them. Out of there.

They left to pursue their untrammeled lives, full of ordinary problems. Their spots were taken by what Tom discerned were a newspaper reporter in a Gore-Tex jacket and a photographer in a complicated vest. At first they talked about someone named Slagle whom apparently they both despised, a colleague in their office. Then they talked about the mushroom girl and the Virgin Mary sighting. Who the hell knows? the photographer said. It's probably too much psilocybin. On those you'd see Tiger Woods in the woods. Or George Bush in the bushes.

Forest Whitaker lolling in the forest.

Tree Rollins up in a tree.

Kate Moss down in the moss.

Stop right there. Let's stick with that one.

Let's try nature names like Ethan Hawke.

You mean bird names like Robin Williams.

I mean water names like Johnny Rivers.

Doc Rivers.

River Phoenix.

Okay. Harrison Ford.

Harrison Ford? What's with that?

A river crossing. Ford a river. River Phoenix, Harrison Ford?

That's incredibly lame.

Try Linda Lovelace.

Monica Lewinsky.

Monica on Hanukkah.

Lewinsky. Stravinsky.

Sikorsky.

No more-ski.

I also have to put in Nijinsky.

What about Nastassja Kinski?

What about Slagle eating your bagel?

What about Slagle reading Hegel?

What about Slagle doing Denny Neagle?
What about Elton John?
They stopped talking and sipped their coffees.
Tom kept his head down and shut his eyes. These
fucks were living on a different plane. Their lives
were not like his at all. They could laugh and talk
about trivial things. Play rhyme games in order to
pass the time. A date with a virgin, he heard one
of them say. Sounds excellent to me.

Tom skipped church and drove toward the campground. He passed a sale he'd shovel-logged in
the fall of '87; the reprod had not been properly
thinned and all these years later there was still evidence of windrowed slash that hadn't burned and
there were rusted cables about. The sky was low
among the trees; it had a metallic cast. The wind
beat against the high branches. The puddles of
standing water looked dark. A case of Budweiser
had been tossed from a car and the broken bottles
littered the road shoulder, some held partly together by their labels. The river ran close to high
water, green with glacial till.
Tom turned east at the campground junction.
There was a driver too close in his rearview mirror—a teenage boy in a Honda sedan—and that
made him seethe. Tom considered rolling down
his window and giving the little asshole the finger,

but instead he slowed to fifteen, taking pleasure from that. The boy turned off at the river road, spinning out as he took the grade, and Tom rolled down his window then to give him the finger while stopped in the junction, honked his horn and yelled Fuck you you little piece of shit!

Even before the overnight pay booth, there were cars parked on the road shoulder, cars, trucks, motor homes, vans, and camping trailers. It was like the approach to a logging show, a county fair, or a circus. Always at the perimeter of those events were throngs of vehicles larger than the events and composing events themselves. A park ranger stopped Tom's truck at the booth, a girl in uniform. She spoke to him with her hands on her knees, her hair falling into her smooth chubby face, a girl who looked like a backpacker type, big tits grown healthy on granola. We're full up, she said. There's nowhere to go. You can use the turnaround.

What am I supposed to do?

Park it down the road I guess.

What the hell is going on?

We're swamped today. That's all I know. Be sure to get yourself well off the road. And be careful walking up.

He went back and parked. People were driving in too fast and banging through the potholes. He walked on the shoulder and found at the booth that the girl had her hands on her knees again, explaining things to someone else, and now there was a line of cars. Tom followed the parade of campsites with their numbered stanchions and picnic tables and here too the cars were everywhere, eased in between trees, pulled in without a scheme. Some were blocked by other cars, by camping trailers or tents. Motor homes were docked like ships but staggered for access to their doors and here and there in the incidental places were arrangements of aluminum lawn chairs. Damp campfires spit popping sparks and people walked with their toiletry kits toward the campground's only rest rooms. Tom saw the contractor from town off-loading chemical toilets. At one campsite an awning had been rigged to protect a corral of display tables. A banner read KAY'S RELIGIOUS GIFTS; under it were plastic statues, crucifixes, books, cassettes, and videotapes. Farther along someone else sold rosaries, scapulars, prayer books and medals from a pop-top Volkswagen van.

Tom spoke to the sales clerk at Kay's. A chinless woman with a blanket across her legs and the bulbous waxen throat of a bullfrog, she sat on a lawn chair by a kerosene heater, wetting her forefinger occasionally with her tongue to turn the pages of a magazine. What's this? he asked her.

It's an Immaculate Heart of Mary figurine.

Those others there on the left are different they're Sacred Heart figurines.

Where are you from?

Near Pocatello.

That's probably over five hundred miles.

It's seven hundred and fifty miles.

So when did you leave there?

Friday night.

But how did you even know this was happening?

How did we know specifically? We knew because of a chat room we're into. More than one chat room we log onto regularly. That's an Infant of Prague statue please be careful with that.

Two other women stopped to look. There's a video I've been looking for, said one, called *Why Do You Test Me?* all about Conyers and I'm also looking for a video I heard about that's all on Veronica of the Cross.

I wish I had them, said the chinless woman. I have this other great video on Conyers, that one there called *Miracle at Conyers* that's just to your right and down a little, and lots of things on Veronica of the Cross I can order out of catalogs just let me grab you an order form.

Tom wandered over to the Volkswagen van and examined one of the rosaries for sale while an impassive bald man pointedly didn't watch him, a man with the superior, fastidious air of certain sales clerks. I just came from Kay's, Tom told him.

I've known Kay for a long, long time. We don't view ourselves as competitors in the least. We have different product lines.

Where are you from?

From near Salt Lake. Packed away I've got a lot more t-shirts. Hundred percent cotton heavy-weights that are on sale right now.

At another campsite sat a food service truck where coffee was sold in Styrofoam cups as well as breakfast rolls and donuts. The boy working there was from Marysville. He normally worked at horse shows, he said, but this seemed like a de-cent moneymaker. He was gangly, with wispy hair on his chin. I'm wiped out, he told Tom. We didn't get any sleep last night. We slept on the floor in here.

Who's we?

My brother and me and my girlfriend. They took the car and went into North Fork to get some hot dogs and buns and stuff. We ran out last night seven-thirty. You people eat a lot of hot dogs. More even than horse people.

In the rest room men were combing their hair even though there wasn't a mirror and washing their hands and faces with cold water and soap from their toiletry kits. When Tom walked in he heard a man say The sun was spinning, that's what I saw. I don't know if spinning's the word—whirling, I guess, or swirling or something. There were streaks of light the first day, and the next we saw Jesus in the sky, it was one of those shapes in the clouds.

Glory, said another man. Fabulous.

We have photographs from California City.

I'd love to look at your photographs, Ed.

There's a very clear one of the golden doorway. There's another of Gabriel—a cloud shape again. There's a good one of the angel of death.

Tom stood by the river, smoking. A drift boat went by with a guide named Buck Hawes and two clients on board. Buck waved, Tom waved back, Buck shook his head, Tom shook his, Buck called out It looks like madness, Tom said It sure does, Buck said Make them keep the lid on, Tom said I'll give it a try, and then the boat was too far down-current for any further exchange. The river was too high but the clients didn't know it sitting there bundled in foul-weather gear and they were going to have to pay Buck for his time even though there were no fish to find, transferring money to the local economy sometimes involved deceit. So be it. Hallelujah. Praise the Lord for Seattle fishermen. Tom went back up to the food service truck and bought a cup of instant coffee. There was no place to sit so he leaned against a tree while nearby at a riverfront campsite pilgrims engaged in a prayer service. The people there held hands like hippies and stood in a loose-knit circle. They recited the Hail, Holy Queen and then a man with a faint Irish lilt said Lift up your voices as we recite the prayer to Saint Michael together, and someone else put branches on the fire, green branches that smoked. Tom's head still hurt and to placate it he shut his eyes and listened without watching. The pilgrims said the prayer to Saint Michael followed by a prayer for the pope's good health, and when they were done the man spoke again, Mary, Mother of Christ, O Most Blessed Virgin Mother, we believe in the forgiveness of all sin and the everlasting life. We believe that the Holy Mother of God continues in heaven to intercede on behalf of all members in Christ. Plead for us in our hour of need. Be unto us as our mothers have been, our salvation and our protection. Avail us of miracles. Cleanse us of sin and redeem us. Be as a light in this place of dark forest. As I understand it we shall proceed at ten-thirty or whenever Our Lady issues her call; don't forget a supply of water, some food for the hike, and toilet paper if it comes to that; there are no lavatories in the woods. The pilgrims chuckled at the mention of this and the man said A good practice is to take care of business while facilities are available which is something I learned many years ago, the hard way, when I was a wee little boy. More chuckling. The forecast calls for light rain, said the man, and this glorious day unfolds before us, in the name of Our Lady the Most Holy Virgin, she of the Immaculate Conception and of God's Birth. In Jesus' name, amen.

Question, said someone. How far exactly are we going? Because I have an unfavorable condition in my back that shoots pain down both legs and unfortunately I'm not sure I can make it depending on how far we have to go. I guess I didn't count on this, I have to admit, having to walk far in.

You'll get there, the man said. We'll make sure of that, my friend. That's what your brothers in Christ are for, to take you to the Promised Land.

But where are we going? someone else asked. Does anybody know our destination?

We don't know. But we give ourselves to it. We go with God and in God's name and the Lord our Shepherd shall lead us.

Getting lost in the woods is unappealing.

A thousand people can't all get lost.

I'm worried about our impact here. Forests are very sensitive. Even if we all go lightly, a thousand people—which is my estimate too of what we've got here—will trample things unmercifully. Maybe we should organize a path and keep people to it.

Do you mean there isn't a path already?

How can there be a path already since no one knows for sure where we're going?

Is there anybody in charge of this? Who do we ask about basic things? Like what's our destination?

A path isn't necessarily the answer, though, environmentally speaking. You can make a case for dispersion too. It's the same issue in the national parks. Do you build paths and give up on certain areas? Or do you try to disperse the crowds?

How did we get onto national parks? Is this an environmental forum? We all know the Church believes in the common good, responsibility and participation, but on the other hand God is our highest authority and God has called us here has he not and so while we might want to discuss these matters of path versus non-path and save the trees, when it comes to it I say follow God, after all the forest is resilient and Our Lady would not have called us here just to wreak havoc and cause destruction.

Forgive me but that makes me very angry, the idea that we don't have free will enough to exercise a little common sense and take a communal position on things, important things like our environment. I happen to believe that Our Lady expects us to discuss our path to her and find the least destructive way—we're not lambs after all, are we, who can be led to pasture on the one hand, yes, but also just as easily led to slaughter? We're not as stupid as that.

Anyway, said the man with the Irish lilt, we'll each do our best to walk with consideration, I don't think there's any more to it than that; walk with love for the earth, amen, and glory be to God. And as far as logistics I say again we don't know anything until Our Lady calls which is supposed to be ten-thirty.

Where did you hear ten-thirty?

From a woman in the campground named Carolyn Greer who is an assistant to Our Lady's seer.

Maybe we can ask her how far it is.

We can discuss the issue of a path too. An environmentally sensitive path.

A path, amen, said the man with the Irish lilt. But the path I mean is a figurative one. The path I mean is the path to salvation. You there, he said, yes you, beneath the tree. He was speaking to Tom now but Tom didn't move, just leaned there affecting a jaunty repose and taking another slow sip of coffee. Why don't you come down and join us?

I'm fine here, preacher. But thank you for asking.

I'm not a preacher. And I'm not a priest. I'm just a soldier in Christ's good army who can see that indeed you want to be one of us. Come, come join our circle.

Thank you, soldier. I'll hold up this tree.

I don't think it'll fall if you join us, friend.

Thanks but no thanks, answered Tom.

At eleven the army of Christian soldiers amassed with Ann as Joan of Arc in front and Carolyn as Sancho Panza. Carolyn had decided the previous evening as the campground filled with wide-eyed pilgrims that Ann was in fact a fortuitous tide on which she should simply sail. Not an uninteresting development, she thought. And more fantastically entertaining all the time. Maybe if I play things right, she thought, it'll stake me to a winter in Cabo.

Ann had passed the morning in Carolyn's van, taking refuge, blowing her nose, treating her rosary like worry beads, and fretting in the lotus position while Carolyn stretched her ample legs, ate an orange with devilish nonchalance, and talked Ann out of her misery. This is what you should expect, she explained. You're their hotline to God, okay? What should they do, stay home?

Ann peered nervously out the window. All morning she'd told herself that she couldn't afford to succumb to her illness, which felt now like the flu. Why was she ill at a time like this? Running a fever, chilled, lightheaded? She could see the KAY'S RELIGIOUS GIFTS banner tied at its corners to hemlock branches and nearby a larger make- shift pennant reading WELCOME ORDER OF MAR- IAN SIGHTINGS ROCKY MOUNTAIN DIVISION. The food service truck had its awning set up, and through an alley between the RVs, legions waited at the rest rooms. At one campsite a dangerous- looking bonfire sent smoke in plumes through the green of trees while around it at least a hun- dred people sang a muffled hymn. Gargantuan mobile homes impeded Ann's view, but she did catch a glimpse of the county sheriff whom she recognized beneath his hat because he'd come to the campground before to harass the mushroom pickers. He was strolling past with his thumbs on his belt, haranguing a campground ranger. I pray I'm up to this, she whispered.

You're up to it. But you better eat something. And take your Sudafed. A lot of it. And those al- lergy pills you've been scarfing.

I can't eat, Carolyn.

Well what if you faint? You're no good to any- one unconscious, Ann. On the other hand, how sly of you. You could pull a holy-roller kind of stunt. A slain-in-the-spirit kind of thing.

I don't pull stunts.

Come on. I didn't mean it.

Who are all these people anyway?

True believers. It's utterly amazing.

It's weird, said Ann. Who are they?

Carolyn slid on sunglasses and crossed her ankles. They're camp followers and disciples, she said. Groupies, fanatics, monomaniacs. Suddenly you're the rage, Ann. You're Madonna or somebody, bigger than Madonna because she can't sing whereas you, you're a diva in your Mother Mary way, not just more cheap porno dance moves and deceiving camera angles. You're an all-American cult leader, a channeler like what's-her-name who speaks for dead Egyptians, or like that guy who waited for Hale-Bopp, the mass suicide eunuch. And of course this is happening in the American West. Where else but the West Coast for this insane behavior? I gotta say I love what's going on here. It's a completely Dada spectacle. It's Hieronymus Bosch on Budweiser.

The Catholic Church is not a cult.

Okay, the Church is not a cult. From now on I agree with you. Carolyn clasped her hands like a supplicant. We won't, she said, go into argument mode. You've got other things on your mind now, Ann. So take a deep breath and exhale, release. Feel your pelvic floor loosen. Pranic breathing. Vipassana. Just get yourself calmed down.

I haven't picked a mushroom for four straight days.

Me neither. But I remain unflappable. Let the winds blow all around me, the greater the frenzy the greater my repose. My nervous system reacts with disdain.

I'm out of funds. Flat broke right now.

Well so am I. It costs money—right?—getting visits from the Virgin. Carolyn pulled her orange apart. Why don't you eat half? she said.

Ann waved it off, looked again at the pilgrims awaiting her appearance, and said Where did they come from anyway? How did they get here just like that? It's like someone snapped their fingers or something. Ann snapped hers and held her face in her hands like the distorted figure in *The Scream*. All these people. Out of nowhere.

They're not out of nowhere. They're a horde of charismatic Catholics with walkie-talkies and a phone tree.

But how did they hear? Stop joking around.

That I don't know. What's life without humor? They're here, that we can count on.

It's just more proof.

Proof of what?

That all of this is real.

Carolyn began to lace up her boots. Real, she said, and rolled her eyes. What proof do you need that this is real? You're the one seeing the Virgin.

I don't need proof. But you do still. You don't believe this is happening.

Whatever, said Carolyn. But pull yourself together. Pull that hood up or whatever you do. And maybe since you're so unfocused, maybe I should do the talking.

I agree I can't talk.

And why is that exactly?

I don't know. I just never could.

Too much feminine submissiveness training. Too much Mary Mother of God. Too much humble virgin pie. Okay, so she's the mother of God, she gets to tell God to pick up His underwear, but still, she's the one doing His laundry and cleaning up His toilet bowl while He gets all the glory.

I wasn't raised a Catholic, though.

Saying that's just more fodder for my fire. You don't even get what's happened to you. You're the perfect victim of masculine authority because you're blind to how it works.

I don't think you should be saying things about me when you don't even know me, Carolyn.

Carolyn knew this was true in theory. She didn't know very much about Ann, and she'd been cavalier in her criticisms. Calm down, she said. I'm OK, you're OK. Just tell me all about yourself. I'm a licensed Life Issues Counselor with a degree from the Institute for Life Issues Studies. Buy my videotape.

Jesus save me, Ann said.

Anyway, answered Carolyn, maybe I should handle the talking.

Let's pray before we go out there.

You pray. I'll smoke dope.

Carolyn.

We'll smoke dope together.

No we won't.

I'm toying with you.

Mother Mary come to my aid. Be with me in my hour of need. Guide me on this path, Mother. Tell me what to say, what to do.

Carolyn nodded and touched Ann's head as though anointing her. I wake up, she sang, to the sound of music, and her voice was unexpectedly beautiful, a tremulous and operatic soprano that prompted Ann to shut her eyes. Mother Mary comes to me. Speaking words of wisdom, let it be, let it be.

Carolyn hugged Ann maternally and pulled her hood around her face. You look so good bundled up that way. Like Little Red Riding Hood.

I'm scared to go out there.

It's all right, said Carolyn. But still there's one question we haven't answered. Lady Madonna, she sang. Children at your breast. Wonder how you manage to feed the rest?

Get it out of your system now. Before you open the door.

Did you think that money was heaven sent?

Stop.

Tuesday night arrives without a suitcase.

Stop.

And in my hour of darkness she is standing right in front of me.

Carolyn.

The best things in life are free, but you can save them for the birds and bees.

Ann laughed. Give me mu-uh-uh-uha-ney, sang Carolyn. That's what I want!

She pulled open the door, climbed on top of the van, and shouted Good morning! to the crowd of pilgrims, shouted it a number of times and waved her arms like a circus barker until some of the pilgrims, like pigeons spotting bread, flocked in her direction. Gather around, gather here! she said, we're about to set off to the site of the apparitions but before we go, just a few announcements, a few eeny-teeny logistical matters that will help everyone, I'm sure of it, will help us all get along.

She could see the campground moving toward her now and it reminded her of the scene from *Macbeth* in which Birnam Wood comes to Dunsinane, the boughs and limbs of the evergreens and the army of eager pilgrims. The spaces between people were filling up, the empty ground was disappearing, it was beginning to look like one of those spectacles Joseph Goebbels designed for Hitler or maybe Saint Peter's Square. Hear ye, hear ye, someone called through a battery-operated electric bullhorn which was then handed up to Carolyn after passing through a series of hands, making its way with speed to her as the result of on-the-spot cooperation, and she realized that at her beck and call were no doubt a hundred lackeys if she wanted them, slobbering devotees, fawning acolytes, servile adherents. People immediately around her van were snapping photographs with all the zeal of journalists or documentarians and others ran video cameras. Can you hear me better? asked Carolyn. Thank God for the electric bullhorn!

There was a burst of approval at this proclamation, and no one seemed to grasp its irony. Praise the Lord, someone yelled, for all things in service to his ministry!

All right, said Carolyn, and she held up her left arm flamboyantly like the worst sort of flimflamming roadshow evangelist, beginning now to embrace her role, All right, she said, if I can ask you to listen, my name is Carolyn the visionary's disciple, I'm here to speak on her behalf, I'm here because she has asked me to speak; she's very young, a humble girl, a girl who until now has been foraging for mushrooms and living here in the campground by herself, living in that tent over there and cooking in that fire pit, getting by as best she can like all the rest of we mushroom pickers who were dwelling here quietly in this little place and doing our best to put food in our mouths until last Wednesday when lo and behold, our humble labors were brought to a halt because a glorious miracle came to pass, a wonderful and forever life-altering miracle, which nevertheless has had the effect of diverting us from our work.

She paused to let that all sink in but already her inference had been well taken and a five-gallon bucket was going around, a makeshift collection plate. A miracle, said Carolyn. A miracle I have witnessed for myself on each of three successive days unfolding in the woods just east of here at a place we must reach by an unmarked route that should not be a cause for undue duress although I should stress that due to circumstances there is no wheelchair access to date, which is something we'll have to change. We do have a minor creek crossing to make which involves a moderate amount of balance of the sort any sojourner in good health possesses—you'll need to walk across a mossy log that presents a minor difficulty—but other than that, this is a walk within the capacity of any normal human being, a walk of I estimate probably two miles, two miles and no more.

Carolyn wondered if her diction was right, if she sounded credible, authentic. Two miles! someone yelled. I'm in Campsite Fifty-one-A if anyone wants to join me in the work of building a better trail!

Glory be! yelled someone else. But let Carolyn speak!

That's okay, said Carolyn, pretending no interest in the path of the bucket but noting with private giddy enthusiasm the ardor with which it was filled. I see this as a group process. I welcome anyone who wants to join in. Far be it from me to exert leadership. Now regarding the creek crossing I talked about a moment ago it will be important that we cross in single file, the crossing will be a bottleneck and will demand patience from everyone as we wait for the person in front of us however slow or out-of-it, but I must stress that no one should feel pushed or intimidated by the press of the crowd, find your own comfort level in making the crossing and take it at your own speed, I don't want anyone to land in the creek, we can do without injuries.

I'm called to build a safer bridge! Campsite Thirty-seven-A!

First Aid Committee, Campsite Fourteen-B!

And, said Carolyn, please stay together. I have a feeling that some could get lost. Whole legions of you could angle off, following leaders who themselves are lost, the only people present here with a firm sense of the direction we're taking are myself and the visionary. I don't know what sys-

tem we can use, but with this many people traveling in the woods we will have to make it a point
to stay together, I'll keep on babbling through this
contraption to give you a sense of the path we're
taking—and by the way I'm very thankful that
someone thought to bring this thing along, it's incredibly handy and will save my voice I can see
that's the case, praise God!

There was a murmur of vague affirmation.
Let's talk some more about the woods! someone
yelled. Let's talk about not destroying the woods
and being eco-friendly!

Oh yeah, said Carolyn. Exactly right. This guy
has an excellent point. A thousand people in a
great big hurry is probably the worst thing that's
happened to this forest with the exception of
when it was logged in the forties so take it easy,
watch where you step, don't litter, leave no trace,
remember, only you can prevent forest fires, and
follow the Ten Commandments.

The sheriff was coming through the crowd
now. He reminded her of a shark's dorsal fin plow-
ing a firm course through the sea. Here comes the
sheriff, said Carolyn. Make way for that man in the
wide green hat! Part the waters, so to speak, and
let our sheriff through! We mushroom pickers
know this man because he visits us regularly to see
how we're doing here, he checks in with us. Yes,
it's the sheriff of this beautiful county, I can't say I

know his name, I can't give the sheriff the introduction he deserves, but I can see he has a few things to say which no doubt will help advance our cause and suggest how law-enforcement protocols can help us act in an orderly fashion, keep the peace, et cetera, follow the rules and stave off chaos—now here he is, the county sheriff!

The sheriff clambered onto the van's roof while Carolyn was desperately speechifying and raised his own bullhorn like a herald's trumpet. From immediately beside him she sensed his gall and grasped that he was astute enough to understand how thoroughly she'd belittled him in her mean-spirited, lighthearted way. He had that beefy masculine smell of testosterone-infused aftershave. His black leather belt made creaking sounds. He was physically strong and appeared to be dangerous. A patina of adolescent acne scarring lent his face an aura of moral turpitude. To Carolyn, he looked like a rapist.

Sheriff Nelson, said the sheriff through his bullhorn. My job is to protect the people of this county, keep the peace and enforce the laws, currently we have upward of fourteen hundred people based on our latest count this morning who have descended on our North Fork Campground which was designed originally and has a legal limit of three hundred and sixty-five people primarily for health and sanitation reasons but also to protect the safety of guests and the investment of our taxpayers in maintaining our campground in good condition.

He paused and scratched the side of his face, dropping his bullhorn to his side. Praise God, cut in Carolyn. Sheriff Nelson has come to help us this morning with some of our logistical problems!

The sheriff shot her a *Be Quiet* look and raised his own bullhorn higher. I'm a Christian too, he said sternly. I walk with Jesus and I'll tell you something: Jesus is my supreme boss, I serve him before any other boss, even the law of the land comes second, that's the truth of it. But that isn't going to change the fact that there are too many people right now in this campground and too many cars and other motor vehicles, and campfires outside of designated fire pits and the woods being used like an open sewer and garbage facilities at maximum capacity—over capacity, there's garbage everywhere—and the black bears out here concern me too because food is not being stored properly or disposed of in an odorless manner and there's too much firewood foraging going on, there's insufficient access for emergency vehicles, the septic tanks can't handle the abuse— in short we have a problem here, we're way over capacity, people, I've posted a twenty-four-hour warning, by this time exactly tomorrow morning, ten fifty-two a.m., the North Fork Campground will—and I stress this—the campground will have one vehicle per campsite and registered campers absolutely and only, others will be cited tomorrow, vehicles will be towed off, I have the names of five local landowners willing to take on campers for a fee, these are folks with fields nearby, my deputies are posting sheets right now with directions to these other places, the sheets are also available at the pay booth at the entrance to this campground. Other than that please respect our county, you're guests here, temporary guests, treat our county accordingly, we're a small little backwater place it's true but we have our own way of doing things and we ask you to respect that fact and not cause trouble or raise a flap, in Jesus' name I'm not real concerned—you're all Christians, you're law-abiding people—and I expect you'll follow our laws.

He stopped again to scratch his face. Okay, thank you, Carolyn said, moving close beside him. Let's all pray now for Sheriff Nelson. She held up her left hand, dropped her head, and then without warning put an arm around the sheriff, who stiffened and dragged off his hat. Underneath his hair was thin—each root planted sparsely in his skull—and blackened by grooming gel. Dear Lord, said Carolyn, help Sheriff Nelson in the work that he is doing. Help Sheriff Nelson to find his way. See that Sheriff Nelson is satisfied.

Help us to do as Sheriff Nelson asks and let not the sheriff be troubled by us. May he endure and even celebrate our presence and find us a group of obedient souls, inspired by you Lord to follow your rules as well as those prescribed by Sheriff Nelson, and may we find other places to dwell as the sheriff has requested of us by ten fifty-two a.m. tomorrow, in Jesus' name, amen.

She removed her arm and shook his hand. He gave her again the *Be Quiet* look, a private look of sinister loathing, and then he clambered down from the van with the cumbersome sloth of an orangutan and, clenching his bullhorn between his knees, fixed the trim of his shirt.

One moment please, Carolyn said dramatically. Bear with me now, my fellow pilgrims. She put down the bullhorn, lay flat on the roof, and pressed her face against the window. Arise, fair sun, she said through it to Ann. Come on, Ann. Get out here.

Carolyn swiveled to the other side of the van and hauled open its sliding door. Then with her face hanging upside down she said I hate to present myself this way. The force of gravity inverted like this only serves to accentuate the horrible degree to which my skin has lost elasticity.

Ann made the sign of the cross in reply. Hey, said Carolyn. Did you see that bucket? We're rich like the Duke and the Dauphin!

She helped Ann onto the van's roof. When Ann hid behind her Carolyn said No Way, Shrinking Violet, you're on top of the Aztec pyramid now and they're going to cut your heart out. Then she seized Ann's arm at the wrist and thrust it upward triumphantly as if Ann had just won a prizefight. Here she is! said Carolyn through the bullhorn. Ann Holmes of Oregon!

A refrain of assent was heard from the crowd, and assorted hallelujahs. And the Lord said let there be light, said Carolyn, rejoice O ye sons and daughters of Zion, behold the handmaid of the Lord, blessed is she among all women, and now let us bow our heads and pray. Dear Lord we thank thee for your loving-kindness, all hail Mary of the Immaculate Conception, She of grace and all things good, lover of the meek and our protector, grant us now on this day of your grace the generous charity we shall need. And now Ann will lead us in prayer.

She handed Ann the bullhorn and pulled her forward. Bail me out, she whispered, and winked. I don't really know any prayers.

Ann looked across the crowd and a sea of people gazed back at her. She could feel the tension of their expectation. This is all a mistake, she thought. I can't give them what they need. Nevertheless, I've seen the Virgin. And she raised the bullhorn to her lips with wet eyes and trembling shoulders. Loving members in Christ, she said, and her body gleaned a first intimation, a first inkling, of sacrifice. She was standing on a kind of altar. A peristaltic convulsion moved through her; the hair at the nape of her neck felt the wind that some describe as the breath of the dead as they stir in their separate purgatories. Stand beside me, Mother, she thought. Was this God's test or were his eyes just elsewhere? She sensed that her course was cruelly predetermined. God knew the story, including its end. *He* wasn't asking any questions. This was how the meek inherited the earth, the beggar, the thief, the whore, the dope addict, the vagabond, the pauper, the crucified.

Hail, Holy Queen, Mother of Mercy, Ann began, and the crowd joined her in prayer.

Until she saw the Virgin Mary, Ann had few words for what she knew and sparse means to explain herself. Her mother had called her Dimple as a child, also Button and Mouse. Her father was a rolling stone, said her mother, by way of an explanation. Met at an eight-dollar concert in Salem, five local bands over nine hours. He was twenty and wore a leather coat but no shirt. His angular chest flamed an angry red. His hair was seized into a thick ponytail. He lived in Eugene, didn't work, and took a lot of acid. He believed, mildly, in eco-terrorism without engaging in it. A constellation of light freckles on his face and his fiery abstract disdain for capitalism endeared him to her initially. Ann's mother ran away at fourteen, hitchhiked north to Eugene in the rain, and lived with her winsome rebel for two months before he booted her out. Literally. He planted a boot in the small of her back to assist her passage through the door. It emerged in her period of pleading afterward that he had no soul to speak of. He could cause pain without remorse. He looked good, but that was all. Ann's mother was not prepared for his arctic male distance. Her entire being felt the shock of his cruelty, but after a month he didn't matter and that came as a surprise to her, how quickly she went cold about him even when she found she was pregnant. He was easy to forget, she said. There wasn't much to remember. His name was Scott and the last she heard he'd joined a band of anarchists in Arizona. She hadn't heard anything since, nor cared to. Even her reservoir of bad feeling dried up; it was as if he'd never existed.

When anyone inquired Ann's mother said that the girl was being homeschooled. She was badly asthmatic, very small, and suffered from chronic allergies to dust mites, spring pollens, mold, and mildew. She carried in her pocket an asthmatic's inhaler, which she sipped from surreptitiously when she felt she was strangling. Her allergies were sometimes entirely debilitating and forced her to stay in bed for long hours with a sheet pulled over her face. Hay fever ravaged her mucous membranes. Often her eyes were swollen and red, her nose ran and itched, she sneezed, wheezed, coughed, sighed, and tried unsuccessfully to expectorate. Ann felt inexplicably tormented by the invisible contents of the world. When her respiratory afflictions left her listless she intimated how it felt to die; her tired lungs sent death's message. The body's surrender and defeat made sense. She felt the meaning of submission inwardly. Capitulation, the cessation of breath, and the panic of bronchial constriction seized her. In this she was like the consumptive children found in nineteenth-century melodramas. Illness formed her sensibilities. Antihistamines offered a modicum of relief to which Ann became so thoroughly addicted that she began to engage in drugstore shoplifting—Dristan, Sudafed, Chlor-Trimeton—before she was twelve years old.

With her mother she picked ornamental brush for florists, gathered mushrooms and seed cones, and peeled yew and cascara bark. Another woman went with them often who was known as Sleepy Jane. Sleepy Jane was tall and big-boned and wore her long hair straight down her back, a threadbare fringe of split ends. They would be picking ornamental huckleberry and Sleepy Jane would suddenly decide to sit cross-legged on the forest floor and smoke the roaches of marijuana cigarettes she kept in an Altoids tin. Or they would be peeling cascara bark and Sleepy Jane would decide it was too hot, peel off her shirt, and take a nap. A fly would land on her sunburned breasts which were long and lopsided, uneven in heft, but Sleepy Jane paid flies no mind and absently fingered her rough nipples. She believed that yews held the souls of dead women who had not been able to leave the earth and she could name churchyards in England and Wales where yews shaded the tombstones. She had a book called *The Sacred Mushroom Seeker*, another called *Soma: The Divine Mushroom of Immortality*, and she read not only Ann's palm but her skull and feet as well. Dimple, she said on each occasion, it doesn't look very good for you. It looks pretty bad, actually. What can I say? If I were you I'd probably decide not to believe in readings.

I don't, said Ann. So it doesn't matter.

Once Ann rode with her grandfather in his tractor-trailer to the Florida panhandle where he dropped a container of plastic bubble wrap. In South Carolina they picked up another load and took it to Louisiana. She lived on secondhand cigarette smoke and breakfasts fried in lard. Her grandfather wore a kidney belt and a beard that made him look like one of the Allman Brothers or the guys in ZZ Top. He was fat in the belly with spindly legs, dark glasses, and suspenders. He liked bands named after states, Alabama and Kansas. He also liked biscuits and gravy, Bugler tobacco, and motorcycle magazines featuring silicon-implanted bikini models. At a truck stop in Oklahoma he gave Ann a dollar—he'd never given her a dime before—and told her to go into the convenience store, look at magazines, and watch the clock. It's seven, he said. You stay there until eight. Don't come out until eight o'clock. What for? she asked. Just do it, he said. There's something I gotta take care of.

It happened again in Wyoming. Friends, he said. I just meet friends. I got friends in these little old places and we like to get together privately.

This time Ann caught a glimpse of the friend, a woman in a royal blue windbreaker and those unwalkable platform shoes left over from the disco era. That's Linda, her grandfather said afterward. We have a mutual interest in racehorses.

Her grandfather was ticketed for ignoring the pay scales on Interstate 80 in Nevada. At Winnemucca they turned north and came home via Klamath Falls and Medford. Her grandfather met another friend in Grants Pass, a woman with an interest in deep-sea fishing. Ann stole cigarettes from the cab of a truck and sat in the weeds to smoke them furtively and masturbate languidly. She had started masturbating as a child of six and it had been since then a source of comfort, free of charge and equal in satisfaction to most candy bars. The barest little shiver left her warm and consoled. A little death, a placid tremor.

At home she was not supposed to hear it but sitting on the toilet she heard it anyway, her grandfather in the kitchen saying to her mother Never again with her riding shotgun, driving's bad enough without your love child badgering me for soda pop ever fifteen miles. She's not that bad, her mother answered. You get a job, said Ann's grandfather. Then you can have an opinion.

Sleepy Jane moved in as soon as Ann's grandfather embarked on his next trip. It was August and a series of parties ensued. They played The Band on the stereo, Quicksilver Messenger Service and the Chambers Brothers. There was a fight in the doorway involving beer bottles. A man with a silver hoop through his eyelid stayed overnight with them, off and on, for ten days. Ann's mother cried inexplicably. There was a hookah and wine bottles on the coffee table. It was the nineties but no one seemed to notice that. A group of drummers descended on their apartment, a duplex with its own patch of lawn in front. They were drumming on the grass—Sleepy Jane and another woman dancing with no

Caribbean finesse—when Ann's grandfather pulled up. He got out of his tractor-trailer and asked if he could try a drum and when they handed him one, a homemade conga, he threw it into the street.

Ann began to go to school. It was too embarrassing. She used her inhaler in toilet stalls and doubled her antihistamine dosage, which deepened her school malaise. She started wearing her sweatshirt hood all the time in public. There were some boys who called her Carrie after the Stephen King character. She met other girls who were castoffs as well, diminutive like her and tangential. They were like mice together. They nibbled and stayed in the corners. One girl, Tara, developed breasts early and supplemented by falsies stuffed with toilet paper they constituted her ticket out. She became more popular. Ann didn't develop. She couldn't read and when the school found this out Ann's mother received a letter from the superintendent threatening a child-neglect suit. But there were other students her age who couldn't read and they had all gone to school. So who was neglectful? said her mother. Ann was put in a remedial class where she was taught to read by a computer. She kept sunflower seeds in her sweatshirt's kangaroo pouch, pulled the salty kernels from the left, stuffed the wet husks down the right. There was no money for dope at first but she traded magic mushrooms, which she knew how to find. The dope made her cough at first, then alleviated her respiratory symptoms. She got caught stealing rolling papers from a convenience store a week after she got caught cheating on a math test.

Then she was thirteen. They moved and she went to a different school. Ann wore flared jeans low on her hips, brass buttons rising from her pubis. A boy asked her if she wanted to get stoned and in the woods he unzipped his pants. Touch me, he said, but she refused, apologizing. In class the next day she was minding her own business when the girl behind her whispered *slut*. She wore the hood and her nickname at this school was Holmes said with emphatic irony for reasons she didn't understand. It was code for homely, she found out. Soon she was accused of eating her own boogers. She had three friends in the same category. She showed them where and when to find mushrooms, which they froze in Baggies and sold. With the money they bought dope and went to a roller skating rink and again she went to get high with a boy and this boy too unzipped his pants. She used her hand like sandpaper rolled to smooth a dowel, employing a regular, detached piston stroke, and afterward he wrote down her phone number. This boy was named Evan. He was tall and approximately pear-shaped, spongy.

They spent afternoons in the basement of his house with soft drinks and pornographic magazines. Blow me, he requested finally. So she knew what it was about now. She put her lips around him in resignation and used a slower stroke than her hand stroke but every bit as regular. It wasn't worth it, Ann decided, even while she was at her work, but she took the job to its conclusion anyway, gagged up his seed, and stopped seeing him. There were consequences. Evan spread the rumors of the spurned. A girl called Ann a whore at school. His friends showed their tongues to her.

Her mother's new boyfriend was named Mark Kidd. He lounged in angular, precarious trajectories across their furniture, shirtless and barefoot, dangling a beer bottle by its neck, swinging it a little like a pendulum and looking at the television, or sitting on the floor with his back against the couch and around his neck a Saint Christopher medal, blond hairs on the shanks of his toes, blond hairs on his legs like a surfer's. He had a rocky, bumpy sternum, a goatee, the same eyes Jesus had in *The Last Temptation of Christ*. He looked like Brad Pitt only goofier. Ann watched him shoot up, at which he was expert in a dull way. His tracks were attractive. The veins in his arms were like a nest of undulant worms. He seemed primed to pop. There might have been too much pressure in his eyeballs. At first he was playful and wrestled with her and held her in his lap against his erection. He knew passages from the Bible by heart. A woman of valor who will find? he said. Or, And Miriam the prophetess, the sister of Aaron, took a timbrel in her hand; and all the women went out after her with timbrels and with dances. Can you suss that? he asked. Can you dig it? When she tried to get away he put his hand between her legs. Behold, I was shaped in iniquity, he said, and in sin did my mother conceive me. Let's get it on. She tried to get away again. He had a way of keeping his fist so deep in her hair she couldn't move without suffering. Death is swallowed up in victory, he said. As by one man's disobedience many were made sinners, so by the obedience of one shall many be made righteous. Then he turned her over. The side of her face was against the floor. I love it how you look like a guy, he said. There's nothing there. No curves. Just your sweet and beautiful little ass. He pressed a palm against her upturned temple and laid into her with a snakelike lunge. What I dig, he said, is just to stay in you, all the way up like this. Mmm. Way in. Mmm. In. We just hold like this and after a while you'll beg me for it. Oh. Good. But I won't give it up until you ask. You have to want me, oh.

He shot up while he lay on top of her, in her, demonstrating a relaxed dexterity. She didn't feel anything but his weight. And in the sixth month, he said, the angel Gabriel was sent from God unto a city of Galilee, named Nazareth, to a virgin espoused to a man whose name was Joseph, of the house of David, and the Virgin's name was Ann, baby, oh yes it was, and then he started to grind.

When he cried beside her deep in his throat with tears that dropped from his jaws to his neck she considered springing to her feet propitiously and making a dash for freedom. But he kept one hand in her hair while he threatened her. Jerry Lee Lewis loved a child, he said, and they crucified him for it. So did Elvis have his Lolita. Every guy digs fourteen-year-olds, they just can't do nothing about it no more. Not in today's society. All these guys with their wrinkled old ladies pretending they don't want fresh little girls to bust their cream against! You think your Indian and your African didn't stay busy hosing fourteen-year-olds out on the prairie and getting down and dirty in the jungle, getting it on, breaking their nuts, snakes, vines, buffalo heads, all that shit like that? Little fourteen-year-old tight clean pussy was what the warriors wanted, Ann. Savages didn't never give a damn, they did whatever their manhood commanded so they could walk through the valley of death undaunted when they battled other tribes. Damn, he said while inside of her, this is as good as it gets.

Young girl get out of my mind, he sang, in a horribly off key whispered tenor directly in her ear. My love for you is way out of line. Then it became a medley with his eyes shut. The younger girl keeps a rollin cross my mind, no matter how hard I try I can't seem to leave her memory behind. Girl, you'll be a woman soon, soon you'll need a man. Little sister don't you kiss me once or twice and say it's very nice and then you run, little sister don't you do what your big sister done.

He would cry right after he came, then laugh. It was part of his post-ejaculatory chemistry. You tell your mother and I'll kill you, he said. So go ahead and tell her if you want. But if you do I guarantee there's gonna be a moment between when the cops are at the door and you're like hiding in your closet. And that's when I'll cut your throat, bitch. Just before they cuff me.

She didn't tell anyone. She believed him, his threat; she was afraid Mark Kidd would kill her. So Ann left in September when the air was still dry and the wind still hot and inviting. The first night she camped in the landing of a clear-cut, curled up on the mildewed backseat of the car she'd saved her money for, a machete and a hatchet nearby. The mildew made her sneeze again and her inhaler cartridge was empty. She blew her nose and took antihistamines. She picked a few truffles, some huckleberries. There were Cambodians in the woods who spoke no English. There were also out-of-work loggers. She came across two men cutting cedar bolts who were nervous, she decided, because they had no permit. That's right, bitch, keep right on walking, one of them called when she turned away. Out of their sight she began to run. Before long she turned to thievery. She was bold about it and stole in daylight: a can of gas, a generator, a cooler, a boom box, a backpack, a case of beer, a raincoat, a spare tire, a car jack. In Eugene she sat on the street with a sign PLEASE HELP ME I'M SO POOR AND NEEDY and hustled pocket change. When she thought she had enough cash on hand, she went to a medical clinic. A deep caustic burning between her legs, coupled with a strange discharge. Yeast infection, it turned out, and on top of that, herpes simplex. Mark Kidd's calling cards.

In a campground rest room she found a pocket Bible and stuffed it in her sweatshirt's kangaroo pouch. She read it by her evening campfire, wiping her nose with a handkerchief. It passed the time and in small towns, on rainy days, she sat in libraries and read it. She stole a copy of the catechism from a library. In one town was a Christian Science Reading Room. The man there gave her a copy of the Gospels. She began to feel worse about the abortion she'd endured the year previous. The baby Mark Kidd had planted in her, murdered before it had drawn a breath, was in a state of permanent limbo. Ann read a book called *Letters from Medjugorje* and at a secondhand bookstore found the *1986 Catholic Almanac* and a book on Christian healing. In October she camped near Crescent Lake and picked white matsutakes. The money was good, but it went into the car, which needed first a water pump, then an alternator. She found that if she cultivated silence and wore her hood consistently like a shroud she didn't have to worry about males. It helped to be offbeat, incommunicative. Ann began to understand witches. She hacked her hair short to deepen her strangeness. She sat close to her fire every evening. She wrote a postcard home that said Mark Kidd is a deseased rappist mom get totaly away from him.

She took psilocybin at least once a week. Her hallucinations now had a religious cast and were sometimes rimmed by halos. The car burned oil. Oregon lay poised between two choices, but she felt drawn northward, called. California seemed dangerous, Washington soothing. The deeper the woods, the better she felt. In Washington it rained more often than not, a soft comforting veil. Ann camped for a week by the ocean and read *The Confessions of Saint Augustine* and Stephen King's *The Dead Zone*. A college student tried to talk to her on the beach. He said he went to Pepperdine but was taking time off to travel. She was reading and he wouldn't go away. She knew what sort of person he was. Very sincere, attended class and thought about his future, this trip to the beach was a nature lark, he was probably hauling around a new surfboard and for sure hoping to get laid. He was away from home and feeling rough and ready, but his earring looked fake and temporary. When he put his arm around her shoulder she turned and said Beelzebub and stared into the backs of his eyes, where she noted the slightest tremor. Beelzebub, she said again, and then he got up and walked away.

Invoking the devil successfully worried her. She went into a Catholic church in the town of Aberdeen—birthplace, she remembered, of Kurt Cobain. She remembered being on-line at school, she was supposed to be doing library research for a paper on Edgar Allan Poe but instead she read Cobain's suicide note: *There's good in all of us and I think I simply love people too much, so much that it makes me feel too fucking sad.* Ann knelt in a pew. The body of Christ hung over the altar. She went up, touched it, and put her fingers in her mouth. They tasted salty, like seaweed. God, she said, save me from my sins. This was during a psilocybin binge, part of its crescendo. Ann put her fingers between her legs and touched herself absentmindedly. It was private, comfortable, and reassuring; it involved no one else. She pulled off her hood and lay on the floor. Sun flooded the stained-glass arch. She felt warm and had a dreamer's vision, three women pushing her through a door with a stone lintel, a tribe of dogs running lathered through a forest, a ponderous search for shelter, too late, from a heavy, cacophonous rainstorm. Afterward, this was all she remembered. It didn't add up to a story with a theme. Nevertheless she believed that the forgotten parts would have coherence if her memory could capture them. There was a residue of meanings, no images, but meanings on the cusp of her discernment. She carried what she couldn't recall as a deepening disturbance. There was a fold or field around her now and she knew how to sustain it. A protective cloak of her own devising. In the church foyer she gathered leaflets and pamphlets. Can Anyone Be a Good Enough Catholic? A Radical Change in the Sacrament of Penance. Moral Issues of Human Life. How to Pray the Rosary. She kept them on the seat of her car. She bought a set of rosary beads and hung them from her rearview mirror. She bought a dashboard Jesus, too, one that turned a luminous amber as the evening darkness deepened. And she thought she remembered some trippy lyrics, in stereo, from one of Sleepy Jane's wine-and-dope extravaganzas—I don't care if it rains or freezes, long as I got my plastic Jesus. Though it could have been something else.

Ann used too much psilocybin and passed out on the altar of a church somewhere—what town she was in, she didn't know. The priest there found her and called the police, who delivered her to a medical clinic where Ann came to the next day. A doctor, a woman, listened to her story, which she told while blowing her nose into Kleenex. I'm too tired to argue, said the doctor. But I still wish you wouldn't just lie to me.

I'm not lying.

Whatever you say.

My allergies are really bothering me.

It's dust mites, I'm guessing. This time of year. She got up, slid open a drawer, and pulled out a Sample-pak of antihistamines. This stuff, she said, is Phenathol. It's one pill every six or seven hours. I can give you half a dozen, dear. Enough to get you home to Mother.

Great.

The doctor shut the drawer and washed her hands. You go home to your mother, she said. Right away. Pronto.

I am going home.

You said that, said the doctor. She crossed her arms and squinted at Ann. She wore thick glasses;

her hair was in a rope. If I was smart I'd call in a counselor, she said. Someone who can deal with a runaway.

Ann took one of the Phenathol pills. I don't really need a counselor, she said. But I do need a ride to my car where I left it parked up by the church.

It's only three blocks to the church, said the doctor. But right now rest. For an hour or so. When you're feeling ready we'll sign you out of here and if you need it someone will walk you over. I'm guessing you're asthmatic, too, given that wheeze I'm hearing.

No, said Ann. I used to be. But pretty much I've outgrown it.

It can come back, the doctor said, if you don't take care of yourself.

When she left Ann lay with her head on the pillow and let the Phenathol work. It did. Quickly. Its efficacy surprised her. Her sinuses cleared, her torment subsided. She pulled open the drawer of pills, took all the packets of Phenathol samples, and stuffed them in her sweatshirt pouch.

As anticipated by certain environmentally aware pilgrims, the maple bottom, the copse of alders, the labyrinth of blowdowns, the thicket of Oregon grape and salal, and the dank mossy forest of the Marian apparitions were all poorly served by the mass of travelers, who stormed through them like Roman legionnaires. Much was flattened. And indeed one pilgrim was detained by injury at the site of the crossing of Fryingpan Creek, a woman with excessive fear of heights who convinced herself prior to making the traverse that Mary and Jesus were sure to guide her if she shut her eyes and let go. She fell and broke two bones in her left wrist and badly bruised a hip. Someone else turned back because of a surge of anxiety brought on by disorientation. A third traveler with chronic vertigo was halted by a bout of stumbling and returned to the campground with assistance. And a man in therapy, rendered vulnerable by the forest, retreated when a minor social gaffe impaired his sense of self-worth. There were other digressions like battery-operated children's toys flailing in the corners of rooms. Dead ends. Marital crises. One couple who had fallen behind found themselves oddly eroticized by the lush density of the ancient forest. Finally they stopped to embrace and kiss. The man laughed gently and put his hand under his wife's shirt so as to run his fingers along her back and next he descended into her underwear which prompted her to say, Your hand is cold. Mother Mary, the man said. I didn't expect her to lead us to the sacrament of woodland fornication.

Let's do it, he added. I'm serious. We can't, his wife answered, not out here, are you crazy? Please, he said. For once let's not be so Catholic about this. I'll lean you up against a tree and take you from behind, okay? It's not okay. I don't like that. But why not? Come on, let's do it. Wait until later, she said to him. Wait until tonight in the motel. We have to catch up to the others.

Eventually the main body of pilgrims arrived at the site of the apparitions. Technically they were trespassing on land owned by the Stinson Timber Company but as yet, nobody cared. State troopers attended them with pistols and nightsticks, as did Sheriff Nelson and his deputies; any large group of people was their business, even those bent on salvation. The same could be said of the photographers and journalists who preyed on the pilgrimage like forest gray jays, birds known commonly as camp robbers. A rain fell so light and ethereal that no one could be sure it was rain, perhaps it was a discharge of the trees, splash induced by high breezes. Stragglers perpetually joined the host. People had not stopped arriving at the campground, asking questions, following signs, and probing into the forest. Pink flagging now festooned the way and marked the trail through the labyrinth of blowdowns where it was easiest to lose direction. There was a place where travelers had broken fern stalks and left them tipped over and dead in large numbers and this marked the path as well. The way was heaped with destruction. A shrewd sojourner off the mark could scout from a bolus of freshly dropped human stool to a sandwich bag impaled on the spines of an Oregon grape leaf to a pink pendant hung by a previous pilgrim from the branch of a maple tree. A substantial percentage of travelers had never been in the woods off-trail and felt the natural disorientation that accompanies this condition. The weight of walking brought the water through the moss and soaked their shoes disagreeably. There were people with wet feet, others chilled by the touch of their own sweat, others who had forgotten toilet paper. Arid people who had neglected to bring drinking water and hungry people forced to endure the heedless picnics of others. Religion did not necessarily remind those with provisions to look at things from another's point of view or to remember the importance of sharing. Hence their fellows suffered needlessly. A man doused a hardboiled egg with salt tapped from a minuscule backpacking shaker, then he did the same with pepper while a hungry man watched with concealed longing. They were oceans separated by continents. This same juxtaposition of food and desire played itself out through the forest. It was the same with drinking water—those who needed it hoped for a charity that widely was not forthcoming. They were unwilling to ask and looked comfortable enough. It didn't occur to those in possession of canteens and bottles that they were surrounded by legitimate thirsts. The woods were full of ignorance and pretense. A bespectacled pilgrim seized a beef sandwich between his teeth so he could page through a trailside reference book, and the oblivious, easy extravagance of that soon galled a hungry woman. He was eating while identifying nearby mosses, lichens, and liverworts. Another man read silently from his Bible with his hand in a bag of pretzels. A group of women ate goat cheese, smoked clams, herring snacks, and marinated sliced red peppers. Most of the pilgrims, hungry or sated, arid or quenched, were moved to consider their mortality by the forest's sea-green cathedral light. The trees rose like pillars. Out of the fallen trees grew new trees. A delirious photosynthetic rapture suffused the air of the place. There was so much evidence of decay and birth it was discomfiting and comforting at once. How could this be here and people matter very much? The indications of human smallness and of the great span of God's time—there they were in everything and who could think about it? Fine shards of fear shot through the atmosphere and pierced the pilgrims in vulnerable places. The message of the woods was simple. You are going to die.

Milling and waiting, the crowd grew high-strung. There were upward of a thousand pilgrims now, filling the spaces between the trees and trampling the understory. Carolyn Greer had marked the apparition site with long tendrils of pink flagging, but already it had been indicated further with a plastic crucifix propped against a tree, with votive candles, medals, chaplets, plastic water bottles, an Immaculate Heart of Mary figurine, a display of carefully separated orange segments, a handkerchief cradling a handful of walnuts, a tin backpacker's drinking cup filled with Skittles, everything set in a bed of plucked ferns so that the spot now looked like a holy site for animists recently proselytized. A depository of relics from some forest hagiography in which the saint was still named Raven. An altar freighted with amulets and fetishes. A shrine in accord and perfectly organic; a tabernacle of totems.

Lines of sight became difficult to maintain. The fiercely selfish carved out views and turned territorial in a neurotic way—the sort of people who suffer the illusion that in a crowd, individuals have rights. But no angle of vision was sacrosanct. Early postures could not be defended, even by those unabashedly obnoxious. Uh hey, excuse me, we were here first, we got here forty-five minutes ago, you can't just squeeze in front of us like that, but already there were more invading pilgrims committing even more grave offenses and oblivious to the complainant. So few could see. The gathering took on a claustrophobic cast. Given the wet ground, it was difficult to sit. The less fastidious accepted damp pant seats, but the majority stood or sat on their rain gear. A group of women took solace in the rosary, concluding with the Fátima Ejaculation, an appellation that induced sniggering among certain nearby males who knew themselves to be perennially immature but nevertheless couldn't help how they were struck. To them, it was funny. The Fátima Ejaculation. O my Jesus, forgive us our sins, save us from the fires of hell, and lead all souls to heaven, especially those in most need of thy mercy. You shouldn't be laughing, a woman said. I can't seem to help it, a man answered. It's like trying not to . . . ejaculate. At this the men laughed all the harder.

There was too much anticipation to be suf-fered. A disturbed zealot filled the emptiness of waiting with a high-pitched soliloquy, while those around him feigned disinterest or lack of consciousness. Conspiracy in the Vatican! he pro-claimed. An Italian actor travels to Austria and is altered by the finest Viennese plastic surgeon to look like Pope Paul VI! Cardinal Casaroli and Cardinal Villot are the villains behind this das-tardly plot in league with the Freemasons and international banking, the Rothschilds and their cronies in Brussels, for which we will suffer World War Three and after that the Ball of Redemption, a comet such as this world has never seen, more deadly than the asteroid of Armageddon! Indeed! We are sure to see episcopal censure and an attempt to unleash satanic forces against our undefiled Ann of Oregon since the Red Hats are all fallen today and the Purple Hats surely are next! The devil is strong! Be not misled! The pope you see is an evil impostor and the one true pope our conduit to heaven has been subdued and is today sequestered in the Roman catacombs where he languishes under the influence of drugs and awaits our crusading intervention! Indeed the symbols of Beelzebub . . .

In another bay of the sea of pilgrims, a woman had taken up juggling rubber balls purchased expressly for that purpose and stowed in the bottom of her backpack. She was skilled and modestly entertaining, passing the balls behind her back and underneath her long raised legs, but someone nearby took offense at her antics and began to argue that such a spectacle was appropriate to a carnival perhaps but unsuited to the matter at hand and an insult to Mother Mary. So there was no more juggling. Some pilgrims played card games. Others examined photographs—Polaroids of cloud formations resembling Jesus, the door to heaven, angels. Cells of devotees arrayed themselves in tight-knit circles and prayed together feverishly. A woman sighted a butterfly about which there were various opinions, Painted Lady, Lorquin's Admiral, Anise Swallowtail, Mourning Cloak, but the time and place was inauspicious for all these and the only possibility, a bearded pilgrim loudly proclaimed—after labeling himself a "poor man's B-league lepidopterist"—was *Nymphalis californica,* whose name, he added, chortling, was a juxtaposition not inappropriate for a number of Hollywood strumpets. Think Neve Campbell, he said. Or Cameron Diaz. *Nymphalis californica.* That's not anything we need to hear, a pilgrim nearby admonished him. Butterflies are harbingers of Mary.

Another woman smelled roses in the woods, a second harbinger. Again, skeptics in proximity to this revelation were quick to point out how improbable it was: there were no roses in the woods in mid-autumn. Exactly, said the woman. That proves my point. The roses I smell, they're holy roses. The invisible perfume of Mother Mary. The roses I mean are not real roses. Did you know that at San Damiano rose petals fell in showers from the sky and then from the hands of Mary herself, and that the seer there was Rosa Quattrini, and that Our Lady appeared to Rosa with a rosary made out of white roses, white symbolizing Our Lady's grace, and also with a cross adorned in red roses, red symbolizing suffering? But no one knew these things. The woman pressed on, a small-time pedant. At San Damiano there were many healings. Rays of light fell to earth from the Madonna. A pear tree bloomed in the autumn of the year, as did the branch of a plum tree on which Our Lady stood. On the day of the feast of aviators, American pilots bore witness there. And Rosa was blessed by the Capuchin stigmatic known as Padre Pio. There was joy and light from heaven! There were graces and comforts from earth!

Two precocious high school boys from a Catholic school in Olympia climbed a tree and looked down on people. There's idiots, said one, who think Christian rock is heresy. Or even a band like Jesus Jones, just because of its name.

I don't get that. What's wrong with their name? In Latin America, there's hombres named Hey-sooz. Does anyone down there worry about it, like they're all going to hell?

No.

It's a gringo El Norte uptight thing.

This is freaky.

Best seats in the house.

This is da bomb.

Totally.

It's happening way up here.

Ann had decided to sequester herself in a small defile full of sword fern. The journey had exhausted her and left her feeling deeply chilled by the cooling of her own feverish sweat. She drank her water and took a Sudafed and two of the Phenathol pills. Then she sat with her back against a log and her knees pulled up against her chest in a limber attitude most adults can't achieve, Carolyn sitting like a yogi beside her, the two of them circumscribed, loosely, by self-appointed churlish sentinels, men who kept their arms across their bellies, chewed gum, and wore billed caps, a group of eight who'd gathered cumulatively during the course of the pilgrimage and made themselves into a convoy. Get it together, whispered Carolyn to Ann. People are twiddling their thumbs.

I can't force it, you know. It's not like this is a performance, a circus, with shows at noon and four. Whatever happens, it's up to Our Lady. I'm not really in charge here.

It's kind of a show, though. Like Billy Graham live at Madison Square Garden. Or Jim Bakker or Oral Roberts. You think those guys aren't showmen, Ann? There's such a thing as inspiration. There's willing her—what do you call it? Summoning her, invoking her. Now get on your knees and say your rosary. And put a little pizzazz into it. Whatever it takes. Get it started.

It's Our Lady who'll get things started, not me.

I beg to differ. It's a two-way street. You want the Virgin, you have to invite her. Open the door. Let her in. And take your hood off, sweet thing. It's not polite to wear a hood in the house, especially when you have company.

You don't believe in Our Lady, Carolyn.

Utterly beside the point.

I don't know why you're even here.

I'm here because I love you, girl. She took Ann's hand and pressed it to her cheek. Don't worry. I'm not a lesbian.

Neither am I. I'm nothing.

So we're just two women holding hands. No sexual implications in that. No one should read between the lines, she called out to their male sentinels. Hands touching. That's all.

She pulled Ann into a standing position. The crowd was singing On This Day, O Beautiful Mother in a manner reminiscent of Tibetan monks chanting *om mane padme hum,* the gathering of voices by some principle of acoustics more than the sum of its parts. Carolyn found it moving. She wrapped her arms around Ann tightly and put her mouth to Ann's ear. The sweatshirt hood now reminded Carolyn of the grim reaper's empty cowl, his faceless comic presence. You're

beautiful, she whispered, baby doll. And kissed
Ann's cheek with tender force. But you need a
bath and some mouthwash.

I'm really sick, answered Ann.

They went out to the altar of ferns with its
baubles and offerings. The great crowd stretched
around them in all directions, plebes in the
Colosseum. But Carolyn felt more like a Mayan
high priest when Ann dropped suddenly to her
knees in a choreography of resignation, pushed
back her hood like a condemned prisoner, and
pulled her rosary from her sweatshirt. Now her
young face with its wan complexion was visible
to her followers. They saw that she was a child
and rejoiced, that her hair was cut like Joan of
Arc's, that she reeked of humility. Behold, someone yelled, the handmaid of the Lord! and the
voices of the singers lifted in a crescendo. There
was a palpable, militant stirring through the
crowd, pilgrims jockeying for position. Carolyn
took cover behind a tree. One of the sentinels
frowned at her, a man in a blaze-orange hunting
vest. Alms buckets, she saw, were going around,
and people were eagerly filling them. Huzzah! she
thought. Was that the word? It was easy for
Carolyn to feel greed and detachment. Eventually
this would all be behind her. A lot of bad movies
ended with people basking frivolously in tropical
climes, laughing and drinking margaritas, taking

their leisure in the ample sun, primed for a twilight of hedonism. Carolyn knew she was one of those characters. There were worse fates, but few so meaningless. She understood that she should not get attached to suntan lotion and Third World discos as philosophical propositions. There was a valid critique to be made of sensualism, one that was selfish, not ethical, since worship of the flesh led to premature despair and an investment in cosmetic surgery. Either that or roomy floral dresses and exile to retail boutique clerkdom in Tucson or Boca Raton. Fine to be an adventurer now among the young in exotic locales, but well-sunned, somnolent, geriatric tourists were a dime a dozen in Key Largo and Palm Springs and died without marring the landscape too much, except for the time-share condos left behind and the scent of cocoa butter. Ugh, thought Carolyn. Celluloid shades could conclude with a million dollars, beach recliners, and cocktails decorated with festive small umbrellas, but what of those flickering, gorgeous phantasms subsequent to the final credits, when the theater is strewn with sad spilled popcorn, and the cinephiles have all gone home to work on last-minute dishes or bills before going quietly to their beds? What of starlets and promiscuous heroes in the silence of living afterward, while no one watches and they grow older by the second? What then? thought

Carolyn. A confirmed old biddy with sun-leathered skin? A lonely spinster with skin cancer?

Ann's raptures began in the midst of endlessly repeated Hail Marys. She stiffened, first, like a pointing dog, then quivered epileptically on her knees, then tilted forward past her center of balance as if frozen during a springboard dive, a trick that fueled her followers' fire because it was as eerily unsettling as a Hindu mystic on a bed of nails or a yogi folded up like a pretzel with his ankles behind his head. There seemed to be a principle of physics abrogated by her very posture that might well be divine in origin. Ann raised her eyes toward the treetops and stretched her arms like Jesus at the Mount and those close by could see her weeping in a manner suggestive of a thorough catharsis, nodding her head, mouthing silent utterances, conversing with her invisible interlocutor, her face kindled from moment to moment by the nuances of a conversation no one else was privy to. Someone yelled Hallelujah! Glory! and someone farther back yelled Mary Mother of Redemption save us from our sins! The boys in the tree were seized by the spectacle such that neither could be cynical temporarily, and each considered in private the priesthood, the prospect of hell, his own myriad sins, the pulsing thralldom of the ardent crowd, and the sexual charm of the visionary. The girl was pornographic in ecstasy, a male projection of female religious passion, as if God had entered her. She looked like the limp wilted models in magazines who have been arrayed so as to call attention to the sexual allure in the poverty of their bodies, their awkward features brought to the fore, their odd angles championed, pouchy stomachs, sagging shoulders, starved cheeks, dead eyes—heroin addicts on 42nd Street in the era just after disco expired; Patti Smith on the cover of *Horses*—the better to make them human, responsive, is there anything sexier than a flagrant flaw, a nipple off center, a port-wine-stained hip, limp hair, uneven breasts, a mole on the throat, bad shoulder blades? Ann was, potentially, all of these. She stood, naked without her hood, unkempt, disheveled, incandescent. Spiritually aflame, it was palpably clear, and trembling as if in postcoital meltdown. It had stopped raining. Shafts of light now penetrated the trees. Beams from heaven! a pilgrim cried, and began taking Polaroids feverishly.

Our Lady's message, Ann said suddenly. I greet the many pilgrims who have come today to—

Louder! yelled someone. We can't hear out here in the boonies! We can't hear anything you're saying!

Carolyn dashed up with the electric bullhorn, held it to her lips and exclaimed Oops!, then handed it to Ann with parodic obeisance and retreated again, a vaudevillian. Hello, said Ann, tinnily, and her voice evoked less mysticism amplified, she sounded like a junior high school thespian nervously engaged in a talent show. She also sounded adenoidal, asthmatic, and seriously phlegmatic. I'll start over, I guess, sorry, okay? I'm sorry that you couldn't hear me.

There were thumbs up, OK signs, and approval from the back. Ann held one hand forth like an orator and with the other clutched her bullhorn. Rejoice, she said. I greet the many pilgrims who have come here today to this beautiful place in the rain forest. Followers in Christ, amen. The Mother of God asks that you serve her now by practicing charity and good deeds. Our Lady asks that the selfish and greedy change their ways immediately, before her Son Our Lord Jesus Christ raises his arm and hurls the world into such dark sorrow as was never seen before. A darkness that will befall us all if our ways are not soon mended. Jesus is angry and his rage will not be stopped until the selfish and the greedy are redeemed. Now your Mother intercedes, your Mother of the Divine Mercy, Mother of the poor and Mother of the world, a woman clothed with the sun, as it is written, who leads you away from suffering. Away from the snares of the devil, Beelzebub, who is with us here in the world today, here even in this forest. Our Lady brings peace and is merciful, just like any mother. She who holds you to her breast and nurses you in your eternal sorrow. Go with her. Take heart in her. For she is the miracle of miracles, Mother of the perfect heart, Mother of God and the Handmaid of the Lord, she is Mary the Queen of Heaven, and by her assumption into paradise she sits now at the right hand of God and comes to you here in order to warn you: be not deceived by Satan the devil in his many forms and disguises. Be not deceived! But follow in her a true woman of valor, a woman who chose by her own free will to become the servant of God!

Ann paused. There were tears in her eyes. Just as Eve chose disobedience, she said, so did Mary say unto God, Be it done unto me according to thy will, and lo, it was done! And now she stands as a mother might between her children here on earth and God the Father in heaven, between all of you and a terrible judgment! She is like the north star to you, a guide to the gates of paradise, leader of the heavenly choir, Mother of Sorrows who stood in witness as her only Son was crucified. Our Lady is all these things and more. It is she who holds back the hand of the Lord, a woman of glory and divine holy power. The Holy Trinity is incomplete without her grace and understanding. She is Mary Light of the Forest whose church will rise in this very place by our hands, our work, and our sweat. Let us begin our task together. Take heart, rejoice, and follow me! In Jesus' name, amen.

Ann fell silent, her message complete, and pulled her hood across her forehead. The drawing of a shade or veil, met by a din of silence. Carolyn stepped forward ebulliently and stood beside Ann with her hands clasped thinking, I like that speech, female energy, Tepid Feminists for Catholicism, a little lukewarm feminist theology never hurt anybody. She looked at Ann with a feigned expression of unadulterated spiritual awe—not entirely feigned, however: the elevated diction of Ann's recitation was genuinely spooky, she had to admit, as if indeed Ann had channeled someone else's rhetoric and intelligence—and noted at the same time that Ann's nostrils were flaring reflexively and the vermilion border of her lower lip remained tremulously aflutter. Mellow, said Carolyn. Let me take over. I've got it, Ann.

Simultaneously a woman stepped from the crowd, prompting a defensive lurch from two sentinels whom Ann held back with a raised hand. It was the ex-bartender, Carolyn recalled, the woman who'd mentioned Paul Simon's "Kodachrome" and who'd chain-smoked her way through the forest on Friday; the woman who'd knelt with the rest in deference to Pascal's pragmatic wager. Forgive me! she cried now, hoarse in the way of some nicotine addicts, but I'm called to testify to a miracle, I'm called to testify! On Friday I traveled with Ann of Oregon to witness for myself her visions of Mother Mary and at that time she prayed for me about which I'll admit I was pretty skeptical, a doubting Thomas, but guess what? Guess! All my warts have disappeared and on top of that I stopped smoking, without any trouble nicotine is gone, I tried patches, Nicorettes, everything you can think of under the sun, but Ann prayed for me and bang, like that, the two things Ann said she would help me with, the warts and the smoking—they're gone! I'm bearing witness to her, she's a miracle worker, I've never been particular-religious but here I am to share with you the amazing truth of her healing glory, Ann of Oregon has cured me!

At this the crowd became raucous. Cries and shouts of affirmation, raised arms, leaping in place, utterance of shards of scripture, prayers of petition and adoration, the Ave Maria could be heard recited in monk-like unison, Holy Mary, Mother of God, pray for us sinners, now and at the hour of our death. There arose a general piety, a cloud of witness and convulsive homage—during which the ex-bartender stole off, returning demurely to her place in the crowd—a clamor like that at the foot of Sinai when Moses appeared with the tablets of God, or maybe like that at

Calvary when Jesus was fixed to his cross. On the other hand, some pilgrims fell contemplative and were turned inward toward silent prayer even as around them unfolded a riot of bald spiritual excess. But these were meditative souls by nature, not prone temperamentally to hysteria, even made fearful by it. Such arousal as they felt surrounding them seemed to their minds the devil's work, like the paroxysms that seized German clerks and burghers during the pageants of the Third Reich.

To Ann it felt like something to shun and produced along the nape of her neck a tingling of despair. Was this really what the Mother of God desired, this surfeit of sudden adulation? She dropped the electric bullhorn, waved, and retreated to her defile of sword ferns, where once again she sat with her hood up and her face concealed between her knees, like a Mexican asleep on a Texas boardwalk at noon in a Western. Carolyn, watching her, felt grave for once. What am I getting her into? she wondered. She sat beside Ann with her head down too, held the girl's hand and whispered to her, You gave a nice speech, it was good.

It was growing dimmer, late in the day, and the prospect of darkness provoked urgency. People began to leave the woods, though not the journalists and photographers, many of whom did not believe that darkness could affect them and felt certain they could thwart it with cell phones. She won't talk to reporters, said Carolyn to the sentinels. Tell them to go their merry way. Tell them to leave her alone.

They were told. They went. They made a variety of manipulative noises in lieu of any farewell. Straggling pilgrims gave petitions to the sentinels, which were summarily passed to Carolyn. Small slips of paper, like a lottery or contest. Pray for me, Susannah Beck. I suffer from irritable bowel syndrome, very uncomfortable and disturbing. I am Leslie Weathers, from Kent. The doctors say I have lupus. My name is Steve, heal my daughter Chastity Ferguson, she was born two years ago with cystic fibrosis. Laurie Swenson, sciatica. Pray for my relief from pain. I also have bursitis in both shoulders. Tom Cross. Pray for my son. He's paralyzed from the neck on down.

Tom hiked back toward the North Fork Campground with the sheriff who'd addressed the crowd that morning—a person he knew from high school wrestling—and a deputy named Ed Long. Tom had dislocated Sheriff Nelson's shoulder when the two of them were juniors. The injury still lay like a shadow between them, but since then the sheriff had gathered around him the penumbra of a martial artist and carried himself with cheesy bluster. Nelson was out of shape but solid in a stiff unassailable way. It was clear whenever he walked into a room that he had come to believe in his girth as a bulwark against both criminals and opinions he loathed. He was slow and sure of his view of the world. What Nelson needed, Tom thought, was his other shoulder dislocated as a reminder that his vulnerability wasn't abstract. It might make him less certain of everything.

Tom walked listening to the officers talk. After all the babble about loggers, said Nelson, this is what brings in the tourists.

We need a turnstile, Ed Long answered.

The thing of it is, Nelson said, all of these people are trespassing.

But it's Stinson, said Long. Do they care?

I don't know yet. But I'll hear from them probably.

They let people hunt.

This is a thousand four hundred people trampling everything in their path. That's a little different from hunting.

A little.

Either you guys get a buck this year?

Neither had. They walked for a while discussing past bucks. I've been teaching my kid to shoot BBs, said Nelson. Also a little basic kung fu.

A couple of blocks, some kicks, some hand strikes. He's five years old. It's cute.

Good discipline, said Long.

Nelson nodded.

But get him a .45, Long added. It'll save you both a lot of effort.

They laughed at this. Boom! said Long. Cross, said Nelson. How's Junior?

Paralyzed, said Tom. Still paralyzed.

I heard he was like that guy who played Superman.

Yeah, said Tom. Like that guy.

That guy's still alive. He wrote a book. He played in a Alfred Hitchcock–type movie. I read about him somewhere. At the dentist.

Yeah.

First he wanted to kill himself.

Yeah.

I guess his wife can still . . . get satisfied. How that works, I don't get.

Me neither.

How could that work?

I don't know.

There's guys who aren't paralyzed can't satisfy their wives.

Yeah, said Ed Long. But they're not Superman. The Man of Steel, right?

Nelson gave Long a look of consternation. Jesus, he said, and sniggered.

It has something to do with the nervous system, said Long. It's automatic, a hard-on.

Fuck you, Ed.

There's Viagra you know.

Fuck you again.

Maybe this vision girl can help you with it, Randy. Maybe she can rectify your problem.

She can't rectify shit, okay? She's just a skinny little mushroom eater. She eats psychedelic mushrooms.

I like chicks skinny, answered Long.

This is a scam. It's a scam, said the sheriff. And that other girl's in on it. The one on top of the Volkswagen bus. That smart-ass redhead hippie with the bullhorn. They're playing games with everybody. That's what's really going on here.

Nelson put a hand on Tom's chest in order to bring him up short. Look here, he said. Whoa. Hold on.

A man wearing a complicated backpack and two women with lesser backpacks were waving at them from between the trees, stumbling in their direction. One of the women was carrying a skull. Hello! said the man. Yo! Sheriff!

Look at this, Nelson said. Granola eaters turned headhunters.

The trio of travelers caught up with them. Nelson pulled on rubber gloves of the sort Tom associated with cavity searches conducted at the prison. Ever since AIDS we gotta wear these, said Nelson, and immediately took possession of the skull in lieu of any other greeting. Where did you find this thing? he asked. You know you should have left it where it lay. Left it exactly where it came from.

Sorry, said the man. We didn't know that.

We're really sorry, said one of the women. But the whole maxilla's intact, as you can see. And there's a handful of premolars in there still. So with dental records, if there's someone missing, it should be an easy ID.

You sound like you watch too much television, said Long, laying his thumbs on his belt. This is real life, not *NYPD Blue.* And the rule is, Don't touch a crime scene.

Excuse me, said the woman. I'm sorry.

She shook off her backpack with difficulty. Her legs were like sausages encased in spandex. The other woman drank from a plastic water bottle and had a savage eczema on her forehead.

We came from north-northeast, said the man. About forty, forty-five degrees.

Don't listen to him, said the woman with eczema. He's terrible with directions and always gets lost. He never knows where he's going.

I took good bearings the whole way, said the man. I worked out my line of travel, made notes. He pulled a compass from under his shirt, worn around his neck on a string. I can get you back there, if you want.

What I want is an answer, the sheriff said. I want to know where you got this.

The woman with the eczema said they'd gotten lost, thanks to the man with the compass: her husband. They'd made the classic hiker's mistake so often warned against in outdoor manuals of blustering forward frantically even when they knew they were lost, until they came to a precipice. Here she'd ventured off with toilet paper and was winding her way through moss-draped maples that were eerie and somehow frightening, she said, because they were so throughly moss-inundated, as if they were being throttled alive, and underneath one of these disturbing trees she found what she thought was an elk or deer bone, desiccated and green. She brought it back and the three of them examined it, especially the other woman in their party, the one in the spandex hiking gear, who had gone briefly to medical school at Johns Hopkins University. This woman seemed to know with certainty that what they had was a small human femur, a leg bone, a child's thigh bone. On the basis of this they'd searched some more and had come up with the green-tinted skull.

And we found these, too, said the man.

He fumbled inside the top pocket of his pack,

pulling out a water purifier and a plastic bag of trail mix before finding what he wanted. Then he handed Nelson a long green bone, the tattered remnants of a rain poncho, and a plastic hair barrette.

Nelson's face had the same pinched look Tom remembered from wrestling practice. The coach would demonstrate a difficult new move that Nelson couldn't quite comprehend and his face would constrict a little. As if the thought required to learn it overwhelmed his faculties. The sheriff seemed patently dumbfounded now and stood in silence with his lips pursed, blinking, holding in one hand the small worn skull and in the other these three forest icons, the bone, the poncho, and the hair barrette.

Lee Ann Bridges, Long said.

Probably, replied Nelson.

Tom sat down on the remains of a log and stuffed his hands in his pockets. The mushroom girl had called this one, she'd told Bridget Bridges exactly this, that Lee Ann had died in the forest. It was—Jesus—spooky. Such clairvoyance unsettled him. The mushroom girl appeared authentically to have the gift of visions. Plus she'd cleared that woman of warts and put an end to her smoking. Tom thought of the bumper sticker back at the motel: DON'T TAILGATE: GOD IS WATCHING. Maybe, he thought, I'm scared, like a child. Or maybe it was just comforting to think that in the end, or after it, lay darkness, stillness, instead of something he wasn't ready for, like heaven, hell, another life. Now his Catholicism seemed like yearning, not belief itself. And his sessions in the confessional seemed like jaw-flapping when the stakes were all or nothing. But what now? So what? He needed someone to tell him what to do. A million Our Fathers and a million Hail Marys. This god damn priest didn't seem to know his shit. Words weren't going to get him anywhere. Tom's condition was serious.

The man with the compass had a map out. The woman who had castigated his navigating skills was poring over it with him. Long and Nelson had turned their backs to engage in a private confab. The woman who had used the word *maxilla* was eating trail mix with undignified haste and washing it down with Gatorade. And how are you? she asked Tom, smiling. I'm doing great, Tom answered.

III

Woman Clothed
with the Sun

NOVEMBER 14–NOVEMBER 15, 1999

O n Sunday evening the priest mastur-
bated. It happened without his intend-
ing it. He was sitting in his reading chair
with *The Ginger Man* propped open on his lap
when it dawned on him that his idle self-fondling
might usefully become less idle. The priest, as always, could not go forward without pondering
moral and spiritual implications, but these he set
aside sufficiently to indulge with only the barest
shame in that feat of deliberative stimulation
which is, according to the catechism, intrinsically
and gravely disordered.

Afterward he felt ashamed, self-conscious,
aware of himself as a celibate priest who'd en-

gaged in onanistic pleasure, in sinful self-gratification. He was, at the same time, vaguely wistful, regretting that he hadn't taken the time to squeeze more pleasure from the act. It had been swift and perfunctory and he was not that sort of self-lover generally, reasoning instead on most occasions that an indulgence was at least partly wasted whenever it wasn't thorough. And since sporadic self-abuse was the whole of his sex life, such omissions of attention meant more to him than they might to other people. Oh well, he thought. Maybe next time. Greater discipline next time. He was tidying up when someone knocked on his door, three insistent raps. My God, he said aloud, it's the Thought Police already. Panicked, he tucked himself quickly away and checked the vicinity of his zipper for stains. I'm completely ridiculous, he thought.

There was a humorless-looking man on his doorstep, behind him the girl who claimed to see the Virgin Mary, and behind her, another man. Their car was idling with its wipers running, and the priest could see, in its headlight glare, a puddle that looked like a pond. As usual it was raining with bland insistence, not a downpour but a misty effervescence, diffuse and weightless as snow. Are you Father Collins? said the man at his door. Father Donald Collins?

The priest tried to look around him. He was a

man with a belligerent mustache, squarely built, wearing a vapid zealot's expression and a hunter-orange nylon raincoat. The other man stood at a short remove, an obscure and forbidding background figure with his arms folded across his chest, a pose like Superman's. Ann, said the priest. Good to see you.

These guys gave me a ride, she said. I—

You should never accept a ride from men. They could easily turn out to be dangerous or something. You never know—I hope you gentlemen will excuse my saying this, but I think you'll agree my point is valid—you never know about men, Ann. You shouldn't trust them, period.

We're not dangerous, said the man with the mustache. I see your point but in this case, Father, you can be sure we're fully to be trusted.

The priest looked past him, out into the rain. Ann, he said. What happened to your loyal female friend? The cynical chairwoman of the Karl Malden Fan Club? Why didn't you get a ride with her? Carolyn, right? Where is she?

Her friend may or may not be loyal, the man with the mustache countered. That's been difficult to pin down.

What? said the priest. Excuse me?

Carolyn Greer. The woman you mention. You talk about issues of trustworthiness, I bring up her name.

He's right, said the second man. We're a little suspicious. It's best to withhold any judgment on Greer until a few answers come in.

The rain was starting to saturate the priest's hair to the point where he felt how cold it was. Let's go inside, he said to Ann. To you gentlemen I say, thank you very much. Thank you for your kind service. Thank you for your help.

It's nothing, replied the second man. You go in. Go ahead. We'll wait out here. In the car, right here. You don't have a back door, do you, Father? A second point of ingress?

The priest took Ann's small hand in his and pulled her into his living room. No, he said. Just the one. Good night now, gentlemen. Thank you.

He shut the door before they could respond, hoping his trailer wasn't tinged with his shame, with the telltale odor of spilled seed one notes in the bedrooms of teenage boys. The priest recalled with terrible embarrassment that the collage of his masturbatory fantasies, unfolding only minutes before, had fleetingly featured the very girl who stood before him now. There was something residually erotic, he found, in her fleshly presence at the very moment when he had just arrested temporarily his desolate sexual desire. In fact it was sexual serendipity. It was as though he had made her from degenerate thoughts—like God making Eve from clay or a rib, except that God was not corrupt—as though he had conjured her.

As I remember it yesterday you were sans bodyguards, he said. You were still yourself, for the most part.

Ann loosened the drawstrings on her hood but didn't lower it. Her pallor, clearly, had worsened since the day before, and he worried, again, about her health. Those two just appeared, she answered.

Are you saying they're apparitions too? Maybe that's the way to think of them.

They sat and she accepted his offer of a cup of chamomile tea. A little something for your cold, he said. I don't think it's just a cold, she answered. I think I'm coming down with the flu.

Are you taking something?

Sudafed.

Is it helping, do you think?

For some reason, no.

You need to see a doctor.

No I don't, Father.

Your health comes first.

No it doesn't. Building Our Lady's church comes first. Before my health. Before anything.

The priest excused himself delicately and went to put the water on to boil. A domestic task that calmed him a little in the face of such fierce dedication. Alone in his kitchen, arranging biscuits on a plate, he thought of words like *vicar* and *parsonage* with their pastoral associations. Finger sandwiches with cutaway crusts. Chocolate madeleines and Wiltshire Haystacks. Mr. Collins from *Pride and Prejudice,* invited to the Bennets' as entertainment. Mr. Collins the clergyman. Father Collins' namesake.

When he returned, the girl still hadn't removed her hood and was sitting with her kneecaps pressed together, as if thwarting an urgent bladder. It's really uncanny, Father Collins said, but you look a little like a visionary. As if you were born to the role.

What's a visionary supposedly look like?

Like Bernadette at Lourdes, I guess, who was fourteen when she saw Our Lady. Or the three shepherd children of Fátima. Or the two cowherds at La Salette. Like you, they all needed showers, Ann. They all needed to do their laundry.

She smiled, thinly, and chewed on a cuticle. You're welcome to clean up here, said the priest. I'm blessed with a washer and dryer on the premises, and plenty of shampoo and soap.

Thank you, said Ann. But what about the church? We have to get started on the church.

Is it okay for you to take a shower first? Before you put on your tool belt?

Nothing's okay for me, said Ann, except to do what Our Lady asks.

The priest sat down beside her on the couch. That sounds hellish, actually, he observed. Like your life isn't yours any longer.

It isn't.

I can see that.

I serve Our Lady.

It sounds like a form of possession, though. You don't even have time for a shower.

Yes I do.

There's a clean towel in there.

What about the church first?

What about today? asked the priest. Back up to today, Ann. Did you have another vision today? Another visitation?

Yes.

At the same place? Out in the woods?

With, like, a thousand people watching. Called there. By Our Lady.

A thousand people.

The sheriff said there were fourteen hundred. The whole campground's full.

The sheriff?

He was there too.

How come?

Crowd control.

A thousand people?

More than that.

You're kidding me.

No I'm not.

Father Collins experienced a lurch of his heart, a stroke of arrhythmia; a catch. He'd understood from the gossip at church that a crowd had gathered for today's apparition, but a thousand people? A thousand? Well, he thought, I'm calling the bishop. This has gotten over my head. This has become a phenomenon that cries out for church investigation. How did a thousand people get up there? he asked. Way out into the woods?

They walked.

I see.

Just like you did.

Father Collins hooked one leg over the other, as if he was just warming up to the subject, as if he was in it for the long haul. So in this context of a thousand people, a number I'll presently take at face value, what did she say to you?

The same message. Jesus is angry. There's too much sin. Believers are supposed to act on her behalf, perform deeds of loving-kindness. She'll return, she promised—two more visits. I'm supposed to tell you everything. We're supposed to get started on the church.

The priest sighed. Okay, he said. Okay—the church. Let's get started building the church. But first we'll need to see who owns the property. Then we'll need to buy it, right? Then we'll need an architect, won't we? Someone to come up with a design and plans who isn't too busy with other jobs? And maybe the architect finishes in nine months. He has to work with an engineer, and that takes, maybe, three more months. Meanwhile, we hope to find potable water—reasonable here-abouts, I guess, fortunately for us. And we also hope the land perks—less reasonable: clay soils. We take the architect's plans into town and submit them for review and approval to a bureaucrat who asks us, four times, to resubmit. This takes—oh, nine months, a year. Meanwhile the county wants a septic design. There will have to be an environ-mental assessment. An environmental impact statement. A cataloging of environmental assets. Botanists will want to count the plants; someone will check for eagle aeries, yew trees, pileated woodpeckers, and then count the newts and voles. Not to mention a wetlands delineation. After twelve to eighteen months, if we're lucky and everything goes without a hitch, maybe we'll have a construction permit and the right to go ahead. Then we can hire a road builder, so we have a way to get equipment in. The road builder will put us on his schedule. There's always a window of op-portunity for road building when things dry out, which is never. Then we'll bring power up from the campground over a distance of probably two miles, which might cost a hundred thousand dol-lars, I'm making up that figure. Again, the power company will have a schedule. And then—then we can build the church. Once we have power, permits, and a road. All we'll need is two or three years, probably two or three million dollars, blood, sweat, and considerable tears, and then we'll be ready to start.

I don't see how you know all this.

I'm already trying to build a new church. Because our current site is dying of mildew. Mildew and carpenter ants.

Ann shrugged. So the first step, she said, is to see who owns the property.

I'll make the phone call. First thing tomorrow. Or I'll go to the county assessor's office and look it up in person.

The kettle in the kitchen began singing. Excuse me, said the priest. You stay right here. Relax for a while. Calm yourself. Think about something other than the church. There's nothing wrong with just relaxing. Quiet repose. Meditation. It's very good for the soul.

I can't relax.

That's not good.

There's things to do.

There are always things to do in life.

There's things Our Lady has asked me to do.

First, said the priest, just relax.

But instead she followed him, bolting from the couch, and while he fussed with the tea bags over his stove she stood in the doorframe, pulled off her hood, and revealed her sickly young face. There's something else, she said.

Okay.

It's personal.

That's still okay.

It's actually a bunch of things.

A bunch of things. That's okay too.

I'm sort of embarrassed. Really embarrassed.

Don't be, said the priest. I'm a priest.

She stood in silent scrutiny of him, as if to verify this statement. The priest picked up his plastic tray with its teacups and nicely arranged biscuits. You can tell me in the living room, he suggested.

It's this, replied Ann. I'm full of sins.

No you're not.

Yes I am.

Do you want to confess?

I can't. I'm not baptized.

Pretend you don't have to be baptized, then. Pretend you don't have to worry about that. Consider me less of a priest right now and more . . . a friend, a good close friend. Baptism isn't required.

He motioned with the tray. Living room, he said. The living room of this trailer house is my unofficial confessional.

In the living room, she perched on the couch. She didn't touch her tea or look at him. He sipped from his own tea, took a bite from a biscuit. He was patient and held to a siegelike silence. Finally the visionary blew her nose and spoke. I'm going to hell, she said.

No you're not. Don't say that.

Satan has a hand on me. I'm going to burn in hell.

The priest, unnerved, bent toward her paternally. He took in her odor of long-soiled clothing. Ann, he said. You don't believe that. You don't believe in Satan, do you? You don't have to think that way.

Father, she said. I've used a lot of drugs. Magic mushrooms and marijuana. I've cheated. I've lied. I've ripped off people. I even stole my catechism. I had an abortion. I ran away from home. I've suffered from . . . venereal diseases. And I . . . you know . . . touch myself constantly. I did it twice, Father, on the day I first saw Our Lady.

That all sounds very normal, the priest said, though he had to admit, privately, a misguided, prurient, tantalizing interest in her obsessive masturbation. You sound human to me, Ann. A human being with faults and a history. Like everybody else. Like everybody.

But everybody else doesn't see Our Lady.

That doesn't change the nature of your sins. Which for the most part are venial. Venial as opposed to mortal.

Father, said Ann. You have to help me. Help me get away from the devil.

There is no devil; begin with that. If you mean a guy with a tail and horns, there's no devil, period.

There is a devil. There has to be. If you believe in Jesus, the son of God, you have to believe in the devil.

Why?

Because how else do you explain all the bad things?

The devil is just an idea, said the priest. A notion. A concept. An abstraction.

If that's true of the devil then it's true of God.

God is a ceaseless mystery.

Then why isn't the devil a mystery too?

The devil is a mystery.

I just feel strange, Ann said. I feel him breathing down my neck. Like he's right behind me, watching me. I want to be purified.

You're nervous.

I guess.

You're alone.

Sort of.

Why did you run away? asked the priest. Do your parents know where you are?

I don't have parents. I have a mother. But she's . . . out of it, you would say.

Father Collins rubbed his chin, the gesture, he knew, of a pedant. Out of it? he asked. How so?

Totally out of it.

Well does she know where you are?

No, said Ann. But she knows I'm somewhere.

Everyone is somewhere.

I don't know.

It's true, though. They are.

Their conversation, the priest concluded, had steadily devolved toward the inane. They'd been reduced to commenting on their mere existence. Look, he said, standing now. You're hungry, Ann, you're tired, you're sick, you're wet, you need a shower. You're under duress from all of this. I think we ought to table our discussion. You take a shower, get into clean clothes, eat something, get a good night's sleep. Then, tomorrow, we'll talk, you and I. Believe me, things will look different.

Her smell—her stench—was discernible across the room. She needed toothpaste, soap, and mouthwash. Father, she said, and the word made him sad. Coming from her it made him sad. He found himself thinking of mortality, which was the subject inspired by her tender impoverishment, which was always the subject behind all subjects—sex, the universe, God. Father, she repeated. We have to get busy. We have to build a new church.

• • •

The priest devised a logistics for her shower that was more than mildly self-serving. Even as he uttered it he knew this was so. Shame, he thought. Incorrigible. Untenable. But the visionary did what he told her to do. She went in the bathroom and shut the door. When she was naked she opened it a few modest inches and dropped her clothes outside on the floor. The priest saw only her thin white forearm and the pale inside of her elbow. He waited until it was clear from the sound of it that she'd stepped beneath the spray of water and then he examined the articles of clothing which did not include a bra or panties, she was too shy to put them in with the rest or she didn't wear such things. Either way it was erotic to think about, though not as erotic as the missing articles, the little catches on the back of a bra, the elastic waist in panties. The priest upbraided himself for being disappointed, for his perverse interest in her underwear. He picked up the other things and held his nose all the way to the washing machine, they were that foul and awful, redolent of sweet high sweat. He turned the pockets of her jeans inside out and found a folded burrito wrapper. In the pouch of her sweatshirt were a half dozen Starbursts, the wet empty husks of sunflower seeds, her Sudafed and Phenathol pills, and three small white seashells. The priest mused. He thought of her beachcombing. He thought about her finding the shells. Fondling them, deciding to keep them. He doubled his normal detergent dose and set the washing machine to use hot water all the way through its cycle. Sterilize, he thought. Purify.

The phone rang four times while the priest squinted at his Caller ID unit, which 90 percent of the time identified no one and told him nothing but Unknown Caller, the indefatigable Unknown Caller, he let the answering machine take such calls including the one coming in at the moment, You've reached Father Donald Collins of Saint Joseph's of North Fork Catholic Church—the priest thought his voice sounded tiny and feeble, he wished, fleetingly, that it wasn't so—and then he heard a more sonorous voice, Hello, this is Father William Butler, I've been asked by Bishop Tracey to look into this matter of Marian apparitions out your way—and Father Collins picked up the receiver, Yes, he said. It's me.

Father Collins?

Right. Yes.

Bill Butler.

Yes Father Butler.

Have we met somewhere?

I don't think so. Maybe.

Your name is familiar.

There's another Father Collins in Federal Way. You're not him?

I'm Donald Collins.

I guess we haven't met before.

I don't think we have either. Bill Butler. It isn't familiar. But my memory for names is terrible.

Mine as well.

It's something of a problem.

This girl out there. I'm calling about that. It's starting to show up in the newspapers.

That doesn't surprise me, said Father Collins. Apparently today a thousand people followed her into the woods out here. I was going to call first thing tomorrow.

First thing tomorrow I'll be in North Fork. So I would have missed your morning call. Where would I find you, Father Collins?

Father Collins felt, already, admonished for his lack of activity. He felt, already, like Father Butler's son. The man sounded older, wiser. Where would you find me? Father Collins asked.

Where would I find you to get a briefing.

At the church, let's say. Nine-thirtyish. Anytime after nine-thirty tomorrow. Because I have to go out to our prison at eight and take confession for an hour.

Your prison?

Yes.

The town has a prison?

The state's way of giving loggers work.

So where are you exactly? Your church out there?

Left at the light. The only light. Two blocks east on the left.

Left at the stoplight.

North Fork Avenue.

If I'm late it's because the roads were bad.

Well I'm in my office anyway doing desk work so it isn't a problem to wait for you. I'll be busy until you arrive.

I think I heard you say a thousand.

I don't know for sure, but yes.

Where did you get that?

It's rumor, hyperbole. This is a chatty little town, North Fork. It might be closer to a hundred.

I've never been to North Fork, Washington.

Logging mostly. Or used to be. Before they opened the prison.

A prison sounds ghastly.

It is ghastly.

A prison casts its shadow on a town.

I'm afraid this town already had a shadow before its prison was recently installed because it rains eighty-five inches a year, if you can believe that number.

I'll bring my raincoat. Nine-thirty or so.

And rubber boots.

You're serious.

Unless you want wet feet all day.

Are we going somewhere?

Out into the woods. That's where she has her apparitions. Two miles back in the woods.

There was a pause at the other end of the line. Father Collins made no effort to fill it. Last year, sighed Father Butler, I looked into the case of a girl near Yakima who was hearing the Blessed Virgin's voice rising out of an irrigation canal at the edge of a cherry orchard. That one, I nearly froze to death. Something like twenty degrees over there. So this—this should be better.

Forty and wet is worse than twenty and dry in my humble, unprejudiced opinion. This place will chill you to the bone.

Sounds miserable. All right then. I'm warned.

I only want you to be comfortable.

Anything else?

She's young, said Father Collins. A teenager. Just a little girl, so expect that.

And a child shall lead them, said Father Butler.

That's it, said Father Collins. So go easy on her.

When he'd hung up he had to ask himself, as in the old rousing Wobbly hymn, which ineluctably he began to sing, Which side are you on? This Father Butler sounded vitriolic and highly unpleasant to be around. Father Collins did not look forward to lugging him around North Fork the next morning.

He put a small neat packet together—a pair of
sweatpants he rarely wore, a clean white t-shirt, a
v-neck cardigan, winter-weight woolen socks.
All of that seemed innocent enough. He didn't
need to castigate himself about choosing this essentially loose-fitting and androgynous wardrobe.
When the shower went off he called through the
door, I've got clothes for you, right out here, I'll
leave them here, I'll be in the kitchen, there's lotion if you want it, do you see where it is? I
should have showed you before, I'm sorry. It's on
the shelf. About eye level. And down below, two
shelves down, if you look around, poke around
back there, there's a toothbrush still in its packag-
ing. And dental floss—you'll see where it is. It's
right there beside the sink. Next to the bottle of
mouthwash, Ann. Anyway, I'll set these clothes
down. How was the shower, by the way?

Good.

It's a little hard to adjust sometimes.

He guessed from the muffled sound of it that
she was rubbing her hair with the towel just now,
that was why she didn't answer, maybe she hadn't
heard what he said, not that it mattered very
much, he was lingering for no legitimate reason,
he liked the idea of talking to her while she was
naked just beyond the door, which he also knew
wasn't right. Okay, he said. I'll leave you to it. I'll
just be in the kitchen.

Where?

I'll just be in the kitchen.

Pulling back one corner of the shade, he
looked out the window at the two men in the
car, vigilant sentinels like baleful shadows behind
their rain-smeared windowpanes, and then he
waited in his reading chair where he worried that
his thinning hair was more unattractive all the
time, there were always methods of intervention
like Rogaine or plugs, but he urged himself to
consider these things from the perspective of his
highest values. He had mentioned the kitchen
only because it was as far away from the bathroom as he could get and he wanted her to feel
entirely confident that he was not in the vicinity,
that he was thoughtful enough to give her privacy while she showered in his house. Like everything else, mentioning the kitchen had a sexual
subtext and sent a libidinous message. Even pretending that everything didn't had a carnal objec-
tive, too. What man could help it? Who wasn't
human? Even a priest was subject to these rules.
Lust, said the catechism, was a disordered desire,
an inordinate enjoyment of sexual pleasure, but
every man felt lust all the time, the question was
how to contend with it, on this the Church was
not silent either, it urged liberation from earthly
passions, it also urged self-mastery which was an
infinite and exacting work, never acquired like a

car or liver spots or season tickets or herpes simplex, instead self-mastery was a permanent quest, it presupposed renewed effort at all the stages of life.

The priest meditated on his celibacy. As in Sirach 1:22: Either man governs his passions and finds peace, or he lets himself be dominated by them and so remains unhappy. As in the Presbyterorum Ordinis: Accepted with a radiant heart, celibacy radiantly proclaims the Reign of God. As in Saint Augustine: While he is in the flesh, man cannot help but have at least some light sins. As in Romans 11:32: God has consigned all men to disobedience, that he may have mercy upon all. It was enough material for a sermon, thought the priest, who usually wrote sermons on Tuesday afternoons, brooded and revised them carefully on Wednesdays, let them sit on Thursdays and Fridays, and reconsidered their contents on Saturdays so as to deliver them with confidence on Sundays. In fact he'd sermonized that very morning on the communal character of the human vocation and on the human desire to come to God, the latter a little bow toward the visionary, whose presence in the forest north of town had infected the mood of his congregation, whose presence was like an agitation to his poor beleaguered flock. Only through God, the priest had said— aware that he was jealous of the visionary's magnetism—only through God can human beings find the happiness they restlessly seek; only through God lies surcease from pain and an end to that perpetual discontent informing every second of life. Father Collins believed this without irony. He believed that his personal ceaseless anxiety was a universal ceaseless anxiety that could find no salve in the things of this world but only in God expansively defined, how life-effacing the thought of that was, how rarefied, abstract, bloodless, conceptual, unreal, and transcendent. Certainly God was complicated, Father Collins had never meant to suggest to his friends who were thoughtful worldly atheists that the God he meant was otherwise or easily assailed by arguments, that wasn't the God he meant to propose when he told them he believed in God. But what did he mean? they wanted to know, to which he could only shake his head and reply, like the arcane Jews who read the Kabala, There are no words, God is ineffable, the name of God cannot be spelled, to look for God with the tools of man is like trying to capture the sun's light in our hands, perhaps, he thought, I should have been a Jew, that quaint Jewish simile makes perfect sense, he was thinking this when the visionary appeared, dressed in his sweatpants and cardigan sweater, her hair combed sleekly and wetly back, white lotion at one wing of her nose, and it occurred to him in that incidental moment that attraction was wonderfully capricious. All right, he said. All showered.

Yes.

Your clothes are in the washing machine.

Thank you.

So now would be a good time for dinner.

What about those guys outside?

I'll go talk to them about it.

He went outside beneath his umbrella, which had caved in on one side, sprung a rib. They were not even listening to the radio. They were sitting on watch with a dour discipline. The windshield had been fogged by their breathing, though they'd cracked their windows to defeat this. Who were these men and why were they here? Gentlemen, said the priest, let's ponder for a minute. Are you sure you want to sit here in the rain? Because I don't think we need any bodyguards. And we're going to be a while.

We'll wait, Father.

I don't want you to.

It isn't a problem.

It is a problem. For Ann and me, we both feel this, it's a problem, a definite, serious problem. You're making us nervous. Sitting here. You're making us feel uncomfortable. We can't concentrate on our important discussion. Because we keep thinking of you out here. Just sitting here doing nothing.

Don't think about us.

That's impossible.

We're committed to providing security, Father. We can't leave our visionary exposed.

Exposed to what, though? Have you thought about that?

Danger, said the man in the passenger seat. Any kind of possible danger.

What kind of danger worries you?

All kinds, said the driver.

The priest tipped his umbrella back and leaned aggressively into the window. He smelled after-shave and pine car freshener. Understand, he said. You'll be here all night. I'm not going to let her go back to that tent. That damp little tent in the campground.

She has a cold, so that's kind of you.

Anyway we're fine with all night.

But, said the priest, how can you be? A miserable night in your car?

We have a cell phone. We'll do it in shifts. In fact, it's already been organized. Twenty-four-hour protection.

Who are you anyway? asked the priest. I don't understand where you come from.

I'm Mike, said the driver. This is Bill. I'm from Butte, Montana, and he's from Boise, Idaho.

That's not what I meant.

Then what did you mean?

I mean, how did you come to be sitting here like this? Don't you have jobs? Families?

I came because of the sighting, said Mike. And then—then I felt I knew. That I was called to provide protection.

Me too, said Bill. I felt called.

People are differently called, said Mike. This is what I feel I have to do. Come to the defense of those in need. Provide for their security. I guess you could say I'm a Christian soldier. Same with Bill here. A soldier in Christ. We're willing to put up with the rain and whatnot. With sitting here all night if we have to. Second Timothy Two, verse three. Thou therefore endure hardness, as a good soldier of Jesus Christ.

If we suffer, we shall also reign with him, said Bill. If we deny him, he also will deny us.

Think not that I am come to send peace on earth, said Mike. I come not to send peace, but a sword.

Dangerous language, warned the priest.

It's just that sometimes the wicked rise up. And the righteous must answer with arms, said Mike. And we're the guys for that.

Nay, said the priest. I'll pray for you. Because I don't think our Lord indeed wants violence. Violence of any sort.

Neither do we, they both answered.

The priest went inside. He took three deep

breaths. Dinner, he said to Ann, pumping dry his umbrella. We're going to eat now. Something healthy, good for your cold. Or your flu—forgive me. Your flu.

What did they say?

They're fine where they are.

In the car like that?

They say they're fine.

What are they doing?

Reconnaissance, they say. I don't really follow it. They're on the lookout, on watch.

Lookout for what?

Dragons, I guess. Or infidels. The British, maybe. Or Bigfoot.

The visionary sat poised on the edge of the couch, her hands stuffed between her knees, her feet pointing toward one another. I don't understand, she told the priest.

Nor I.

Is there some kind of danger?

There's absolutely no danger.

Is it, maybe—someone is after me?

No one is after you.

I feel like there is.

Who could be after you?

I don't know. Someone.

What you need, I think, is dinner, Ann. Dinner and a little downtime, rest. How are the clothes. Okay?

Great.

You're comfortable enough?

I feel good. Clean.

I'm sorry I didn't have anything better.

These are fine. I'm great.

I have, said the priest, a nice piece of halibut. Halibut, rice, and a tossed green salad. It'll take about thirty minutes.

I can't eat, though. I'm not even hungry.

You have to eat.

I can't.

The priest sat down in his reading chair. *The Ginger Man* lay on the table beside him, a symbol of his own transgressions if a book can be a symbol of something, *the throb of his groin pumping the teeming fluid into her throat* and other episodes of poetic pornography, Donleavy on the back of the book looking dapper in knickers and carrying a walking stick, the priest had the complete and unexpurgated edition sold for ninety-five cents by Dell, and now as if by casual caprice he picked up his hardback *Ship of Fools* with its black-and-white photo of Porter at her desk, wearing pearls and clutching her typewriter, and set it on top of the Donleavy. The priest felt a little like Ichabod Crane, agitated by hormones and racing nerves, though not quite so hyperthyroidal. He held his chin between his fingers in order to pose as an intellectual and said I'm sorry I have to slow down

I'm acting like your father or something it's just that I don't have visitors too often I don't really know how to be a proper host of course we'll eat when you're hungry Ann and not a moment before you're hungry and in the meantime we can just relax I have a collection of cassettes over there I'll put one on say Gorecki or Brahms or maybe chamber music classics do you have a preference?

No.

He put on the Gorecki, symphony number 3, the Symphony of Sorrowful Songs with its Lamentation of the Holy Cross dominating the first movement. Its stairway of fifths, its eight-part polyphony, its eerie Goreckian tempo. An antagonist for his Id, he hoped. There was nothing like Gorecki's Number 3 except perhaps intestinal distress to induce a shriveling woe.

That's sad music, Ann said.

Shall I change it then?

I want to be sad.

How come?

I don't really know.

Well I won't invade your privacy. I won't pick or probe. I'll just say that in about twenty minutes I can put your clothes in the dryer.

Or I could do it, answered Ann.

And I've saved all your pocket things. Your flu pills and shells and candy.

Thank you.

So in the meantime there's tea which I'll warm up for you and please help yourself to biscuits. The priest sat down and delicately sipped. Your confession, he said. Earlier. I'm thinking of the mushrooms you mentioned. The hallucinatory psilocybin mushrooms and of what a committee of inquiry might want to make of them.

I haven't done any mushrooms for a while. If that's what you're thinking—I haven't done them.

As I understand it, nevertheless, there's a phenomenon commonly known as the flashback which attaches to hallucinogens like LSD or peyote buttons or psilocybin mushrooms. Are you aware of this? The flashback?

Sort of.

Well how can I explain it?

I don't know.

Someone uses a hallucinogenic drug. They experience an episode of immediate effects that subside within say twenty-four hours. Arbitrary. It could be twelve hours. Who knows? That's not the point. Well a flashback would be an episode of effects occurring sometime afterward. The next week. The next month. A year later or two years later. You're going about your normal business, eating a sandwich and reading a magazine, when the sandwich turns into a little bird and the magazine grows little hands and feet— this is what's called a flashback.

That's not what's happening.

How do you know?

I know cuz I know. That's not what's happening.

How long has it been since you used psilocybin? How many weeks or months?

Our Lady is real so it doesn't matter.

But how long?

Like a month maybe.

What about dope?

I don't smoke dope.

But how long?

You know. Weeks.

So not too long.

A couple weeks. At least two weeks before I saw her.

The priest sipped his tea and arched one eyebrow, his little finger bent and held aloft. He felt comically smug. He felt villainous. What do you think? he asked the visionary. Could I have maybe been a celebrity interrogator during the Inquisition?

She didn't answer, didn't smile or laugh, so that he felt, next, like a pompous cleric full of sanctimonious ridicule. Forgive me, said the priest. It's an absurd line of thought. You haven't used dope in at least fourteen days. You haven't used mushrooms in at least a month. And this doesn't sound, to me, like a flashback. It's too concrete. Too vivid for that. But maybe; I don't know.

Ann fingered the nap of his cardigan sweater. Before, she said. What did you mean by a committee of something? Like a minute ago? When you said that?

A committee of inquiry. Of investigation. Into this episode of Marian apparitions. A process known in the Church as discernment. To discern the validity of your visions, Ann. To discern their legitimacy.

The Church has that?

It has for centuries. Because what if someone was faking it or was out of balance mentally? Or consciously manipulating followers for the selfish purpose of material gain? What if their visions were false in some way? It is the duty of the Church to ferret this out. To determine if it can sanction an apparition or deem it worthy of belief.

Well I haven't used anything for like a few weeks. So it isn't that. Not mushrooms, Father. Not mushrooms or marijuana.

Let's not discount the flashback, Ann. It might go a considerable way toward explaining what you're experiencing.

But why don't you just believe me, Father? I'm telling you—Our Lady is real. I'm not hallucinating.

The priest interlaced his fingers slowly and set them in an attitude of child's prayer just beneath his chin. I'd honestly like to believe you, he said. Believing would make this so much easier. I don't want to be a skeptic or cynic. I'd like to make that leap of faith, but in all honesty I can't just yet. I just don't have enough information. So tomorrow morning I meet with a priest the bishop is sending out our way. And I think, given the numbers of people who seem to be attracted to this event, I think he will appoint a committee. A committee of investigation on which he will want me to sit. And then I'll approach it formally, if and when I'm called to the task. But until then, let's be tea drinkers.

I can't just sit here drinking tea though.

But this is soporific—chamomile. And highly therapeutic, too. For somebody with the flu.

I was trying to tell you before, Father. I'm here because I need to be cleansed of my sins. And we have to start building the church.

Sins, said the priest. Let's start with that one. I—

I mean I stole stuff constantly, okay? I stole a sleeping bag from the back of a truck. I told these two women I'd watch their stuff, then I took their cooler and their boom box. I pawned stuff left and right, Father. A chain saw once. An air compressor. I also pumped gas and drove off without paying. Many times I did that.

Before or after you stole the catechism?

Everything I did was before that point. Before I gave myself to Jesus.

I see.

But I already knew—everyone does—thou shalt not steal. It's wrong.

Yes.

So I need to be baptized.

You're back to that.

I can't be saved unless I'm baptized.

You didn't grow up with the Church, Ann?

I didn't grow up with anything, Father.

I suddenly have an idea, said the priest. Why don't you call your mother right now? You can use my telephone.

I'm not like one of those posters, answered Ann. One of those posters you see at the post office of somebody who's like official or something. An official runaway or something.

Well maybe you could just call socially. For no good reason. Just to say hello. Just to check in. A phone call.

No, said Ann. That's the last thing I want to do.

But why wouldn't someone want to call their mother?

I just don't want to. It's a long story, Father.

Long doesn't matter, it doesn't matter, does it? Because after all, we have all kinds of time here. We're sitting here talking, isn't that the case? And I'm a priest. A listener by nature. Not to mention an inveterate talker. So I don't mind if your story is long. I even kind of like that.

I didn't mean long the way you mean it. I mean: I just can't explain it.

You mean you can't explain to me why you don't want to call your mother? Or you can't explain what you mean by the word long? Or both? Maybe it's both.

I'm lost again.

Why don't you want to call your own mother?

I don't know. Can we leave it at that?

Tell me about it.

I can't.

The priest sighed. Okay, he said. It's just that you seemed in a mood of disclosure. Disclosure and contrition. Confession.

Ann drank her tea. His mind turned to that. A lissome teen with a teacup at her lips. Tell you what, the priest offered. You spend the night here. Don't go back to that damp tent of yours. Stay here tonight. Nurse your flu. The couch folds out into a comfortable bed. You'll be warm and clean. Please stay.

He tried to remember which corner of hell was reserved for sexual connivers. Was it the First Bolgia with its Panderers and Seducers like Jason of the Golden Fleece or the Second Circle where lustful souls are forever driven on the wind? Ann got up to use the bathroom and he closed the shades tightly, leaving no gaps, in order to prevent the spies outside from looking in on them. Then he waited in a heat of agitation while Ann washed, brushed her teeth, and peed—he heard the hard long stream of her urine rebounding off the porcelain only because he was listening for it—next he performed his own neurotic toilet, brushing his teeth, flossing carefully, massaging his gums, swallowing his multivitamin, lathering his face and hands with scented lotion, combing his hair, swilling with mouthwash, and sitting on the toilet like a woman to pee in order to make less noise about it, in case Ann was listening. Why did he care? He didn't know. Father Collins assessed himself critically in the mirror. I'm still okay, he decided.

In the living room they knelt together and recited the Salve Regina. Hail Holy Queen, Mother of mercy, our life, our sweetness and our hope. To thee do we cry, poor banished children of Eve. To thee do we send up our sighs, mourning and weeping in this valley of tears. Turn, then, most gracious Advocate, thine eyes of mercy towards us. And after this our exile, show unto us the blessed Fruit of thy womb, Jesus. O clement, O loving, O sweet Virgin Mary.

Fruit of thy womb, the priest said afterward. Those underwear people stole that metaphor. Is nothing sacred? he asked.

They're Fruit of the Loom, Ann answered.

It sounds like something left in drawers, if you understand my meaning.

I like that prayer, it's one of my favorites.

So do I. Very much.

It makes me feel better.

As it should, as it should. Since Mary is the Consolatrix Afflictorum, she who consoles us in our afflictions. Our comfort and our hope, our Mother.

Amen.

And on that note, I bid you good night. Don't neglect to take your flu pills.

I guess those guys are still sitting out there.

I've taught myself to ignore them already. Let them sit in the car if they want. What can we do about it?

She lay, at last, on the sofa bed. The light from the reading lamp fell across her and suffused her with a boudoir glow that filled him with a terrible yearning. Good night, she said. This really feels good. Thank you for everything, Father.

Whatever I can do, the priest replied. Whatever I can do to serve you.

He walked down the hall, shut his door, and leaned against it with his eyes shut. Lord be with me, he whispered. And lead me not into temptation, but deliver me from evil. The priest moved forward, mentally, in Matthew. Watch and pray, that ye enter not into temptation: the spirit indeed is willing, but the flesh is weak.

He arranged his own weak flesh on the bed. Twice he got up to pull back the shade and peer out at the strange sentinels but there was no sign of movement from their car, he couldn't see beyond the veil of rain, the halo of light from the porch lamp was insufficient to include them in its reach. The priest curled up beneath his sheets and reluctantly acknowledged his insomnia. He wasn't going to sleep tonight, not with the visionary just yards away, the two of them alone in his house, it was not just her essential femininity, the proximity of a desirable female, it was also her strong strange spiritual aura, which moved and disturbed him both. It was Ann in her totality, a thing he would not have expected. It was Ann of the Immaculate Vision. Was there any difference, he asked himself, between legitimately, actually seeing the Virgin and believing to have seen the Virgin? An epistemological question at heart—or was it ontological? The priest rolled over, turned on the light, and picked up his copy of *The Catholic Reporter*. ATTACHMENT TO CORE BELIEFS ENDURES, LINK TO INSTITUTION WEAKENS, NCR–GALLUP SURVEY REVEALS, that was the subhead across page one, against the backdrop of Father Michael Moynihan leading a prayer service in Connecticut. There was an article on the European synod—PASTORAL IDEAS NIXED AS CURIA HOLDS THE LINE—ALSO PHILIPPINE DIOCESE BACKS INDIGENOUS IN MINING CONFLICT, BISHOP CALLS SENATE TREATY VOTE A MAJOR ARMS CONTROL DEFEAT, POPE AGAIN ASKS CLEMENCY FOR TEXAN GARY GRAHAM, and CARDINAL O'CONNOR RETURNS TO HOSPITAL FOR TESTS. The priest read all. He read the letters. He read MARRIAGE TRENDS SIGNAL DECLINING ROLE OF CHURCH and ACCOMMODATIONS TO CONTINUING PRIEST SHORTAGE. Why were there fewer priests? It was much discussed. God's call, some said, was constant, but men did not hear it as well anymore, there were too many tempting distractions in the world, others said we could not be sure that God's call indeed was steady. The priest agreed with the former argument. Tempting distractions, obviously. The world was one big Sodom and Gomorrah. Did God make sense, though, in the end? The God who turned Lot's wife into a salt pillar merely for looking back at the brimstone falling as prophesied across the plain, the God who spoke with Abraham as though they were negotiating the price of a used car to determine the number of righteous men it would take to save the two cities? God wanted fifty but Abraham worked him down to ten by employing deference, humility, and flattery, I who am but dust and ashes, let not the Lord be angry and so on, the same God who later toyed with Abraham by asking him to bind his son, arrange the boy on a sacrificial pyre, then slit his throat with a knife. Just kidding, said God at the last moment. Just checking to see how loyal you are. God the insecure Mafia don. God the malevolent psychotherapist.

The priest brooded and indulged his self-absorption, rationalizing that a sleepless man had a right to unrestrained thought. It had been a day full of obligations and endless ministerial duties, including a meeting with Larry Garber regarding his drawings of the sacristy, revised based on their telephone exchange, and a general review of the floor plan for the nave, the baptistry, and the choir. Garber was a plodding interlocutor utterly devoid of irony and bereft of those cultural reference points on which Father Collins' humor depended. They were over a half million dollars short, a fact that seemed lost on Garber. He used sharp pencils and a three-sided scaler. He took notes on a laptop, kept his blueprints rolled in a cardboard tube, and made use enthusiastically of tracing paper. Father Collins had checked his watch three times while pretending to wring his hands. Then it was over. Good work, he said. The entire congregation appreciates so much your hard work and generosity. I'm invested in this, said Larry Garber. I enjoy what

I do. It feels very good. I'm excited about it every day. I can see that, Father Collins said. It's obvious, your personal investment.

He'd gone in the late afternoon on his rounds, Sunday visits to the bedridden of his flock or to those by other means indisposed, and he'd felt like a country doctor. A toothless logger dying at home of pancreatic cancer, another logger convalescing from triple bypass surgery, and then Tom Cross the younger. How are you today? he'd said to Junior. I'm catheterized, the boy had answered in his disturbingly aspirate exhaling whisper. I have. An infection. And pain. In my legs. Phantom pain. I'm on a drug. It makes me. Makes me tired.

His mother had left them in the kitchen alone on the principle that confession was a private matter so it was just the priest and the paralyzed boy with the vent tube disconcertingly at his throat and his faint sad smell of urine. He'd twitched in his chair, which was tilted back, his legs and arms flopped involuntarily but he was well secured by a seatbelt. Father Collins had asked if he wanted to confess and the boy had said no and took communion, Father Collins wearing rubber gloves to serve this particular paschal banquet and quoting spontaneously from John 6:53: Truly, I say to you, unless you eat the flesh of the Son of man, and drink his blood, you have no life in you.

Okay.

Your suffering is inexplicable, Tom. But in suffering we glimpse God's mystery. In suffering we know Him better.

Okay.

And suffering can have redemptive meaning. In pain we are drawn much closer to God, not merely he who suffers himself but all those around him also, all right? Everyone in his presence.

Yes.

And the prayer of faith will save the sick man, and the Lord will raise him up—the Lord *will*—and if he has committed sins, he will be forgiven.

Okay.

I pray for your soul every day, said the priest, and took the boy's limp hand in his own. I ask the Lord to comfort you, he said. I ask the Lord to be with you.

Now Father Collins turned restlessly in bed and pondered the sinewy corpus of Our Savior that seemed to watch him from the wall. Soon he would sit in conference with the bishop to review his initial year of service and to jointly reflect on his future as a man of God, a servant of the Lord, a slave of Christ, a proclaimer of the Gospel. Had he acted *in persona Christi Capitis* and in a manner consistent with his priestly sacrament and did he wish to continue his ministry? On these matters the bishop would pontificate, though he mostly seemed a preoccupied man, distracted by the complexity of his calling—at heart an administrator in vestments. A dour weary traditionalist with beady eyes, expressive hands, and extremely bad halitosis. Father Collins imagined himself suggesting that prayer and reflection had led him to believe in the need for an introspective hiatus from his duties as a priest. His rhetoric would incorporate an air of confession. He would seem to be forthcoming about his inner life. He would use the phrase *the will of God* as if his own will were not involved in the outcome of the matter.

But all of that lay in front of him. In the meantime here was this Marian apparition unfolding, apparently, in bizarre full force in his own backwater parish. The priest imagined busloads of pilgrims bent on divinely inspired chastisements and evangelical devotional fever, hailing the advent of Mother Mary, saluting a cardboard ephemeral church, Ann as substitute for authentic worship, for the mundane daily variety of faith that composed his own enervated ministry. A thousand people, the girl had said; more than a thousand, probably. And how many more by tomorrow? There came a perplexing knock on the door. How did he look? Accoutered in briefs and a crew neck t-shirt? He arrayed himself in a more manly posture, on one elbow, recumbently regal. Yes, he said. Come in, Ann.

His heart fibrillated—moral confusion. She opened the door, a silhouette, a vision. I can't sleep, she said. My allergies are acting up. And I keep thinking about . . . a lot of things.

It's all right to think, Ann.

I have a bad feeling.

Don't you worry. God is with you. Sometimes we just need someone to talk to. Someone to share our deepest thoughts with. A little honesty sometimes.

Yes.

So be honest, Ann.

Okay. I will.

What are you really thinking about? What is it really that's keeping you awake? Your deepest thoughts. Confess them, Ann. Ask yourself what you're really thinking and tell me without hiding anything.

That's easy.

I'm glad you can say that, the priest answered. His heart was more gravely aflutter now. He could throw it all over, he knew he could. Everything to lose himself. Disappear, become somebody else. She was exactly what he thought he desired, the nexus of God and lust.

You know what I'm going to say, Father.

I hope I know what you're going to say.

I'm thinking about building Our Lady's church.

That's exactly what I thought, the priest lied.

She sat on his bed—sniffling, sneezing, blowing her nose—and it took him nostalgically back to high school, teenagers engrossed in late-night profundity replete with unspoken eroticism. She pulled up her knees and set her head against them; one of the things that made her pornographic was her mindless flexibility, the suggestion that with comfort and ease she might attain the positions described in the Kama Sutra. She'd stripped off the cardigan, so here she was now on his bed in his sweatpants and through the t-shirt he'd loaned her he could see one nipple. But what was the point of looking at it, a man could look and never stop looking, at a certain point he had to turn away, what was wrong with now, immediately, the nipple seemed rather large to him in relation to the size of her breast. I think, she said, that if I understand what the catechism says I'm going to need to be baptized.

What?

I was just looking at your catechism—checking. I can't be saved unless I'm baptized.

Is this a part of your vision? From Mary?

She hasn't said anything about it, Father.

So why are you feeling this all of a sudden?

It isn't sudden, the visionary said. I told you—I'm scared of the devil.

Father Collins felt awkward beneath his sleeping

bag wearing only his briefs and t-shirt while conversing with this girl. It was perfectly possible that
she was insane, sitting on his bed at one in the
morning with her pall-like flu and sallow complexion, her allergies and rapt expression, assailing him
with talk of the devil, a manipulative vamp, a psychotic seductress, secretly out to ruin his life, the
intentional undoing of a priest. Or maybe not. He
didn't know. But what was she doing on his bed
like this? Look, he said. We better put things on the
table. Because this is getting a little weird, Ann.

Weird?

Well I'm a priest and you're a sixteen-year-old
female. Sitting on my bed in the middle of the
night. I mean, you have to admit this would look
pretty compromising, say to those men keeping
watch outside, if anyone were to see this situation
it would have to look pretty compromising and
more than mildly suspicious, right? People would
say that this is just wrong. There's no moral justi-
fication for it. A photograph of it—that would
end my career. I'd have to leave the priesthood.

Ann descended into the fetal position, a closed
flower, a snail. I'm not here for . . . that, she
told him.

Good, said the priest. Because I'm celibate.

I'm here to get baptized, Father.

Father. Despite himself he felt wounded by her
lack of interest, which seemed to border on dis-

gust. But after all he was nearly twice her age. A gaunt wry priest with thinning hair. Baptism, he said. You mean right now? You want me to baptize you now?

Could you?

Is there a reason to be in such a big hurry?

I don't want to die unbaptized, Father.

Well I don't think you're going to die tonight. And if you read your catechism carefully, Ann, the Church indeed makes room in heaven for those who expire with the explicit desire to receive the sacrament of Baptism.

But it also says that in a case like that I'd have to have already repented my sins and performed acts of charity.

True.

So maybe it's better if we do the baptism.

But do you mean right now? Literally? Because it can't be done. It just can't be. You would have to complete a conversion course. A course known as the catechumenate. An initiation into Christian faith. It generally takes a full year.

I think I'm ready right now, Father.

How so?

I've seen Our Lady.

For me to baptize you now, Ann, would be tantamount to affirming the veracity of your visions. Lending my priestly support to them. I'm not quite sure I can do that.

Why not?

Because I don't yet believe your visions are real.

What would it take to make you believe?

It would take—well—hard evidence. The evidence yielded by the process of discernment. A set of facts and circumstances that appeared . . . incontrovertible. All that would make me believe.

But do you have evidence of God, Father?

Your visions, Ann, are different from God.

So you don't believe.

No. I don't.

So you're not going to help me build the church. Or baptize me. You won't do either.

As soon as I believe I'll do both, Ann.

Then, said Ann, I'm really lost.

At the prison Sunday night Tom Cross drew shit watch; he sat on a chair in the medical unit hallway and stared through an observation window, waiting for a naked prisoner to pass a balloon full of crack cocaine. The prisoner wore his hair in greasy cornrows and slept on the floor with his back to Tom, and whenever he rearranged his limbs, which was often, he reminded Tom of a zoo animal, almost no trace left of pride in his movements, a languid choreography of animal defeat, a slack heavy lifer in his thirties or early forties with raised gray burn scars on his back and shoulders and silver psoriatic elbows. The job of watching his restless sleep grew boring in the most obvious and inevitable manner, so that Tom sat literally twiddling his thumbs, nodding off sporadically, checking his watch absentmindedly—and forgetting what it said immediately—massaging his neck, staring at nothing, thinking of Eleanor and of Tammy from the Big Bottom, thinking of the impossible depth of his debt and of the way Jabari scrubbed the toilet bowl, her chocolate-brown arms and yellow rubber gloves, the long-haired girl in the booth at the campground bent so that her breasts came to rest against her ranger shirt, the woman with her mouth full of fancy trail mix, her fat legs sheathed in black spandex. For a while he mulled Lee Ann Bridges' skull, her hair barrette, green-hued thigh bone, and shreds of nylon rain gear. Ann of Oregon's brief oration, darkness falling across the world, the greedy, the selfish, the true believers, the woman whose warts had disappeared and who felt no need for cigarettes now, his own capricious petition. Ann of Oregon clutching her bullhorn, Ann canted forward improbably on her knees, Ann in ecstasy.

Dullness and ennui. Guilt and sorrow. Tom pulled out the Gideon's pocket Bible he'd borrowed surreptitiously from the nursing station desk and perused its tripartite indexing system:

WHERE TO FIND HELP—When Afraid, Anxious, Backsliding, et cetera; TEACHINGS ABOUT SOME OF LIFE'S PROBLEMS—Adultery, Adversity, Anger, Anxiety; CHRISTIAN VIRTUES AND CHARACTER— Abundant Life, Citizenship, Cleanliness, Consecration, Contentment, Courage, Diligence. He turned with curiosity to Facing a Crisis, which took him first to Psalm 121, I will lift up mine eyes unto the hills, from whence my help will come, and then to Matthew 6:28, Consider the lilies of the field, how they grow; they toil not, neither do they spin.

Lilies of the field? What? thought Tom. He tried Adversity: Are not two sparrows sold for a farthing? Divorce: What therefore God hath joined together, let not man put asunder. Worried: Take therefore no thought for the morrow. In Trouble: The lines are fallen unto me in pleasant places. Disaster Threatens: He shall cover thee with his feathers. Defeated: For thy sake are we killed all the day long. The prisoner defecated and Tom barged in with rubber gloves, a plastic probe stick, a nose plug, and a surgeon's mask. There was no balloon and he said to the prisoner I guess we ought to go back to the unit and turned away leaving him foul and naked with a packet of sterile wipes. Tom went down the hall, dropped the probe and the rubber gloves in the Medical Waste bin, signed off for the prisoner's clothes, and brought them back still folded. Here's your clothes, he said. Damn, said the prisoner. You can wash up back at the unit, Tom told him.

They went out. Tom made note of the Time and Outcome of Feces Watch in the logbook and initialed it. They left the medical unit and crossed the courtyard side by side. It was raining softly and there was something medieval and Teutonic about the black expanse beyond the razor wire and the watchtowers and high lit walls. Barbaric Goths dressed in wolf skins; vats of hot tar poured from crenellated ramparts. They put you through the ringer for nothing, said Tom. Exactly, said the prisoner. I tried to say it. But nobody listens to me.

Me neither.

That's different.

But I don't expect anyone to listen anymore.

I say this: You don't know the half.

Come again? asked Tom. What don't I know?

You don't know shit. How you going to know it?

I don't know shit?

That's what I said.

What don't I know? Name something specific.

I can't tell you about it because you haven't been in here.

I'm in here now, though.

You leave when your shift's over.

I'm still in prison.

You can quit, said the prisoner.

And do what? asked Tom. Exactly what?

Whatever they do out there right now. Fix leaky roofs or make umbrellas. Sell rubber boots. Sell raincoats.

They're not doing anything.

They're always doing something.

Anyway name something you think I don't know.

I can't even do that. Because you don't speak my language.

Well pretend like it's possible.

I can't do that either. Because you're on the outside. And it's all good if it's on the outside, man. It's all good, you know.

It isn't all good, not true, said Tom.

Have it your way, said the prisoner.

Tom stopped beneath the overhang at Building D and pointed a finger at the guard in the booth, who nodded and buzzed the door open. What if I said I'd let you out? he asked the prisoner. But only if you let me break your neck beforehand? So you're a free man but paralyzed?

Break my neck?

Like I said.

Break my neck?

Answer the question.

Hypothetical don't mean shit. It don't mean shit, all right?

Well don't say it's all good on the outside, okay? Things can be messed up anywhere.

You still don't know shit, said the prisoner.

Tom waited in the day room while the prisoner showered and then he celled him in. He and another guard named Marvin Meriwether who had been a faller like Tom for seven years and who had worked another seven as a millwright took the 4 a.m. watch at Unit B, the Youthful Offenders Program. Murderers, rapists, armed robbers, arsonists, all of them not eighteen yet, some of them not even fifteen. They couldn't be in the general population because the older guys beat and raped them. Tom didn't speak to them very much, it seemed to him that distance was best, he attached an aura of threat to his mannerisms, he let himself symbolize moral apathy, his rare comments were cold and cheerless. You act like a girl you get treated like a girl. Don't go looking for sympathy. You're on your own—no one gives a shit.

Tom and Marvin Meriwether did nothing together; they stood in the rotunda talking. Loggers they'd known. Equipment. Places. The Mar H-39 High Pressure Boom, the M.A.C. Thunderbird Mobile Yarder, Max Taylor, Frank Combs, Marvin Meriwether's father who'd been a high climber in the early fifties and then a rigging boss. Marvin's sister, married a second time, the new husband had daughters eighteen and sixteen, they were living in Winlock, the new husband drove a tractor-trailer, he liked Harley-Davidsons. Marvin's son, on a crab boat in the Bering Sea, second season, he'd lost an ear there. The Seahawks, the Sea Gals, swing shift. Marvin's knee. Clyde Williams' hip replacement. The high school basketball team's muddled coach. The point guard, Sonny Schmidt's son, his brother had been the point guard too, three years before. Neither saw the court well, dribbled with their heads down. Spin fishing for steelhead. Brine salting salmon. Whitetail trail in wet packed snow. At five-thirty a prisoner wanted out, claiming sick, on orders from the booth they put him in the dayroom, a white kid with plump hairy legs in briefs, lamely holding his doughboy gut, long hair, tattoos on his shoulders, he was in because he'd participated in the beating death of a homeless man, he was going to puke he insistently warned them, and then he did on the dayroom floor, what he wanted next was to shower, clean up, go and see the doctor. What a plan, said Tom. But here's a better one. You swab the floor and we'll cell you in. Come on, said the kid. I'm tied up in knots. You should have just puked in your toilet, said Tom. Come on, said the kid. No, said Tom. I'm seriously sick, man, the kid complained. A person at home pukes they clean it up, said Tom, why shouldn't you have to do the same? I'm royally sick, the kid insisted. All sorts of people puke at night, said Tom, but do they get in their cars at five a.m. and drive to a hospital to see a doctor? No, they get back in bed and wait it out and that's what you're going to do too, you don't get special treatment. You can take a shower, put in Meriwether.

Meriwether went for a mop and bucket while Tom stood over the prisoner. The boy rested his head on a table like a student falling asleep at his desk so that Tom had the chance to inspect his tattoos, the one on the right read TMDF, the one on the left was a swastika. Tell you what, Tom said. Let's cell you in until your clean-up gear arrives.

What?

Back to your cell.

Jesus. Come on.

You want to argue?

Come on, man.

It sounds to me like you're arguing.

I'm sick like a dog.

Back to your cell.

The boy didn't move. Okay, said Tom. I've asked you three times. So you'd have to say I'm within my rights. He looked up at the guard in the monitor booth, who was watching with what

Tom construed as an endorsing, if casual, interest. Tom turned his head toward the dayroom loud-speaker. I'm going to cell him in, he called. Go ahead, the booth guard replied, leaning into his microphone. I'll buzz his door for you.

Okay, said Tom. This is it—last chance. The boy still had his head on the table. Tom seized his hair at the nape of his neck and with his other hand twisted the boy's arm back until he had him in a shoulder lock. God damn, said the boy, and stood up.

I can make it hurt more or you can start walking.

God damn, the boy repeated.

Traction, said Tom. Traction can hurt.

Jesus Christ you motherfucker.

This is a progressive thing that ends with your shoulder dislocating depending how far you want to take it.

I'm fucking sick.

I'm celling you in.

Back off—Jesus, man.

I will if you walk.

I'm trying to walk.

Let me give you a hand, you fuck. Tom steered the boy toward the door of his cell. Let me go, said the boy.

Cooperate first.

I'm trying to cooperate.

No you're not.

Yes I am.

What's happening to you now, you earned this, said Tom.

You're breaking my shoulder, the boy answered.

This, said Tom, is all your own doing. And felt a hardening sense of glee, a torturer's simultaneous immersion and detachment. This didn't have to happen at all. You should have cooperated earlier.

The boy squeezed his eyes shut. What's your problem? he asked.

I don't have a problem.

You're warped, dude. Twisted.

Don't tell me that, said Tom. Don't say that.

He tightened up on the shoulder lock beyond what circumstances required. He knew he was past his job description now, in the realm of personal matters. But it felt good. It was what he wanted. Darkness falling, darkness ascendant. I don't want to hear that, he told the boy. I don't want to hear I'm twisted.

The boy was in too much pain to answer. Tom felt panic contorting the boy's body. Marvin Meriwether came in then with the mop, a bucket on wheels, and a handful of rags. He stared at Tom and coughed politely. Tom, he said. Here's the clean-up stuff. Let him clean things up.

Okay, said Tom, and let his prisoner go. Now you can mop your own puke.

At 8 a.m. they went off shift, Tom with his hands stuffed deep in his pockets, Meriwether kneading his forehead. They crossed the courtyard in the early light, the rain still falling like a dream of rain, barely tangible, mist, vapor. The hills beyond the prison walls were blurred gently by a laggard fog, by slow fog tendrils sinking through the trees, down the morning ridges. Across the rec yard, out to the west, beyond the wall and between two watchtowers was a clear-cut Cross Logging was responsible for, a neat forty-acre hillside rectangle, a view of Tom's work as it once had been, wreaking that particular havoc in the spring of 1985 without hesitation or second thoughts. It was highly addictive, cutting trees, he'd dreamed about it frequently or sleeplessly pondered tomorrow's tactics, a fan-shaped felling pattern, butts together, one drag for the skidder instead of three, logical efficiencies, creative means to maximize profit, how good it had felt to advance that edge between open space and uncut timber, broadening up the felling lanes, a solid advance and movement, progress, the crew in sync in that wordless way when everything was going well, no disorder, confusion, or discussion, most of the equipment sort of holding up, out of that unit they'd taken a good number of pricey special-mill-grade logs, they'd done a lot of bucking at the grade break, they'd also done some long butting, there'd been some fast taper trees.

Passing between buildings B and C on a causeway adjacent to the visiting room they saw the priest from the Catholic church in the no-man's-land between checkpoints. It's the priest, said Tom. That guy? said Meriwether. He doesn't look like a priest.

He is though.

Well where's his collar and all?

He doesn't dress that way.

He was dressed instead in jeans, chukkas, leather gloves, and an overcoat. Urban Casual, Tom thought. Fading hip guy dressed for getting bagels at ten on a Saturday morning. The priest elicited in Tom, always, a muted if vast antagonism. A disapproval fraught with private vehemence. Why couldn't he just dress like a priest, carry himself with priestly composure, wear clothes suggesting disdain for the worldly; wasn't that his task in life, to embody twenty-four hours a day the exalted life of the spirit? What was the point of a priest in jeans, a priest with no outward sign of his calling and no clear symbol of deference to the Church, a priest who looked like an earnest young lawyer on his way to a date at

Starbucks? Tom blandly hailed him—pausing in the razor-wire checkpoint cage—by saying This is Marvin Meriwether, to which the priest replied with false cheer, A pleasure to meet you. Father Donald Collins. I forgot you were employed here, Tom.

Yeah.

I knew it once but then I forgot. I'm sorry I already forgot your name.

Marvin, Marvin Meriwether.

I'm terrible with names it's a curse of sorts or maybe a symptom of something deeper. I need to do a better job remembering names: Marvin Meriwether.

Yes.

Donald Collins. From the church in town. Tom's church. Marvin Meriwether.

Meriwether nodded. Excuse me, he said. But can I ask you a question? Sorry to ask you something like this but—what's a priest doing in a prison?

A priest in a prison, the priest shot back, takes confession from certain individuals, it seems, who have much to confess.

Meriwether tapped his broad dimpled chin. A large, blond, red-faced alcoholic, the doltish giant from a fairy tale who is eventually killed by an ax to the forehead or by a kettle of boiling pitch. Makes sense, he said. When you think about it.

Every Monday, the priest said pleasantly. For one hour: eight until nine. Or on request, of course.

I always wondered, Meriwether pressed on. What if somebody confesses to you that they murdered someone or robbed a bank? Don't you have to report it?

No.

That, said Meriwether, I don't understand.

What don't you understand about it?

Hearing about crimes from criminals, I guess. And then just sitting on your hands.

The priest's high forehead furrowed. He wagged his forefinger: priestly admonishment. What the penitent makes known to the priest, he said, remains shrouded under a sacramental seal. The penitent must be certain of this principle in order that he might be willing to come forward, emboldened by the assurance of privacy to deliver the contents of his soul. For this good reason I am not at liberty to divulge one iota of a penitent's words as spoken to me in the confessional.

I mean you could know who shot JFK. You could know that Cross here killed somebody. But you couldn't do anything about it.

No, said the priest. Except absolve them of their sins. And of course the conditions of absolution would include a public acknowledgment, a public confession, of guilt.

I guess that works, said Meriwether. Unless they just . . . refuse.

If they do, I carry their secret to the grave.

Me, said Meriwether, I couldn't do that. I'd have to tell somebody.

And I wouldn't be seeing them in heaven, said the priest. They wouldn't be going there.

So they can't win, said Meriwether.

Who can't win at what exactly?

The criminal who confesses to you.

He surely can win, the priest replied. By finding his way to the Lord.

Not too great of a win, said Meriwether. Because look it's either prison or hell—hell on earth or hell afterward, take your pick about it.

The priest smiled a thin wan smile. Tom saw he didn't mean the things he said, as if they were only metaphors. Well put, said the priest. Nicely articulated. But smart to always choose prison over hell. Eternity's a very long time.

Meriwether nodded. Hey, he said, and his eyes brightened as Tom had seen them brighten before for Jack Daniel's and Jimmy Beam. Changing the subject. You're probably in a hurry. I know that. But real quick. Sorry about this. But this is my one opportunity to ask. The mushroom girl. What is that?

The priest blinked, his jaw tightened, he bit his lip momentarily. She claims, he said, to have seen

the Blessed Mother. She claims to have had . . .
visions.

What do you think? Tom asked.

I don't think anything either way. It's premature to think anything without facts or evidence.

I went up there. I saw her in the woods.

Yes—we missed you at mass yesterday.

I hardly ever miss, said Tom.

Saturday night you can always attend. As well
as twice on Sunday. The priest absentmindedly
picked lint from his overcoat. So you went to the
woods, he observed.

With a huge crowd. From all over the country.

The priest nodded agreeably but his smile
looked contrived. Sounds to me, he said, like a
revival meeting. Was there any speaking in
tongues?

She cured a woman of warts, said Tom. And
she helped her get off cigarettes.

Worth considering, the priest replied. The
warts and cigarettes both.

I didn't hear about this, said Meriwether. I
mean cigarettes, that's one thing, a person can decide they're going to stop smoking, but warts—
do they just go away like that?

They do, said the priest. Spontaneously. Warts
are a viral phenomenon, so immunity can rapidly
develop. Not to mention the psychosomatic, the
salutary effect of belief.

Neither prison guard answered. What in God's name was the priest trying to say? Tom asked himself. Established medical fact, said the priest. It helps to believe in one's treatment, one's medicine. It helps to be convinced of a therapeutic effect inherent in some pill or other. Even if it's merely a placebo, a fake, with no bona fide benefit.

Hey, if it works, agreed Meriwether.

We can all celebrate good outcomes, said the priest. There's nothing wrong with good results—as long as the means that yield them aren't evil—though we can't extrapolate backward from good results to validate a particular Marian apparition. On the other hand, bad results would surely be cause for the church's definitive invalidation of a seer. Ill effects would not arise from a genuine manifestation of Mary. And so far, regarding the thwarted warts—not to mention the snuffed-out cigarettes—so far, so excellent, no cause I can see to denounce our local visionary. Though these particular positive outcomes still don't mean anything.

We'll let you go, said Meriwether.

And I you, replied the priest.

He tipped an invisible hat in their direction and, it seemed to Tom, fled. There was a long vent at the back of his overcoat, and when the priest turned toward them, one hand on the gate as the tower guard buzzed it open, a gust of wind made it flare. Come see me sometime, he called back to Tom. We ought to talk more often.

About what?

About . . . matters.

I don't get much out of talking, Father.

Through me you can talk to the Lord, said the priest. Come see me, Tom.

Then he was gone. Meriwether made a show of scratching his forehead. Bizarre, he said. Real strange guy. When I was growing up our pastor was . . . I don't know. You couldn't even speak to him.

What religion?

Lutheran.

This priest is new, Tom said.

You like him?

I don't know.

He's a liberal.

I see that.

He's probably for fags getting married and all. Or probably he's a fag himself.

Maybe.

How is it priests are so far left?

That's something I don't claim to get.

You'd think it'd be the opposite.

I don't know what goes on inside his mind.

He's thinking, said Meriwether, about guys I'll bet. About fondling altar boys.

Town was a zoo. Cars everywhere. The parking lot at Gip's was full for the first time Tom could remember. There were even lines to get gas at the minimart for the first time since OPEC. The Sportsman's Motel had no vacancies, and neither did the North Fork Motel. The parking lot at MarketTime was full and cars had spilled over into the Assembly of God lot, which was full as well. It was not even nine but the drugstore was open for business as were the auto parts store, the Dew Drop Inn—until today serving only lunch and dinner—and the hardware store, its front window filled with a banner reading SALE! Tom decided against going to MarketTime. He waited his turn at the four-way stop, rolled down his window, leaned out, and called to Jon Hicks, who was walking in the gutter, It's like the Alaska Gold Rush Jon you better put your hat out.

Up yours Cross.

Where you going?

To hell—same as you.

You need a ride?

How's your son?

Still paralyzed.

When you coming by the Vagabond with us?

Get your hat out right now.

The parking lot at the Tired Traveler's Guesthouse was no better than the rest. There was still the trailer from the Greater Catholic Merchandise Outlet and the car with the DON'T TAILGATE—GOD IS WATCHING bumper sticker, plates from California, Arizona, Colorado, and Nebraska, a man in rubber rain gear checking his motor oil, another man loading up suitcases, a woman with a poodle on a retractable leash, an old woman sitting in an idling car who made brief frightened eye contact with Tom before looking the other way. Tom had lost his parking space. He drove in between two trees, killed the engine, and walked toward his cabin still wearing his guard garb, pausing to light a cigarette so he might have reason to ogle Jabari with her hair bundled up beneath a paisley scarf and her wide South Asian derriere sheathed in baggy red sweatpants. Making her sad lonely cleaning rounds. Did anybody else in the world wear red sweatpants? Scarlet jodhpurs—gay Englishmen on polo ponies. She had on cheap gaudy running shoes, too. He could see brown skin above her thin white socks, between the socks and the bunched anklets of her sweats. Not that she meant to show anything; her clothes were dedicated to concealing her figure. She was pushing the clean-up cart across the gravel like a Bengali peanut vendor. He imagined her drowning in Bangladesh, squatting on a rooftop over murky floodwater, doe-eyed

victim of another famine, sunken ferry, over-
turned bus, CNN train wreck, malaria. Good
morning, he said, it's still raining.

The most fleeting eye contact of all time—
made the old woman in the idling car seem
brazen by comparison. So Jabari could claim to
have acknowledged him and yet not acknowledge
him. Why? Who was she? She turned the key in
Cabin Eleven. Were they Muslims or Hindus? He
didn't know for sure. He didn't even know their
real names. What had Pin said about the Ganges?
They might be Sikhs or something else. Or those
people who swept the road before their feet so as
to not end the lives of insects. Her ass was indeed
a wide brown sailor's chart of spicy India. And the
red sweatpants were ridiculous, clown's clothing,
but she seemed so ignorant of their absurdity that
her ignorance was ultimately alluring. She probably wore matronly underclothing, navel-high
briefs and grandmotherly bras. The image of
Jabari stripped to her underwear presented itself
to Tom's mind.

He stood in the doorway of Cabin Eleven,
leaning casually against the jamb in an attitude of
sexual aggression. She was already plugging in the
vacuum cleaner. Busy around here, he said.

Very much.

Wouldn't it be nice to slow down and relax?

Very busy.

So what needs fixing?

My husband in the office will answer this question.

He loved that lilting birdlike trill, her low throaty soprano. Also the stink of curry in her clothes—or maybe it was saffron and sweat. But can't you think of something I can fix? he asked. Something you know needs fixing?

Jabari wouldn't look at him. My husband will say, she answered.

But what about you? Tom asked. You must notice things as you go from room to room. Things you see with your own eyes.

If you will please now speak to my husband, sir.

But—

He is in the office. Speak to him. There was a new pressure in her voice suddenly, a female householder, upper caste, claiming authority in a tone she'd used in wherever, maybe the Punjab.

Okay, said Tom. I'll talk to him. But in the meantime think what you might need fixed and holler—I'll fix it for you.

In his cabin Tom sprawled wide on the bed and watched the television. Or rather changed the channels restlessly, stopping only to consider an attractive woman or to wait for something violent to unfurl. No sports. He didn't really care about games. That was an act, something communal.

Tom napped with the heat on as high as it would go. It was not really sleep although in this state he noted that time seemed to pass more quickly. He looked at the clock and when he looked at it again it was significantly later than he would have projected, so in some form he must have slept. But it didn't feel to Tom like sleep exactly. Did he ever really sleep? In the way he used to? His limbs felt dead but his mind stayed active. He thought of his son: his mind alive but his body . . . dead weight. Tom hadn't seen him since before the restraining order, but he guessed Junior still watched television constantly. Not hard to guess—what else could he do? Junior had his own remote controller, a special remote with very large buttons that Eleanor had gotten from a catalog for invalids, there seemed to be a catalog for everything these days and Eleanor had them all. Junior could work it with remarkable speed for someone who was paralyzed, a plastic rod seized between his teeth, he viewed each image for a fraction of a second, the satellite dish—forty dollars a month—could hardly keep up with his dental dexterity, it gave him fifty or sixty options, the boy would cycle through them twice before pausing for a respite. It was irritating but who was going to stop him? Who had the heart to halt this routine? It wasn't possible to spoil Junior. Whatever he wanted he ought to have, including his own big Compaq computer, compliments of the Cross Family Committee. Somebody's retired desktop, charity, Tom's needs were other people's tax write-offs now. Pulled up close on a swiveling tray, outfitted with something called a Sip 'n Puff in lieu of your normal mouse. If the TV wasn't on, the computer was, sometimes the two were on together, Eleanor had put in a second line, it was almost thirty-three dollars a month, it didn't cost them any more than that because Junior had free Internet service, somehow or other he'd figured that out, how to get something for nothing. What else could he do, lying there? Tom had looked over Junior's shoulder at the endlessly shifting monitor screen, Virtual Paraplegia, Quadriplegic Bulletin Board, Spinal Cord Injury Information Network, Miami Project to Cure Paralysis, Junior sipping chat-room messages or puffing them into the ether. *Have worse pressure sores with this new wheelchair, need info on cushions that actually might work, regarding assistive devices for gait I can only say they're a mixed blessing, really, you fall you're in for more injury, it doesn't feel like walking anyway, maybe a little once in a while just for the change of pace.* Or: *This morning I went to a pool for therapy; the transfer was really dangerous on the wet floor, does anyone have a good design for a really effective brake? Arnie B., Charlottesville.* This sort of thing made Tom depressed. Quadriplegic computer nerds. Invisible paralyzed strangers sharing tips. Static ghosts in rooms across the world. Ephemeral presences exchanging ephemera. Net surfing, Web sites, chat rooms.

Midmorning he went to see Pin in his office. The small television was on, as always—a cable news program airing a feature on two Seattle lesbian performance artists who were opening a coffee shop. There was that curious smell of something Indian, Pin's pomade, rank sweet sweat, carpet shampoo, cardamom. I am very glad you are here, said Pin. I am very glad to see you, Mr. Cross. I am wanting to speak to you.

There's probably a few things to do, said Tom, with all these people around.

Pin was perched on his stool, ensconced—a caged bird clutching a dowel. I am very happy to have customers, he said. Very very happy for business.

Anyone would be, I guess.

So I am happy for the Virgin Mary. That she has decided to come and bring so many customers to stay at my motel.

A gold mine, said Tom. Except—they break things. And tax the septic system.

Pin tangled his thin caramel arms in front of him so as to lean on the back of one wrist. I do not understand, he said. Gold a mine?

Gold mine.

Is that somebody?

A mine. Where you dig gold. Where you dig gold out of the ground.

We are not digging gold.

It's a saying—you know. It means with the Virgin Mary here this motel is like a gold mine.

Pin rubbed behind one ear with the flat of his little finger. An unsanitary public gesture, thought Tom. But apparently that's how they did things in India. How I wish, said Pin, that yes, for a gold mine. But I possess seventeen cabins.

He didn't get it. A figure of speech. Well maybe you can build some more soon, said Tom. With all the money coming in.

Pin raised an eyebrow. Yes, he said. In the future more cabins will help my business. But for now I am having seventeen.

Tom began to grasp what was coming, but only with raw disbelief. More cabins, more maintenance, he said.

Yes more maintenance always, said Pin. But right now I must rent sixteen cabins. Because you are living in one, Mr. Cross. You are in Cabin Seventeen.

Seventeen minus one is sixteen—right. So that's sixteen still needing maintenance.

Pin untangled his arms slowly and began to straighten up the things on the counter—his stack of business cards, his check-in slips, his motel

postcards, his pen. Every day, he said, the followers of the Virgin Mary are asking me do I rent a
room even when they can see from the road my
No Vacancy sign.

What a nuisance. Can't they read?

I must wish to have more cabins, Mr. Cross.

Why don't you just stop beating around the
bush?

I am not beating.

You're playing games. You know what I mean.
Don't pretend you don't know English. You all
speak English in India. It's one of your national
languages.

Pin now folded his hands in front of him. A
clerk or bureaucrat at his desk, protected. Please
do not be angry, he said. Please let us be peaceful.

Tom drummed his fingers against the counter.
It is every day each room single bed forty-nine
dollars, said Pin. In one week three hundred
fifty dollars. In one month one thousand four
hundred dollars. So you can see—very difficult.

A plumber's forty an hour, answered Tom. A
gardener is fifteen or twenty dollars. I already give
you one-sixty a month. I don't think you're really
behind.

So I must increase your rent payment every
week to two hundred and fifty dollars.

Tom felt himself clench inwardly. Jesus, he

said. Jesus Christ. In this country we've got a name for that. It's god damn highway robbery.

Please do not be angry, Mr. Cross. I am very much sorry. No angry.

Jesus, man. You're ripping me off.

Nobody is ripping off, Mr. Cross.

Tom picked up the stack of business cards. Tired Traveler's Guesthouse, he read. I liked it better as the R&M. I understood those people.

Pin said nothing. He looked cowed but defiant at some obscure level. Somebody who knew the rules, if nothing else. Somebody counting on the rules. Be that as it may, his chin now trembled. Tom tapped the business cards against the counter. Fuck you Pin, he said.

Please you must not say bad things, Mr. Cross.

This is the bottom, Tom said. You people . . . you come in here. Treat me like this. In my own home town. Screw me over. Try to jew me. It doesn't get any lower.

He threw the stack of business cards at Pin's fax machine. They hit the wall with a slap and scattered. Pin picked up the telephone receiver. I am calling a policeman, he announced.

Go right ahead, Tom said. You don't know anyone in this town.

He pushed through the door and went to his cabin, where he sat on the bed for a few minutes

first, then at the table smoking calmly until
Nelson showed up in a cruiser. Tom watched
with a calculated distance. Nelson got out and adjusted his shirttail, pulled at his belt, and ran a
hand through his hair, eliciting in Tom an immense disdain and the memory of wrestling
Nelson in high school, of dislocating his shoulder
junior year, the expression of pain on Nelson's
face, he hadn't handled pain with dignity, he'd let
himself look pathetic when injured, and so be it,
thought Tom. It was not a bad thing to have at
hand. Nelson locked the door to his cruiser, no
doubt according to some protocol, the 12-gauge
shotgun was still inside, and went confidently into
Pin's office. Tom smoked with giddy patience. Lit
the next from the butt of the last. Enjoying the
veil of inevitability that lay over everything now.
Finally Nelson crossed the parking lot, swagger-
ing, and knocked on Tom's cabin door. Open,
called Tom, it all felt foreordained, and Nelson
came in without caution. Throwing business
cards—Nelson sniggered. What is it with this
little brown greaseball? I got better things to do.

Like what?

You know you don't even have to ask. I was
just heading out to the campground.

Sit down if you want.

I gotta get out there.

There's a chair if you want it.

For a minute, said Nelson. Then back to Ms. Mushroom and her fans.

He looked more tired than usual—his eyelids were gray and swollen. His cheeks had a jaundiced, sallow cast, the plastic complexion of a corpse, a cadaver. And he was carrying more weight than ever before, fat everywhere, Nelson was swelling, his gut, thighs, face. The brunt of cop jokes—donuts, maple bars. I never met this guy, he told Tom.

From India.

I figured that.

That little Hindu raised my rent a million dollars suddenly. Now that he's got all these people coming in the guy turns on me.

Your place looks like a gun shop, Tom.

I helped him out a million times. Tried to get him straightened out. Went out of my way for him.

What's that over there?

It's a forty-four-caliber black-powder revolver. Take a look if you want.

Nelson didn't, waved Tom off. My brother had one but in stainless steel, he said. Except with a nice brass trigger guard. Which he got in Texas when he went down bass fishing.

That greaseball wants me out of here.

Well what do you expect?

I don't learn I guess.

This Korean's got the laundromat. Same deal. Slant-eyed money-grubber.

Well forget it now, Tom answered.

Nelson nodded sympathetically and set his elbows against his knees—locker room tête-à-tête, halftime. The easy thing—don't throw his business cards. It makes me have to do something, okay? It makes me have to react.

Fuck you.

It puts me in a bind. He's scared of you. I'm supposed to be reaming you out right now. Kicking you out. Restraining order. The guy feels like you're dangerous, Tom. He doesn't want you around.

I am dangerous.

Don't tell me that.

I want to kick his little brown ass.

Don't do it, Tom. I'm telling you not to do it. You smack him around, it comes back on me. Because here I am just slapping your wrist. And then let's say—assault, you waste him. You kick his head in. Kick his ass. Well then that Hindu's going somewhere else. And I get accused of racism or something. The state or someone gets down on me. The department of whatever kicks *my* ass.

Things are fucked up.

I gotta show I'm following the rules. This is America. Land of the free. You ever listen to these rap people like this nigger who calls himself Snoop Doggy Dogg? Kill cops, freedom of speech? So how we gonna stop your landlord?

Tom shook his head. It's bullshit, he said. Jesus.

Calm, said Nelson. Keep it together. I'm way too busy for this type of call. So don't throw his business cards next time.

I can't afford to pay a thousand bucks a month to park my ass in this miserable dump.

Well you rob a bank I'll catch you, Tom.

Isn't there some rule about notice or something? He's gotta give me a month or something? Before he can raise the rent?

Nelson smiled. Hey, he said. Come on. Slow down. You're the one threw the business cards. That little grease monkey didn't do anything the law doesn't let him do anyway. It's a free country—didn't I say that? He can charge whatever he wants, can't he? For a room in his motel?

Tom snuffed his cigarette against his bootheel. Maybe you could get him deported, Nelson. Why don't you check his green card or something? Get him out of here?

Nelson stood, tucked his shirt, felt his belly. It isn't him that's gotta get out. It's you, Tom, if you can't meet his price.

All right, said Tom. I see where you stand.

I stand just where I have to stand. Not necessarily where I want to.

Right.

It is right.

Fuck you too.

Why don't you talk to him? Apologize? Try to work something out?

Tom put his boots up casually on the table, laced his fingers at the back of his head. Apologize my ass, he said.

Calm, said Nelson. I appeal for calm. I think you should give it time, calm down. You've got too much on your plate now, Tom. Try to be peaceful about it.

His wife's got an ass.

I noticed that.

Well let me sit here and think about it.

Good move, said Nelson.

He left and Tom thought for less than five minutes. Then he began to pack his things. Packing felt redemptive, cleansing. There was always the option of clearing out and it felt right to embrace that. How easy it was; flight, retreat. Tom didn't own much. He liked it that way. Traveling light and unencumbered. A fugitive and his earthly possessions. He didn't pack in orderly fashion, but neither was he careless about it. His rage, as always, was pointed outward—a searchlight blinding whomever it illuminated. At the same time he felt like a deer caught in headlights. The moment before roadkill. Deer and driver. His rage reflected back on him. Tom knew well about dire straits but these were deeper circumstances. Yet there was no point in ruining or losing anything, his binoculars or steelheading reel. His possessions had value, suddenly, as possessions do for the shipwrecked.

When everything was laid out across the bed he double-locked the door behind him and walked toward the maintenance shed. Maybe Pin was watching from the window. It didn't matter. Tom didn't check. Let Pin feel how Pin felt. Jabari's cleaning cart, at Cabin Fifteen, was tucked up under the moss-covered eaves. She knew everything by now, of course. Well let her stew while she cleaned her toilets and turned up her nose at American excrement. Let her ponder the maintenance man who smelled of nicotine and wouldn't go away. Intrepid of her to have ventured forth while Tom the Terrible yet lurked on the premises, man-eating tiger drags woman to her death, villager washing sari in stream pulled under by massive crocodile. But were there crocodiles in India? It hadn't been covered at North Fork High School. He'd never seen it on the Discovery Channel. Pin, on the other hand, was holed up, a house rat. He wasn't going to show his caramel face. So Tom went into the maintenance shed and took a tarp and skein of twine, an act of petty larceny. They weren't his. But who used them other than he, Joe Maintenance? Pin didn't even know the tarp existed. Tom had folded it, kept the twine neat, and left them there in their places. It wasn't theft except technically. He was borrowing his own work supplies. It was raining and he would need a tarp. Tom went out with it under his arm. Tom Cross, tarp owner.

He ran the defroster. More deliberation. He double-parked in front of his cabin, trapping a Chrysler minivan. In plain sight of Pin if Pin was watching. Tom put his firearms and fishing rods on the seat where rain couldn't get to them. Also his cartons of shells and rifle rounds, his tackle boxes, his reels, his binoculars, his knives, his fifth of Crown Royal, and his hunting boots. Collected talismans—he locked them in.

At the table he wrote a note—all caps. I FIG-URE THE MATTRESS IS WORTH FIFTY DOLLARS SO HERE'S YOUR FIFTY FOR IT. That was all. Three tens and a twenty. He was not a thief, wouldn't stoop to stealing. They were going to have to be happy with that. What else was there to say? The whole time I wanted to fuck your wife and I'll bet you Pin she wanted to fuck me? In fact we did it in Cabin Nine every day while you watched *As the World Turns?* Tom spread the tarp across the floor with the twine placed in forethought un-derneath it and hauled the mattress in one move off the box frame with his clothes and worldly possessions piled on and wrapped everything, the mattress and his personal items, afterward it looked like something from a horror movie or perhaps recovered from an archaeological dig, the jute twine lashed a tight dozen wraps including a pair of slipknotted loop handles, the clean mean package of a physical perfectionist, of someone devoted to the things of this world, to trim and tackle, gear, equipment, everything always had to be right if it involved objects in the spatial realm, but what other way was there to do things? It only felt good this single way. It was always worth the effort it took. Tom felt primeval satisfaction.

He broke camp. Last go-round. Heat off. Shades pulled. Drawers checked. Under the bed. Tom allowed himself a weird short pause, a paltry sentimental moment. Bachelor-pad blues? Well better than homeless. Pine board walls and cable television. He'd hung his hat, put his feet on the bed. Anyway, he thought, go fuck this place. He pulled the wrapped mattress out into the rain and muscled it into the bed of his pick-up, shut the cabin door and double-locked it. As usual in his adult life, everything unimportant was in order.

Tom knew he needed his pick-up canopy and so drove straight to his old lost house, where he'd left it rotting in the backyard. There was of course the issue of the restraining order enjoining him against just such a retrieval—technically Tom couldn't be on his own premises—but more tangible was Heidi Johnston's Corolla, parked by the force of sheer bad luck so as to block his access route. Tom had hoped to snake under trees, repossess his canopy unmolested, start the hold-down nuts with his fingers, and be history in less than two minutes. He could tighten the bolts a mile up the road with a hijacker's grin on his face. Only now this impediment: a Corolla. Plenty of times driving by for a glance he'd seen strange cars parked in front of his house and had fantasized mostly for the wounding pleasure of it but also as a disenfranchised husband that Eleanor had taken a variety of lovers, that everyone in town knew about her antics but kept a straight face when he was around, though on the other hand he knew full well that these cars belonged to the volunteers who called themselves the Cross Family Committee. To the women from church who came to help Junior, wipe his ass, change his clothes, shampoo and shave him, range his limbs, splint his arms and legs in place, count his pills, prepare his meals, feed him and then wash the dishes, comb his hair, clip his nails, change the bandages at his breathing tube and swab clean his piss tube. Massage and knead his gut each morning to make him pass a stool on a plastic sheet and empty his piss bag in the toilet. These women

Father Collins applauded weekly, an institutional-ized part of his mass—Heal the sick, cleanse the lepers, raise the dead, cast out devils: freely ye have received, freely give. Or: So we, being many, are one body in Christ, and every one members one of another. Or: And above all things have fervent charity among yourselves: for charity shall cover the multitude of sins. Or: Be ye steadfast, unmovable, always abounding in the work of the Lord. Father Collins listed the CFC members by name during this weekly, dutiful interregnum: Constance Pedersen, Julia Corn, Julia Neiderhoff, Tina Van Kamp, Heidi Johnston, Carolyn Meyers, Carol Boyle, Marilyn Davis, Grace Weaver, Beatrice MacMillan, Leah Long, and Annabelle Fletcher, whose grandfather was a North Fork pioneer—Annabelle had written a book about him—and who herself had Parkinson's disease. *Cedar Shakes and Prairie Potatoes*: Tom had read it with froward interest. A book of myths: old Fletcher had been a royal jerk, according to those who knew him. Owned a lot of river bottom. On Sundays dressed like an East Coast dandy. His granddaughter idolized him, obviously. The other women were unremarkable and uniformly dull and dowdy except for Julia Neiderhoff, who had the throat and calves of a mare, dark hair, and a classical chin.

Almost from the day that Junior came home

they'd taken over running Tom's household and had ruined his privacy. A coven of sounding boards for Eleanor, too—Tina Van Kamp was twice divorced and goaded Eleanor onward. They all commiserated, certainly. Some were married to loggers themselves and so brought familiar complaints to the table. Tom's house became a women's club, a coffee klatch, a radio talk show, a touchy-feely caucus. The smell changed—antiseptic deodorizer alchemized by high furnace heat into a damp effervescence. Lipstick stains on coffee cups, a thing he'd always found loathsome. And clutches of dried flowers in his bathroom. Eleanor's vocabulary suddenly changed—I'm not sure you value what I'm saying, Tom, I don't hear you honoring my feelings, Tom, Well fuck you then, he eventually came to answer, and get these witches out of my house! Except, it was true, they took care of Junior. Without them, forget it— Tom knew that. But why couldn't they just be good Samaritans and leave off doubling as marriage counselors? Why did they have to meddle in his marriage and get inside his wife's troubled head, talk her into despising him? When he came home he'd find say Marilyn Davis seated at the table next to Eleanor, Diet Pepsis, carrot sticks, open Bibles, heavy talk, Hey, he'd say, how's Junior doing?, but it was like he'd brought cold weather with him, they suddenly fell conspiratorially silent, when he went upstairs they started again, or sometimes he found three or four together praying like nuns and holding hands, their heads bowed, their eyes shut: Heal the sick, Give us the strength, Pray for us sinners now and at the hour of our death, other times someone read Bible verses: And when they were come in, they went up into an upper room, where abode both Peter, and James, and John, and Andrew, Philip, and Thomas, Bartholomew, and Matthew, James the son of Alphaeus, and Simon Zelotes . . . Tom would slip past them with a beer in his fist, take a shower, and lie on the bed with the door shut and the television on, when Eleanor came in he'd steel himself, it was time for combat again.

So what to do? He could open the door to Heidi Johnston's Corolla, slip her transmission into neutral, and gently prod her car out of his way with the front bumper of his pick-up. Or he could bluster afoot into his forbidden backyard and drag his canopy around the side of his house like Arnold Schwarzenegger or Neanderthal Man, a savage making off with shelter. Or he could knock on the door with polite humility and explain to Eleanor obsequiously that if possible he would like to collect the canopy and that he hoped for her dispensation. In other words, there were no good options. His life had come to this absurd pass: merely mounting a canopy on his truck was now freighted with tumultuous questions. Hog-tied, hamstrung, pinned, pincered. Wherever he turned, complexity. Tom tapped his steering wheel with his thumbs and quelled the urge to bash the Corolla. Then he parked and groomed his hair in the rearview mirror because looking good was a kind of revenge and he wanted Eleanor to feel pain.

At the door she said Restraining order, Tom. Don't make me have to make a phone call.

She didn't look good. Washed out, severe. He didn't even like her anymore. Here was a woman he'd come inside of probably at least three thousand times and he didn't want to touch her any longer. That was the strangest part for Tom—the cavernous depth of his revulsion. But she was drying up: crow's feet, frown lines, sexless religiosity. And always adding new inner strictures. Knobby fingers with knitting needles in them, he couldn't face that kind of future. But it was already here. Ellie wore sweaters and had a loose ass, a paunch. Sorry, he said. I know this is wrong. But all I want is the canopy for the pick-up. I don't even have to come inside or bother anybody, Ellie. I just need to get around back, grab the canopy.

He was standing in the rain but she wasn't. It was clear to him that she was afraid, outweighed by eighty-five pounds. In the presence of an irrational opponent who in prior meetings had demonstrated, to her mind, how fully he was prone to rage. Nine-one-one, she said to him. I was told that if you ever came around to call nine-one-one.

I'm not coming around. I'm just picking up my canopy, that's all. I'll pick it up and then I'll be gone. Just let me in the backyard.

No Tom.

Yes Ellie.

Eleanor set her chin a little harder. I've also been advised not to argue with you should you happen to show your face illegally which is what you're doing right now. I'm not even supposed to speak with you, period. So this is it: good-bye.

Wait.

She tried to shut the door but he put his foot in its path and the door stayed open halfway. Wait, he said. Eleanor. Just wait a minute. Come on, wait. Just let me get my canopy.

Heidi Johnston appeared behind Eleanor, or part of Heidi Johnston. He probably outweighed her by fifteen pounds, but Heidi was only five two or three, a woman with a grotesquely mammoth chest, pruny all around the mouth and clearly short on estrogen. One of those manlike adipose women North Fork harbored in very large numbers, the town's most prominent genetic marker: fat and masculine androgynous females buying cake mix at MarketTime or selling raffle tickets at Burger Barn. Heidi, he said. Hi-dee-hay.

Be careful, Heidi, said Eleanor. He's very violent.

I'm not violent.

Yes you are.

Come on, said Tom. I just want my canopy. How complicated is that? A truck canopy? Why is it such a big deal?

But it's a very big deal to Eleanor, said Heidi. It's very important to her.

She's not here? said Tom. Eleanor? She can't maybe speak for herself?

She's very capable. If you'd only listen.

I'm right here listening.

No you're not.

Then what am I doing?

I don't know.

Well get out of the way then. This isn't your business.

I'd go for the phone, put in Eleanor, but I don't want to even risk it right now. Unless—wait— I'm going for the phone.

You go ahead, Heidi urged her. She faced off with Tom, stared him down, beady little angry animal eyes. Eleanor, said Tom. Be reasonable. I'm not here to do something criminal. I'm only here for my canopy.

That canopy, said Heidi, is community property. This is a community property state. So one you don't own that canopy anymore and two you *are* doing something criminal by breaking the terms of your restraining order and showing up here at all.

Wasn't it usually a guy in this role? The slick new boyfriend standing up to the hapless discarded ex-husband? Tom moved more boldly into the doorway. Look, he said. Eleanor. All I want is the god damn canopy. I'll tell you what you can have the house, even your lawyer would agree to that. I'll trade you the house for the canopy, Ellie. Take advantage of me.

Nine-one-one, said Eleanor.

This is a waste, said Tom.

He went out again, yanked opened the Corolla's door, and moved the stick into neutral. Don't you touch my car! yelled Heidi, but he made himself deaf to her shrill entreaties even while she advanced on him like an overweight pit bull. I don't have a beef with you, warned Tom. It's just that your car here's in the way and right now—I have to move it.

Heidi briefly quickened her pace, but at ten feet suddenly halted. Her eyes were wet. Too much adrenaline. That's my car, she said.

I'm going to move it, answered Tom. It's in my way—I'm moving it.

No you're not.

Yes I am.

You touch my car I'll get you arrested.

I thought you were a religious person.

I'll press charges, get you arrested.

Didn't Jesus say to turn the other cheek? Have mercy on the desperate?

Stay away from my car. Last warning, Tom.

You aren't threatening to shoot me, are you?

Stay away from my car like I said already.

Your car's on my property, though, said Tom. I have a right to move it.

He laid his shoulder into her bumper and rolled the car ten feet. She called him names and yelled while he did so: Everybody knows all about you you sinner this whole town knows how abusive you are, everyone knows what happened you know, you paralyzed your own son for the rest of his life, how can you even live with yourself? how can you even stand to be you? everybody knows what a lowlife you are, what scum you are, what a jerk you are, you're screwing Tammy Buckwalter, you're down to living in a motel cabin, now get your hands off my car I mean it get your hands off my car!

Tom maneuvered his pick-up through the trees and was hauling the canopy into place when Eleanor slid open a window behind him and said The cops are on their way Tom they're on their way right now.

I just want the canopy, Tom answered.

That's not the point.

It's the only point.

You always think you know so much.

I only know one thing—I need this canopy.

Tom—you're pathetic.

I love you, honey.

You're out of control, said Eleanor.

There was no time for the hold-down bolts. Tom tipped the canopy into the bed, weighted it down with a few sticks of firewood, and drove toward the street again. Heidi had blocked his path with her Corolla and was standing beside it, daring him, and looking self-righteously arrogant. Fat-ass hog. Piece of shit. How tempting it was to slam her broadside with an unexpected acceleration but instead he smashed through a tangle of blackberries that for a moment concealed his view through the windshield and when he hit the street again he rolled down his window and called to Heidi Have a nice day, ugly bitch.

Child of Satan, Heidi replied. Go join your father in hell.

IV

Mediatrix

NOVEMBER 15, 1999

One of Ann's followers knocked on the van door and handed Carolyn a stack of Monday newspapers, a thermos of tea, a bag of oranges, a box of extra-strength Tylenol, and four small containers of yogurt. Pray for me, she entreated Ann, struggling for a glimpse over Carolyn's shoulder. I'm Elizabeth Hoynes, your servant. She'll try, said Carolyn. Now please go in peace. Please give Ann some privacy. But the servant hesitated, lingering hopefully, and Carolyn saw behind her a throng of followers pressing toward the van like rock and roll fans, devotees who, with the door open, were calling out their assorted petitions and exclaiming their adoration. I could always douse them with pepper spray, she thought, if it turns into genuine chaos.

Fortunately, though, there were nearby sentinels arrayed in a defensive perimeter. New unbidden male presences who had appeared the night before. Carolyn noted that the campground, this morning, looked suddenly like a refugee center, full of refuse and unwashed people milling with desperate zeal. Her van was like the United Nations truck with its load of soy powder for the starving. Already it was past ten o'clock and there was a rain hiatus that wouldn't last, the trees were dripping, drab clouds blew past, North Fork's eternal, oppressive pall darkened everything preternaturally and dimmed the faces of the hopeful acolytes, beneath it all of them, Carolyn included, were dank damp prisoners, citizens of a gulag, a colony of rotting mushrooms. Earthbound strangers locked in gray straits. Hollow refugees yearning toward whatever God they could construe. Or toward nothing, as in Carolyn's case, except, perhaps, the god of the sun, that pagan equatorial potentate. The ramshackle campground made Carolyn yearn impatiently for Cabo San Lucas. She would sleep naked there and eat fruit and rice, drink margaritas, get high at 9 a.m., take pick-me-up tokes as needed. Shop for limes and tonic water; read travel books beneath palm trees. South of the border the past four winters her slogan and mantra had been *mañana*—everything could wait for another time—but for now, hey, breakfast and the papers, delivered by an earnest servant. Pray for me, please, the servant repeated. And I hope you enjoy your breakfast this morning. Carolyn, nodding in the manner of a dowager who expected just such offerings, pointed at an errant photographer and pronounced, Make him follow the same rules as the others, he has to stay behind the lines. But already a sentinel was at the business of thwarting the wayward cameraman with a hand thrown across his lens. Carolyn considered the herd of petitioners urgently waiting for an audience and said, She's engaged in fervent prayer just now, tell them so, do that for me, then raised an arm in benediction until the servant turned to the crowd and announced: She's at prayer everybody, be patient and calm, and God bless you all! Thank you, said Carolyn, that's it for the moment, and a sentinel drew the van's door shut: with the shades drawn too, for privacy, Carolyn had a chance to laugh. She'd redecorated her inner sanctum with votive candles, hung a crucifix from her rearview mirror, and left the Gospels, a prop, on her dashboard. All to the good, presto, a miracle—tea and morning news. Instead of grazing for mushrooms in the rain. Instead of wandering, damp, in penury. Didn't all of that call for a heartfelt wicked cackle? Carolyn ate yogurt and perused the headlines. TEEN SEER SWAMPS LOGGING TOWN. RUNAWAY AT EPICENTER OF VI-

SIONS. HUGE CROWDS DRAWN TO MARY SIGHT-
INGS. THOUSANDS GATHER FOR FOREST VIGIL.
BISHOP TO STUDY APPARITIONS. MUSHROOM
PICKER CLAIMS TO SEE VIRGIN. PILGRIMS TEST
TOWN INFRASTRUCTURE. LOCAL SHERIFF "OVER-
WHELMED." WOMAN CLAIMS SEER HAS CURATIVE
POWERS. LOCALS RESPOND TO VISION FRENZY.
Carolyn browsed, in search of her own name, ac-
knowledging as she did so that yes, all is vanity, her
ego was a pack of drunken monkeys, it wanted
what it wanted, period, and now it wanted her
name in the news, however tawdry and puerile
that was, however empty and ridiculous. So be it,
thought Carolyn, I've sold my soul to the material
world with its infinite array of fascinations, to be
alive is better than not, than ashes or the afterlife,
than worm fodder, Saint Peter's Gate, nirvana, or
the Elysian Fields. A willing slave to the corporeal
quotidian, which included press notes such as this:
*Ms. Carlton claimed her warts disappeared about three
and a half hours afterward.* Carolyn read on, increas-
ingly astounded. *MarketTime checker Sue Philips,
27, described Ms. Holmes as "quiet, meek, somebody
you wouldn't even notice." Phil Peck, Media Affairs
Officer at Stinson Timber, said the company would issue a statement Monday morning. A spokesperson for
the diocese expressed the bishop's concern over reports of
hysteria and said a full Church inquiry would soon be
under way. Sheriff Nelson cited safety and health con-*

siderations. Mushroomer Steven Mossberger, 29, said the visionary "mostly kept to herself—the rest of us just couldn't see this coming." Ms. Holmes, born in Medford, Oregon, was reported missing September tenth after dropping out of East Valley High School. Mayor Cantrell, speaking outside his office, was "guardedly optimistic" that North Fork could handle the growing flood of religious pilgrims. Lyman Sylvester, president of the North Fork Chamber of Commerce, described events as "a shot in the arm for a patient in serious cardiac arrest." Father Collins refused comment and referred questions to the bishop's office. At the Vagabond Tavern local out-of-work loggers expressed dismay at the sudden influx. "It's not that we're against outsiders," said Dale Raymond, 41, born and raised in North Fork. "But when people come here they better pay attention. They need to understand who we are in this town. Don't just roll right over us."

Ann sat with a pillow behind her head, opening the thermos slowly. She'd passed the night in the priest's sofa bed and been whisked away by sentinels at eight, her clothes clean, her allergies suppressed by a double dose of Phenathol, her fever as yet unmitigated. Perturbed, too, by Father Collins' recalcitrance. How could she make him see the Blessed Mother? That Our Lady had reached to embrace him too? Arriving that morning at the North Fork Campground she'd lowered her head to the reporters and cameras—a television news team producer beckoned—but had clasped her hands at her chin for petitioners, who'd shouted her name and called their praises, Glory, Hallelujah, Our Ann! Carolyn, quickly emerging from her van, had embraced Ann publicly with dramatic flair, Spent the night with your priest, aye? she'd whispered, I'll have the cameras cleared right away, these media people are like vicious scavengers, they'll bite your fingers if you feed them. She'd trundled Ann inside, slammed the door, then turned like a press agent and said, emphatically, Not giving any interviews this morning, I'm sorry there won't be comments. And we're going to establish a media-free perimeter. You'll all have to stay outside the flagging our friends are about to put up for us so the business of Mother Mary can be conducted unencumbered by media.

Now, in the van, she peeled an orange with flippant grace and leaned closer to her newspaper. Hey, she said. Check this out. This quote—right here—this quote's from me. *Greer, describing herself as the visionary's disciple, estimated Sunday's crowd at two thousand and projected even larger crowds today, with "accompanying stress on local infrastructure."* Unquote. I mean, check it out, said Carolyn. I'm like your spokesperson or something now. I'm totally in the newspaper.

Do you know what it means to be a disciple?

Does it mean I have to buy your dope?

Ann didn't answer. She poured a cup of tea. Your helper, said Carolyn, in spreading the teachings. A devoted follower of Saint Ann of North Fork. That's me—want a part of this orange?

No thanks.

You should, though. For the vitamin C.

Saint Ann?

Bad joke. Sorry. Now take this Tylenol—three or so. Unless your priest gave you some this morning after you slept with him.

I slept on his sofa.

That's what they all say.

What do you mean?

His other girlfriends.

He's a priest, remember? He doesn't have girlfriends.

Did you see *The Thorn Birds*? Richard Chamberlain? Hitting on Rachel Ward?

No.

So is he into handcuffs?

Carolyn.

So what did you do if you didn't sleep with him?

We talked about things.

What kinds of things?

About the church.

Which church is that?

The church we have to start building right away. Our Blessed Mother's church.

I see, said Carolyn. That church, yes. I've been thinking about that church also.

She pointed at her five-gallon picking bucket, half full with small bills and change. See that? she said. There's your church right there. Money translates into a church. You get aggressive about asking for money, your church will, I don't know. Materialize.

How much is there?

I don't really know.

Maybe we should count it.

We'll count it later. In the meantime make an announcement today. More than once. Repeat it, Ann. That you can't fulfill Mother Mary's wishes without more alms, contributions, tithes, offerings, greenbacks, tax deductions.

Carolyn put the bucket on the table. Look what I wrote right here, she said. Our Lady of the Forest Church Fund.

Our Lady of the Forest?

Nice ring, don't you think? And I've got three more buckets just like it.

There was a tentative knock on the van's sliding door, courteous and deferential. Carolyn tucked the bucket away. Not a moment's privacy, she complained.

A new devoted follower this time, this one a woman in a parka patched with duct tape, a clear plastic rain scarf over a hairdo swirled stiff like gray cotton candy. There's a priest here who says he's from the bishop, she said. And another priest from the church in North Fork. They both want to speak to you.

Oh they do, said Carolyn. How interesting.

Should I let them in?

We'll talk about it.

What should I say?

Tell them to wait.

For how long?

Until I say.

No, said Ann. They're welcome.

The woman moved aside and the clergymen peered in. They stood in the open door of the van, Father Collins in his overcoat and leather gloves and the bishop's representative in ecumenical black garb and a high white priestly tab. With his gray bristle cut and wire-rimmed glasses he looked like a high school gym teacher dressed as a priest for a faculty Halloween party or a six-foot-two Harry Truman. Hello, said Father Collins, good morning, salutations. The crowd is exceptionally huge today. I'm just astonished at the size of this crowd. This is my . . . colleague. Father Butler.

Good morning, said Father Butler. Sorry to intrude on your breakfast this way. We're barging in, apologies. And yes, this crowd is exceptional.

You're from the bishop, said Carolyn. Or so my associates report.

Yes, from the bishop. That's right. Yes. Getting right to the point with it, yes. I'm sent by the bishop. To look at things. To have a look out here.

To have a look?

Exactly.

The visionary sat against her pillow with the thermos cup of tea in one hand, the other settled in her lap. She was under blankets like a convalescent in a turn-of-the-century sanatorium, minus a thermometer stuck in her mouth and a hot water bottle by her head. Her pallor, now, was almost ghostly, her complexion so flawless as to seem surreal, a Kabuki character with anorexia, girl from the West doused with rice powder. Father Butler, she said dreamily. Welcome and peace be with you.

And you must be the girl we've heard about and read about in the newspapers.

Father Butler, repeated Ann. I'm glad you're here. My name is Ann Holmes. Please come in and sit with us. You too, Father Collins.

Father Butler hesitated. Such extreme politesse, he said. I don't know when I was last invited into one of these clever Volkswagen vans. It's really . . . efficient, isn't it? Would efficient be the right word?

Germans, said Carolyn. Lebensraum.

The priests sat at the fold-down table so that

the four of them now were like teenagers in a booth at a small-town soda shop. Father Butler smelled like brittle leaves or a very earthy pipe tobacco, Carolyn could not quite tell, or possibly Bay Rum aftershave. Bugs in a rug, he said.

It's cozy, she answered. Cozy or claustrophobic, depending on your point of view. Cup half empty or cup half full. I hope neither of you gets Ann's flu, by the way. Maybe I should open a window.

No need, Father Butler replied. In New Guinea I worked among the sick every day, but the Lord kept me well—indeed wherever I went in the Third World the Lord always kept and blessed me. But 'sixty-two to 'sixty-five in Popondetta, not far from Port Moresby, why those were some of my heartiest days, despite the presence of malaria, typhoid, and assorted, shall we say, jungle fevers. I lived on simple food there, slept when it fell dark, got up with the light, played a bit of soccer, badminton, and never once a speck of illness.

You're lucky, said Carolyn. That's not me. Just tell me you're sick I get sick, too. Or tell me you were sick last week. I can talk myself into serious disease without even really trying.

Ho, said Father Butler. Hypochondria. But you're looking hale now, Ms. Greer. You're looking relaxed, I must point out, for someone so close to the center of things. Someone so close to—excuse me—purported visions. And with this clearly feverish girl at your side, convalescing in, shall we say, close quarters. It reminds me a little of my navy days. Bunking shipboard in shifts.

Purported or not, said Carolyn, there's no point in stressing out.

Father Butler didn't blink or waver. Composure, he said, is certainly admirable. A trait of martyrs, oftentimes, who know they go to the Lord.

Well I'm no martyr.

And yet you sacrifice, clearly, Ms. Greer. You might be miles from here, unencumbered. Instead of offering your services so generously. As Ann's friend and confidante.

Carolyn began playing with an orange peel. Kneading loose the white inner meal. Father Butler, she saw, was an inquisitor. He seemed already to have looked right through her. On the other hand he couldn't know that underneath his priestly posterior was four hundred and fifty-five dollars she'd appropriated from his fellow Catholics. The night before, her shades drawn tight, she'd tediously counted all the small bills Ann's followers had so virtuously coughed up and hid more than half in the empty catch basin of her van's never-used chemical toilet, directly underneath the very bench on which Father Butler sat. Whatever you say, she told him.

Father Butler smiled, pulled loose a handkerchief, and began cleaning his glasses. He was ag-
onizingly slow about it, blowing hot air
repeatedly on the lenses and holding them up to
a seam of light, examining his polishing work
critically. As you may or may not know, he said to
Ann, there are each year in this country alone a
considerable number, hundreds shall we say, of
claims made regarding the Blessed Virgin, that
her face has appeared on a freshly dug potato, that
a pizza maker throwing dough in Syracuse saw
her silhouette in the wrinkles of a crust. The details are unimportant. The details are not my
point. Shorn lamb's wool, cow dung, snowdrifts,
children having epileptic seizures, road-show
evangelists, psychotic nuns, runaways addicted to
marijuana—go ahead and take your pick. These
claims are manifold, absolutely, commonplace and
everywhere, rest assured you are not the first such
claimant, nor will you be the last. So commonplace as to be banal in certain circles of the episcopal college which I think shall go unnamed
right now, to name them would be a certain di-
gression, but the important point is that your experience of Mary is not in the least bit unusual,
dear, as far as the church is concerned. It has seen
the likes of this a thousand times, and each time
the likes of me is dispatched to try to make sense
of it. Although, I should say, your case is unusual

in that the scope of it is quite impressive, you've succeeded in attracting considerable attention, more than the average Marian event, that fact is not contestable, this is a significant episode that requires a significant investigation, such investigation to pursue, at its core, the fundamental truth of your claims regarding the Blessed Virgin. Which the Church does not take in any way lightly and which it is determined to explore thoroughly with all due seriousness.

A change of tone had crept into his voice, an increasing gravity that made Carolyn think of the immolation of Joan of Arc. She knew very little about religious persecution, but perhaps this was it.

Father Butler looked up from his polishing work in order to settle his eyes on Ann, who responded by clasping her hands to her chin and saying I want your questions, Father. I want your interest. Thank you.

You're very welcome.

I'm blessed by your presence.

You may not feel that way later on.

I'm sure I will, replied Ann.

Father Butler went back to his glasses, giving them a final scrutiny before slipping them onto his face. Their presence was prosthetic and increased his severity. Fortunately for you, he said, I'm not a psychologist. I don't operate in the realm of science. If I did I would dismiss you out of hand as suffering from a patently self-evident delusion, the ready and obvious explanation. But for a priest it isn't that clear and simple. It can never be clear and simple, Ann. What is the nature of God's plan, God's reality? How can we know the good Lord's truth? Father Butler shook his head, as if to suggest the innate futility of every metaphysical inquiry. You can see that the task I have in front of me is grave, deep, difficult, challenging. How do I decide what is real?

I don't know, answered Ann.

Like floating about in a void, said Father Butler. Devoid of reference points.

Ann tightened her blankets around her. Outside she could hear the din of the crowd. She was calm and listless yet she burned with fever. An inchoate truth had hold of her. She could see Father Collins had misgivings about the tone of this prelude to an inquisition. He fidgeted and watched her with a conspirator's empathy, as if to say I'm not his friend, these are unavoidable circumstances. Ann watched Father Butler pull back a shade and peer outside as if he was dumbfounded. But it was all an act, she could easily see this. She could see his shrewd and driven performance. He was already fashioning his clerical noose, there was nobody who could talk to God except the pope himself.

In here the questions are abstract, said Father Butler. But out there a thousand fervent pilgrims are waiting for us to emerge.

More than a thousand, said Carolyn. And all of them believers.

Father Butler let the shade fall back. Right, he said. More than a thousand. I meant a thousand figuratively. At any rate, here we all are. Contemplating, once again, the eternal attraction of the Mother of God. A thing so easily . . . exploited.

He smiled beatifically at Ann, then raised his hands like Jesus sermonizing. In my job, he said, there are wonders, of course. It isn't all just flim-flam artists. And one of these wonders is our Church's recognition that God in all his mystery and power has in fact historically communicated with us, and if he so chooses can communicate again, and can choose to do so via private revelation, by presenting himself, if I can put it this way, to the inward perception of an individual, to Abraham or Moses, say, who in turn is called to deliver God's message in a public fashion, as you feel you are, and this has been one of God's great means, to deliver himself to his followers through the conduit of such revelations, a divine technique which the Church affirms may not be confined to the Lord alone but may extend as well to Our Lady, the Blessed Mother, as we've witnessed in Bernadette at Lourdes, whose visions the

Church deems worthy of belief, in Lucia dos Santos at Fátima, in her cousins Jacinta and Francisco Marto, in Sister Catherine Labouré, in Mélanie Calvat and Maximin Giraud, these are all individuals, Ann, whose claims were very similar to your own and whose revelations were carefully scrutinized, examined by local diocesan committees, approved by pertinent local bishops, and ultimately accepted as legitimate by the Church—a mere handful of cases, my dear, among the thousands investigated; nevertheless, there they are, and because they are, why, there are men such as me, appointed to pursue these claims.

So the odds aren't good, said Carolyn. Because the Church holds all the cards.

Father Butler locked his fingers together. Cards, he said, are an improper conceit. But on the other hand it is the province of the Church to make a determination, is it not? The Church revealed by the Holy Spirit, the Church perfected in glory? Who else might do so?

Only the Church, Ann agreed. There isn't anybody else.

Father Butler tried to lean back and stretch, but there simply wasn't room. He looked oversized, a rat in a mouse den, an adult in a child's playhouse. In these matters, he explained, the Church is careful. Exhaustive, always, in its consideration. Not wishing to err in either direction.

In the end quite delicate about its wording. The opinion of the Church is rendered exactingly. The question of discernment is taken seriously. We must decide if this is merely a case for secular psychologists to yawn about or, instead, a bona fide apparition. Or—a third disturbing alternative—one of the tricks of Satan.

Father Butler allowed a beat of silence for the obvious purpose of heightened drama. I know what you're probably thinking, he said. The concept of Satan is . . . antiquated. Perhaps you're waiting for me right now to use the word diabolical so you can have a laugh at my expense.

No, said Ann. I'm not.

I was thinking more of Arch Fiend, said Carolyn. Arch Fiend or Prince of Darkness.

A rose by any other name, Father Butler shot back. But it's always possible that the force of evil, to give Satan more secular clothing, is active in fomenting apparitions, so we must take this possibility into account, we can't dismiss Satan's subterfuge. Greed, ambition, personal gain, the name of evil is irrelevant, name it as you must, Ms. Greer. According to your lights, such as they are. As you please, as you must. Lucifer goes by any number of titles, but always his endeavor is exactly the same, to destroy, subvert, bring anarchy and chaos, pave the way for hell on earth.

The Great Deceiver, said Carolyn. You're saying maybe it's the devil in disguise when Ann sees the Virgin Mary?

I'm saying, said Father Butler, that it's possible. That we can't overlook that prospect.

I'm just not much for talk of the devil.

We'll put him in the back of our mind for now then.

Do you think that's really a good place for him?

Foremost is our effort, generally, at discernment. A broad endeavor, certainly. So we can afford to leave him there temporarily while we press forward in other areas.

We, said Carolyn. Forgive me but that sounds like the royal plural.

The priestly plural, said Father Butler. Father Collins and I.

Father Collins smiled sheepishly. He looked, thought Carolyn, disposed to defend himself, prepared to distance himself from Father Butler, but instead there was a saving knock at the door and she threw it open with muscular force on two sentinels in rubber rain gear and on the woman with the transparent plastic scarf battened down against her hair who was poised between them like an actress on whom the curtain has risen. I'm here, she said, on behalf of your petitioners, and handed Carolyn a wad of paper on which, she explained, were requests. They want to see you,

Our Ann, she added. They need you to hear their appeals.

She has to go to the woods now, said Carolyn. Tell them to clear a way for us so we can get through them, please.

She shut the door, turned to the priests, and picked up her bullhorn with belligerent enthusiasm. Well, well, she said. How interesting. We're about to embark on a forest journey to the site of these purported apparitions. But won't it appear, if you come along too, that you've decided to sanction us?

Appearances are not of interest, said Father Butler. Only reality. Truth.

I agree, ventured Father Collins. We only want the truth.

Brave of you, sneered Carolyn.

Father Butler raised one hand. Whatever your sentiments might be, he said, we'd like to continue this dialogue with Ann. Would it be possible for you to meet with us—tonight, say? At seven o'clock? Would that work for you? At Father Collins' church? In town at seven o'clock?

Our day is long, said Carolyn. Make it nine o'clock.

Ann pushed her blanket aside. Her thin forearms, the knobs of her wrists, suggested emacia-

tion. The pallor of illness had left her white in dis-
concerting fashion. Father Collins, she wheezed.
I ask you again. I ask you in the name of Our
Lady, please. Help me build her church.

They set out into the forest at eleven-thirty,
slowed by the volume of the campground crowd,
and the trees were a relief to Ann, though her illness made walking difficult. It helped that
overnight a way had been cleared as obvious as
the Oregon Trail. Ann led, leaning on Carolyn,
who carried only her bullhorn. The two priests
walked immediately at their backs, next four sentinels hauling alms buckets, and behind them five
thousand pilgrims. The sheriff had deputized
three out-of-work loggers, bringing the county
contingent to nine; there was also his department's canine team, a leashed pair of fat German
shepherds. The state had sent a half dozen patrol
officers whose pressed uniforms and wide-
brimmed hats made them look like colorless dop-
pelgängers of Royal Canadian Mounties. In the
forest their shined shoes were loudly out of place.
Soon they all had wet feet.

Most of the photographers darted ahead in
search of advantageous postures from which to
shoot in the forest gloom, but the trees made it
impossible for them to capture the magnitude of

the crowd. The journalists were consistently thwarted by sentinels, though one managed briefly to walk beside Ann and ask Do you have a Web site yet or an e-mail address where I can reach you? Carolyn replied, Yes we do, it's Ann at North Fork dot org. All one word. Ann with no e. Caps where appropriate. You'll find our e-mail address there and you can e-mail us your questions conveniently and we'll get back to you.

I sense you're lying.

Okay—it's a lie.

What if I ask some questions right now?

Now really isn't a very good time.

How do you feel about everything that's happened?

Now isn't a good time to talk.

Would you say you expected a crowd this large?

She isn't answering questions, sir.

Who are you?

Carolyn Greer.

Right, but who are you?

Carolyn Greer. Double-e Greer. Spokeswoman.

Spokeswoman?

At a later date I'll pencil you in.

Ms. Holmes, is this person really your spokeswoman?

Yes. She is.

Leave your card, said Carolyn.

The log at Fryingpan Creek was still intact but had now been circumvented. The trail turned downstream fifty yards to where a makeshift bridge had been erected by someone with a rudimentary background in construction. There were slip-proof treads nailed over rough planks, neat one-by-two safety railings, and plywood wheelchair ramps. On the near bank two men waited. One wore a green wool timber cruiser's jacket, the other a Highlander raincoat. They were standing with their hands in their pockets, observing the approach of Ann's processional, minions of the local land baron. Greetings, said the one in the Highlander coat. I'm Richard Devine. From the Stinson Timber Company. And this is Richard Olsen.

So you're both named Richard, said Carolyn.

And who might you be?

Carolyn Greer.

And your friend here beside you is the girl with the visions?

That depends, said Carolyn.

Two of Ann's sentinels moved silently forward with a distinctly martial air. Their manner prompted Richard Devine to put a fretful hand to his temple. He had a patrician's gesticulations; the hand to his temple, though liver-spotted, was elegant and debonair. I see, he said. And you've brought along a crowd. Something like a medieval army.

Well observed, said Carolyn. Though it's hard to miss five thousand people.

The other Richard, who was implike and stumpy, a thirtyish retainer with a crescent of red hair—a friar's ringed pate, thought Carolyn, on a classic victim of male-pattern baldness—took from his jacket a neatly folded map and began to unfold it meticulously. This, he said, is a company map. But everything on it can be verified with the county. And we thought you might want to have a look.

Pilgrims were now making dashes through the creek, walking the log, and boulder-hopping. Richard Devine watched with what Carolyn divined was a mock and artful anguish. He peeked under the hand at his brow, grimaced, and peeked another time. I'm afraid they're trespassing, he said, wincing.

The map will show that, said Richard Olsen. Everything on the other side of the creek is Stinson Timber land.

Which we wouldn't mind, added Richard Devine. Except that you've got enough people here to fill a football stadium. Plus you've plowed a trail through our holdings. There's serious damage to the undergrowth and a considerable amount of garbage.

I hear what you're saying, answered Carolyn. Your issues are excessive littering and modest environmental damage. So let me assure you we'll pick up our garbage. A committee will be appointed right away to police your property thoroughly. And now that we have a trail established, there won't be any new undergrowth damage. We can organize trail supervisors, we can keep our people to the path.

But up where you have your religious meetings, Richard Olsen said. All of these people disperse out there. Fan out. Fill the woods. That's where the damage is occurring.

Extreme damage, said Richard Devine. We made an inspection of the site this morning. For us it's tantamount to devastation. The erosion and plant loss is significant. And there are also sanitation issues. We're not sure our woods can recover.

In the grand scheme of things it's a small area, said Carolyn. You own, what, ten billion acres? Why not give five acres to Mother Mary?

It's an ecosystem, explained Richard Olsen. Things in it are contiguous. Interrelated. Mutually dependent. There's a ripple effect from five acres.

Spare me, said Carolyn. You're Stinson Timber, not the Sierra Club. It's lost timber you're worrying about, so cut the enviro-babble.

Timber for profit, said Richard Olsen, is not

inherently evil, is it? We're also stewards of the land.

Stewards of the land, said Carolyn. The last time I checked you were Stinson Timber. The biggest devastators of land in the state. Owners of ten thousand poorly planned clear-cuts you keep hidden behind locked gates. But from the air, you know what? Everyone can see. In between bites of their airplane food. Your land is completely defoliated. Vietnam after the air force got through. Your land looks utterly and completely tragic. Stewards of the land. Stewards of the land. If you're stewards of the land I'm Julia Roberts. Talk about Newspeak! War is peace. Freedom is slavery. Stinson Timber is steward of its lands. I don't want to hear more lies.

Richard Devine clutched his forehead again like someone with a dawning migraine. My God, he said. Let's stick to the point. The only issue in front of us is trespassing. Trespassing plain and simple.

From your point of view, said Carolyn. By the way, where's your coterie of lawyers? Hiding behind the trees?

We don't need lawyers, said Richard Olsen. We just need calm. And common sense.

Carolyn raised her electric bullhorn. Pass the word back among the others! she called. We're going to take a short break right here! A ten-minute break! Pass it back!

I'm glad to hear, said Richard Devine, that you feel we can resolve this in ten minutes.

We can totally resolve this, Carolyn said. Because I know exactly how to speak your language. Your language—obviously—is cash.

What we want to talk about is trespassing, said Devine. I take that back. We don't want to talk about it. We're just asking you not to do it.

And you're asking us not to because you think we do damage. And damage can always be mitigated, right? Offset with cash on the barrelhead, right? So look—my people will call your people. And we'll work things out, we'll get to it. It's just that for now—guess what?—we're here. And no one really wants to go home. No one exactly wants to stop. They all came out here because Mother Mary is making appearances on your land. Is that something you can blithely ignore? The fact that the Virgin is appearing on your property? Doesn't a phenomenon such as that make "trespassing" somehow trivial, irrelevant? Open your eyes to reality. There's five thousand people backed up behind me who are bent on crossing this bridge.

Point well taken, said Richard Devine. Nevertheless: no trespassing on our property. And I'm sure that with your bullhorn there you can suppress reluctance on the part of your followers to conform to the state's no trespassing law. These are religious people, after all, not hooligans or rabble-rousers. Despite the behavior of those people over there on the other side of the creek.

Wow, said Carolyn. Unbelievable. I mean I don't think you're even hearing me. I can see you're going to make this difficult. So let me try another approach. Bear with me while I start all over. Now I'm betting in the pocket of your deluxe fancy raincoat is a very small and elegant cell phone and I'm also betting that you can hit one button and be in touch with your CEO or with the vice-president in charge of trespassing issues or with the department of access approval forms or with whoever actually makes decisions and I want you to get that person for me and put she or he—I know I'm not grammatically correct—put her or him on the line.

The decision's been made. It's a moot point now. There's nobody for me to call anymore. Except, maybe, the sheriff.

Carolyn smiled. Let me page him, she said. She raised the bullhorn and glared at her adversary. Sheriff Randolph Nelson, she said. Paging Sheriff Randolph Nelson.

She lowered the bullhorn and shrugged with loose ease. Wherever we go we bring him, she said. The sheriff likes to tag along with us.

How convenient, answered Devine.

They fell into waiting. Carolyn sat beside Ann, against a rock. The immense flock of pilgrims squatted in the trail, perched on logs, leaned against trees, ate, sang, and prayed. Father Butler remarked to Father Collins, You were absolutely right about the weather out here, it's clammy underneath this canopy, I'm chilly and a little damp. But, said Father Collins, the forest is truly marvelous. I feel when I'm here the presence of God. You do? said Father Butler. All well and good. As long as you're not seeing Our Lady.

The sheriff blustered into view with two straight-faced deputies in tow: three men carrying firearms. What's the trouble up here? he asked. There's five thousand people in these woods.

The trouble, said Carolyn, is that guy there with the ironic name of Richard Devine. You'd think that with a name like Devine he'd see the light or something.

Devine handed the sheriff his card. We're trying to do something simple, he said. We're trying to put a stop to trespassing.

The sheriff gave the card a cursory perusal, then handed it back absentmindedly. There's five thousand people out here, he said. Approximately five thousand people.

Precisely the problem, answered Richard Devine. If it was five rather than five thousand, that would be dramatically different. We probably wouldn't much notice or care. But five thousand? That's another story. A difference not only in degree but in quality. We can't allow them on Stinson land in such utterly devastating numbers.

Nelson rubbed his chin, befuddled. He hung his thumbs from his belt buckle, a habit, zipped his jacket and unzipped it. This is a bad situation, he said. You've got your five thousand people here who want to get through to where they're going and set against them me and my deputies and some state patrollers in shiny shoes and that's what we've got to try and stop them. Now if each of us handcuffs one of these people and drags him forcibly out of the woods that still leaves four thousand nine hundred eighty-five to swarm right past us and across the creek, in other words I don't have the logistical capability to enforce your property rights.

In other words, put in Richard Olsen, the mob rules.

Sheriff Nelson frowned at him. These are Christian people, he said. It's not like they want to spike your trees.

No matter their religious affiliation, said Olsen, they pose a danger to the ecosystem here. They threaten the health of this forest.

And, Richard Devine added, while you yourself may not have at hand the means to enforce our property rights, this girl certainly does.

He gestured toward Ann the way a ringmaster gestures at the sequined girl who will put her head in the lion's mouth. Ann had endured the entirety of the debate with her eyes cast down, her face in her sweatshirt hood, but now she looked up at the company factotum with his crown of distinguished silver hair, his ruddy geriatric face. She could do it, said Devine, looking back at her sternly. A few judicious words from her, spoken into that electric bullhorn—a few words from her would resolve this matter. And if she won't comply, won't cooperate, arrest her when she steps across that bridge. That, sheriff, would settle it.

And start a riot too, Nelson replied. Can you imagine me dragging this girl through the woods past five thousand of her followers?

Talk about bad PR, added Carolyn. On top of everything else.

Richard Devine began to knead his fingers. It occurred to Carolyn that he had arthritis, that no place in the world was worse for arthritis, a November morning in the sodden rain forest, frost in the metacarpal joints, mildew in the phalanx bones. You should have brought your gloves, she said. Your cashmere fur-lined gloves.

It's not funny. I have arthritis. I'm not so young anymore.

We'll pray for you, Ann answered quietly. For an end to your arthritis suffering.

Devine let a scoffing chortle escape. My hands especially, will you? he asked. And a special plea for my finger joints?

Somewhere in the forest, far to the rear, a considerable number of pilgrims were singing. The sound of it was ethereal, enchanted, it might have been mere wind in the trees or a distant band of woodland dryads who were also exceptional ventriloquists. Ann stood straining to discern it. She could not quite make out its tone, celebratory hymn or funereal dirge, canticle or lamentation, chant or elegy. But its faint hue seemed aimed at her or came to her as if aimed. As if to her ears privately, a choir of nymphs or angels. I'm called by the Mother of God, she said. I'm called into her presence now. I beg you to let us pass.

Richard Devine blew into his palms, sharp, whistling gasps. Come again? he asked.

Our Lady has blessed and chosen you, said Ann. She's chosen your forest for her appearance. She's calling to you this way.

Who are you to speak for her?

Just a girl. No one else.

What makes you think I should listen to you?

I speak in the name of Our Lady, our glory, our life, our sweetness, and our hope.

She stepped forward. She put her small hand on Devine's right arm. She's like, she said, a light in the forest. A beacon of hope in the woods out here. She's Our Lady, God's love, calling you. Calling to you through me.

Richard Devine removed her hand as though it were a small lizard. Come on now, he said. I guess I appreciate your . . . spirituality. Your zeal and passion for what you believe. But in my book this is plainly psychotic. I don't mean to be insulting, really, but maybe what you need is to see a psychiatrist, get some help, some counseling.

That *is* insulting, said Carolyn. You should apologize to Ann.

Sheriff Nelson shot her the *Be Quiet!* look with which she was already familiar. It implied, she knew, the depth of his revulsion, and even in these current circumstances, demanding, as they did, her undivided attention, she found herself pondering her femininity, wondering if greater sexual allure might alter the sheriff's sentiments. That was Ann's unspoken advantage—her obvious, unearned beauty. Her unblemished skin, her thin little legs, her hard little no-sag breasts. Genetic-luck-of-the-draw features, totally undeserved. Carolyn had never been like that but had acquired, rather, a set of learned wiles that were ultimately a paltry substitute. She had always yearned to be naturally beautiful while knowing, too, that this sort of yearning was humiliating, small, pathetic, misplaced, and starkly, completely embarrassing. I'm ugly, she thought, and it doesn't help me. Not really ugly. Just not attractive. Life is completely unfair.

The sheriff said, We'd better do something. And do it quick. Because these people are going to cross this creek one way or the other, I feel that.

You do something, said Richard Devine. Because I'm finally just exasperated with it. And you're the law around here.

This isn't the Wild West, said the sheriff. I'm not the law, I'm law *enforcement*. When I can, that's what I do—enforce. But I can't enforce the law right now. Not right now, in these circumstances. If you want to give some prior warning, put up signs, make things clear, let people know ahead of time—all right, we can probably make that stick. Probably. No promises. You all have a history of letting people in, deer hunters in particular. But I guess we could arrest people on account of prior warning. You'd have to get your message out. You'd have to let people know, No Trespassing, and give them time to get used to it. Maybe we can agree on twenty-four hours? Twenty-four hours of getting the word out, plenty of advance work, legwork? So people know a line has been drawn? People know you're serious? The land can be posted with No Trespassing signs. You get your signs up, make announcements. Twenty-four hours sounds right.

That's twenty-four hours of damage, though, Richard Olsen countered.

I don't know, the sheriff said. Maybe you could plant new trees or something. If that's a concern. Plant new ones.

Trees are money, said Carolyn. That's all they really care about—money. Not trees or anything. Money.

You shut up, said the sheriff.

Devine did indeed have a cell phone that was even smaller than Carolyn had predicted and after he'd used it at ridiculous length, standing an aloof twenty yards downstream, redialing a number of times, talking to a variety of people, waving his arms and pacing the bank, holding his temple again in his hand with his eyes shut, grimacing—after all his gesticulating and animated hobnobbing, he tucked the cell phone angrily in his coat pocket, stumbled on a root walking back upstream, and told the sheriff that the Stinson Company agreed to the twenty-four-hour proviso and would allow today's pilgrims to proceed.

Carolyn immediately raised her bullhorn. We're about to move forward again! she announced. You will find a small new bridge at the creek which you should cross with care and as you do, don't neglect to put something in the bucket, two of Ann's followers will be on hand to accept your wonderful contributions in support of Mother Mary's new church!

That's the next step, she said to Devine, arm in arm with Ann again and making her way toward the bridge. First you give us twenty-four hours. Then we build a church on your land. That's the way these things work.

On the wheelchair ramp she swiveled like royalty. Excuse me, she said to the nearest follower. But could you maybe stand here and collect a toll so we can build the church Our Blessed Mother wants? And, she said to those nearby, please give us space on the other side. Ann needs space now in which to meditate and prepare to meet Our Lady.

She and Ann crossed at a stately pace Carolyn enforced. The others waited and let them walk ahead, though two sentinels followed at the minimum distance for private conversation. In the forest of blowdowns, hung from trees, were crucifixes, rosaries, crepe-paper roses, and a wooden cross clearly carved on the spot by a pilgrim adept with a pocketknife and adept at braiding strips of cedar bark into a rudimentary twine. Along the trail—tucked into the furrows of the firs, spiked into rotting logs with twigs, weighted down under spruce cones and stones—were bits of paper bearing petitions, some in small plastic sandwich bags, others in sealed envelopes, others folded into origami birds, others embellished with artwork or calligraphy, and these were collected by a pair of Ann's followers and dropped into mushroom buckets. Set about on stumps and logs were statues of the Rosa Mystica, the Black Madonna, Our Lady of Lourdes, the Infant of Prague, a lamb, Our Lady of Fátima, and Our Lady of Scottsdale. There were also lighted votive candles, miraculous medals, and a variety of small framed photographs—of the pope smiling beneficently, Teresa of Ávila, John of the Cross, and Christ beneath his crown of thorns, suffering cryptically. This is a little weird, said Carolyn. All these strange little forest totems. All of this weird religious stuff just sitting out here like this.

There's going to be two more visits, said Ann. Our Lady has promised to come two more days. So twenty-four hours—it's not enough.

Hey, said Carolyn. Don't complain. I got you over that bridge, didn't I? So let's cross the next one when we come to it, okay? We can worry about other stuff later.

They're going to put up No Trespassing signs.

Well what do you want me to do about that?

I want you to talk to them and get them not to do it.

Carolyn hugged tightly Ann's small hooded

head. Tell you what, said Carolyn. Why don't you talk to Mother Mary? And get her to talk to God and Jesus? Maybe they could have a family conference and straighten these problems out.

Family conference. That's not right.

Well I don't know what you're supposed to call it. It's all unimaginable anyway. Like what is the deal with Christians in the first place? Are God and Jesus really the same person or could they like have a conversation, a father-and-son heart-to-heart now and then, Let me show you how to catch trout, Son, or Hey Jesus, did I tell you how sex works? And Mary who's now your closest friend, where does she fit in exactly, is she just a woman who stepped out on her husband and came up with a bad explanation like—it's God who got me pregnant, Joe, now stop worrying about me and go herd your sheep—or is she part of the so-called "Godhead" which also includes this bizarre third party known only as the Holy Ghost?

She's Our Savior's mother. You know that.

Yeah but it seems like if you throw in Mary what you've really got is a quartet, Ann. A group of four, not a trinity. The Fab Four, with Ringo as Mary, Paul as God, John as Jesus the crucified one, and George as the Holy Ghost.

Stop thinking, Carolyn. It's a mystery.

Thought is my way. My path. My yoga. How am I not supposed to think? How do I turn off my brain?

Your brain can never get you there.

Then I guess I don't really want to go. And where is *there,* by the way?

They left the forest of blowdowns behind and negotiated the steep hill northward. Last Thursday, said Carolyn, it was just you and me. Up here rooting around for mushrooms and eating apricots out of my handkerchief. You were just plain Ann from the campground. Just that girl in the next little campsite. Now we're dragging around five thousand fanatics who bring us tea and yogurt for breakfast. It's just so completely unbelievable, Saint Ann. It just makes me want to laugh.

Our Lady brought her followers here.

Whatever you say.

She brought you too.

Okay—she brought me.

Well why are you here then?

I really couldn't tell you, said Carolyn.

It's because of Our Lady. That's why. Our Lady.

Whatever you say, repeated Carolyn.

The path through the Oregon grape and salal was as though trimmed artfully with electric shears and put Carolyn in mind of topiary in a Victorian English garden. They stopped here to rest momentarily while Ann blew her nose and coughed in her fist so that first the sentinels caught up with them, then the spryer journalists and photographers mingled with impatient pilgrims. The sweating priests eventually arrived too, Father Butler wiping his brow, Father Collins with his overcoat draped across one forearm like a gentleman on his daily constitutional. The priests, it seemed, had engaged each other in a stringent theological row, the sort of altercation that passes time during a woodland hike. But I have, said Father Butler, always decried the image of Mary as an avatar of passive femininity and propound her instead when I propound her at all as an icon of genuine female empowerment. You may decry such, said Father Collins, nevertheless the Church plays its sorry part in perpetuating her image as handmaid of the Lord, juxtaposed against Eve. I wouldn't be so certain of that, said Father Butler, there are factions and then again there are factions. Father Collins gravely shook his head, The basic thrust from Rome is the same, barefoot and pregnant and exclaiming after Gabriel Be it done unto me according to thy Word, Be it done unto me, it's sexual passivity, anyone reasonable can see that. The Angelus, said Father Butler, is an exaltation. Or a devotion composed in the twelfth century. I wouldn't read too much into it. More to the point is the

OUR LADY OF THE FOREST

Magnificat, Collins, if I were making your spe-
cious argument. The exultant prayer of Our Lady
herself. But I don't know how much you could
make of it. I'm not sure it's really of assistance to
you while you devise your tangled web.

Here, said Father Collins, is where the Hebrew
comes in. The missing Aramaic no one adheres to.
Ecce ancilla Domini. Fiat mihi secundum verbum tuum.
Does the Latin catch the original substance? Be it
done unto me according to thy word. "Done unto
me." Is that quite it? As opposed to your reference
from the Gospel of Luke? Wherein we have "be it
unto me according to thy word," note the sense of
"done" is not included, at least in accurate transla-
tions. So no one is doing anything to anybody, no
one is getting "done," Father Butler—unless
Rome says so, I guess, afterward. Having excised
the feminine principle entirely from the godhead.

You sound like Graves regurgitated.

Graves makes sense. So does Jung. And Goethe
too, *Das Ewig-Weibliche.* We aren't going anywhere decent, you know, without the Woman-
Soul.

Father Butler began cleaning his glasses. It's the
times, he said. The tenor of the times. You're simply full of sixties backwash and can't help being
faddish and foolish any more than, I don't know,
let me think of somebody. What about Timothy
Leary?

You're out of touch, Father Butler. Father Bill. I humbly submit you're out of touch.

Well I look for what is universal. Universal and timeless, I suppose. Not merely the flavor of the moment. Because fads are ephemeral by definition. But God—God remains.

So does Mary. Insistently.

Yes, but as handmaid of the Lord.

The procession pushed into the dank-smelling forest with its moss-veiled vine maples, nursery logs, devil's club coverts, and fern grottoes. It came to the dark and uneasy grove where Ann's apparitions had ensued. The limbs of the trees here were seized by moss as if in suspended animation. Like crab claws on the sea floor, desiccated by years. A vast photosynthesis covertly went forward and its hallmark was utter stillness. No birds sang. Sojourners in this silent landscape expected something imminent ahead which on reflection couldn't be named. They felt as someone in a landscape painting looks whose purpose is to indicate scale and imply his own insignificance. The density, girth, and magnitude of trees made feeling small transcendental. Some of the pilgrims experienced religious awe and indulged an instinctive animism. Others felt like gentrified adventurers with knapsacks, walking sticks, and volumes of poetry reciting Whitman on a New World promontory overlooking an abyss. Theirs was a majestic claustrophobia, a darkness infused with largesse. For them this was a chilly northern jungle shot by Ansel Adams on an optimistic day or a Bierstadt landscape if Bierstadt had wandered into forested higher latitudes. All was green and good and godly. All was God's evidence, God's sign. Except what belonged to Satan.

Ann walked with eyes cast down, as much the attitude of the highly devout as it was of the humble mushroom picker still instinctively casting for chanterelles. She retrieved a handful of petitions from the ground and picked up a Saint Christopher medal that made her remember against her will the Saint Christopher medal Mark Kidd had worn and how on more than one occasion he had forced her to clutch it between her teeth because that gave him an erotic charge while he held her by the throat and raped her. At those times she'd felt asthmatically strangled, close to death by asphyxiation; she'd felt the world of the living slip away in a flood of phosphorescent darkness. Walking, Ann tried to deflect her shame as she had tried many other times. She was sometimes seized not as much by memory as by the acute recognition of her haplessness in the face of physical aggression. Was rape, too, the will of God, like earthquakes, mud slides, and Sudden Infant Death Syndrome? Like everything that happened to Job? Like Jesus' crucifixion? Ann unfolded a petition and read, *Dear Blessed Ann of Oregon. My name is Sydney Ellen Mullen. Six weeks ago I was diagnosed with leukemia by a doctor in Reno, Nevada, where we live. I am married, 29 years old and have two children, a boy Joel 5 and a girl Erin 3. My husband is a firefighter and I have left him at home with our children in Reno so I could come here and, I pray, be healed by you. God bless.*

I tried Christian Science but was not impressed, especially because I still have leukemia even after doing what it says in Science and Health with Key to the Scriptures *and am supposed to be getting radiation this week and at the start of next week. A lot of thoughts go through your head when you're traveling alone (plus I slept in the car on the way, so that meant lonely night hours). One is that radiation and chemo are gifts from God and in turning away from both those treatments maybe I'm turning away from Him, which I don't want to be. So I guess I should take the radiation and chemo. A lot of people are helped by them. Maybe what God really gives us are miracles like radiation and chemo. What do you think about that possibility?*

There's a verse from Isaiah *I like a lot: Fear thou not; for I am with thee: be not dismayed; for I am thy God: I will strengthen thee; yea, I will help thee; yea, I will uphold thee with the right hand of my righteousness. This gives me strength. But it also raises issues. Maybe radiation is the right hand of righteousness. I think this trip up into the forests has convinced me I should just do the treatments, trust to the doctors and just do them, have faith. But I'm afraid of nausea. In radiation they slowly kill you in order to kill the cancer cells, which scares me. I'm afraid. That's the bottom line. I'm scared.*

I believe in Our Lady and in prayers to Her & hope you will keep me in your prayers & will help me to find a miracle today & will ask Our Lady to intercede when you speak to her next time, please. And God bless & keep—Sydney Mullen.

There were a few hundred of these.

While the multitudes gathered at the place of apparitions, a report circulated that somewhere in the forest a statue of the Black Madonna had begun to glow a copper hue and that all around it in a shaft of light gold dust fell from the sky. In another version, rose petals fell as silently as snow while the Black Madonna radiated light in a nimbus or a halo. It was also said that these phenomena accrued in fact not to the Black Madonna but to a statue of Our Lady of Lourdes. Either way, pilgrims discussed and celebrated this meaningful adjunct spiritual occurrence. Some wandered off to see in privacy to their inevitable personal needs. Carolyn made a bullhorn speech about proper woodland sanitation, the principles of which were far easier to describe than to put into present practice. Most of the pilgrims did not want to dig or saw no valid reason to dig or would not entertain the possibility of digging without a tool. Instead they lifted out a swatch of moss, did what they came to do, and replaced the moss in, at best, superficial and cursory deference to etiquette. There were soon five hundred of these barely disguised shitholes and, before much longer, at least a thousand. Richard Olsen pointed some out to Sheriff Nelson and said, It's just what I warned you about, Sheriff, a health inspector who came up here would shut this all down right away. We already decided on twenty-four hours, said Nelson. And believe me, nature will clean things up. Shit don't really hurt dirt.

Pilgrims came forward to the altar of ferns and left more candles, photographs, petitions, crucifixes, rosaries, and flowers. They left money, an umbrella, a sweatshirt, a camera, and a packet of chewing tobacco. A group had hauled in a half-life-size plaster statue of Our Lady of Fátima which was propped against a hemlock tree and garlanded with a crown of moss. A little like Aphrodite there, said Father Butler to Father Collins. These people are closet polytheists.

Well welcome to the real Catholic Church, Father Bill. Which is really composed of real people, isn't it. People with valid spiritual instincts instead of endless liturgy.

This is *not* Catholicism.

I suppose you're still for the Latin mass.

I am, yes. If you want to know.

Well there's no going back to pre–Vatican Two.

I think that's a shame, said Father Butler.

Someone handed him a packet of photographs as large as a deck of playing cards. On top was a Polaroid marked "Door to Heaven," a large rectangle of blinding sunlight referred to briefly in Revelation, *After this I looked and lo, in heaven an open door!* Very nice, remarked Father Butler, examining it with clearly feigned interest. Very interesting. Exceptional. He handed the photos back, stifling a yawn. The door to heaven up among the clouds. Be sure these get well circulated. There's no need to leave them with me.

There's one charlatan, he said to Father Collins, who claims to have invented what he calls the Photonic Ionic Cloth Radio Amplifier Maser. I'm not pulling your leg, he said. That's what it's called. Acronym PICRAM. B-movie science-fiction apparatus. The visionary is supposed to hold it in her hands during the course of an apparition and it produces, I don't know, waves on an oscilloscope. Telltale waves. Our Lady's sine wave. It looks like pre–Buck Rogers technology. Like it's full of radio tubes.

I never said this whole business was otherwise. Father Collins' hip felt sore, inflamed and tight from woodland walking. But I think you should give her a fair chance.

Well just so you know where I stand, no matter what.

Except that it's such a biased posture from which to begin an investigation.

I suppose so, said Father Butler. But I do have a bias against fakery. Against shams perpetuated in the name of our Church. Is there something wrong with that?

Maybe Lourdes looked like this in the beginning.

Maybe it didn't. Or if it did, so what?

So consider both possibilities equally.

That's precisely my job, said Father Butler. My mission and my mandate.

From her place in the vale of concealing sword ferns, squatting on her heels next to Carolyn, listening to the swelling crowd now singing an antiphon called Alma Redemptoris Mater, Ann shut her eyes, made the sign of the cross, and said the Apostles' Creed. She said an Our Father, three Hail Marys, Glory be to the Father, and to the Son, and to the Holy Ghost, As it was in the beginning, is now, and ever shall be, world without end. Amen. Then she moved out to the fern altar and knelt with her back turned toward the crowd, removed her hood, dropped her head, and silently announced the first Joyful Mystery while all went silent watching her, the Joyful Mystery of the Annunciation, whose fruit, she knew, was humility. She said privately another Our Father and ten Hail Marys, during which she tried to imagine the moment in which Gabriel appeared to Mary exclaiming, The Holy Ghost shall come upon thee, and the power of the Highest shall overshadow thee: therefore also that holy thing which shall be born of thee shall be called the Son of God. Was there fear then? Did Mary suspect the devil's work, that Lucifer, disguised, might be the supernatural one who intended to plant his seed? Was her fear greater in the dark hours, did she flee from sleep and dreams? Did she consider sticking herself, breaking her water? Was she horrified by this inexplicable pregnancy and did she suspect a monster would split her legs at the moment of birth in Bethlehem? Did she hope for a stillbirth? Did the baby himself disturb her initially? Did she suspect—in retrospect—that the advent of Gabriel was merely a hallucination? Did she blame Joseph for believing she lied, for surely he must have felt cuckolded? How could she be married, a virgin, and pregnant—all three? Did she wonder if Gabriel would appear again and did she yearn for that because after his visit her ordinary life paled by comparison to the experience of an angel saying she was highly favored, blessed among all women? Was that humility? Or was she frightened of his reappearance and wanting nothing other than the peace and suffering of an ordinary peasant existence? And was that arrogance? What was this growing in her belly—trouble, insanity, a miracle, faith, the seed of an angel, the seed of the Lord, the seed of a terrible incubus? She labored and it seemed like nothing in particular, nothing out of line, out of order. Then here came these prostrate worshipers with their gold, frankincense, and myrrh. Did she want that? Would she make something of it? Parlay it into more? Was he a monster? Seraph? Cherub? Demon? Later the boy is lost in Jerusalem and discovered impressing rabbis. Is she proud or afraid of the prophecy now? He turns water into wine—is he the son of Beelzebub, and is she Beelzebub's consort? Scary. Who is that person sleeping over there, the issue of my womb? But then he's crucified. While it might be Our Savior who expired at Calvary it is also her child, dead in her arms, could there be anything more painful? Woman, behold thy son! said Jesus, and those were real thorns, a real stab wound, who could look at real nails, spikes, piercing the hands of a son? The ankles crossed, the head hung. No, no, no, that is just my son, what kind of cosmic misunderstanding has brought him to this tortured death? The Fifth Sorrowful Mystery, Crucifixion, whose fruit was perseverance. Ann said another Glory Be. A decade of Hail Marys, then O my

Jesus, forgive us our sins, save us from the fires of hell, lead all souls to heaven, especially those who have most need of your mercy, and she heard Mary say Behold daughter, it is I again as promised. And fear not for I know your thoughts.

Standing in a wheel of light, an incandescent disk. Her hands before her spread generously. And dressed in white, the beauteous one. Fair, maternal, shimmering shade, her expression beneficent but cryptic too, seeing the world from the right hand of God, from the other side of death.

Hail Mary, full of grace, whispered Ann.

Fear not but call my followers forth. My Son is angry. Call them forth. They shall renew their service to Our Lord through me.

Yes Mother.

And through me they shall spread his message. And I shall stay the hand of my Son, as only a mother might.

Yes Mother.

The greedy shall turn giving, selfless. And there will be an end to poverty, so be it.

Yes Mother full of grace and kindness.

I will return once more, be sure of this, daughter. Daughter, you must build our church. You must enlist the support of your priest.

May I speak, Mother? Just for a moment? Forgive me. I am nothing. Nothing but your willing sheep. But I am asked by many to plead with

you—to beg of you—to please intercede,
Mother. Sydney Ellen Mullen, who has leukemia.
Others too—hundreds of them. To help them in
their time of need.

I know your thoughts, daughter. Be not afraid.
I am with thee. I am your Mother. Now dig in
the earth. As I say. Dig in the holy earth.

Ann did as beckoned. She pulled the stratum of
moss aside and clawed into the black humus with
its effluvium of death and leaves. Immediately,
water welled up in the tiny pool she'd formed,
black water that smelled of the grave. More muck
than water—mud. When she looked up, the
Mother of God was gone. Carolyn knelt beside
her now. I should have expected this, said
Carolyn. You people always find holy water.

The roads had numbers, not names. At one time,
not even numbers. But before the Forest Service
became bent on digits there was a grassroots system of reference. So for Tom, FS 171 was the
South Fork, east at 171D was Ford Creek, south-
east at 1711 was Ford Mountain, south at 1711A
was the Ford Ridge Units, otherwise known as
the Ford Sale. By virtue of so many turnoffs—and
so much distance—this area of the forest was little
frequented. An unnumbered spur road ran below
Ford Ridge into Ford Unit Two for three-quar-

ters of a mile before coming to a lazy Y. One leg was a cat track dead-ending higher up while the main spur ran to a log deck landing where in '86 Tom ran a skyline show—eleven guys, a haulback and carriage, a yarder, and a good-sized loader. A sale in the boonies, on the way to nowhere. Tom had hunted blacktail here. Camped in the landing sometimes alone and sometimes with Greg Kruse, his hunting partner. Kruse was divorced, remarried, divorced again. Two ex-wives, five kids. Decked out in his camo jacket, drinking quart bottles of beer by the fire and talking about important matters like the smell of snatch and big tits. Perched on a log amid the charred remains of Tom's sixty-acre clear-cut. Stumps, stick alder, vine maple, drifts of unburned slash, old cables, beer cans, fireweed, snowbrush, bracken, and the cassette drive in Kruse's truck playing Lynyrd Skynyrd. *Won't you gimme three steps, gimme three steps mister, gimme three steps toward the door?* Saying, She smells . . . skanky. And Tom going along because it was easier than saying he wasn't interested. Answering, Well that's a good smell, you notice they get older you don't get that smell. Shit sticks to you, Kruse noted, self-absorbed. Can't wash it off—like skunk or something. Why would you want to? Tom asked dutifully. Smell it all day. Lay back and suck it in. Skank, said Kruse. That's a good word. Even if technically it ain't a

word. Is skank a word? Who cares? said Tom.
Bury your nose in it and be grateful.

The place was haunted by this tiresome business. By two lengths of rebar in the fire pit. Tom
recognized his own crimped beer cans still there
among the damp gray ashes, Budweiser washed
out by the elements. Greg Kruse. Where was
Greg Kruse? He hadn't seen Kruse in a year at
least. Tom bolted down his truck canopy, squared
away his gear, rolled his sleeping bag out across
the mattress, and lay down listening to the rain
rattle the fiberglass shell above his head. At least,
he thought, I have a job.

Though maybe not. Did the world want a
prison guard who carried with him assorted mis-
demeanors and medium-weight legal baggage?
He didn't know. Maybe it didn't. Anyway, he'd
find out when he found out. Tonight, he knew,
was a possibility, they could fire him when he
showed up for his shift, though he doubted
Nelson had the time or inclination to clue them
in just now. Not with North Fork seized by
strangers, the whole county inundated. So there
was a plus to these new circumstances: Nelson
was so frazzled and distracted it freed Tom up for
petty crime. Minor infractions Nelson couldn't be
bothered with, what he had to deal with was
crowd control. Tom shifted in his sleeping bag
and turned onto his side. Pin had probably called

Nelson about the mattress around the same time
Eleanor called about the canopy. What did that
mean? What could it mean? For one it meant Pin
couldn't rent the cabin until he got a new mattress
delivered. Tom hadn't thought of that. An added
expense, lost revenue. But probably those Hindus
looked at it such: This is the price we had to pay
to get rid of that horrible maintenance man, you
have to take the good with the bad, at least he's
hightailed it out of here, we're clear of all his dan-
gers. Okay, they were right. Tom knew he had
gone off, been pissed and irrational, but at least he
could breathe now. Nobody would hassle him
way out here. This felt good. This was better. He
climbed out, unlocked the cab, and retrieved his
.44 and a 12-gauge shotgun. He placed them in
easy reach of his right hand and tried to fall asleep.

He'd done this long ago with Junior—slept in
the pick-up with firearms ready. They'd gone to a
rodeo in eastern Montana just for the hell of it together. And because Tom wanted Junior to go.
Thinking maybe a change of scene would kick-
start him, the dust and the broncs with their nuts
cinched up, the gimpy rednecked riders. But
Junior hadn't much cared for rodeo and got bored
during the calf-roping event so they went for chili
dogs and jo-jos. They rode the Ferris wheel which
Junior seemed to dreamily enjoy, commenting on
the generous view of grasslands underneath the

widespread stars, and then Junior sat through three bumper-car sessions getting bashed around continuously but never figuring out how to bash people himself even though Tom yelled instructions. There were a lot of drunks around. There was an Indian encampment with dancers in headdress and stick games played by leathery old people and it was this Junior seemed most fascinated by, he'd wanted to hang around the Indians, he'd wanted to watch the dancers gyrate and the old people move their sticks in the dust, he'd wanted to listen to the Indian singers and the beating of the Indian drums. So be it. That was fine. They stayed until Junior got tired, drowsy. He was eleven years old and had cotton candy stuck to the corners of his mouth and a sunburned forehead. They'd walked back through a boisterous night crowd to the pick-up. The parking lot was full of campers and horse trailers and people sitting out on lawn chairs drinking and listening to loud music and watching, in the distance, the bungee jumpers lit by a spotlight, and there were dogs milling about. They'd left their own dog, a mutt named Jack, tied off to the rear bumper with a bowl of water and when they came back at 2 a.m. Tom fed him kibble with leftover jo-jos and then he and Junior got in the pick-up bed and lay there with the rear canopy window open because it was a tepid summer night.

There'd been boozers and lowlifes everywhere though, shouting, carrying on, and carousing, and the drums and singing from the Indian camp, and Tom heard someone taunting his dog, he'd listened more closely and discerned it was two Indians, you could tell by their clipped, closed manner of speech, the way they buried their words in their chins, they were taunting Jack and he knew right away he wasn't putting up with that, fuck these god damn motherfucking horse people, I'm a god damn motherfucking shit-kicking logger, and he'd nudged Junior awake and whispered Watch this, then thumbed two shells into his shotgun's magazine, one for each of the assholes outside, and kicked the tailgate open hard with the Indians shocked by the drama of that into a freighted silence. And in that interim Tom chambered a shell with forceful, meaningful emphasis and said, Get away from the dog.

They did. Right away. Nothing. They were gone. Junior sat up, breathing hard. A telltale irritating sickly wheeze. Dad, he'd said. Was that all right? They were messing with Jack, Tom said to him. You don't let anyone mess with you. You put 'em on their heels when you have to.

The boy had talked about it all the way home. He'd brought it up in Butte and again near Spokane. What if they'd had their own guns? he'd asked. What if they hadn't gone away? What if there was an argument? Tom said, Stop worrying it. You point the business end of a shotgun at somebody things generally go your way. But you weren't going to shoot those guys, were you? said Junior. Not just over Jack, right? Don't you like Jack? Yeah—I like him. Shouldn't we protect him? I guess, yeah. Isn't it our job to protect him? Because he's our dog? So we've got to protect him? I don't know, said Junior.

Tom had told that story to Kruse, who'd argued Junior was probably right, unless you were actually willing to shoot people just because they were teasing your dog you probably shouldn't push the stakes so high right off the bat. I *was* willing to shoot them, Tom had answered. Now he wondered again why he hadn't heard from Kruse, who'd disappeared after Junior's accident. Tom could guess. For the same reason he would have disappeared himself if a tree fell on someone else's son. You put some money in the can, said you were sorry a couple of times, maybe offered to help with something, but then, after that— what next? Dwell on it? Let it in? How could you go on with logging that way? Didn't everyone prefer that you go about your business and let the miserable have their misery? No, thought Tom, I don't blame Kruse. Things are bad enough around here without me spreading grief.

And that was right. Why make people uncom-

fortable by showing up? They couldn't concentrate with Tom around, Tom could see that
without much effort, how his walking into
MarketTime was highly upsetting, just his walking in was nerve-wracking, made people jittery,
uncomfortable. So fine. He knew how to go
away, not show up, travel through town like a
shadow. And at least other loggers knew what was
up, knew what he knew about things. They all
knew—accidents happen. Some poor fool has to
be aggrieved. You had to hold up your end of the
bargain and let other guys walk away from you
when bad luck took over your existence. Because
other guys had work to do. And what was left
over at the end of the day? Just enough to straggle in, lay on the couch, and work up the energy
to get the garbage out. Maybe now and then give
lip service to caring about the chance calamities
of others because women demanded it and it was
easier to pretend you gave a shit than to tell the
truth: that you didn't.

And that was the truth: he didn't. What could
he say? He didn't. Instead he enjoyed killing animals. Fish, deer, grouse. He liked having a freezer
full of meat. He liked to get laid as long as it
wasn't either too complicated or too simple,
which meant he thought about it way more than
he did it. He liked knowing he could beat the shit
out of most other men. He liked to work and at

the same time hated to work and wished he didn't have to—but then what? Did the things he liked mean indeed he was twisted, as the boy at the prison had asserted? Tom didn't think so, but he believed other people would. Any marriage counselor or psychiatrist would charge him plenty to call him twisted yet he considered himself normal and the men he knew were the same. Though he didn't know many men these days. At a certain point he'd stopped wanting company. He liked things exactly the way he liked them and that meant accommodating no one. So of course Kruse was gone. Kruse probably wanted to hunt by himself too. It wasn't any sort of falling-out. Eventually they would see each other and nothing, so what, as if they had never stopped hunting together, stopped carrying on their friendship. Because there was no friendship to carry on; women didn't understand that.

Tom slept fitfully, in the throes of morose reveries. At four he thought he'd put a twilight hour into tracking blacktail and laced his boots, loaded a rifle, poured water into a canteen, polished the lenses of his binoculars, ate beef jerky, and all these preparations felt purifying. He worked down the unit to the bank of Ford Creek where he washed his face in the swirl of an eddy, laid out over a rock. No breeze. The water gave him a headache. He immersed his face twice. He

boulder-hopped and hiked upstream staying out
of the brush, his walking covered by stream noise,
thinking this was one of the problems with Kruse,
the guy was just too noisy on the move. Tom had
said to him Just think about it Kruse, if I can hear
you then they can hear you, but that didn't
change the way Kruse did things until finally they
hunted separate canyons and just spent camp time
together. He snuck up on Kruse once silently and
broke a branch at twenty yards and when Kruse
turned bringing his rifle up Tom called, See what
I mean, Greg? You heard that, didn't you. That
was me stalking you like you were a buck and
when you heard the branch, you were on to me.
And they've got better ears than you do.

Fuck you, said Kruse. I almost shot you.

Tom wasn't really hunting now. He was just
out walking with a deer rifle for the hell of it.
And looking for sign along the creek aimlessly.
And staying out of the open places where there
were long views a buck could use while descend-
ing toward feed and drink. Tom sat for a while
doing nothing on a slope of mountain blueberry.
He'd passed a lot of time like this watching does
pull the horsehair lichen from tree branches and
browse fir needles and twigs. Now the light was
lower. The November twilight was tangibly brief.
He lay back and let his rifle rest across his hips and
stared up through the interstices of the blueberry

into the dark branches of the trees. Eleanor, he said out loud. He recalled one of their blueberry expeditions, driving back into town for cream, eating the blueberries and cream in bed, eating them from her breasts at first, then from the triangle of hair between her legs, he felt a transitory urge to jerk off which he suppressed in favor of moving upstream again where he saw a red-legged frog on a rock and collected a handful of chanterelles. He hadn't shaved in four days. He would need to shave before work tonight, which he could do in the rest room of the minimart in town. Things had come to that.

He didn't worry about the dark. He wasn't afraid. He had an unusual ability to see nocturnally. Where other people tripped and led with their hands, he saw well and easily. All it took was the last of the sun or a little moon or starlight and he was perfectly capable of finding his way to wherever he was going. He boulder-hopped and walked downstream to the lowest corner of Unit Two and stood on the first scorched stump inside the fireline with its fringe of dead fireweed and bracken. There'd been a tailblock somewhere down here and he looked for its telltale markings. Unit Two had cleared him, he recalled, something like four thousand dollars. If you didn't count interest payments. For sixty acres of trees.

There were no deer. He hadn't expected any.

There were no stars; thick cloud cover. Tom shouldered his rifle and fired at the clouds. The sound of it rippled over the hills. The sound of it ripped a hole in the heavens, albeit a small hole. But a hole nonetheless. Joy nonetheless. His thunderstick was powerful. He loved the magic of it. A man making a loud noise and wielding death from a distance was surely more than nothing. Or could pretend to be. To himself and to the world, but not to God of course, because God knew the difference. In spite of that he fired again, a shot nearly as gratifying. The only thing he knew as pleasurable was felling a large tree perfectly. Back when Cross Logging was a viable entity he'd sought perfection as a matter of course, as if there were no alternative. He'd made his back cuts and his finish cuts with art, as if his saw were a scalpel. One delicate row of fiber at a time. As much holding wood as physics would allow. There would come a point of no return and he would shut his saw down, beat his retreat, crane his neck, and tilt his hard hat while the tree creaked, poised, a slow death. He could raze a whole forest for that satisfaction and never have enough of so doing. He'd liked it all, the ride to earth, the litterfall, the new shaft of sunlight riddled with gnats, the tree on the forest floor. He'd liked directing the fall of trees, guiding them into their resting places. It was what he knew and it was useless now.

He drove toward town on Forest Service roads sinuous and hypnotic in his high beams. The rain had slowed to the merest steam, a mild carbonated mist. It seemed rather to condense on his windshield than to fall out of the sky. There was no right speed for the windshield wipers, which demanded sporadic attention. Tom pulled over when he came to the South Fork to stand by the river with a cigarette in hand and watch the rain strike the current. The fishing would not have improved yet, he thought. The rivers were all high, out of shape.

At the highway he turned north and pulled in at the minimart, where he stood in line for coffee and two hot dogs. All of the burritos, fried chicken, bundles of kindling, gallon cans of white gas, toilet paper, and motor oil had been sold. There was mud on the floor and a line at the rest room, lines of cars at the gas bays, and a line of campers at the propane tank. The clerk at the cash register, Suzanne Rhoades, said I guess all this craziness is good for business but Tom what's it doing to my peace of mind? and handed him his change without touching his fingers or looking him in the eye. Tom ate sitting at the wheel of his truck and decided to come back at eleven to shave because right now shaving in the minimart rest room was a selfish proposition. By eleven—maybe—things would be different. So that gave him evening hours to kill. He drove down Main behind a throng of cars, splashed into a mud-puddle parking spot at Gip's that opened fortuitously while he'd circled for parking, and checked his post office box. Health insurance bill, therapy bill, lab bill, electric bill, collection agency threatening letter—the one piece of mail he felt compelled to open—bank statement, and three advertising circulars. Tom stuffed all of it back in the box as if to make it disappear that way and walked with his plastic garbage bag of laundry and his nearly empty carton of Borax toward the Korean laundromat. Its name had been changed under the current proprietors from North Fork Laundry to Kim's. Why? What was wrong with North Fork Laundry? What private sentiment or business principle had inspired Kim to make the change, which after all must have cost money? Was it pride and defiance, like the Jews? Anyway the place was cleaner, he'd have to give Kim that. The grime was gone from the windowsills and the lineoleum floor had been waxed. Tom had seen Kim himself only once, a small neat man collecting his coins before sweeping the place with a push broom. Tom had pretended to read a magazine while noting Kim's high-strung Asian efficiency when it came to sweeping a floor. The little man had shuffled near wearing his squinty-eyed poker face until finally they traded expressionless glances and then both looked away rapidly. Otherwise Kim was invisible. He might have lived in Timbuktu. An absentee profiteer, probably busy with a chain of laundromats. Or maybe, Tom thought, he and Mrs. Kim and Pin and Jabari played mah-jongg together on Friday nights and discussed new ways to appropriate the town while drinking ginseng tea and smoking opium from a hookah. Who knew? Maybe they all got naked together and did the positions in the Kama Sutra, The Pancake Flip, The Foul Ball, Camel With Three Humps, Around The World, Tiger About To Pounce. . . .

Kim's was crowded. Everyone there doing laundry was a stranger. The locals had retreated into their rat holes. There were no good-looking women present. Tom liked glimpses of damp bras moiled up among other laundry as it was moved from washer to dryer. He liked to hear the catches of bras clanking against dryer drums. He associated the smell of newly washed laundry with the promise of sexual activity because Eleanor had habitually showered at night and come to bed in a clean nightie, smelling washed. Back in the old days, in the olden times, when there was plenty of that married good stuff. But every woman in the laundromat now was fundamentally unappealing. There was no one he could even work himself up to. Tom found a machine, poured in quarters, and started a load of whites. Kim's getting rich tonight, he thought. Then he checked his watch and walked down Main to the Big Bottom.

He could have one or two. Three at the outside. He had to be straight for work at midnight. Tom thought the Big Bottom might be a haven but even it was full of strangers. Mother Mary's followers, apparently, needed drinks as much as anyone. And Monday Night Football. Was that a sin? The Raiders led the Broncos by two touchdowns and a field goal. Some of the Mother Mary people were cheering after tackles but locals held down both the pool tables, a minor depressing triumph. Tom took a chair and waited for Tammy Buckwalter with lascivious anticipation. For some reason, he was needy tonight. He would not have predicted feeling this way but you could never predict such a thing, he'd found, it happened whenever it happened. He watched Tammy working the tables, plump and delectable inside her jeans, attractively disheveled and out of shape. She ignored him, he saw, intentionally, pulling beers and laying them down, wiping tables and collecting money as if she didn't know he was there. Which was telling. It meant she *did* know. A sense of professionalism must have finally kicked in because at last she showed up with a tray in hand and an expression of exaggerated disdain. He noted her midriff hanging over the waist of her jeans which he had to admit was sexy. Carnal memories have their own kinetic energy, their own internal impetus, and he felt he wanted to do Tammy again, but this time more languorously, really go with it. Tammy, he said. I'm a loser, baby. You heard that song? My daughter listens to it. She gets in the truck and puts it on. I'm a loser baby so why don't you kill me.

Okay.

Go ahead and do it. Kill me.

On second thought it's too much trouble.

I'll make it easy for you this time, Tammy.

We already tried that.

We can try again.

I vote no. Definitely. Now what kind of beer do you want?

Tom said, Whatever's on tap. You think it over, Tammy.

She tucked the tray beneath her armpit. If I think it over I'll puke, she said. Your tap beer is on the way.

Tom watched football and scrutinized strangers. He was back at the Big Bottom drinking beer and couldn't explain the fact. A recurring dream. His beer arrived with no pleasantries attached except Tammy's ass in flight. The Broncos kicked a field goal. Tom suddenly missed his daughter. It occurred to him that the strangers in the tavern had been dragged to North Fork by their wives. By women for whom Virgin Mary apparitions were a hobby like bird-watching. The sort of men who went along for the ride in order to minimize conflict. The sort of men who knew how to stay married by getting with the program. When the pressure grew, they went for a beer and commiserated halfheartedly. Tom could hear two of them bullshitting nearby, men of his own age in raincoats. Raincoats, tennis shoes, and soft indoor faces. They didn't seem to know they were over their heads in showing up at the Big Bottom, where they could easily get their asses kicked. Tom tuned in to their conversation: No, *north* of Santa Fe, one was saying. Like you were going up to Los Alamos. You kind of head north at the Los Alamos turnoff instead of heading west.

The other man nodded an ambivalent affirmation, as if to suggest how obvious it was that without a map in front of them these directions were absurd and pointless. It's like taking the back road to Taos, said the first man. Do you think you're going to go there?

Maybe. Sometime. Sure.

They call it the Lourdes of America. Or so Paige informs me. But it didn't look like much to me, an adobe church and a dirt parking lot, you can do it quickly between Santa Fe and Taos without any extra pain. Chimayo. Something like that. There's a good place to get burritos right by it—a hole-in-the-wall kind of place out there which I always think are the best kind of places, in fact the burrito I had there for lunch was probably at least two hundred times better than the spendy dinner we had in Taos.

We don't do much Mexican food. Sharon can't eat tomatoes.

I'm allergic to milk lately. All of a sudden. Lactose intolerant. It's terrible.

They gulped their beers, babies clutching flagons. Well I wouldn't mind New Mexico, said the one who didn't eat Mexican food. New Mexico and Arizona both. My brother is in Arizona.

Younger or older?

Younger brother.

What's he doing?

Plays a lot of golf. And bicycling. I guess he bicycles competitively or something. He works for the Prudential.

It'd be worth it to go up to this place Chimayo because the drive is beautiful and Sharon would enjoy it as long as she doesn't eat the food but it's an interesting little hole-in-the-wall place there.

What's this about the dirt now exactly? You were saying about the dirt?

That people take dirt from there in plastic bags like I described to you before. From a little well. A hole in the ground. Like they take the water from Lourdes I guess they take this dirt from this place Chimayo and hold it or pour it on their hands or something and hope for a miracle. For miracle healings. And like I said, Paige got some for her Manhattan uncle who was far down the road with emphysema.

And?

It didn't work. He passed away and she felt bad about it because she'd made all these claims. About the dirt. Or implied them. She didn't really claim anything.

What's to feel bad? She just tried to help.

I know that but she doesn't look at it that way.

She's a good person.

I tell her that constantly.

I'll tell her too.

That would be nice if it helped and it might if she hears it from more than just me. She could use more reinforcement.

So they must have a sizable hole in the ground there.

They don't though. I asked about that. I asked around because I wondered about that. Just like you. Same thought entered my head. I wondered why it wasn't all dug out with so many people taking the dirt. And I guess this guy comes around every day and puts new dirt in the place.

What?

He brings in dirt, the priest prays over it, it's ready to go in the bags, I guess, even if it came from a dairy farm. I don't know. These things are . . . what can you say? They're funny, sort of. It's all kind of funny. I'm not sure what you think of these Virgin events but to me, they're ridiculous. What can I tell you? I don't know what else to make of it all. I mean, what are we doing here if we can't laugh, okay? What are you going to do?

Laugh or cry.

My point exactly.

She and I could visit my brother and then hop over there.

If it works out maybe that would convince her and you could get in eighteen holes.

Are you going to have another beer, Wally?

I'm definitely having another beer.

Excellent, said Wally's friend. I'm with you.

Tom thought that maybe he himself would go ahead and kick their asses. It would be impersonal and cathartic at the same time. Just take it out on two assholes without any strings attached. But instead he knocked back the rest of his beer and resolved to escape this quagmire. A tensile restlessness had a hold of him tonight. He wanted to throw Tammy Buckwalter across the bar and show her what he was capable of, use the goatish power in his loins to put her in thrall to him. I'm a loser, he thought. So why don't you kill me? On the way out he said, I'll be back, Tammy. Soon as I can. You take your time, she answered snidely. And pay up for the one you drunk already.

At the laundromat he stuffed his whites into a dryer and checked all his pockets for change. There was none and furthermore the change machine was out of order or rather emptied by pilgrims. So where was Kim when you needed him? Tangled up doing Spin The Cobra or Reeds In The Wind with Jabari? Bring some god damn change already you little Korean kike! And Kim wanted a buck an hour to dry, up from seventy-five cents. Greed and inflation. Maybe the Koreans had learned that from the Jews. Maybe the Punjabis took Jew lessons too. What could you do except reach into your pocket and shell out to all of them bitterly? And who was willing to admit to the world that he kept track of quarters? Tom walked across the street to HK's, where everybody was sullen and white. HK's was gloomier and smaller than the Big Bottom, with an exceedingly crusty and grim drinking crowd, dried-up boozers intimately acquainted with the world of delirium tremens. It was locally famous for a brawl that occurred there on the Fourth of

July in '79 between bearded bikers from out of town and loggers affronted by the presumptuous way the bikers had parked on Main Street. The angles had been too jaunty, maybe. And the bikers were lighting M-80s in the street. So there was major carnage contained by logging trucks blocking all points of exit. Since then HK's had gone into decline, but there was still a Polaroid of the battle damage taped to the back of the cash register, a couple of choppers laid on their sides, a felt-penned caption reading OLD FASHIONED ASS WHUPPING, you could also make out some broken glass already swept into the gutter.

Quarters, Tom told Bob Hill, the bartender. Hill was a notorious drinker himself with leaky eyes and a parboiled look. I need quarters to give to the Koreans.

I had to quit giving out laundromat quarters when I ran dry two hours ago with all these wackos coming in here.

Religion wackos, yelled a drinker named Cunningham. They're chewing quarters like communion wafers. And chugging holy beers.

I only need two, Tom said.

There's none, said Bob Hill. I don't have any. They cleaned me out, all my quarters.

He wiped the counter and Tom said Jesus, it's got to where you can't even turn around in this god damn town anymore.

Hill leaned back with his bar towel and shrugged. If they want to buy a drink, fine, the more the merrier, bring it on and bring your wallet, but if all they want is change for the laundromat they can go to hell. I'm not a bank, he added.

Holy water, Cunningham barked. They're all gonna get swamp fever from it. They all gonna get giard-ya.

There was muttering from other unemployed loggers sitting at the bar and tables. I bow down to idols, someone called. Hey loan me some quarters, someone else called. Sid down Tom god damn it and drink you're making me nervous standing there.

They'll all be shitting holy water next. We'll be cleaning it out of the streets.

Be quiet, Cunt-ingham. Cross is Catholic.

Fuck all you people, Tom said.

He went out. He got quarters from a stranger at the laundromat, a woman painted up like Tammy Faye Bakker, so much eye shadow it was tragic and ghostly and made you think of dead people. Of walking dead people. Maybe they were real. So here was this woman who looked lovelorn and dead but who carried a ten-dollar bank roll of quarters in her curio-shop acrylic coin purse. Men don't do laundry, she said to Tom. They can't figure out these machines.

You just gotta kick them around, he answered. Push any button and kick.

He shoved in his quarters and started the dryer. The lovelorn dead woman was folding her laundry and stacking it in a plastic basket and there was something nauseating about her perfume and Kmart wardrobe. Well did you get yourself any of the holy water? she asked. What holy water? Tom answered. I guess you weren't up in the woods this afternoon. No because I work at night and that means I have to sleep in the daytime. Well today Our Ann found holy water in the ground. What do you mean found holy water? She dug it straight out of the ground up there like she was Bernadette at Lourdes.

The dead woman had long fake fingernails and eyelashes and she made him feel that what she'd said must inherently be suspect or dubious. Her appearance cast a cloud of doubt over everything she uttered. We waited in line for two hours, she told Tom. And then we filled our water bottles with it. Healing water. From the ground.

Healing water. Did she heal somebody?

A lot of people are being healed.

Is that true?

There are miracles unfolding.

Is that true? repeated Tom.

The woman fluffed her lashes up with the plas-

tic tip of a fingernail. Her makeup looked uncomfortable to Tom, the chemicals in it eating
through her skin. Her eyes watered and a small
ball of black detritus floated on her viscous
cornea. She blinked incessantly in an attempt to
dislodge it, painted mouth thrown open. I can
see, she said, that you don't believe me. But I
swear by Jesus, it's so, in his name. But maybe . . .
hold on . . . are you saved?

I guess I don't know if I'm saved or not.

Oh you'd know if you were, praise the Lord.

Then I'm not I guess.

Then I'll pray for you.

You wouldn't be the first.

Sounds like the devil's got ahold of your soul.

In a big way, answered Tom, and smiled.

The dead woman shook her head as though
saddened. Then she reached for more tangled
laundry. A man's briefs, a dish towel, dark slacks,
a knee sock. Cosmetic surgery, Tom concluded.
She'd had something surgical done to her face, the
skin sanded down with a disk sander, blurred, so
you couldn't quite focus on it.

Back to these miracles. These healing miracles.
These miracles you mentioned, he said.

Amen and glory.

Get back to them. Get back to that subject.

The blind made to see, the lame made to walk,

a child with illness sanctified, a man in darkness redeemed.

All of that happened?

The Lord is good.

A blind person got their sight back today?

There was a terrible alcoholic called to the Lord. And a man who gave a hundred dollars to the Church of Our Forest Lady. And a child with psoriasis healed by the holy water. And a woman with arthritis cured!

But what about the blind person?

If there was one brought to the holy water I'm sure he'd come to see.

So there wasn't one.

You ought to have seen that woman with arthritis begin to dance the rumba!

So there wasn't any blind person then.

Ever one's putting up a supply. Because they're shutting it down tomorrow in the morning. They're getting up No Trespassing signs and after that there won't be any access to the holy healing waters.

She'd folded her last washed article now. Tom imagined that with a high-pressure hose he could wash all the makeup from her face in ten minutes and see what she looked like, who she was. He wondered how long it took her in the morning and how long again at night to struggle with her artificial face. Now it dawned on him that underneath her cosmetic mask was somebody's wrinkled grandmother. He could see how she'd look on a sofa, crocheting, or at a quilting bee or at a senior center eating lunch from a tray. If you didn't look closely she was a whore in her mid-forties, Jezebel at the laundromat, but if you did she was a senior citizen desperate to be younger. Wearing a disguise wherever she went. She picked up her basket like someone with lumbago and said, I'll pray for you.

Prayers never hurt, Tom answered.

She left. Tom started a load of darks and sat atop his machine listening to the dryer drums spin and to the agitators in the washers. Kim's was warm, industrious, and friendly and he didn't feel like leaving. Another woman came his way looking for a free machine and he said to her Pardon me, excuse me, sorry, I wasn't up in the woods today, what's this I hear about holy water?

There's holy water in the ground up there.

That's what I heard.

It's a miracle.

Did she heal anybody?

There were many healings.

What kind exactly? What kind of healings?

A man with a cane who didn't need it any longer. He threw it off to the side and walked. I saw that with my own eyes, him throwing his cane away. And a woman who had that ringing in her ears. Tinnitus, they call it. Gone.

While Tom waited for his laundry loads he interrogated whoever came close. Rheumatism in the right kneecap—gone. Migraine. Intestinal distress. Toothache. Bursitis. Heartburn. Tennis elbow. Nervous anxiety. Paranoid delusions. Neck pain. Constipation. A woman in a parka with liver spots dappling her face claimed that she herself had been freed from the constant misery of bunions. Ann of Oregon had blessed her at the altar, poured holy water across her feet, and after that the bunions on her toes which had been the bane of her existence until then ceased to cause her pain.

Tom said, But are the bunions still there?

They're still there, but they just don't hurt.

How do you explain it?

I don't explain it.

No pain?

None at all. And I got healed in the nick of time. Because tomorrow the woods are shut down.

Tom didn't believe her. How could it be? Be honest, he said. Maybe you've got yourself talked into it. You talked yourself out of your bunions, maybe. Because you wanted to believe in being healed.

If I did I guess that's a miracle too.

In a way, said Tom. You can look at it that way.

I do, said the woman. Praise Mother Mary. It's a miracle however you look at it, isn't it? As long as the pain is gone?

He still had time before night shift started, so he drove toward the North Fork Campground. He drove with less patience than usual and with a terrorizing frustration about other cars and twice he passed drivers who were doing fifty-two where the speed limit was fifty-five. Predictably there was no good radio reception except for a station that had once played country but now played pop music aimed at teenagers so he put in a cassette called *The Legendary Hank Williams Senior* chiefly because it was in the glove box—somebody had left it behind years before—*Chains from My Heart* and so on. Tom listened with resistance to it. Its emotional tenor was a mystery to him, an alien sensibility. No one could be that cheerful about sadness in a place where it rained with such unrelieved constancy, a long slow piss from heaven. He rifled through the glove box again and came up with Eleanor's Dixie Chicks tape and threw that out the window—*flip*—with a therapeutic glee. *My fishing pole's broke, the creek is full of sand, my woman run away with another man. . . .* With that frog in his throat like Gomer Pyle.

At the campground Tom left his truck on the road shoulder and hiked toward the glow of the campfires and gas lamps and the lit windows of the campers and trailers. The scene reminded him of a Civil War painting he remembered seeing on the History Channel, crowds huddled close to comforting flames, a gargantuan army in abeyance for the night but in expectation of the morrow. A whole town of new Port-A-Potties was set up by the fee shed and two state patrol cars were parked on the median, side by side and head-to-toe so that the officers inside, hats off, radios crackling, could shoot the breeze, make comments about women, and chew gum with their elbows in the window frames, which taken altogether was bad PR, they ought to get out and off their asses and do something for their tax-paid salaries. Tom walked by feeling vaguely criminal: mattress theft, truck canopy hijacking, assaulting a fax machine with business cards. He made his way past Kay's Religious Gifts which even at this hour was doing a lively trade in the garish light of kerosene lanterns, as was the bald man from Salt Lake City selling t-shirts from the back of his van, as was the food service truck run by Marysville teenagers who normally worked at horse shows. There was another retailer set up now with a banner reading NORTHWEST CATHOLIC SUPPLY and beside it a booth hawking soda pop, potato chips, candy bars, plastic water bottles, kindling, and flashlights. When the vendor turned around it was Eddie Wilkins Junior wearing a blue coin apron and a knit watch cap that made him look like a small-time burglar and making change from the apron pockets like a peanut peddler at a baseball game, Eddie who had at one time worked for Cross Logging and been arrested twice since then, once for growing marijuana plants, the other for pirating cedar. He had a small goatee now and indistinct sideburns and when he saw Tom he said, in a furtive aside, If you can't beat 'em join 'em and praise the Lord for your conversion. I bought most of this crap at the Wal-Mart in Tacoma and just sell it off at markup.

Ten sticks of kindling for five bucks though?

Hey I'm a capitalist like anybody else.

Whatever happened to business ethics?

Whatever happened to supply and demand?

Don't you need a state business license?

I got one for my booth at the Jubilee. Eddie stepped back out of earshot of pilgrims examining the bags of potato chips. But Tom—what're you doing out here? I can give you a discount on the kindling.

I'm a tourist, said Tom. Looking around. Think of it like the circus is in town and I'm hanging around behind the tents.

Jesus, whispered Eddie. Sell 'em some popcorn. Or better yet—go fill some jugs in the river and sell 'em holy water.

They can get it themselves, they don't need me.

Well sell it to the ones who can't walk two miles between now and tomorrow morning.

You do it. But get the right bottles. And labels. Get the right labels.

You're giving me, said Eddie, big ideas. Great big holy water Web site ideas. Want to go into it with me?

I'm computer illiterate.

That doesn't matter.

In the meantime get rich selling candy bars.

Okay I will, said Eddie.

Farther down the loop road of numbered campsites Tom saw coming toward him a battalion of pilgrims carrying empty jugs and flashlights. He stood aside to let them pass—they seemed to him like earnest children—and then he lit a cigarette and squatted with his back against a tree. Two days of sick leave, he remembered. On the other hand, if he didn't show up, would that be the last straw on top of Nelson calling? And, he thought, what if it was? What if they fired him? His prison guard's pittance, set against the vastness of his debt, was like throwing a handful of sand at the ocean, like pissing on a raging forest fire. Pocket change. Penny ante. What he really needed to do was skip town, set himself up with a fresh start somewhere, and just live quietly like a million other deadbeats down-and-out in small western places where nobody noticed or gave a fuck. Head south. Modesto or Flagstaff. Warm winds and barren spaces. Get another dumb-ass mindless job and a half-decent television set with rabbit ears until he worked his way up to cable. Sit around at night with a six-pack of Schlitz and a copy of *Penthouse,* jerk off, eat lunch-meat sandwiches, doze on the couch, every once in a while go fishing if he could figure out how to do it without a license. Live somewhere with a low heat bill and a lot of Mexicans always looking the other way, get beer at convenience stores, fast food in a bag, keep the truck full of gas, topped up. And fuck everybody. What did he owe? He was already worthless. Eleanor could come after him for alimony and his answer would be Hey, look, check my pockets! You can take home all the lint you want. And my television and my leftover beer, my boots and this package of taco shells.

There was a booth that said AID STATION/LOST AND FOUND where a woman sat reading *Reader's Digest* with a flashlight in her fist. Tom approached her with a straight-faced game plan. Hello, he said. Praise the Lord. Did anyone turn in a little lost cell phone? The woman folded back the corner of her page and he knew right away from that unconscious gesture that he had her number. Nokia? Yep. Flip phone? Yep. Afterward he called in sick for the night, it was a line where you left a recorded message, Tom felt grateful he didn't have to bullshit directly to a warm living ear. Even so he allowed his voice to subside into a listless register, as if indeed he was flu-ridden. This is Tom Cross. . . . I can't make my shift. . . . I'm sick tonight and sorry for the late notice but all day long I was hoping to make it and . . . uh . . . now I see I'm not going to get out there. Hoping to get better by tomorrow, thank you. Tom Cross. Thank you. Click. They probably figured the cell phone static meant he was parked in the woods somewhere, bent over a luscious divorcée's tits, ever since he'd separated from Eleanor he could feel that assumption trailing him, that he lived now like an alpha dog in heat, the married guys always rooted for him, Go for it, they'd say. Get some!

Tom went back to Eddie's booth with a fresh cigarette stuck between his lips and his hands slipped into his jacket pockets. There were pilgrims buying soda pop so he had to wait while Eddie winked at him like a gypsy scam artist and suggested the pilgrims add candy bars to their transactions. Then Tom was up front. Old trick, he said. Real old trick. Except this time it's serious, Eddie—no shit. Hey Eddie look over there, and he pointed just over Eddie's shoulder and when

Eddie turned he picked up a water bottle and put it inside his jacket. What was this, he said. Ninety-eight cents? For one of these plastic water bottles from Wal-Mart? I'll tell you what I'll give you a buck for it. He dropped a dollar on the table.

Take two and bring me some holy water, Tom.

How much are you going to mark it up?

You getting water for your son that's paralyzed?

I'm getting it for you. Because you're impotent, Eddie.

Well I hope it works. Here, take a Snickers. Eddie tucked one into Tom's jacket pocket and thrust a second water bottle at him. It's all fucking crazy, he observed.

Holy water in a Wal-Mart plastic bottle.

That's America, said Eddie.

Tom walked out of the campground on the trail marked, with a makeshift sign, OUR LADY OF THE FOREST TRAIL. In the sodden woods candles shimmered under trees and pilgrims hiked toward him announced by their roving flashlight beams. You're late going up. It's after ten-thirty. Well now or never, I guess, Tom answered. He met another group at an uphill bend. You're going to need a flashlight with you it's dark up there in certain sections. There's a little one here in my pocket, lied Tom, but I'm trying to get my eyes to adjust. Farther along, close to Fryingpan

Creek, a third party rested on a log, three women. Hello, said one. You're a late-night traveler. Last chance for holy water, answered Tom.

They've got the pool good and excavated now. It just keeps filling with holy water. You won't have any problems.

At the bridge a white gas lantern cast light and a man stood waiting with a five-gallon bucket. Who goes there? said Tom. That's my line, said the man. A seeker, said Tom. Bless the Mother of God. We're taking cash donations, urged the man, for building the Church of Our Lady of the Forest. Tom dropped a nickel into the bucket. You can put this job on your résumé, he said. That way if you apply for a toll-booth position you'll have a little head start.

On the far side of the bridge, nailed to trees, were two NO TRESPASSING signs, two PRIVATE PROPERTY signs, two STINSON TIMBER LANDS signs, two KEEP OUT signs, and a small box, mounted on a post, containing a notice on Stinson letterhead, probably two hundred copies or more beneath a plastic shield. Tom read it by the light of three matches, Hello, my name is Q. Robert Stinson, Chief Executive Officer of the Stinson Timber Company, and grandson of our company's founder, Joshua Waddell Stinson.

For three generations the Stinson Company has dedicated itself to careful stewardship of its forest holdings and has sought to preserve their pristine beauty and delicate ecosystems.

Our North Fork Quadrant is home to mule deer, elk, black bear, cougar, lynx, and bobcat, and to hills carpeted with magnificent fir, hemlock, and cedar trees. In these woods, yew bark is harvested to make taxol for cancer patients, and cascara bark is harvested for laxatives.

Timber harvested here is used to build homes, schools, and hospitals, and our trees shade rivers and creeks in which salmon and steelhead spawn.

For many decades the Stinson Company has allowed hunters, fishermen, and other outdoor recreationalists free use of its lands and has also allowed the commercial harvesting of mushrooms and floral brush on a small scale. We have always welcomed the public with open arms and in the spirit of a good neighbor.

Unfortunately, we must now close the North Fork Quadrant and prohibit public access due to excess use.

It is in the best interest of our forests that we do so. As stewards of our lands, it is incumbent upon us to act on their behalf, even when such actions are difficult. Yet we can do nothing less. We must ensure the health of our forests in order that future generations might continue to benefit from them and enjoy them.

The North Fork Quadrant of the Stinson

Timber Company is hereby closed until further notice. Trespassers will be prosecuted to the full extent of the law. Tampering with or removal of signs is a misdemeanor and subject to fine and/or imprisonment. We thank you in advance for your compliance.

Cordially,

Bob Stinson.

Tom tightened the lids on his water bottles and entered the forest of blowdowns. The trail wound around fallen trees and passed lit votive candles and pieces of merchandise he'd seen for sale at Kay's Religious Gifts—crucifixes, rosaries, statues, figurines, all left in the forest like sacrifices offered to furtive gods of the night. Tom sat for a moment on a rock in the forest and by the light of a votive candle contemplated a gallery of miniature framed photographs arranged on an altar of moss and plastic flowers. A label had been affixed to each—Sandro Botticelli, *Madonna of the Sea,* Hans Memling, *Virgin and Child,* Andrea Mantegna, *Madonna of the Caves,* and Georges de La Tour, *The Adoration of the Shepherds,* in which the Christ Child looked strangely like a corpse. Across the trail was a second gallery, Pietro Perugino, *The Deposition from the Cross,* Dirck Bouts, *Lamentation,* Giovanni Bellini, *Pietà*—in this one Christ's wounds were exceptionally vivid because of their dimension of graphic depth—and

Michelangelo da Caravaggio, whose Christ in the moment of deposition was as muscular as a steroidal weight lifter. Tom scratched his head and pondered the Bellini, attracted to its wounds and to the turquoise pigment applied to Christ's face suggesting the pallor of recent death.

The trail turned steeply northward now, and darker and gloomier, and the numbers of pilgrims in exodus dwindled, and Tom hiked steadily taking a strange pleasure in the extraordinary nature of present circumstances, alone in the night woods on a desperate mission to retrieve two bottles of holy water. He felt like a soldier. Purposeful. He felt the grief and bitterness of the past like a secretion suffusing his gut. He began to search for redemptive memories or an alternative way to look at things but nothing legitimate welled up. Striding through the sheared salal and Oregon grape he passed more lit and flickering candles and a group of pilgrims who had stopped to rest, one of whom greeted him by calling out It isn't far now to the holy water you've already gone three quarters of the way and there aren't any more steep hills. Tom thanked him for his travel information but didn't stop to hobnob any further and before long passed another group coming his way with flashlights. Just around the corner, someone said. Miracle of miracles, said another.

There was a bonfire burning in the dank-smelling forest where the apparitions had un-furled. There were pilgrims with shovels, hoes, and picks digging out a large pool. There was an altar of ferns festooned with petitions and with more framed photographs and candles. Propped against its tree, illuminated grotesquely by the bonfire light, stood the half-size statue of Our Lady of Fátima garlanded with its crown of moss. She looked sinister somehow, like the guest of honor at a wake.

Tom came forward tentatively with his water bottles and warmed his hands amid the crowd at the fire. Welcome, brother, someone said. Join us in thanksgiving. Hail Holy Queen, called some-one else, an ardent voice from across the flames. Mother of Mercy, our life, our sweetness and our hope, to you do we cry, poor banished children of Eve! It was closing in on midnight now; neverthe-less there were at least fifty people gathered close to the fire's heat, filling plastic jugs at the pool and milling about with restless fervor as if unable to leave. The blaze burning deep in the woods, the altar of ferns and the macabre wreathed statue, the firelight reflected in the gleaming black pool—it all felt to Tom like a witches' coven or a sylvan gathering of warlocks. It all felt dangerously su-pernatural and disconnected from God.

The flames hissed. The forest floor lay wet un-derneath. Sparks from slowly combusting moss rose through the tree branches like miniature wraiths. Tom turned his back to the people at the bonfire and went down to kneel by the pool of holy water. It was black and smelled of mud and moss and a woman with a hoe who was working nearby—in the dark he couldn't make out her face—said Praise the Lord and Hail Our Lady, what miracle are you seeking?

I'm seeking my ill son's health and salvation.

What illness does he suffer from?

Paralysis, said Tom. He's paralyzed.

He can't move?

His neck is broken.

An accident?

No, said Tom.

What happened then?

I did it to him.

You broke his neck.

That's right. I did.

But how can that be?

I broke it on purpose.

But how can that be? How? Why?

Hatred, said Tom. I hated him.

He filled his water bottles, wiped his hands on his pants. The woman let him do so in silence and then she reached to touch his shoulder. Hail Mary, full of grace, she said. The Lord is with thee. He is.

Leave me alone, answered Tom.

In the woods, by the trail, not far off, he set down the bottles, sat on a log, and smoked the last of his cigarettes. Tom knew he wasn't acceptable now in his language or demeanor. He could still see himself as others saw him. And he was not surprised to be not surprised. He asked himself, Is it me or them? The world or me? Who doesn't see? Who doesn't know? How long have I been going in this direction? When did I start this way?

He hated women. Bitches. Cunts. The faceless whore with her pious pity, Jezebel at the laundromat, Tammy, Heidi Johnston, Jabari, Ann of Oregon, the Cross Family Committee, Eleanor, they were all the same when it came to it, they all wanted to get inside you.

Tom hiked out and drove his truck toward town. The moon was risen. A rare night of few clouds. Wind-driven clouds across the moon reminded him of his Ford Unit hunting camp. Sitting by the fire drinking Budweiser with Kruse and frying backstrap in margarine, listening to AC/DC.

In North Fork Tom found a mob at the church. Cars pulled in: a revival meeting. A candlelight vigil, Bible thumpers. A mass of pilgrims, three state patrol cars, even a couple of television cameras. Okay, he said. All right. This is it. Tom drove up onto the sidewalk, spilled out, and waded into the crowd.

V

Assumption

Father Collins unlocked the door to his church and noted immediately the odor of mildew perpetually inhabiting not only the vestibule but the sanctuary, hallway, storage room, kitchen, sacristy, and especially his own office. A clammy green must exuded from the carpets, which were laid over concrete subfloors. Church volunteers with mildewcide-laced rug shampoo had sought unsuccessfully to purge this aroma, obstinately repeating their vigorous attempts and applying a variety of chemical products essentially to no avail. For a day or two one noted an improvement, a sterile antiseptic balm, and then the mildew smell returned, putrescent and freshly incubated.

Father Collins admitted Father Butler to his

church and locked the door behind him. It was eight-thirty-nine and he had come to feel—in fact it had been the tenor of his day—that Father Butler was tiresome. They'd gone from the woods to the campground to the trailer court, where Father Collins had turned down the sofa bed and plumped his colleague's pillow. Always there'd been Father Butler's voice, sonorous, grating, presumptuous, categorical, and full of ministerial self-regard. He'd expounded on the Holy See, the Catholic Theological Union, Vatican II, Cardinal Martini of Milan, and the recent Synod of Bishops. He'd related a number of Third World narratives unified by the theme of difficulties. Absurd difficulties regarding basic matters—water, housing, transportation, sanitation—that Father Butler found comic and telling. The strapping young priest with his quinine water, buzz cut, and stalwart good humor, abroad among *backward indigenes.* Father Collins had to remind himself repeatedly that his brother-in-Christ had been a young adult during the Eisenhower administration and therefore had missed out on diversity as a worldview and had not been inculcated into the nuanced semantics of the multicultural sensibility. He had never learned to be PC, which actually was a kind of relief. Nevertheless it was still galling to hear him prattle on about *natives* and to hear him pepper his speech with unfashionable, antiquated, and objectionable locutions like *primitive, oriental,* and *uncivilized*. And eventually it was also exhausting.

The two priests out of boredom had supped early at Gip's, where they'd argued about Western metaphysical dualism after Father Collins asserted that racism was an organic product of European philosophical thought—trotting out Luther, Calvin and Descartes, Saint Augustine's platonic theology, and Freud's insinuation that leadership of the human species fell to the European nations—a debate neither clergyman cared very much about though it nicely passed the minutes until their hamburgers arrived, at which point they called a cease-fire. The heady smell of grease and meat and a brief silent prayer from Father Butler. Father Collins liked a hamburger now and then more than he cared to admit to himself and ate them with guilt because good forest land had been destroyed to make graze for South American beef cattle, though on this evening Father Butler's red-faced presence suppressed his carnivorous appetite and inspired in its place an idealist's ascetic self-denial. Father Collins picked at his french fries, played with his ketchup, and took note of the brightly decorative mustard festooning the corner of Father Butler's mouth as he dispatched his hamburger with unabashed relish and much labial noise.

Now they sat in the church office digesting grease and listening to the baseboard heater click, and Father Butler picked at his teeth and repeated something he had said before dinner, I think you've misread your Augustine, Collins. With all your talk of the Manichean Realm of Light and Christ's place in the Manichean cosmogony, to use your term—cosmogony. I don't think it works in your argument. Your abstruse racism argument.

So let's leave it then, said Father Collins. We've done enough with that tired subject. Though I'm well acquainted with *The Confessions,* I'll have you know. I still refer to them often.

With their emphasis, Father Butler said, on control of the restless passions, Collins. Control of the restless passions.

Your point being what?

That you have a ceaselessly roving eye. Come on, now, don't play dumb, I've noted it more than once today—and look, proof, you're turning beet-red, as scarlet as the scarlet letter! Noted it among the goodly women who follow your little friend Our Ann, and again with our prim pert hamburger waitress. Father Butler wagged an admonishing forefinger. Not good for a priest to look so much. Not good for a celibate brother-in-Christ. What was your Saint Augustine's phrase? The broiling sea of fornication?

I'm only a man like other men, brother. I don't pretend to be otherwise.

And didn't he say that the impulses of the spirit and those of the flesh are at war with one another?

It's the impulses of the spirit and the impulses of nature.

For all intents and purposes the same. So I got a bit of the language wrong. Father Butler pressed his fingers together, forming a tent or rafters. That mold smell is awful, he announced.

It's a nasty sort of peculiar mildew. Peculiar to rain-beaten logging towns.

Well it's perfectly evil. Perfectly wretched. As if the door to Pandemonium were located beneath your church.

That would be, technically, a sulfurous emanation, brother. Fire and brimstone, et cetera. Very drying to mildew.

At any rate can't you do something soon? It's abhorrent, this much must.

Well, said Father Collins. I'm glad you're here. Taking notes on our humble physical plant. And soon going home with notes in hand. Taking our message to the diocese. The message being that out here in North Fork we need to do something about a mildew crisis. Not that they haven't heard from me. Not that I haven't informed them incessantly. Made like a fly in the bishop's ointment.

Offered elegantly simple choices. A, start over and get a vapor barrier under the slab, or B, build a brand-new church.

Your lighting is drab as well, said Father Butler. The general atmosphere is depressing.

Father Collins, sulking behind his desk, thought of Father Butler as a cross to bear and reminded himself that this sort of irritation was incidental in the long run. If Christ could wear a crown of thorns, couldn't he suffer Father Butler? In the past twelve months he'd learned prodigiously about the nuances of professional endurance and become a seasoned veteran when it came to forbearance. Yet he worried that Father Butler's investigation would drag on interminably and that perforce he would have to bear at length this chattering, orotund, clerical fool who resembled the wrestling and football coach at Father Collins' prep school. Father Ted with a whistle around his neck. And now here came this Father Bill. Everyone's friend but a tough sergeant too who knew his rote theology. You know, said Father Collins. Out here like this. So far away from the bishop's office. I haven't gotten much of a chance to see for myself what he's like.

The bishop? Father Butler replied. Are you asking me about the bishop?

In a nutshell maybe. Don't feel the need to write his biography. But in a nutshell—yes.

The bishop as I know him is a pragmatist and compromiser. A realist about what can actually be accomplished. And relatively above the fray. Anything but a detail man. He likes to delegate wherever he can. Middle-of-the-road but canted right by nature. Yet malleable when circumstances demand. I've seen him turn left against his instincts. I respect him, ultimately, yes I do. He's a politician, unlike me. And in the long run he gets things done.

So in other words he's no ordinary Ordinary.

Clever wordplay.

Fun with homonyms.

Well what is it exactly you want to know? Is he going to build you a new church out here? I don't think that happens anytime soon. Because he's fully cognizant of budget constraints. In fact he's excellent at crunching numbers. In another life he might have kept books. Anyway, he's hard to ruffle. I guess I have seen him become impassioned about aggressive proselytizing by Protestant groups. That sort of thing really bothers him. Fundamentalist fanatics.

Father Collins leaned back in his chair. It was a cheap padded task chair from Office Depot with a pneumatic height-adjustment lever, plastic casters, and molded arms, utterly homely but enormously comfortable in a way that was bad for his lumbago. Eighty-eight dollars. Father Collins had paid for it himself but didn't plan to keep it after he left because it had come to smell like mildew. It had been a tax deduction once as an office expense and would be again as a charitable contribution. The next priest could douse it with mildewcide.

It's closing in on nine, he said. Maybe we should discuss Our Ann a little. Preliminaries. Before she arrives. Some thoughts about her. In preparation.

Father Butler pulled at his priestly tab like a man loosening his tie. I'll be frank, he said. I'll be quite frank. She's a dope-smoking runaway, period. She isn't going to stand up to scrutiny or even take very long.

How do you know?

Because I can just about smell the dope on her and see it in her eyes. In her case I can use what I call Procedure A, approved and recommended by Father Groeschel as he recapitulates Father Poulain, namely that there are some simple considerations which permit an open-minded observer to dismiss a reported revelation without doing too much investigation. And one of these—I'm extrapolating from Poulain now, because Poulain didn't have to endure the sixties— one of these is drug use.

So you see, Father Butler droned on, it's the short version out here in North Fork this week, short by the Church's historical standards which means very long by anyone else's—but you know that as well as I do. I talk to her. Or we talk to her. We talk to everybody. One at a time. Anyone who's had dealings with her. I have my assistant back at the office do extensive research, too. Where she was born, school grades, arrest records, credit history. Whatever we can dig up, specifics. Then I put my report together and the bishop broods for five minutes.

There's something tragic in all of that.

Well I'm not required to entertain such notions. Tragic or not there's a job to perform. There are motions we have to go through.

Father Collins bit his lip and thwarted his impulse to comment further, to suggest that for him the tragedy of it lay not just in the girl's undoing but in the length of the Church's paper trail, in the Church's bureaucratic imperatives and incessant record keeping. The grottoes underneath the Vatican were no doubt filled with slate and vellum, desiccated rag pulp ledgers, and meeting minutes recorded on parchments made by eighth-century Moors. How many scriveners and amanuenses had toiled in service to the Vicars of Christ, their secretariats, councils, and tribunals? Was there any institution on earth that made greater use of ground wood fiber? The Prelate's Recommendation to the Holy See Regarding the

Phenomenon of Our Ann of North Fork would be filed in front of the six-month fiscal report from the Pontifical Council for Laity and behind a European Synod position paper on special papal appointees. Going through the motions, said Father Collins. I suppose that must be necessary.

Dot *i*'s, cross *t*'s, and, to paraphrase Sir Thomas More, keep your affairs . . . regular.

Father Collins checked his watch. I'll tell you what, he said with false authority. You wait here. Relax. Unwind. I'm going to put some water on for tea and wait for Our Ann in the vestibule.

Tea?

Yes.

I'll have some then.

Our Ann has a flu for which tea might be good.

As you say, said Father Butler. I'll take mine as a digestive.

Father Collins strode down the hall like a harried parish beadle bent on a mission, lit a burner on the stove in the kitchen, and ran the rust through the pipes thoroughly before filling the teakettle with cold water. *Our Ann,* he thought, ashamed of himself for having used the name ironically in deference to Father Butler's dominion. The kitchen had a close, water-stained ceiling, curling squares of linoleum, rotting baseboards, chipped Formica counters, and that air of occasional sporadic use that renders the contents of a refrigerator suspect and suggests that the biscuit flour, corn meal, and cooking oil comprising its depressing contents should all be immediately thrown out. Over the sink, typed in a capital Zapf Chancery font, was a set of instructions for kitchen use inside a plastic sheath. Its syntax was atrociously mangled, as was much of its spelling. SCRUB SINK WITH CLENSER AFTER UTLIZING. FOR HY-GENE'S SAKE GOOD HOT WATER SHOULD BE UTLIZED. DRY DISHES ALL THE WAY BEFORE PUTTING BACK. WIPE COUNTER TOPS COMPLETELY DOWN WITH RAG. DISPOSE OF USED COFFEE FILERS. USE TWISTEES ON GARBAGE BAGS WHEN BAGS ARE FULL. THANK YOU AND GOD BLESS OUR KICHEN!

Father Collins took solace in his moment of privacy, standing over the stove. He had not had a moment alone all day in which to contemplate the befuddled embarrassment he'd felt that morning in the presence of the visionary, appearing, as he had, as feeble handmaid to her stern, dogmatic inquisi-tor. As Father Butler's whipping boy, yes-man, and valet. There he'd sat beside Father Butler in that claustrophobic Volkswagen van where there was no escape from the visionary's scrutiny of his pusil-lanimous shit-eating face. Father Collins' embar-rassment was partly moral—the young priest seething with contradictions—but also, he knew, partly romantic: he'd felt as action hero compromised and even metaphorically castrated. He'd stood before Ann with his soul excised and displayed in Father Butler's hands. And no doubt it had revealed itself as the dead gray matter it was in truth so that he could no longer hide from her. She would know that his reluctance to support her cause arose from his systemic male malaise and from the same inherent cowardice that had driven him toward the priesthood, out of the realm of corporeal struggle with its sex, blood, and animal violence, its frightening Darwinian rules.

He'd given up plenty to be outside the game, and not just the opportunity for sex. Or rather he'd chosen to lose without playing—quit after the first few adolescent skirmishes—and so wouldn't pass on his genetic complement via the fleshly consolation of orgasm. He would also not know love's vaunted madness, its tragicomic mystery, except through God, an abstraction. He would love only an idea. So losses piled up. Including children. His nonexistent children's children. Finally an old priest in a home for old priests—maybe his sisters would visit him there if they weren't suffering from Alzheimer's disease or simply dead already. He would be, inevitably, a geriatric castaway; he could see that far into the future. It wasn't far in cosmic terms, as the poets insistently reminded him: brief candle, wingèd chariot drawing near, Oh my God, Father Collins thought, it was all of it a lot to ask! It was lonely and left him with reservations and riddled him with wounding doubts.

There was succor, as always, in the sound of the teakettle, though the succor he felt at this juncture in his thoughts only deepened his sense of personal crisis: he was an indoor male of domestic contents, beaten, gelded, impotent, unmanned—celibate and, by that fact, neutered. Ultimately it came to this: a hot cup of tea served scrupulously as perhaps the zenith of Father Collins' day, lending it an aura of meaning.

So he performed his daily tea-making rites: Monday, it must be orange pekoe. There was a cozy sewed by one of his parishioners into the shape of a hen at nest and he pulled that over the little teapot. Followed by the discipline of a thorough steep with its silent call for perseverance. He mused and meditated, shut his eyes, and imagined himself quitting the priesthood. But then what? Finally he poured himself a cup of tea and took it with its matching saucer as nursemaid for his vigil in the vestibule. He felt like a fussy baby with a bottle. But I'm a priest, he thought, on watch for a visionary. It ought to be shot in black-and-white by an understated European director. And he looked out the window into the night. There were puddles shimmering in the church parking lot. He paced, balancing his teacup carefully. He thought of checking on Father Butler. Instead he sipped his cooling tea and read the flyers on the bulletin board because reading and tea were his habitual manner of whiling away idle time. The Cross Family Committee. The Build Our New Church Fund. Acronym BONC. The parishioners on the steering committee preferred it as an exclamatory: BONC! Carolyn Greer's battered Volkswagen van pulled suddenly into the parking lot and behind it was a queue of cars as long as—longer than—a funeral procession, disappearing around the corner.

Father Collins set his tea on the table, unlocked and held the door ajar, and watched while Carolyn stepped from her van, followed by the visionary wrapped in a blanket; already cars were filling the spaces, pilgrims storming out of them with fervor. Father Collins recognized the humorless sentinels who had kept their earnest night-long vigil while he'd preyed ineffectually on Ann of Oregon. Greetings, he called. Good evening, Ann. And good evening to you, Carolyn. I'm afraid we'll have to keep the others out. The church isn't officially open right now. We're not holding services or anything.

The church is always open, said Carolyn. The church is owned by the people.

We're not socialists, said Father Collins. This isn't some kind of collective.

It ought to be.

But it isn't.

The visionary's fever had turned convulsive. Her pale lips, he saw, were trembling. Her glassy eyes were open wide—a fish cast up on his beach.

Carolyn had one arm around Ann. I thought, she said, of bypassing your church and going directly to a medical clinic but I didn't know where to find one.

Please come in, replied Father Collins. Ann, he said. You're looking worse. You'd better let me take you to a doctor.

The church, she answered robotically. We have to start building the church.

He admitted them and then blocked the doorway, and because looming there felt a little heroic it also felt like an antidote. God bless! he called. To all of you. You're welcome to keep your vigil here. In our parking lot. For as long as you wish. God bless you all!

He shut the door rapidly and turned the thumb latch. Two sentinels ran up to plead with him through the glass and he waved at them courteously and smiled dumbly. I brewed tea, he said to Ann. And there's a couch in my office. You can lie down there and be comfortable and put your head on a pillow.

Tea and a couch, said Carolyn. And maybe you could call a doctor.

I don't want a doctor, said Ann.

Shrouded in her blanket she looked biblical—an ancient Hebrew wrapped in a shawl, a beggar of Galilee, a peasant of Jericho, a Midianite languishing beside a well. There was also something medieval, monastic, and hairshirtish about her blanket and her pale face in shadow. Her afflicted appearance gave him pause and made him think first of diabolical possession—there were dark circles under her eyes—then of victim souls. This way, he urged her. Down the hall.

Mother Mary bless you, Father.

I'll run for the teapot, he answered.

He brought it on a tray with cups and saucers as if tea were the point of this gathering. His brother-in-Christ was making false civil noises about turning up the baseboard heater while examining the thermostat through his bifocals. Father Collins sensed that in his brief absence Father Butler had shrewdly established a tone of smarmy, tender condescension. An unctuous priest full of phony regard for an ingenue's decidedly ill health—the man was a cunning, sanctimonious fraud, but then, so was he himself.

Fever, Father Butler was saying, is the body's

way of cooking out illness. As long as your temperature doesn't run too high, fever is probably a good thing.

Are you a doctor? asked Carolyn, seated on the couch alongside Ann with the ankle of her right leg propped on her left thigh, the casual posture of a man. A doctor, a detective, and a priest?

Father Butler smiled, bent at the knees, finessing the thermostat higher. In the Third World one becomes a jack-of-all-trades out of dire necessity and happenstance, Ms. Greer. I'm also an auto mechanic of sorts, an electrician, a plumber, a drainage engineer, a social worker, and a soccer coach.

And a witch-hunter too, Carolyn added. Don't forget about witch-hunter.

Father Butler sighed flagrantly to announce his irritation. Come now, he said. That's a little unfair. I'm only doing my duty here. Pressing an obligatory investigation into the claims Our Ann has made.

Father Collins, pouring tea, could not, at this, hold his tongue. We're genuinely interested, he said. We bring to the table no presuppositions. No assumptions regarding anything. What we want to discover is simply the truth. The truth and nothing more, Carolyn. So this is not just obligatory questioning. But it's also not a witch-hunt.

Well, said Carolyn. Straighten out your stories. Or is this good cop, bad cop?

Father Collins began to parcel out the teacups. The visionary bent to remove her damp shoes, drew her legs up under the blanket, and arranged herself in what appeared to be—he could see, in outline, the protuberances of her knees—the Buddha's lotus position. With her teacup and saucer, her head still covered by the blanket cowl, she looked to him like a frail swami being interviewed by the BBC.

Father Butler, in an act of sudden unilateral aggression, seized Father Collins' desk. He sat down behind it and took up a pen, which he began absentmindedly to fiddle with. Sometimes, he said, I use a tape recorder, but in this case I don't feel it's necessary. Not for the sort of informal dialogue I'd like to have right now.

Right, answered Carolyn. Just trading recipes. Or chatting up a Tupperware soiree.

Father Butler turned his stern gaze on Ann. Perhaps you remember from this morning, he said, the word I used to describe the process I'm trying my best to initiate here. A process the Church finds necessary for good reason. A process called discernment, Ann, whose purpose is, as I've said before, to discern the validity of your claims.

She's very ill, said Carolyn. I—

From the Latin *discernere*—to separate or distinguish between. With a special emphasis on accuracy. What I seek to do is to distinguish accurately between what is true and what is not true. Between hallucination and illusion on the one hand and a bona fide Marian apparition on the other. And from there—assuming that indeed we have a vision, which can be the case on rare occasions—to discern whether it is divinely inspired or diabolical in origin.

Ann said nothing. She sat with her teacup poised in her lap, a Mongolian in front of her yurt. Her cryptic expression, Father Collins thought, was appropriately unassailable and impervious to her inquisitor's rhetoric. Saint John of the Cross, said Father Butler, warns us to assume that extraordinary experiences must certainly arise from the forces of evil unless it can be proven otherwise.

Yes, said Ann. I welcome your questions.

Why is that? Why would you, Ann?

Your questions lead us where we're going, Father. Because Our Lady's message includes you too. Whether you know it or not.

Father Butler maintained his dismissive facade without the slightest waver. You understand that for the Church, he said, at the very best—*the very best*—a revelation such as the one you claim can have only limited significance? That even were I to find truth to your claims, your claims will never be part of the canon, part of Catholic theological faith, but only something a good Catholic *might* prudently accept as probable? Prudent acceptance of probability is approximately the Apostolic See's position on Bernadette at Lourdes, Saint Hildegard, Saint Bridget, Saint Catherine of Siena—the lot of them saints, let me underscore—and still the Church can go no further than to affirm a prudent acceptance of the possibility that their revelations are legitimate. That's it. No further. Not even with saints. So you see—we need some perspective.

Yes.

Yes, said Carolyn. I can see what you're saying. That the Church doesn't seem to trust women.

And if I might speak sweepingly, in generalizations, you should understand that for the Church, Ann, Our Lord Jesus Christ is the final word— through Christ, Our Father has spoken with finality and has embodied his full revelation. *Full* revelation, *entire* Word: nothing new to be added.

Yes.

So that a claim of visions involving revelations is potentially heretical in the sense of impertinent. At the very least, an insult to God. Saint John of the Cross is excellent on this when he tells us that anyone desiring visions is guilty not only of foolish behavior but also of offending God himself by living with the desire for novelty. So you can see—we take a hard line on this. On the possibility of heresy.

A person has to be baptized, said Ann, to be guilty of heresy, right?

You're not baptized?

No I'm not.

You're not a Catholic?

Not really I guess.

What are you then?

Nothing I guess. I've never gone to church, Father. I've never been religious until lately.

Father Butler tilted back in the desk chair and stuck the pen behind his ear, as if to say with these small gestures that his work was abruptly terminated. Why didn't anyone tell me this? he asked. Why are we even here?

You're just old-fashioned, Carolyn said. Loosen up. Free your mind. After all, Jesus was a Jewish guy. So he couldn't even eat the wafers at your church. Is that any different from Ann having visions? That a Jewish guy is your ultimate Christian? So why couldn't Ann see the Virgin Mary? I just think anything is possible.

I don't recall a case, offhand, where the purported visionary was not even Catholic. Not even a member of the faith in question! Surely this case is open-and-shut. Surely I have a reasonable query—Why would Our Lady reveal herself to someone outside Her church?

On the other hand, put in Father Collins, that Mary should choose someone so unexpected is not, I think, without precedent. The peasant visionaries at La Salette were young cowherds, after all. Bernadette Soubirous was out gathering firewood. The children at Fátima were humble shepherds. So who's to say that a girl gathering mushrooms is not, possibly, an appropriate candidate? A possible conduit for Our Lady's message? I'm not saying that she is or isn't. I'm only saying that the matter of baptism ought not to preclude an investigation. A thorough, complete investigation.

Father Butler drew the pen from behind his ear like an archer unquivering an arrow. Well, he said, our report on matters is duly expected. Even with this development. He tapped the pen against the desktop and sighed with weary sufferance. Well, he repeated. I suppose you're right, Collins. I suppose we had better proceed with this. Just to keep things to form.

How lucky for us, said Carolyn.

The visionary coughed, dropped the veil of her blanket, and pulled back her sweatshirt hood. She balanced her teacup delicately on the armrest. I'm so hot, she said. All of a sudden. And began, brazenly, to pull off her sweatshirt. She stood and Carolyn rose automatically and held down Ann's dirty t-shirt hem while she peeled herself, in a frenzy, out, Carolyn taking artful pains to ensure that the visionary's slim young midriff did not reveal itself. We'll turn the heat down, Father Collins said. Sudden turns of temperature, added Father Butler, are how a fever runs its course.

Carolyn hugged Ann and stroked her damp neck. It's all right, she said maternally. You're going to get better—I know you will. Just ignore these two strange clerics. Honey, she said. Your health. Come on now. You've got to get focused on your health.

The visionary passed an interlude in the bathroom lasting more than twenty minutes, during which Carolyn dropped in on her nervously half a dozen times. You need a doctor. No I don't. What's the problem? I'm having my period. Cramping? They're like terrible cramps. On top of your flu you're dealing with that. Let me just sit here a little while. Do you have any tampons? I don't use tampons. What about pads? I don't use those either. So what do you do? I use handkerchief and napkins. That's like barbaric or primitive or something. Well anyway it's what I do. That's like unsanitary and totally depressing. Anyway—I don't feel good. You don't sound good from out here either, I'm afraid you're going to pass out on the toilet. Can you bring me my sweatshirt? Carolyn brought it. I still have

some of those Tylenol from breakfast. Maybe I'll
take some. And my allergy pills. I'll get you some
water, Carolyn said. She went to the priest's office to get Ann's teacup. How is she now? asked
Father Collins. It's a girl thing, answered Carolyn.
You guys wouldn't understand.

She took the teacup down the hall and handed it
in along with the Tylenol and a packet of Phenathol. Ann looked cute in the toilet stall with her pigeon-toed pose and her jeans at her ankles and her
perfectly white trim teenage legs with their calves
tensed, firm arches of muscle. Carolyn felt a pang of
jealous angst. God, she said. You're sweating.

I'm sick to my stomach.

Something's like wrong. Seriously.

I've got what they used to call at my school
Montezuma's Revenge I guess.

The runs.

Yeah.

At a time like this. Flu, cramps, the runs.

Yeah. Not to mention I'm wheezing again.
My asthma is acting up.

Sometimes it's time to call a time-out. You
know what I mean? Do you know what I'm saying? Because the body speaks, my dear sweet
Ann. And what your body is saying right now is,
Help, let's go see a doctor.

I'll go tomorrow. Tomorrow afternoon. After
Our Lady comes. Then.

Carolyn rolled her eyes at this. Too many oranges, that's all, said Ann. I just have to ride it out.

Carolyn shuttled back to the office. The priests were slumped in their chairs trading yawns. We were just reflecting, said Father Collins, on the phenomenon of the victim soul that Ann's ill health brings to mind.

Victim soul, said Carolyn. That sounds like a reggae band.

It's a soul appointed by God, said Father Butler, to suffer various pains and ailments in penance for the sins of man. A soul participating in the suffering of Christ. Supposedly—that's the gist of it. For crackpots who believe that sort of thing. The best example that comes to mind is the eminently absurd Veronica Lueken, otherwise known as Veronica of the Cross, the seer of Bayside, in Queens.

Never heard of her, said Carolyn.

She suffered from everything. Diabetes, gallstones, I don't know what else, problem after problem for decades on end, all manner of ailments. There was also a seer named Mary Ann Van Hoof who ranted famously about Yids and Commies. She supposedly manifested painful stigmata and vomited all the time.

Enough, said Carolyn. I don't want to hear this. I'm going back to check on Ann.

Excellent, said Father Butler.

In the bathroom Ann stood washing her hands. She wore her sweatshirt hood cinched tight. No more oranges, I agree, said Carolyn. They're too acidic or something.

She helped Ann back down the hall to the priests, settled her on the couch again, and wrapped her in her blanket. I hope you're better, Father Butler said. I don't want to press this interview if it means further strain on your health.

I'm okay.

Are you sure about that?

I feel okay.

All right, said Father Butler. Then I'm going to ask you to tell me a little more about your religious background.

What do you mean? said Ann.

Father Butler looked fleetingly exasperated. I mean, he said, before all this. What was it that made you feel spiritual?

Spiritual? said Ann. I guess . . . the sea. The sea did. The sea does. I like the ocean a lot—I like to go there. When I see the ocean I get . . . spiritual. But I guess a lot of people are like that too. When they're at the ocean.

And stars, she added. Definitely stars. I got into camping on ridges this September where I could check out the stars if we had a clear night and def-

initely that was spiritual. I mean it's kind of obvious to say it but since you asked, okay, it was, to
see the stars that way.

And a bunch of little things. Like if I see the
little whatchamacallits that fall off maples when
it's windy in the spring I think about how few of
them will grow into trees and you know what?
That's spiritual. Or I end up looking at a beetle
for a long time or an oyster mushroom or something like that and the feeling I get is . . . spiritual.
From looking at those things. All the time. It happens to me constantly. It's totally all the time for
me to feel spiritual about just the wind or
something.

I love this, said Carolyn. You're a nature poet.

Father Butler, hulking over his notepad, said
Please Ann, go right ahead talking, I'd love to
hear more of your thoughts.

What should I tell about?

Whatever you want. Free association is dandy
with me. Old stories, memories, high points, low
points. I—

She's not insane, said Carolyn. If that's what
you're getting at. She's not.

I didn't say that.

You're implying it, though.

No I'm not.

Yes you are.

I'm not implying anything.

I'll bet you suspect schizophrenia. Paranoid schizophrenia. Or a borderline histrionic.

Please now, Father Butler said, and sighed. Why don't I just ask a simple question? He scratched the corner of his mouth and winced. I hate to ask. I really do. But honestly I have to— point-blank, just ask. So here we go. Drugs and alcohol. I have to ask about that.

Neither, Ann said. I don't use either.

I don't use either can mean many things.

I mean it to mean just one thing—I don't.

But have you ever?

Yes. I admit it.

How recently then?

Like a few weeks ago.

A few meaning what? A few means how many?

Like three, maybe. Three or four.

Drugs or alcohol?

Marijuana.

Only that?

Marijuana and magic mushrooms.

So I don't use either means, then, that you last used marijuana or magic mushrooms three or four weeks ago, yes, correct? Isn't that what it means?

The mushrooms more like four.

Father Butler scribbled notes with a knit brow. Excuse me, he said. I write very slowly. He looked up and the light struck off his glasses so that they obscured his eyes and appeared luminescent. This is important, he muttered.

He put down his pen and clasped his thick hands in the traditional manner of a Church functionary, fingers intertwined above his heart. In the considered view of our Church, he said, the character of the purported visionary is as critical as the character of the purported visions. The two are considered inseparable. There is no true vision without a true visionary. And a true visionary is free of drugs. So of course the admitted use of drugs not only argues against your legitimacy but also provides us with a ready explanation for the phenomenon at hand. In an obvious way, inarguably. I think you'll all agree with me. The authenticity of an apparition is naturally compromised by the very good and reasonable question of whether a chemically induced hallucination isn't the best and foremost explanation. A magic mushroom specter or phantasm is not, after all, a Marian apparition. We can all agree on that.

Granted, answered Carolyn. But Ann hasn't tripped in a month or so and she's seeing Mother Mary right now.

Father Butler set his elbows on the desk. You know, he said. I've been at this for years. I've been from here to say Haight-Ashbury investigating Marian apparitions. So this isn't my first time coming across mushrooms of the genus *Psilocybe*.

With their well-known and documented power to elicit vivid psychoactive experiences long after the waning of primary effects. Otherwise known—known in the vernacular—as flashbacks, but of course you know about that. Certainly you know all about flashbacks.

I'm not having flashbacks, said Ann.

She's not having flashbacks, Carolyn said. Flashbacks are kind of mellow and dreamy. What's been happening to Ann every afternoon is hugely extreme and intense.

I wouldn't know, answered Father Butler, how best to describe the foggy parameters of the delayed psychoactive psilocybin experience. I'm not sure anyone has described it scientifically or determined its maximum intensity—there's nothing I know of extant in the literature—but I do have to say at this point in the proceedings that we have to take into account, strongly, the possibility that the visions in question are induced by the psilocybin mushroom.

Ann shook her head and tried to answer, but no words emerged. Carolyn took hold of Ann's small hand, held it tightly in her own ample lap, and said Now wait a minute, hold on here, I've never heard of someone beshroomed seeing the Virgin Mary every day at the same place and about the same hour and the rest of the time they're completely normal, right up to the minute

before it happens, and normal right away afterward, no tripping up and then coming down, and
for sure I've never heard of any flashback that
sounds remotely like what's happening to Ann, so
your explanation doesn't make sense.

Your opinion is noted, Father Butler replied.
But not in the official record I'm keeping of this
initial discernment interview.

He swiveled a few degrees in Father Collins'
chair. Ann, he said. Help me with something. Do
you remember exactly when you started in using
psilocybin mushrooms?

Sixth grade.

That seems sadly young.

We sold them. My mom and me. Ann covered
her eyes momentarily. I'm confessing right now
to a crime, she said. We sold 'shrooms. To make
a living. And I took them too. Sometimes.

You know, said Father Butler. This reminds me
of something. And turned his gaze on Father
Collins. Have you heard of Pahnke's Good Friday
experiment? Does Walter Pahnke ring a bell with
you? It was written up in *Time* magazine I'm
guessing approximately thirty-five years ago or
somewhere thereabouts.

I wasn't even born, said Father Collins.

Pahnke gave psilocybin to twenty Protestant
divinity students on Good Friday in 1962 in the
chapel at Boston University, I think, or I guess it

was in some sort of basement of the chapel, not the main but the secondary chapel, and he broadcast in the Good Friday service to see if that wouldn't maybe induce some sort of mystical religious experience in these spiritually inclined volunteers. And perforce they had these religious experiences, feelings of timelessness and eternity, of tasting everlasting life, of dropping away from the world as we know it, as if they were saints or visionaries, there were various sorts of hallucinations, in short the drug indeed facilitated full-blown religious and mystical interludes, I repeat, the drug known as the psilocybin mushroom facilitated in Pahnke's well-known study these intense subjective mystical interludes: now doesn't that apply to Our Ann?

Wait, said Carolyn. Let me say it again. Ann hasn't tripped in four weeks, okay? And her visions are happening now.

Another study, said Father Butler. Another tidbit from my years of files. This one, if I remember correctly, from the newsletter of the Multidisciplinary Association for Psychedelic Studies, of all things—can you imagine such an organization actually existing in the world? Father Butler shook his head, chagrined. At any rate this little story was about the fact that certain psilocybin users are prone to hearing an audible voice. A positive, insightful, reasonable voice. Perhaps a voice like the Mother of God's. Hearing a voice like Ann here does. Ann who is also a psilocybin user, not incidentally a psilocybin user. Doesn't that sound like it means something?

It's not just a voice, though. I see her, too. I don't just hear her, Father Butler.

Now I'm not saying—I'm trying not to say—that the use of psilocybin resolves this case. Only that the use of psilocybin is a factor that absolutely must weigh in. We'd be wrong to leave it out, I'm certain of that. Wouldn't we be wrong, Father Collins?

Father Collins concurred, wincing. But Carolyn has a point, he added. About the four weeks. And the nature of flashbacks. Carolyn makes a valid point.

Waffle on a tightrope, said Carolyn.

There was nothing to do in the face of this but serve more tea and quell the urge to sneer in return. Father Collins, good host, made the rounds. He poured Ann's tea and sought to catch her eye in order to remind her that the night before they'd lounged on his bed together. In order to confirm the intimacy he felt, if he could only elicit that confirmation from someone so natively off-kilter. Ann was now in a lather of sweat, bathed as if dying of fever. Her unblemished face, though gray, shone wetly. A sheen of fierce and passionate conviction was one way this might be

read—death, suffering, God, rapture, an ecstastic
bliss he might have envied if he had not already
surrendered himself to a more mundane variety
of faith and simultaneously, to doubt. Father, she
said. Baptize me now. Keep me from the snares of
the devil. And help me build the church, our
church. The Church of Our Lady of the Forest.

He felt emboldened by Ann's plea to speak to
her now as if Father Butler had ceased to inhabit
the room. Ann, he said. I want you to understand. I want you to know why I can't do those
things. Even though I like you very much. Even
though I want to do them. I want you to know
my thoughts, who I am. I—

I know who you are already, Father Collins.
Because Our Lady sent me to you.

I'm quoting Saint Thérèse of Lisieux. The
Little Flower. The Carmelite. To ecstasy I prefer
the monotony of sacrifice. And that, in a nutshell—that's me, Ann. The monotony of sacrifice:
I personify that. Or have. Or did. Or did for a
while. Because right now I'm riddled with questions. Shot through with terrible questions. My
humble path is so uncertain I'm afraid it will
dwindle and end.

Father.

I'm just a man. Do you understand? I'm a man,
weak. Just a man.

Jesus was a man, said Ann.

I'm not Jesus.

But we are all in his image.

I know that. Or I think I do.

The important thing, said Ann firmly, is to build the church Our Lady wants, and also to get the Stinson Company to let me go into the woods tomorrow. And I need your help with both those things. Father Collins—help me.

I wish I could.

You can, though. Help me.

But I don't believe, he said.

Ann rose and pulled her blanket around her head so that both the blanket and the sweatshirt hood cloaked her face in shadow. I'm going into the sanctuary, she said, to pray that the Stinson Company is touched by God and opens our path through the woods to the Blessed Mother. I'm going to pray for that, Father Collins. And for you. And for Our Lady's church. Excuse me now. I'm going.

Let me help you, said Carolyn. She rose and draped an arm around Ann's shoulder. My poor little girl, she added.

Father Butler dropped his pen on the desk and tipped back in Father Collins' chair with his hands clasped behind his head and his elbows spread like wings. We'll continue later, he said.

God bless you, said Ann. Thank you.

She went out, leaning on Carolyn. Father

Collins hauled along the tea things, feeling like an overgrown altar boy. From the vestibule it was now evident that the parking lot of his little church had become a new locus of Marian obsession—throngs had massed to sing, pray, hold forth tapers lit against the night, and exhort Ann of Oregon steadily by name, more intensely when she came into view through the vestibule's dirty windowpanes. Some had their faces pressed to the glass, the better to see inside, no doubt, and at the sight of Ann they passed word of her presence so that others rushed forward to peer in too, until Father Collins feared the windows would fracture from the weight of all their zeal.

He put the tea set on the counter in the kitchen and hurried back up the hall to the sanctuary, where Father Butler was now seated in a pew, as was Carolyn, farther up, apparently studying a missalette. Ann stood at the communion rail with her head craned toward the crucifix suspended above the tabernacle. It was canted forward and hung from guy wires so that it looked like a monstrous bird of prey in the moment before its stoop. Father Collins felt personally responsible for the generally unexalted state of things, as if it reflected on his tenure. The pews in the nave were scarred by years of use and a lack of consistent maintenance and the kneeling boards sagged and creaked. The communion rail was also well-beaten by time, friction, and circumstance, and the organ pipes appeared tinny, warped, and in need of a muscular polish. Most embarrassing was the chancel addition, commemorated in 1963 according to a plastic wall plaque. The arch dividing it from the nave was poorly built and let precipitation in; buckets were needed to catch the drip that compromised the atmosphere at services. Father Collins, performing the mass, had often been distracted by the sound of water. Pock, pock, pock, pock. During interludes of silent meditation it even seemed to reverberate.

Ann knelt inside the tent of her blanket and teased out her rosary beads. That floor is cold, called Carolyn. Don't you kneel there, please.

I have my blanket.

That doesn't matter.

I have to kneel.

No you don't. You don't have to kneel. God isn't that unreasonable, is he? He's sitting up in heaven, sweetheart, shaking his head and saying to himself What on earth is she doing on the floor?

The answer is: I'm praying the rosary.

I'm sure God will let you dispense with that in favor of securing your health right now. Because God is logical, isn't he?

No.

And anyway, you're wheezing.

Ann made a feeble sign of the cross and began to mumble her rosary. Father Butler sighed and joined his hands across his belly. The sanctuary light, thought Father Collins, made his face look furrowed. A pruny shriveling at his upper lip, a telltale geriatric feature, revealed itself for the first time. Psilocybin mushrooms, he whispered.

One thing to remember, said Father Collins, is that Abbé Peyramale, the parish priest at Lourdes, was Bernadette's paramount skeptic and doubter before becoming her paramount supporter.

Yes.

So anything can happen.

In principle, yes.

You yourself have pointed out that the whole question is inherently vague. Inherently vague and difficult.

Yes.

Father Collins straightened up missalettes left in disarray by parishioners. I just don't think we should be premature, he said, in coming to any judgment. I, for one, wouldn't want to be hasty, sign my name to some document or other, and then be proven wrong.

No.

You've gotten terse.

I've done this before.

Then you know about caution, said Father Collins.

I know about going through the motions, brother. Especially when drugs are involved.

Father Butler removed his glasses, settled them on his lap—against his gut—and began to massage his eyes. You're difficult to understand, he said. Do you really think the Church will sanction the claims of a girl who admits to the use of a potent hallucinogen? To recurrent use of psilocybin? Why in God's name do you defend her?

There's no answer to that, said Father Collins.

They sat in silence contemplating this and feeling weary together. They were silent for a long time and in the absence of their constant noise Father Collins was aware of mildew and of not wanting to age any more. He was aware of his superficiality, of the incessant power of vanity. He noted the visionary's durable stillness, her labored and obstructed breathing, her ability to sit in a motionless trance like a meditating monk. He began to yearn for a good night's sleep, partly as an anodyne for his overwrought senses and partly to anesthetize his soul. He wanted to disappear. He wanted sleep's forgetfulness. It seems to me, said Father Butler, that my work is probably done for this day. So I'll hie myself to bed, I think. And see you again in the morning.

Father Collins gave him the trailer house key and the key to his battered station wagon. I have to stay, he said.

Duty can be an awful thing when what you need is a good forty winks.

So make yourself comfortable. You know where the towels are. Make yourself entirely at home.

Good of you, brother. I'm with you in spirit.

Hold down the gas pedal when you start the car.

We'll weather this beautifully, you and I.

I suppose we will. After all.

We'll laugh about it one day, hoisting a pint. Quaffing a pint together. Someday.

Carolyn came up the aisle toward them and halted with her hands turned backward on her hips like somebody with mild lumbago. Okay, she said. She's fine for now. So I'm going out to the parking lot because I have to address her followers.

And I'm off to bed, said Father Butler. I can't waste time any longer.

This isn't a waste of time, said Carolyn. She's asking the Lord to soften the hearts of the Stinson Company pharaohs. And you two clerics ought to join her in that. Make phone calls to the bishop, send telegrams to the Vatican. Lead already. Like Moses.

Go on, said Father Butler. Address your followers.

Her followers, said Carolyn, not mine.

Father Butler worked his way out of the pew. I'll make myself scarce through the side door, he said. I can't take any more of this business. He gave a chilly automatic wave and went in search of his coat.

Father Collins accompanied Carolyn to the vestibule. I'm worried about Ann's health, he said. Her breathing is just so seriously congested. I think she has to see a doctor.

Solicitous of you. You're a man of compassion.

I don't know why you've decided to hate me.

I don't hate anybody. It's not worth the effort. Carolyn hugged Father Collins stiffly and thought of Judas Iscariot's kiss. I'm sorry, she said. I just think you're weak.

I am weak. You too are a seer.

I also think you're totally confused.

Yes, said Father Collins. I am.

Carolyn zipped her jacket to the throat and said I have to go out there now and deal with this crowd a little.

I'll lock up behind you.

Then how will I get back in?

I'll give you the key, said Father Collins.

Carolyn took it, went outside, and made her way through the crowd of pilgrims with her palms joined in the prayerful position and a be-atific smile. The gathering had the feel of a protest now, a swelling militancy. Glory! she called. Praise to the Lord! Our Ann is at prayer in the sanctuary. Abide with me, rest for a while. Have patience, friends, like Jesus.

There were, she estimated, two thousand fanatics, keeping a manic evening vigil and spilling into the side streets. Their faces were illuminated by flickering candles and by the halogen lamps on North Fork Avenue and a group had joined hands to sing a hymn recently familiar to Carolyn, so that as she walked she sang too, casually, as if she'd known it her whole life. We pray for our Mother, The Church upon earth, And bless, Holy Mary, The land of our birth, bestowing the blessing of her smile.

In her van she locked up, drew the shades tightly shut, and made up a sign—DO NOT DISTURB: SILENT MEDITATION—which she propped on the dashboard. She lit two votive candles and drank long from a plastic jug of orange juice. After stuffing a handful of hazelnuts in her mouth she ran her hands through the money in the collection buckets, shaking her head and exulting. Praise the Lord! she said aloud, as the candlelight glinted among the coins. Yea, though I walk through the valley of the shadow of death I will fear no evil: for Mammon is with me! Carolyn laughed, bolted more hazelnuts, and fingered her vial of pepper spray. The buckets were full, it was surely a miracle, and she took ten minutes to pick out the large bills and ten more to organize them into neat packets and hide those in the chemical toilet chamber underneath the rear bench seat. By her most conservative, cursory count, she had twelve thousand dollars. She also had the option to exit, depart town quietly at 3 a.m. and make tracks for Cabo San Lucas. She could stop at banks along the way and convert the cash into traveler's checks that would not be questioned at the border crossing where every year she drew Mexican suspicion because of her hippie-ish Volkswagen van and generally left-wing demeanor. Twelve thousand dollars tucked beneath the seat would definitely raise another red flag labeled, in bold, YANQUI DRUG DEALER. And who needed that? Carolyn just wanted to get where she was going, settle into a beachfront flat, and not be bothered by anyone while she worked on her tan all winter.

The prospect of ennui—of tropical doldrums—presented itself to her mind. In winters past she had noted this: that her Mexico was enticing and seductive from a distance but inert from closer up. The rhythm of life as she'd once known it there—dance clubs, hangover, beach swoon, dance clubs—had been replaced by morning marijuana and light nonfiction reading. Paperbacks on trekking in the Andes, camel-riding the Outback, and bird-watching on Bali. But the stoned frugality of her last few years, it turned out after not very long, was simply newly boring. In fact, she'd found, most things were boring. She was thirty and bored by everything. Most of the time she felt tense and aimless. Free-floating anxiety informed her existence. Being sardonic and wry was a ruse. Inside she was seething with existential turmoil, just like everybody else. Why are we here? Et cetera. Half the time her life seemed meaningless and the other half she felt tormented by her appearance, which would only get worse with the years. Getting older just could not be faced. She would have to descend into the pit of despair in which, she guessed, the elderly wallow and learn the mystery of subsisting there—but not before she went south of the border with a major pile of money.

Money! She flipped through a thick wad of legal tender as though it were a deck of cards. Money, she thought, was a lease on life she hadn't known before. It occurred to her that with enough of it she could visit a liposuction clinic. What I wouldn't pay to be sexier, she thought. Streamlined, svelte, sleek, honed. As trim and nubile as the models in *Cosmo*. Were there side effects from liposuction? Especially the type done in Guadalajara? She made a mental note to research this. My legs, too, she told herself. Thinner legs would be excellent. She thought of her mother's cellulite, the black-and-blue clots behind her knees, the varicose calves, the spider veins, My

God, pleaded Carolyn silently, please never, no, help, give me death or give me surgery, I don't want to look like my mother!

Carolyn picked up her travel book, *A Short Walk in the Hindu Kush. We were in a great meadow of level green grass, springy underfoot and wonderfully restful to my battered feet.* She hadn't read from it since the previous Friday and she missed Eric Newby's cantankerous mirth and extra-dry British bafflement. She missed vicarious travel and escape. She thought with pleasure of hitting the road. A drive in darkness down the interstate, lounging by morning on the Oregon coast, drinking a demitasse of potent espresso and indulging in a chocolate croissant, her wallet stuffed amply with fives, tens, and twenties. *On the far bank sheep and goats browsed in a deep water-meadow.* Carolyn decided to begin her diet immediately after that breakfast celebration. One perfect morning, with sunglasses, in Bandon. She would wear a scarf like Melanie Griffith, tilt her demitasse with European class, and think of herself as wanton. A voluptuous and mysterious single woman. She liked that word— voluptuous. So maybe she should skip the chocolate croissant. What was the French term for one of those? They were always greasy anyway. Full of butter and calories. There was no way to eat one and remain *très chic. A pain au chocolat* would undercut everything, make her feel like the hog from Indiana she felt like most of the time.

Carolyn peeked past a curtain. Twelve thousand dollars was very good—especially since posing as Ann's disciple was a fantastically farcical pell-mell lark, far easier than foraging in the damp for mushrooms—but as long as there remained a crowd outside there remained more money to be pilfered. And why stop now? Why not twenty thousand? A big grift rarely presented itself, if Carolyn understood Hollywood correctly. To not go with it or to go halfway was to miss this god-given, holy opportunity. Carolyn thought she could double her money before it was time to pull out.

Double or nothing, she said out loud, tinkering with the dial on her compass and noting its insistence on north. Yet she had to admit to a strained moral doubt. To a compunction grounded in fear and trembling. There was Pascal's wager, always, to consider. And in truth she felt no sympathy for the devil. She thought of herself as a decent person who didn't cause harm to sentient beings. So what was this about right now? This fraud she perpetrated on a major scale? Ripping off the religious faithful—not to mention Ann of Oregon—was certainly no way to hedge one's bet against that ultimate, looming cardsharp, vast, colorless eternity.

No atheist, she thought, is ever firm. Even at

near complete conviction the pittance left over was consternating: fire and brimstone, geysers of flame, those popes in Dante stuffed head to toe down orifices in Beelzebub's cellar. Chilling. Gruesome. Popes in a chute. In college she'd memorized twelve lines of that canto for the express purpose of anticapitalist recitation. *Ah, Simon Magus, and you his wretched followers, who, rapacious, prostitute for gold and silver the things of God which should be brides of righteousness, now must the trumpet sound for you, for your place is in the third pouch.*

How ironic, thought Carolyn. But I'm committed already. A secular humanist. A material girl. All I wanna do is have some fun. And I definitely can't be one of these Christians with their myriad insanities: God's *son,* of all things, ridiculous! So what does that leave? Nothing, I guess. All I can say at Saint Peter's Gate is, I'm sorry, I went with Mexico and science, Darwin and margaritas.

Carolyn picked up Ann's catechism and quickly rehearsed the Hail Mary, since it was very short, a few sentences. She made sure of it. She said it aloud. Then she grabbed her electric megaphone, slid open the van door, and set all the picking buckets on the roof. They were full of change and one-dollar bills with an occasional five or ten mixed in, and they made her feel clever and deceitful. She clambered up after them and said exultantly, addressing herself to two thousand people who waited in the deep damp part of the night, My friends, praise be to Mother Mary, hallelujah, hail thee, Immaculate Mary, all praises to thee, Ave Maria, Hail, Holy Queen, our life, our sweetness and our hope!

The gathering moved in her direction with the collective will of a school of fish and she paused for a moment of self-adulation and private congratulation. I'm good, she thought, and getting better. This mob of pilgrims is at my command. I've grown into the job, I guess. From this high vantage she could see to the street where deputies milled uneasily, two cars from the sheriff's department and three from the state patrol. Hallelujah! she called again. Hallelujah, hail thee! Our sweet and wondrous Mother Mary!

As if there was no need to give it thought she passed four picking buckets down from the van's roof and into the nearest outstretched hands desperate to be of service. Reserving the last bucket, she held it aloft with the drama of a torchbearer. A sea of people stood before her now, squeezed into the spaces between the cars, as mesmerized as the audience at a magic act. Looking up with wonder and hope and what Carolyn thought was adoration. Our Lady, she said, who is full of loving-kindness, asks us to build her church!

She reached into her own pocket, drew forth

five twenties, and cast them into the bucket. She passed that bucket to the crowd too and said Now let us pray together. Hail Mary, full of grace, she began, and everybody joined in unison. It was frightening to Carolyn, robotic and fascist, as if they were all in a trance. The Lord is with thee; blessed art thou among women, and blessed is the fruit of thy womb, Jesus. Holy Mary, Mother of God, pray for us sinners, now and at the hour of our death. Amen.

Amen, repeated Carolyn. Amen to that, my friends. We have before us a set of grave circumstances. Circumstances brought on us by the Stinson Timber Company, which has chosen to deny us tomorrow's pilgrimage in the name of private ownership of land and in flagrant opposition to the will of Our Lady, who has called Our Ann to come forth tomorrow into the woods once again.

Praise Mother Mary! somebody yelled. Let Ann go to the woods!

This arrogant, cut-and-run timber corporation which is a subsidiary of a larger multinational conglomerate has opted to set itself against us, my friends, as it has set itself against the will of common people for I don't know how many years. Stinson doesn't care about you and me, only about its pocketbook and fat bloated bank accounts. Its CEO needs another swimming pool,

the members of its board need estates on the
Riviera. Friends, when the Blessed Mother talks
about greed, she is talking about them—Stinson
Timber.

There were chuckles of agreement, a ripple of
mild laughter, and Carolyn paused, as if for effect,
but in truth she didn't know where to go next or
what she wanted to say. For the first time in her
life she had an audience at hand—her own audience, in thrall to her voice—and all that occurred
to her was to babble on long enough to make sure
the buckets went around. God I'm an empty person, she thought. And so, she said, we are at an
impasse. Irresistible force meets immovable object. Us against No Trespassing signs. The people
against our global oppressors. Carolyn knew her
rhetoric was wrong but she seemed to have no
choice in the matter; what came to her was what
came. So we will have to make a decision tomorrow. Are we going to back down, back away, retreat, or will we protect our Ann of Oregon on
her path to the place of apparitions, the place of
healing waters? Will we do what is right by the
laws of God or by the laws of man? I hate to speak
such dangerous language and I am not advising a
turn to violence, after all we're righteous
Christians, we know it's good to turn the other
cheek, walk peacefully in the name of Jesus,
deeply respect these law-enforcement officers

who are good men doing a difficult job, standing by in the street over there—Hello, you guys, we love you, peace!—but there is such a thing as disobedience, organized civil disobedience like Martin Luther King or Mahatma Gandhi, we can trespass tomorrow in orderly fashion, accept the inevitable arrest of the few in the name of the victory of the many. And in this I ask: Are you with me?

There was a chorus—*Yes!*—but not loud enough, and Carolyn, raised on eighties rock concerts, saw that a degree of repetition could contribute to her onrushing filibuster. Are you with me? she said again, emphatically, to which she received an emphatic *Yes!*, Are you with me? she repeated, and when they rejoined with more raucous power she said, softly, Then you're with Jesus, yes my friends, then you walk with God.

The buckets were filling. What else was there to say? Bail, said Carolyn. Our arrested martyrs will need to make bail. She displayed another twenty-dollar bill and waved it feeling like a game-show host. We're going to build that church, she said. With the Lord's help, and yours too, we're going to walk into the woods tomorrow to the place of healing waters!

Shouts of consent, a raising of hands, and Carolyn said, For tonight we must have patience, friends, while Our Ann keeps vigil inside the church, praying for a righteous outcome. Our Ann has sent me to tell you all that you must keep vigil and pray with her, offering your prayers up to Our Lord and to the Blessed Mother, Queen of Peace, that the woods will be open tomorrow!

Stay, said Carolyn. Keep watch. Bear witness. And be as generous as you can, please, in the name of Our Lady of the Forest.

She picked her way down from the roof of her van, where she was intercepted by a sentinel she recognized, the man in the blaze-orange hunting vest with the Slavic-looking Cro-Magnon cranium and the salt-and-pepper mustache. All the buckets are out there, she said. Still, I'm locking my van.

Is Ann safe? asked the sentinel. Inside there?

Come again? What was that?

Our Ann. Is she safe? In the church there?

Carolyn locked her door and tried to move away, but he took hold of her arm with painful force, squeezing it across the triceps. He was strong and she nearly dropped the bullhorn. Wait a minute, he said.

Carolyn looked at his fingers with disdain, as though he had warts or running sores. There are two possibilities here, she said grimly. The first is simple uncomplicated assault defined by your hand on my arm right there which is forcibly and illegally detaining me. The second is complicated sexual assault in which that hand is construed by me as a totally unwanted sexual advance—and believe me, guy, it's definitely unwanted, because not only are you completely disgusting and totally unpalatable as a sexual partner but that orange vest is completely pathetic, dude, and makes you look like Elmer Fudd.

The sentinel released her. I'm assuming, he said, she's endangered in there. Unless I hear you say otherwise.

Carolyn brushed her nails against her arm, whisking away his germs. Smiling, she stepped into the crowd, lost him, and blended in among the Christian lunatics with her beatific grin aglow, as if she wore a nimbus. Hail Mary, she said through the bullhorn, and kept moving, regal and patient.

Carolyn unlocked the door to the church with Father Collins' borrowed key, but when she turned to throw the bolt behind her a somber-looking man was there, appearing by stealth, it seemed, out of nowhere, as if he had tracked her path covertly, not a sentinel and probably not a pilgrim, someone she didn't even vaguely recognize, a guy who looked like the Marlboro Man minus the ten-gallon hat. He had those tacky long truck-driver sideburns, hollow cheeks, wet blue eyes—he looked a little like a wastrel, a vagabond,

and that sent a thrill through her shoulders. But
then she'd always been attracted to vagabonds and
to men who were contained, aloof, and confidently impervious to her wit. The problem was
that her preferred sort was mellow, whereas this
guy looked just plain burned out, your average
boozer in a North Fork tavern, a beer drinker
with Country Western issues like domestic strife
and debt. Mother Mary, she thought. What's
wrong with me? Checking out material for a one-
night debacle. If I fell back into slumming again.
A dark mute cowboy in bad decline, emotionally
bankrupt, in personal default, somebody miserable and interesting. Briefs, not boxers. Glow in
the dark condoms. Everything smelling like nicotine. It was so attractively bleak and depressing.
She'd slept with a guy like that only once. And
he'd had trouble getting aroused. Otherwise, they
never went for her. Bad guys don't like fat legs,
she figured. No guys like fat legs.

Hey, he said. I'm coming in.

No you're not doing anything of the sort.

The man pushed through and into the
vestibule. I don't need bullshit, he told her.

He didn't stop to address her further. She was
clearly a bit player in his private drama. Whoa,
she said, making use of the bullhorn. Halt right
there. Immediately! But he didn't halt, he went

into the sanctuary. She wondered if this was what the sentinels prophesied. An inexplicable madman, obsessed.

She followed him in and saw with relief that he'd stopped in his tracks and stood grooming his hair, caressing it into place with his palms, that Father Collins had risen already and stood uncertainly between him and Ann, halfway down the center aisle, his hands held forth beseechingly, palms high like the pope on Easter Sunday. Tom, he said. Tom, what is it? What are you doing here?

Her, said Tom. I came here for her.

Are you okay?

I'm here for her.

Wait, said the priest. Let's talk about this.

I didn't come down here to talk with you.

I mean for just a minute. Let's talk. What's wrong? Father Collins clasped his hands at his chin. He seemed to be praying for divine intervention. Tom, he said. Now please now.

Carolyn spoke from the sanctuary door with her hands set defiantly against her hips, feeling plump and ineffectual. This is a house of God, she said. I'm going out to find Sheriff Nelson to take care of this.

You go ahead, said Tom.

He resumed his aggressive advance toward the

priest, who for his part kept his hands at his chin in a posture of utter religious submission and hapless passivity. I can't let you pass, said Father Collins. I'm sorry, Tom. I can't.

I'm coming through, answered Tom.

The visionary rose before them now. As though she was weightless, freed from the earth, despite her phlegmatic wheeze. Her face invisible inside its cowling. Her features were shrouded, unreadable, and she still had her blanket seized around her. It's okay, she said. Let him come.

The priest stepped aside to let Tom have the aisle but kept his hands clutched, fingers twined, as if entreating a conqueror and as a measure of self-protection. The Church loves you, he implored, as Tom went past. You're a child of God. You have a beautiful soul. Now let's not do anything rash.

Don't talk to me, answered Tom.

A few feet from the visionary he put his hands against his knees and tried to peer under her sweatshirt hood and the deep mantle of her blanket's hem, where he made out her face in shadow. Also that she was small, ill, and breathing like a lung-shot elk. That she was not much older or bigger than his daughter, that her left boot was split at the welt. He had the impression of rootless penury and smelled what he thought was rain on her clothes and a tincture of campfire smoke. I sent you one of those petitions, he said. Yesterday. On Sunday.

She didn't answer, but on the other hand, he hadn't asked her anything. Tom leaned in further to scrutinize her the way he'd at one time scrutinized children at the elementary school Halloween Fest when he was stumped by an effective costume. Back in the days of domestic bliss and silent desperation. Back when he could feel moderately happy to have won the Black Cat Cakewalk. Are you in there? he asked. Come out now.

I'm here. Yes.

Come on out.

I can't come out.

Why not?

I'm afraid to come out.

What are you afraid of?

I'm afraid of you.

You don't have to be afraid of me. I'm not going to kill you.

There was a pause and then Ann of Oregon said, I am anyway. Afraid of you. Especially when you mention killing me.

Take off your hood.

I can't.

Tom tapped a boot heel against the floor and a clot of mud dropped onto the floorboards. They say you do miracles, he said.

If there are miracles it's Our Lady who performs them.

So you don't claim any miracles then?

It's Our Lady who brings her grace to the world.

So you don't claim any miracles?

No.

You don't save people with holy water?

No. Our Lady does it. Not me.

Tom peered again beneath the hood and again saw mostly shadow. He felt the difficulty of communicating with someone whose eyes he couldn't see and whose expressions were concealed. Well you're her messenger, he said.

Yes.

She showed you the way to the holy water.

Yes.

So that makes you some kind of miracle worker.

No.

They're all talking about you like you're some kind of miracle worker.

It's Our Lady who performs miracles. It's Our Lady who grants peace and salvation.

Tom said, Name one for me. Name one miracle that's happened.

She saves people.

Name somebody.

Anyone who calls to her.

Can you name somebody?

Pray to her.

I've tried before. It doesn't work for me.

You have to believe, said Ann.

Tom looked over his shoulder at the priest, who hadn't moved from his spot in the aisle—spooked deer poised on the road verge. The redhead with the bullhorn was gone already, gone, Tom knew, to find Nelson. That's fine, he thought. I'll deal with that later. Is everything okay? asked Father Collins. No, said Tom. It isn't.

He turned again to Ann of Oregon and briefly caught the barest hint of her eyes assessing him. Tom had once shot a raccoon in a culvert, the animal invisible except for luminous pupils that unsettled him only a little. A penetrating moment of introspection before he'd squeezed the trigger. Ann's shrouded presence reminded him of that. It was obvious, up close, that she was only a child, the tenor of her voice was childlike, she was just another drug-addled teenager, a wasted little runaway who'd slipped over the edge, overdosed too many times, and ended up in North Fork. I've got a question for you, he said.

Ask.

How'd you know about Lee Ann Bridges? How did you come by that?

The Blessed Mother told me.

She did?

Yes.

You're playing me.

No.

You're a scam artist.

No.

So how did you know?

The Blessed Mother. She told me.

Why would she do that?

I don't know.

Why would she tell you?

I can't answer.

You're bullshitting people.

No. I'm not.

You're jerking everybody around.

The visionary made no reply to this. Look, said Tom. You're bullshitting people. Because if Mary's real then all of it's real. God, Jesus, all of it.

Yes.

So that would mean there's a heaven and a hell. And a judgment day coming. And a devil.

Yes.

You believe in the devil?

Yes. I feel him.

The force of evil?

It's in the world.

Something that causes bad things to happen? You believe in that? The devil?

Yes.

You're right, said Tom. And I'm him.

The visionary fingered her rosary beads and fought more desperately to inhale. She was praying now in an aspirate whisper whenever she succeeded in drawing breath; the words he couldn't make out.

I broke my son's neck, Tom said. I paralyzed my son. He's paralyzed. A quadriplegic.

Oh no, said the visionary. No.

I did it to him. I broke his neck.

I'll pray for you.

I'm not asking for that.

What do you want then?

A miracle healing.

I told you, though. I can't do miracles. Only Mother Mary can help you.

Tell me you're real.

I'm real. Believe me.

Tell me you can heal my son.

The Blessed Mother is the only healer.

I want to believe that, said Tom.

These words, he saw, were the right incantation, because the visionary unexpectedly pulled back her hood and let her blanket drop. Her limpid eyes were disturbingly large, her forehead gray and slick with sweat, her cropped hair matted to her skull. She looked, to Tom, like an adolescent mental patient suffering from malaria or tuberculosis on top of being deranged. She looked anorexic and feverish. I have to sit down, she said.

She dropped in front of the communion rail, coughing. On her knees, straight-backed, trembling, pallid, clinging to her rosary beads. Tom knelt too, on his haunches, low, checked on the priest's position once again, and said, I need a miracle.

He heard the door to the sanctuary swing open. Nelson came in with the comic full force of his blustery upper-body language—he'd been a poser since junior high, a pec flexer and weight-room knuckle dragger—behind him the redhead with her electric bullhorn, and finally Ed Long, the deputy.

Hey, called Tom. No guns in a church, Randy.

But it was not the proper combination, he saw, of familiarity and wit. Or it was but Nelson was suddenly impervious to that sort of plea for mercy. Tom, said Nelson. I've been looking for you. And he stepped into the aisle, leading with his chin, his thumbs riding on his belt buckle. Hey, said Tom. That's pretty cool, Randy. Just like a television sheriff.

Nelson sighed and rubbed his temples, or gauged the extent of his receding hairline: okay with him if all pretense was dropped, that was the message in his stout gesticulations: I don't like you, Cross. Cross, he said. Enough's enough now. I'm not going to take any more of your lip. That guy at the motel called in today saying he watched you drive off with his mattress. And then after that I had Eleanor call saying One you were over there bothering her again, Two you trashed her bushes to get your canopy, Three you just about killed Heidi Johnston, Four you were out in the street mouthing off and you know what, Cross? It's enough already. It has been for a real long time. I'm telling you I've had it up to here with you. Guess what, Tom? You've lost your grip. And nobody wants to deal with it. No one can take it anymore. I had a feeling when this girl here tracked me down and described for me what was going on, I had a feeling it was going to be you. And now—you're under arrest.

I'm not a quote girl, put in Carolyn. I—

Excuse me, said the sheriff. You shut up now. I'm in the middle of something here. I've got to deal with what's in front of me. I've got to take this man down.

Come take me down then, Tom said.

Just watch me, Cross. You watch me.

Father Collins stepped again into the center aisle. He had always felt there was a certain bravura in playing the pacifist intermediary and he relished his role right now. Please, he said, no violence; I mean it. Please don't resort to violence, Sheriff. Not in this house of Our Lord, please. We can't have violence here.

The sheriff waved him to the side brusquely. You're in my way, move over, he said. I need to keep him in my line of sight, unobstructed, Father.

The priest moved aside, crushed, deflated, and as he did Tom stepped behind Ann of Oregon and knelt with a hand cupped over her shoulder as though she were a shield. Wait, he said. Okay Nelson, wait. Just wait a minute now. Hold on.

You're making her look like a hostage, answered Nelson.

That isn't what's going on here. You know that.

You better get out from behind her, Tom. Get out from behind her right now, please. I'm only telling you once.

Tom didn't move. He clutched her more firmly. Pray for me, he said to her. Pray for me and my son.

You get your head on straight, said Nelson. Because Ed and I are coming down there and we don't want any trouble.

No, rasped the visionary. Wait.

She put her hand over Tom's hand where it held fast to her shoulder. The sweat on her face looked silver and thick; beads of it fell from her chin. Her trembling was like the trembling of her visions, convulsive, graphic, otherworldly, disturbing, and finally completely mesmerizing. Even Sheriff Nelson was brought to a halt by the distressing strangeness of the scene before him, its spiritual ambience. The out-of-work logger with his long pointed sideburns and air of pathetic last-ditch hopelessness and this frail, sickly, famished-looking girl, holding his hand and quivering as if in the throes of rapture. Hail Mary, Ann wheezed desperately, and sought to follow with full of grace, but the words would not issue from her still-moving lips, her lungs had constricted too thoroughly. She clutched Tom's hand, coughed feebly, and exerted herself to draw a breath.

She can't breathe, said Carolyn fiercely. Let go of her shoulder you jerk.

But Tom felt the small burning force of Ann's fingers and began to hope that her touch alone might induce some kind of redemption. He thought it possible that the girl was entranced and in the grip of some weird holy fit that might be favorable for him somehow, that by virtue of mere proximity and touch he could reap a transformative benefit. So Tom held fast. He focused on Ann's hand. He felt the tremulous connection between them and prayed for something to come of it. Ann's hand was aflame, unexpectedly powerful, and calloused from all her outdoor work.

Through her fingertips he could feel the beating of her heart as rapid, it seemed, as a bird's. Maybe, he thought, this is finally it. After all my suffering. Salvation.

I swear, said Carolyn. She's going to suffocate. It's her asthma, okay? So let her go. Ann, she said. Are you doing okay? Let go of her shoulder you ape.

She's gagging, choking, said Father Collins. Tom, this is an emergency.

Carolyn thought of the vial of pepper spray dangling in her cleavage. Now, she decided, is the time to exploit my talent for verbal trickery and deceit, now is the time for creative action and intelligent intervention. This beer-drinking yokel is no match for me, I'll turn him every which way easily. Pulling the spray vial into view she said, See this thing? This little jobby here? It's Ann's asthma inhaler, okay? It's what keeps her breathing at times like this. Sort of like nitroglycerin pills for people who've had big heart attacks. I carry it for her because she forgets, it's sort of my job to remember to bring it. And now—now she needs it, okay? Can't you see what the deal is here? She needs it or it's like she's strangling.

She pulled the vial free of her neck—a talisman dangling its braided leather cord—and advanced with a wary step. Hold up, said Nelson. You stay

right there. But Carolyn ignored him and kept on
moving. She walked down the aisle with the vial
held before her as if it were a cross and Tom
Cross a vampire. I said hold up, Nelson repeated.
Let her go, said Father Collins. Maybe she can
solve this peacefully.

Thank you, said Carolyn. She needs her
inhaler.

No, wheezed Ann. Carolyn.

I've got your inhaler.

No. Stay away.

Don't be scared. Here I am.

No, gasped Ann. Please.

Carolyn stopped short of the communion rail
and glanced overhead at the corpus of Christ suspended from his crucifix above the tabernacle.
She felt a strange glee, a pang of wicked triumph.
Poor Jesus was helpless to do anything, nailed up
so painfully, but she, Carolyn, with her vial of
pepper spray, was about to make front-page news.

Okay, I'm here, she said.

She looked at Tom Cross. There were tears in
his eyes. She hadn't expected that sort of weak-
ness. Not from a guy so infused with machismo.
The poor wretch appeared to be falling apart,
succumbing, maybe, to Ann's magnetism.
Carolyn looked at Ann's small hand resting on top
of his big dirty fingers, Ann's pretty hand quivering with passion as if driven by a piston in her

forearm. Got hold of another one, Carolyn thought. She's hypnotized another victim.

Ann, she said. I've got your inhaler.

No, answered Ann. Stay away. Stay back.

What's wrong with you?

I can see your aura.

Take your inhaler.

I see you now.

Here I come, said Carolyn.

She moved in for the kill feeling thoroughly focused, imbued with physical courage. Her plan for the winter ran through her head: breakfast in Bandon with sunglasses on, the California coast with its cinematic sunsets, LA carwash, San Diego Freeway, Meh-hee-co on one million dollars a day with a marijuana buzz. Carolyn put her forefinger against the nozzle and checked the direction of the aperture. Okay, she said. Asthma inhaler. Open wide, Ann.

Hail Holy Queen, Ann pleaded.

Hail Holy Queen, said Tom.

Carolyn—head twisted back, eyes squeezed shut, hearing from her throat an involuntary growl—showered Tom's face with the pepper spray. She misted his nose, eyes, and mouth so thoroughly that he quickly let go of the visionary's shoulder, drew both hands across his face, and fell to the floor by the communion rail, where he curled into a large fetal ball, a man-sized baby, a snail, helpless, and Carolyn heard him whimpering a name. Tommy, Tommy, he kept repeating. In between gagging. Tommy.

That's what you get, said Carolyn wrathfully. You shouldn't have challenged me, sucker.

Tommy, answered the fallen man.

He'd never felt so helpless before. Never been reduced in this way. A pain he could neither deny nor accept. It simply was, no matter what. And what to do in the face of such pain? How to propel it forth or thwart it? There was nothing to do; pain was what it was. It seized him again on every inhalation. Tom's own breathing seared him down to nothing. Air itself was a torment, death. Tom was introduced to illuminating blindness. He flailed in search of the visionary's presence but the ordinary world had abandoned him. Where was everyone? Why was he alone? What did all his suffering mean? Imprisoned as he was behind his eyelids he beheld a light as thorough as darkness. Mother of God, he prayed silently. Be inside me now.

Beside him the visionary lay on her back, seeing as if in a dream. The birdlike form of Christ hovered over her, his suffering face, as always, cryptic, his sinewy arms spread wide like wings, his contorted abdomen and chest looming close, his tattered shroud hanging low on his hips, she saw his wound, his alabaster skin, and she said, silently, Come to me, Jesus, and cleanse me of all my sins. Forgive me my trespasses. Save me from hell. And it seemed to her he was about to stoop and take her in his arms.

I haven't been baptized—the thought of that chilled her. I haven't been sanctified for heaven.

She felt the heat of her menstrual blood, heard a pounding in her ears. She sought to implore Our Lord again, but Father Collins' face intervened; he was kneeling over her and blocking her view of the Son of God behind him. Ann, he was saying. Ann. Hey. Then she felt his hands on her face. He was holding her face so lightly in his fingers. She's blue, she heard him say. I don't think she's breathing. I've never felt a face so hot. She's burning up. She isn't breathing. That can't be, said another voice. Her muscles are rigid, replied the priest. She's locked up, and look, her pulse. He laid two fingers against the flank of her throat. It's fast, he said. Call for help.

The priest put his ear against her mouth. I don't think she's breathing, he said again. Forgive me, he said. Oh Ann, please forgive me. Mother of God, Ann gasped. Mother of God, save us.

VI

Our Lady of the Forest

NOVEMBER 12, 2000

The new vesting sacristy had wonderful closets, aromatic, orderly, and large. Father Collins dressed in an alb and stole and was about to slip a chasuble from its hanger when he paused, bent, and removed his glasses in order to examine the items now collected as the foundling Our Lady of the Forest reliquary—two baby teeth, a lock of hair, a swatch of dingy sweatshirt cotton, a bone shard, and a tiny dime-store crucifix designed to be worn as a necklace. False and beautiful, he thought. False and potent totems. They had all been left on his desk anonymously with a letter explaining at length and in detail how Ann of Oregon's relics had been secured: the bone shard recovered from a careful sifting near Toketie Falls, on the road to Crater

Lake, where Ann's mother had tossed Ann's cremated remains; the crucifix and sweatshirt cloth clandestinely purchased from an "unnamed but entirely reliable source who had penetrated the county coroner's office"; the baby teeth and hair obtained from Ann's grandfather, an independent trucker named Melvin Holmes, for $3,500. The teeth, stained yellow by time, were small as popcorn kernels. The strands of hair, held together by a rubber band, were not the right color or texture.

Father Collins laid the bone shard against his palm and nudged it over with a fingertip. There was always the possibility of a forensic test to determine authenticity, but in the end what difference would a test make? This bleak blanched bit of calciferous tissue, unexalted and ridiculous, was, to the priest, sufficient for adoration, even if it came from a deer's flank. Which put him at odds with the Church.

Just as he was shepherding the bone shard away, guiding it back into its reliquary case, there came a small knock at the door. The members of the choir filed in and began—nervously—to enrobe. Father Collins greeted them cordially and hummed a few bars of the Gloria, smiling. Yet he himself felt mildly distraught and undone by anticipation. He was on this morning about to help dedicate the new Our Lady of the Forest

Church. It was a task he wished to perform without a slip and with the proper evincing of his passion. The priest was ignorant of the rites of dedication but had in the last month studied closely the proscriptions in the *Roman Pontifical* and in the *Ceremonial of Bishops.* He had also memorized the Ordo for the day and typed up a script for the ceremony. Despite these provisions he had a case of nerves and felt an imminent acid reflux. He wished the bishop had agreed to appear but also understood his recalcitrance. Impossible, the bishop had told him. In these circumstances. My personal involvement. Though I'm perfectly happy, you might let it be known, to see this growing, joyful interest in our Church and in our faith. The bishop had granted his judicious blessing, saying You understand why it must be so, given what has unfolded. And summarily entrusted the ceremony to Father Butler as a priest of rank and esteem in the Church and of late his Vicar General. An appropriate irony, Father Butler had said, upon his arrival, once again, in North Fork. But we must be cast down, and cast down repeatedly. And perform our duties with an open heart. With that, he passed most of the preparations into Father Collins' hands.

Father Collins reviewed with the choir members pertinent points in the proceedings. He told them they all looked festively accoutered, dressed as they were in new vestments. Twelve women and four men, directed by Constance Pedersen, whose mezzo-soprano pierced the priest's soul, and including the architect Larry Garber, whose meek contralto was strangely moving. Garber, today, had another role—as project architect he would present the building, right after Father Butler's greeting but before the sprinkling of the holy water.

Give it to Garber, he'd welcomed design help, and with the pro bono consultation of two Seattle architects, a structural engineer, a commercial landscape designer, and a Stinson Company environmental specialist he'd formulated a graceful set of blueprints. The building was understated and spiritually evocative—rough cedar beams, sweeping glass walls, a light-washed, spacious, ethereal sanctuary—and the grounds incorporated a fern dell, a grotto, a hall of mosses, and a pool. The road from the campground arrested speed and was closely shrouded by a canopy of trees, and the parking lot, with its split cedar fence, lay a half mile from the church site. Worshipers were made to approach by foot on a path always bending through the forest. Here their souls were moved toward manumission, the ordinary world distilled. Along the Fern Walk worshipers found rest stops appointed with benches and objects for meditation: a statue of the Virgin, another of

Saint Bernadette, a third of Saint Catherine
Labouré.

Father Collins had found, to his surprise, that
he took an avid interest in matters of design when
it came to the Our Lady of the Forest Church. In
his self-characterization he was a lover of abstrac-
tions, a soul afloat in the realm of ideas, so it had
caught him off guard to find that his brain had
fixed on architecture. It seemed to him a trans-
formation related to turning thirty. At any rate
he'd scoured the blueprints with clerical obses-
siveness and had supervised each day of the work
with a fussy nitpicker's zeal. Inexorably he fell into
an alliance with Garber and came to appreciate a
three-sided ruler and a lot of slow careful head
scratching. It was humbling to discover this new
world beside his old one, so he dabbled in sur-
veying and carpenter's math as an exercise in re-
gaining perspective. After all, drain rock and
mortar mix didn't make theory irrelevant; the
universe remained, to the contrary, predictable, as
solidly Newtonian as ever. What a relief to affirm,
with a transit, the platonic basis of everything!
Smitten, the priest learned the lingo of the trades
so as to ingratiate himself with subcontractors; he
felt they might do a better job if they suspected he
knew a little something. He didn't. He couldn't
see inwardly from the plan to reality in any purposeful detail. But at night he fell asleep with his

mind striving anyway toward solutions to physical problems.

The members of the choir filed out in their vestments and Father Collins, after pausing to assess the dignity of his own garments, crossed the hall to the working sacristy. The servers, he found—Tom Cross and Carol Boyle—were engaged in a sacramental inventory. Holy chrism, check, Sprinkler, check, Thurible, check, Corporal, check, Purificators, check, et cetera. I'm dressed, said the priest. So one of you can keep vigil again. I see you're still in your street clothes.

Yes, answered Tom. I have a question about that.

About the reliquary vigil?

About our vestments. Tom was new to the ministry of serving; Father Collins had recently appointed him an acolyte in support of Tom's efforts at self-improvement. Red or white? Tom asked.

The priest primped his chasuble for Tom's edification. White, he said. White is worn for a church consecration. Red has other purposes. We wear it, for example, on the feast days of martyrs. Among other occasions.

Tom nodded as if filing these facts away. There was a deepening patina of gray at his temples and just above his ears. Father Collins understood from their confessional dialogue that Tom had been allowed, lately, to visit his children again. That he bathed and fed Tommy without feeling saved. Salvation, the priest had reminded him at confession, was undoubtedly the work of a lifetime.

I'll put on white, said Tom.

He went out and the priest did Tom's work momentarily, filling the chrism vessel with olive oil and folding the altar cloth. He thumbed with appreciation the Lectionary and took down the censer and incense boat and spoon and counted the candles and candlesticks. A rush of tactile pleasure filled him. The aspergillum looked brilliantly polished. Hand it again to Larry Garber: there was a place for everything, and pleasing order.

For a moment in the presence of Carol Boyle, who was obliviously busy at her work, he paused to remember Ann Holmes. He thought of the shroud of her sweatshirt hood and of her canvas tent in the campground. The priest said a Hail Mary meditatively and crossed himself very slowly. He gave thanks for his winnowing of the previous autumn. He gave thanks, too, for the monotony of sacrifice. There were things to do, there were many things to do, there was a host of things he felt drawn to doing. Then he went out with ministerial resolve, as his schedule on this Sunday dictated. In the vestibule was a rack for the missalettes and prayer books constructed of fir by a furniture builder, and a baptismal font hewn from a piece of granite already naturally convex. The altar boys were straightening the missalettes and, on seeing him, increased their efforts. Father Collins smelled the new stain exuding from the vestibule's aggregate floor. He was pleased to note no tincture of mildew, and this left him feeling vindicated. The project manager had kept to high standards on Father Collins' constant insistence, shaking his head and repeating Overkill, but whatever you want, I'll just do it. Everybody seemed glad, now, to have taken Father Collins' zealous approach. The site was by nature aqueous, spongelike; much money had been spent on good drains.

The priest pondered, once again, the vast funding that had materialized in the wake of Ann's sudden death. The Stinson Company, in an about-face generated from its PR department, had gifted the land for the church to the diocese and had made the front page of both Seattle papers. The Chamber of Commerce had energized the banks to guarantee what its constituency foresaw as a cash cow in perpetuity. The City Council's tourism plan was revised and invoked in light of developments to generate infrastructure tax monies. A wealthy Marianite in California had anonymously contributed a half million dollars, and the hardscaping of the grotto and pool, the walkways, benches, and bluestone terrace, was donated by a Tacoma company driven by Marian fever. A host of moss-backed artists stepped forward, emerging from their drenched forest hovels, to fill the new church with their handiwork.

And in town something called the Super Motel was already nearly completed. On Main Street was the new Country Corner Cafe, featuring homemade pies. The North Fork Campground had been vastly expanded. Three new bed-and-breakfasts had opened. MarketTime was being renovated, a delicatessen and bakery added. There was a new coffee shop around the corner from Gip's called First Light Espresso selling pastries with French names, *biscotti* from a jar, and sandwiches made on peasant bread. There were plans in the works for new downtown sidewalks, angled parking, and improved sewer lines, and as long as the streets were being ripped open highspeed cable would go in. The tourism consultant, Applebaum, had suggested to the town the marketing slogan The Lourdes of the Northwest Rain Forest.

Standing in front of a tableau carved from yew wood—a triptych featuring the Annunciation, Lamentation, and Coronation of the Virgin—was a woman Father Collins didn't recognize. She was peering closely at its rough chiseled detail and as he approached he saw her lean farther toward it, the better to admire its craft. Excuse me, he said. Might I help you?

The woman increased her attention to the woodwork. Maybe, she answered. Might you?

Worshipers assemble in the fern dell, said the priest, gesturing toward a bank of picture windows. Just there, beyond the grotto.

I'm not a worshiper.

Who are you then?

I'm president of the Karl Malden Fan Club, Father. Don't you recognize me, even?

She turned and winked and his first thought was, What a clever and thorough disguise. Carolyn, he said. You look different.

Weight gain, she answered, helps enormously, hugely. I highly recommend an extra twenty pounds to fugitives and spies.

You're not either.

That's good to hear.

Should you be?

If I was that would make my weight gain convenient and invest it with meaning, maybe.

Father Collins stepped closer to the triptych and clasped his hands at his back. Your hair is different too, he noted.

Dyed it this obscene jet black, said Carolyn. And had it cut in this unflattering pageboy. So now I look like what's-her-name—Rosie. And with this huge Gore-Tex anorak and this ugly mascara I'm not even me anymore.

It works, said the priest. I wouldn't have known you.

Carolyn rubbed up the rouge on her cheekbones. I'm incognito for a reason, she said. I didn't want to deal with her hive of followers. Her swarm of glassy-eyed Christian storm troopers. But I did want to come to this . . . thing today. And I figured you wouldn't reveal me.

I might, though.

You wouldn't and you know it.

I'm glad you're here.

Don't pretend that, Father.

You were Ann's friend.

Not really, said Carolyn.

How can you say that? asked Father Collins. You—

I killed her, said Carolyn. Remember?

She feigned even closer inspection of the triptych. Do you have a few minutes? she asked.

The priest didn't. Her timing was bad. He was expecting on the order of ten thousand people in a little less than two hours. There were already reporters assembled in the grotto. Shuttle buses hauled pilgrims to the parking lot. There were preparations to make before the entrance procession, he wanted to review once more his commentary, not to mention his homily, he wanted to seat more deeply in his mind the order of the ceremony, and he felt it necessary to oversee the altar servers and to work a bit with the deacons. Not to mention a review with Father Butler, beginning in fifteen minutes. What about tomorrow? he asked.

Tomorrow I'm going to Seattle, Father. To have truffles or something. For lunch. And shop. And get a massage and a seaweed drape. Unbreakable appointments.

It's just that right now I'm a little preoccupied.

Well this is short, said Carolyn. And they aren't going to start without you.

True.

Carolyn slid on tinted glasses slung from her neck on a silver lamé tether, half-moon reading aids that sat, slightly crooked, low on the bridge of her nose. You look good, she said to the priest. You look . . . vibrant or something.

You're wearing rose-colored glasses, Carolyn.

Five minutes, I swear, she pleaded.

They went into a confessional room, where Carolyn perched on the edge of her chair and for effect and to practice staying in character crossed her large thighs and filed her nails. You remember I was arrested, she said. But I don't know after that what details you got. I kind of lost touch with you.

Very few, said the priest, and checked his watch. I was busy with things. Incredibly busy. And I haven't stopped being busy.

Carolyn filed away myopically, even with the reading glasses. I got released on personal recognizance. After three long boring days in jail. You don't want to be in jail, by the way. And my public defender thoroughly distressed me when he said I might get second-degree manslaughter. Or possibly reckless endangerment. For my stupid pepper spray . . . murder.

It wasn't murder.

Yes it was.

Accidents happen.

Not according to you Catholics.

So you've wrestled with guilt.

Like anyone would.

Is that why you're here?

I don't do confession.

Well, said the priest. As I say, it wasn't murder. You needn't beat yourself up over something that exists only in your mind.

Carolyn uncomfortably recrossed her legs and paused in her frenzied manicure. Ann is still dead, she pointed out. That's not just in my mind, is it? The fact that Ann is dead?

No one is to blame for that fact, though. There

is a conjunction of events that is in the stars, not in ourselves, et cetera, I guess I'm mangling Shakespeare.

So you believe in fate.

Not exactly.

You believe in the stars.

Metaphorically.

Stars as a metaphor for what specifically?

Stars as a metaphor for God.

Carolyn rotated her file once. So working backward through your statements, she said, I guess we ought to blame God.

The priest shrugged. I suppose, he said. Though I would quibble with word choice. Blame.

Isn't it a bad thing that Ann is gone?

It's a bad thing, yes, I'll grant you that, if in return you promise not to walk me through that boorish argument from evil.

Boorish, said Carolyn. Maybe so. Boorish but at the same time completely compelling. Don't you think it's compelling?

And yet, said the priest, so many persist on the path of God despite its admitted persuasiveness.

Carolyn paused, considering this. That just doesn't work, she said. Saying that doesn't change the fact that *God exists* and *Ann died* are logically incompatible statements.

Your mind is finite, the priest explained.

I've never bought that argument, though. You

can't make me see how innocent babes skewered on the tips of Cossacks' swords make the world a better place.

She rotated her file another turn and scrutinized her cuticles. The real point, she said, is that in this present case I myself was the catalyst.

No.

I was the one with the pepper spray.

Yes.

The cause of death was pepper spray.

No.

Are you going to let me feel bad about it?

Of course I am, said Father Collins.

Good, said Carolyn. Because I do.

Father Collins smoothed the creases in his chasuble. At any rate, he said. Enough self-blame. Events seem to have . . . conspired.

The last thing she said to me was troubling, said Carolyn. She said she could see my aura.

Hmmm.

Whatever that means.

I don't know.

Aura, said Carolyn. That's so Carlos Castaneda.

I've never been certain what aura means either.

It's so like cosmic or sixties or whatever.

Well people see things when they're under duress.

But they don't usually see my aura, do they?

I suppose, said Father Collins, it's a nimbus or a halo. An aureole, perhaps.

Carolyn began to file again. That sounds kind of divine, she said. Like the light surrounding an angel's head. The supposed light around an angel.

That could be. I suppose.

Except that I'm not an angel, said Carolyn. So the whole idea is ridiculous.

The priest checked his watch surreptitiously. I'm sorry I'm short on time, he reminded her. But I have to ask what you've been doing, Carolyn. Over this last year. With yourself.

I've been in Mexico. Not far from Cabo. I winter in Cabo every year. This time I stayed much longer.

Father Collins thought of the classified advertisement he'd considered more than a year ago in the pages of *The National Catholic Reporter: parish position in Ecuador, fishing villages on the sea.* Sounds lovely, he said. *Muy* restful.

Actually, it's boring, said Carolyn, scratching her neck with the nail file. And this year I spent a lot of time worrying. Calling my lawyer constantly to see if the prosecutor had charged me yet and—I'm in a confessional right now, right?—I drank a few thousand margaritas.

Not healthy.

And slept around considerably, too.

The priest made a show of plugging his ears.

And got high a lot. Whenever I could.

It sounds depressing and empty, said the priest.

The prosecutor never charged me, said Carolyn. She winked and gave him the thumbs-up sign. This confession business feels good, she added. Did I tell you about the lipo, Father? I had a guy in Ensenada do my thighs. That's when the rest of me blew up like this. The fat just migrates somewhere else. Carolyn pinched her chin again. Those guys rob you, she told him.

She opened her purse, tucked her file away. Also depressing, said the priest.

One other thing, said Carolyn. I've been on-line a little bit lately. Doing my satanic research.

She took from her handbag a pill foil pack. The tiny lids had been pulled open, and the pill compartments were empty.

I found this in my van, she said. Cleaning the place out I found it beneath a seat. You could call it a relic or something, I guess. One of Ann's empty pill packs.

He took it from her. He recognized it. Did you come here to give me this? he said. Is this what brought you here today?

It is, said Carolyn. Yes.

She shifted in her chair, turned sideways, draped an arm. Our Ann had terrible allergies, she said. Dust mites and mildew drove her crazy. And for that she was taking something called Phenathol in doses larger than normally prescribed. Way larger. You remember, right? She was constantly popping a bunch of those pills. The ones in that little pack you're holding. Well you know what I found on Phenathol, Father? Phenathol taken in excessive dosages? It has a variety of pertinent side effects—pertinent, I mean, to Ann of Oregon, to Our Ann the Inspired Martyr and Visionary. I mean like trembling and shaky hands, seizures, muscle spasms, and—whoa: hallucinations. Like seeing things that just aren't there. Like—for example—seeing God's mother. You understand what I'm trying to say? Mary was just a big Phenathol overdose. Phenathol's behind this massive spectacle. This multimillion-dollar film-set church. That's what you're presiding over, Father. A Phenathol trip. A lot of Phenathol.

That might be, the priest replied. Because Father Butler—remember Father Butler?—he made the same point nearly a year ago. After the autopsy results.

I see, said Carolyn. So I'm an idiot.

And you should know, too—since we're talking about her autopsy—that Ann's brain, at the end, denatured. Comparable to cooking the white of an egg. That was the official cause of death, not bronchial constriction or asphyxiation or whatever might happen in response to pepper spray. The priest now folded his hands in his lap. Her brain, he said, was cooked by her fever. By the heat and force of her rising fever. An adverse reaction to Phenathol, perhaps. But maybe, too, the hand of God. However you want to construe that term. However you want to construe God, Carolyn. Because behold—by her fruits, we know her.

Hail Mary, I guess then, Father.

Your cynicism does you zero good.

It's what I have, said Carolyn.

On the thirty-third Sunday in ordinary time— leaves in dark damp molder on the ground—the Our Lady of the Forest Church was dedicated. The procession began at noon in a gray pall that felt to most of the pilgrims present as limitless as the trees. It began to rain while they were under way and the raindrops caused the oxalis to shudder and streamed down the alabaster statues of Mary, Bernadette, and Catherine Labouré. Rain wrinkled the water in the pool and elicited from its opaque surface an effluvium of leaf meal. The crossbearer led, and his cross shone wetly. The presbyters covered the relics with shrouds. Some of the pilgrims carried lit candles, but these went out immediately. They walked and sang God in His Holy Dwelling and Let Us Go Rejoicing.

The forest, though, deadened their voices. Their hymns drifted off and were lost in the trees. At the threshold of the church they halted as one and were further soaked and seized by uncertainty. Something was happening at the front of the crowd but who, really, could tell what it was? Some of the pilgrims soon went inside but the great majority were left in the downpour and shifted inside their rain gear, waiting. Among them was the stooped-shouldered widow who had read Bishop Berkeley and Thomas Aquinas. Were we led all that way for Birth or Death? she thought. Nothing was what it seemed.

The acolytes had set up sixteen loudspeakers, but the sound system produced an irreducible hiss and crackled persistently. The pilgrims listened while inside the church Father Butler blessed the holy water and they imagined him sprinkling it on the church's walls and on people already wet. Then they sang I Saw Water Flowing. The rain increased and, with it, the static. The rain made the liturgy of the Word unintelligible. The pilgrims endured this development too. Some thought of retreating to their cars, but most were trapped by circumstances and anyway preferred to endure conditions as a private measure of spiritual worth. Who would confess to such vanity? This was a veritable storm, though. In truth it was raining with unsettling vigor. Indeed it was possible now and then to discern in the distance the boom of thunder softly pealing across the hills as if muted by the density of clouds. The world seemed flooded, inundated. There had been a downpour the previous day which seemed to have gathered angrily again. Cars on the roads had appeared like boats trailing muddy, rippling wakes. There'd been reports of slides on the highway, and in North Fork, on the west edge of town, a child had been swept into a drainpipe.

What could the pilgrims make of things? There came—they thought—the depositing of relics, but nobody could be certain. Then the anointing of the altar and church walls with holy chrism or—for those who couldn't help the play on words because of a perennial immaturity—with holy jism instead. A man whispered it to his neighbor, sniggering, and they stood there in silent comic communion. What else was there to do? How else to pass the time? The pilgrims looked up at the sky without hope. It was going to keep raining in all probability. What could they do? Where might they go? God had chosen, for this day, rain. The thing to do was to stand in it suffering and implore insistently the Blessed Mother. To thee do we cry, poor banished children of Eve. To thee do we send up our sighs, mourning and weeping in this valley of tears.

A NOTE ABOUT THE AUTHOR

David Guterson is the author of *Snow Falling on Cedars* and *East of the Mountains,* and of the story collection *The Country Ahead of Us, the Country Behind.* A Guggenheim Fellow and PEN/ Faulkner Award winner, he is a co-founder of Field's End, an organization for writers.